Victor H

Les Misérables
Volume 1

Victor Hugo

Les Misérables
Volume 1

1st Edition | ISBN: 978-3-75234-441-7

Place of Publication: Frankfurt am Main, Germany

Year of Publication: 2020

Outlook Verlag GmbH, Germany.

Reproduction of the original.

LES MISÉRABLES

BY

VICTOR HUGO

PART PREMIER

VICTOR HUGO (1828)

PREFACE

So long as, by the effect of laws and of customs, social degradation shall continue in the midst of civilization, making artificial hells, and subjecting to the complications of chance the divine destiny of man; so long as the three problems of the age,—the debasement of man by the proletariat, the ruin of woman by the force of hunger, the destruction of children in the darkness,— shall not be solved; so long as anywhere social syncope shall be possible: in other words, and from a still broader point of view, so long as ignorance and misery shall remain on earth, books like this cannot fail to be useful.

HAUTEVILLE-HOUSE, 1862.

BOOK I.

A JUST MAN.

CHAPTER I.

M. MYRIEL.

In 1815 M. Charles François Bienvenu Myriel was Bishop of D——. He was a man of about seventy-five years of age, and had held the see of D—— since 1806. Although the following details in no way affect our narrative, it may not be useless to quote the rumors that were current about him at the moment when he came to the diocese, for what is said of men, whether it be true or false, often occupies as much space in their life, and especially in their destiny, as what they do. M. Myriel was the son of a councillor of the Aix Parliament. It was said that his father, who intended that he should be his successor, married him at the age of eighteen or twenty, according to a not uncommon custom in parliamentary families. Charles Myriel, in spite of this marriage (so people said), had been the cause of much tattle. He was well

3

built, though of short stature, elegant, graceful, and witty; and the earlier part of his life was devoted to the world and to gallantry. The Revolution came, events hurried on, and the parliamentary families, decimated and hunted down, became dispersed. M. Charles Myriel emigrated to Italy in the early part of the Revolution, and his wife, who had been long suffering from a chest complaint, died there, leaving no children. What next took place in M. Myriel's destiny? Did the overthrow of the old French society, the fall of his own family, and the tragic spectacles of '93, more frightful perhaps to the emigrés who saw them from a distance with the magnifying power of terror, cause ideas of renunciation and solitude to germinate in him? Was he, in the midst of one of the distractions and affections which occupied his life, suddenly assailed by one of those mysterious and terrible blows which often prostrate, by striking at his heart, a man whom public catastrophes could not overthrow by attacking him in his existence and his fortune? No one could have answered these questions; all that was known was that when he returned from Italy he was a priest.

In 1804 M. Myriel was Curé of B—— (Brignolles). He was already aged, and lived in great retirement. Towards the period of the coronation a small matter connected with his curacy, no one remembers what, took him to Paris. Among other powerful persons he applied to Cardinal Fesch on behalf of his parishioners. One day, when the Emperor was paying a visit to his uncle, the worthy curé, who was waiting in the ante-room, saw his Majesty pass. Napoleon, noticing this old man regard him with some degree of curiosity, turned and asked sharply,—

"Who is this good man who is staring at me?"

"Sire," M. Myriel said, "you are looking at a good man and I at a great man. We may both profit by it."

The Emperor, on the same evening, asked the Cardinal the curé's name, and some time after M. Myriel, to his great surprise, learned that he was nominated Bishop of D——. What truth, by the way, was there in the stories about M. Myriel's early life? No one knew, for few persons had been acquainted with his family before the Revolution. M. Myriel was fated to undergo the lot of every new comer to a little town, where there are many mouths that speak, and but few heads that think. He was obliged to undergo it, though he was bishop, and because he was bishop. But, after all, the stories in which his name was mingled were only stories, rumors, words, remarks, less than words, mere *palabres*, to use a term borrowed from the energetic language of the South. Whatever they might be, after ten years of episcopacy and residence at D——, all this gossip, which at the outset affords matter of conversation for little towns and little people, had fallen into deep oblivion.

No one would have dared to speak of it, no one have dared to remember it.

M. Myriel had arrived at D——, accompanied by an old maid, Mlle. Baptistine, who was his sister, and ten years younger than himself. Their only servant was a female of the same age as Mademoiselle, of the name of Madame Magloire, who, after having been the servant of M. le Curé, now assumed the double title of waiting-woman to Mademoiselle, and house-keeper to Monseigneur. Mlle. Baptistine was a tall, pale, slim, gentle person; she realized the ideal of what the word "respectable" expresses, for it seems necessary for a woman to be a mother in order to be venerable. She had never been pretty, but her whole life, which had been but a succession of pious works, had eventually cast over her a species of whiteness and brightness, and in growing older she had acquired what may be called the beauty of goodness. What had been thinness in her youth had become in her maturity transparency, and through this transparency the angel could be seen. She seemed to be a shadow, there was hardly enough body for a sex to exist; she was a little quantity of matter containing a light—an excuse for a soul to remain upon the earth. Madame Magloire was a fair, plump, busy little body, always short of breath,—in the first place, through her activity, and, secondly, in consequence of an asthma.

On his arrival M. Myriel was installed in his episcopal palace with all the honors allotted by the imperial decrees which classify the Bishop immediately after a Major-General. The Mayor and the President paid him the first visit, and he on his side paid the first visit to the General and the Prefect. When the installation was ended the town waited to see its bishop at work.

CHAPTER II

M. MYRIEL BECOMES MONSEIGNEUR WELCOME.

The Episcopal Palace of D—— adjoined the hospital. It was a spacious, handsome mansion, built at the beginning of the last century by Monseigneur Henri Puget, Doctor in Theology of the Faculty of Paris, and Abbé of Simore, who was Bishop of D—— in 1712. This palace was a true seigneurial residence: everything had a noble air in it,—the episcopal apartments, the reception rooms, the bed-rooms, the court of honor, which was very wide, with arcades after the old Florentine fashion, and the gardens planted with magnificent trees. In the dining-room, a long and superb gallery on the ground floor, Monseigneur Henri Puget had given a state dinner on July 29,

1714, to Messeigneurs Charles Brûlart de Genlis, Archbishop, Prince of Embrun; Antoine de Mesgrigny, Capuchin and Bishop of Grasse; Philip de Vendôme, Grand Prior of France and Abbé of St. Honoré de Lérins; François de Berton de Grillon, Baron and Bishop of Vence; Cæsar de Sabran de Forcalquier, Bishop and Lord of Glandève, and Jean Soanen, priest of the oratory, preacher in ordinary to the King, and Bishop and Lord of Senez. The portraits of these seven reverend personages decorated the dining-room, and the memorable date, JULY 29, 1714, was engraved in golden letters on a white marble tablet.

The hospital was a small, single-storeyed house with a little garden. Three days after his arrival the Bishop visited it, and when his visit was over asked the Director to be kind enough to come to his house.

"How many patients have you at this moment?" he asked.

"Twenty-six, Monseigneur."

"The number I counted," said the Bishop.

"The beds are very close together," the Director continued.

"I noticed it."

"The wards are only bed-rooms, and difficult to ventilate."

"I thought so."

"And then, when the sun shines, the garden is very small for the convalescents."

"I said so to myself."

"During epidemics, and we have had the typhus this year, and had miliary fever two years ago, we have as many as one hundred patients, and do not know what to do with them."

"That thought occurred to me."

"What would you have, Monseigneur!" the Director said, "we must put up with it."

This conversation had taken place in the dining-hall on the ground floor. The Bishop was silent for a moment, and then turned smartly to the Director.

"How many beds," he asked him, "do you think that this room alone would hold?"

"Monseigneur's dining-room?" the stupefied Director asked.

The Bishop looked round the room, and seemed to be estimating its capacity.

"It would hold twenty beds," he said, as if speaking to himself, and then, raising his voice, he added,—

"Come, Director, I will tell you what it is. There is evidently a mistake. You have twenty-six persons in five or six small rooms. There are only three of us, and we have room for fifty. There is a mistake, I repeat; you have my house and I have yours. Restore me mine; this is yours."

The next day the twenty-six poor patients were installed in the Bishop's palace, and the Bishop was in the hospital. M. Myriel had no property, as his family had been ruined by the Revolution. His sister had an annuity of 500 francs, which had sufficed at the curacy for personal expenses. M. Myriel, as Bishop, received from the State 15,000 francs a year. On the same day that he removed to the hospital, M. Myriel settled the employment of that sum once for all in the following way. We copy here a note in his own handwriting.

NOTE FOR REGULATING MY HOUSEHOLD EXPENSES.

```
For the little seminary                               1500 francs.
Congregation of the mission                            100  -
For the lazarists of Montdidier                        100  -
Seminary of foreign missions at Paris                  200  -
Congregation of Saint Esprit                           150  -
Religious establishments in the Holy Land              100  -
Societies of maternal charity                          300  -
Additional for the one at Aries                         50  -
Works for improvement of prisons                       400  -
Relief and deliverance of prisoners                    500  -
For liberation of fathers of family imprisoned for debt 1000 -
Addition to the salary of poor schoolmasters in
the diocese                                           2000  -
Distribution of grain in the Upper Alps                100  -
Ladies' Society for gratuitous instruction of poor
girls at D--, Manosque, and Sisteron                 1500   -
For the poor                                          6000  -
Personal expenses                                     1000  -

Total                                               15,000 francs
```

During the whole time he held the see of D——, M. Myriel made no change in this arrangement. He called this, as we see, regulating his household expenses. The arrangement was accepted with a smile by Mlle. Baptistine, for that sainted woman regarded M. Myriel at once as her brother and her bishop; her friend according to nature, her superior according to the Church. She loved and venerated him in the simplest way. When he spoke she bowed, when he acted she assented. The servant alone, Madame Magloire, murmured a little. The Bishop, it will have been noticed, only reserved 1000 francs, and on this sum, with Mlle. Baptistine's pension, these two old women and old man lived. And when a village curé came to D-, the Bishop managed to regale him, thanks to the strict economy of Madame Magloire and the sensible management of Mlle. Baptistine. One day, when he had been at D—— about three months, the Bishop said,—

"For all that, I am dreadfully pressed."

"I should think so," exclaimed Madame Magloire. "Monseigneur has not even claimed the allowance which the department is bound to pay for keeping up his carriage in town, and for his visitations. That was the custom with bishops in other times."

"True," said the Bishop, "you are right, Madame Magloire." He made his claim, and shortly after the Council-general, taking the demand into consideration, voted him the annual sum of 3000 francs, under the heading, "Allowance to the Bishop for maintenance of carriage, posting charges, and outlay in visitations."

This caused an uproar among the cits of the town, and on this occasion a Senator of the Empire, ex-member of the Council of the Five Hundred, favourable to the 18th Brumaire, and holding a magnificent appointment near D——, wrote to the Minister of Worship, M. Bigot de Préameneu, a short, angry, and confidential letter, from which we extract these authentic lines:

"——Maintenance of carriage! what can he want one for in a town of less than 4000 inhabitants? Visitation charges! in the first place, what is the good of visitations at all? and, secondly, how can he travel post in this mountainous country, where there are no roads, and people must travel on horseback? The very bridge over the Durance at Château Arnoux can hardly bear the weight of a cart drawn by oxen. These priests are all the same, greedy and avaricious! This one played the good apostle when he arrived, but now he is like the rest, and must have his carriage and post-chaise. He wishes to be as luxurious as the old bishops. Oh this priesthood! My Lord, matters will never go on well till the Emperor has delivered us from the skullcaps. Down with the Pope! (there was a quarrel at the time with Rome). As for me, I am for Cæsar and Cæsar alone, etc., etc., etc."

The affair, on the other hand, greatly gladdened Madame Magloire. "Come," she said to Mlle. Baptistine, "Monseigneur began with others, but he was obliged to finish with himself. He has regulated all his charities, and here are 3000 francs for us at last!"

The same evening the Bishop wrote, and gave his sister, a note conceived thus:—

CARRIAGE AND TRAVELLING EXPENSES.

```
To provide the hospital patients with broth      1500 francs.
The society of maternal charity at Aix            250    -
The society of maternal charity at Draguignan     250    -
For foundlings                                    500    -
For orphans                                       500    -
Total                                            3000    -
```

Such was M. Myriel's budget. As for the accidental receipts, such as fees for bans, christenings, consecrating churches or chapels, marriages, &c., the Bishop collected them from the rich with so much the more eagerness because he distributed them to the poor. In a short time the monetary offerings became augmented. Those who have and those who want tapped at M. Myriel's door, the last coming to seek the alms which the former had just deposited. The Bishop in less than a year became the treasurer of all charity and the cashier of all distress. Considerable sums passed through his hands, but nothing could induce him to make any change in his mode of life, or add the slightest superfluity to his expenditure.

Far from it, as there is always more wretchedness at the bottom than paternity above, all was given, so to speak, before being received; it was like water on dry ground: however much he might receive he had never a farthing. At such times he stripped himself. It being the custom for the bishops to place their Christian names at the head of their mandates and pastoral letters, the poor people of the country had selected the one among them which conveyed a meaning, and called him Monseigneur Welcome (Bienvenu). We will do like them, and call him so when occasion serves. Moreover, the name pleased him. "I like that name," he would say. "The Welcome corrects the Monseigneur."

We do not assert that the portrait we are here drawing is probably as far as fiction goes: we confine ourselves to saying that it bears a likeness to the reality.

CHAPTER III.

A GOOD BISHOP AND A HARD BISHOPRIC.

The Bishop, though he had converted his coach into alms, did not the less make his visitations. The diocese of D—— is fatiguing; there are few plains and many mountains, and hardly any roads, as we saw just now: twenty-two curacies, forty-one vicarages, and two hundred and eighty-five chapels of ease. It was a task to visit all these, but the Bishop managed it. He went on foot when the place was near, in a carriage when it was in the plain, and on a mule when it was in the mountains. The two old females generally accompanied him, but when the journey was too wearying for them he went alone.

One day he arrived at Senez, which is an old Episcopal town, mounted on a donkey; his purse, which was very light at the time, had not allowed him any other equipage. The Mayor of the city came to receive him at the door of the

Bishop's Palace, and saw him dismount with scandalized eyes. A few cits were laughing round him. "M. Mayor and gentlemen," the Bishop said, "I see what it is that scandalizes you. You consider it great pride for a poor priest to ride an animal which our Saviour once upon a time bestrode. I did so through necessity, I assure you, and not through vanity."

On his tours the Bishop was indulgent and gentle, and preached less than he conversed. His reasonings and models were never far-fetched, and to the inhabitants of one country he quoted the example of an adjacent country. In those cantons where people were harsh to the needy he would say, "Look at the people of Briançon. They have given the indigent, the widows, and the orphans, the right of mowing their fields three days before all the rest. They rebuild their houses gratuitously when they are in ruins. Hence it is a country blessed of GOD. For one hundred years not a single murder has been committed there." To those eager for grain and good crops, he said, "Look at the people of Embrun. If a father of a family at harvest-time has his sons in the army, his daughters serving in the town, or if he be ill or prevented from toil, the Curé recommends him in his sermon; and on Sunday after Mass all the villagers, men, women, and children, go into his field, and cut and carry home his crop." To families divided by questions of money or inheritance he said, "Look at the Highlanders of Devolny, a country so wild that the nightingale is not heard once in fifty years. Well, when the father of a family dies there the boys go off to seek their fortune, and leave the property to the girls, so that they may obtain husbands." In those parts where the farmers are fond of lawsuits, and ruin themselves in writs, he would say, "Look at those good peasants of the valley of Queyras. There are three thousand souls there. Why, it is like a little republic. Neither judge nor bailiff is known there, and the Mayor does everything. He divides the imposts, taxes everybody conscientiously, settles quarrels gratis, allots patrimonies without fees, gives sentences without costs, and is obeyed because he is a just man among simple men." In villages where there was no schoolmaster he again quoted the people of Queyras. "Do you know what they do? As a small place, containing only twelve or fifteen hearths, cannot always support a master, they have schoolmasters paid by the whole valley, who go from village to village, spending a week in one, ten days in another, and teaching. These masters go the fairs, where I have seen them. They can be recognized by the pens they carry in their hat-band. Those who only teach reading have but one pen: those who teach reading and arithmetic have two: those who teach reading, arithmetic, and Latin, have three. But what a disgrace it is to be ignorant! Do like the people of Queyras."

He spoke thus, gravely and paternally. When examples failed him he invented parables, going straight to the point, with few phrases and a good deal of imagery. His was the eloquence of the Apostles, convincing and persuading.

CHAPTER IV

WORKS RESEMBLING WORDS.

The Bishop's conversation was affable and lively. He condescended to the level of the two old females who spent their life near him, and when he laughed it was a schoolboy's laugh. Madame Magloire was fond of calling him "Your Grandeur." One day he rose from his easy chair and went to fetch a book from his library: as it was on one of the top shelves, and as the Bishop was short, he could not reach it "Madame Magloire," he said, "bring me a chair, for my Grandeur does not rise to that shelf."

One of his distant relatives, the Countess de Lô, rarely let an opportunity slip to enumerate in his presence what she called the "hopes" of her three sons. She had several very old relatives close to death's door, of whom her sons were the natural heirs. The youngest of the three would inherit from a great-aunt 100,000 francs a year; the second would succeed to his uncle's dukedom, the third to his grandfather's peerage. The Bishop generally listened in silence to this innocent and pardonable maternal display. Once, however, he seemed more dreamy than usual, while Madame de Lô was repeating all the details of their successions and "hopes." She broke off somewhat impatiently. "Good gracious, cousin," she said, "what are you thinking, about?" "I am thinking," said the Bishop, "of something singular, which, if my memory is right, is in St. Augustine. Place your hopes in the man to whom it is impossible to succeed."

On another occasion, receiving a letter announcing the death of a country gentleman, in which, in addition to the dignities of the defunct, all the feudal and noble titles of all his relatives were recorded,—"What a back death has! what an admirable burthen of titles he is made lightly to bear," he exclaimed, "and what sense men must possess thus to employ the tomb in satisfying their vanity."

He displayed at times a gentle raillery, which nearly always contained a serious meaning. During one Lent a young vicar came to D—— and preached at the cathedral. He was rather eloquent, and the subject of his sermon was charity. He invited the rich to give to the needy in order to escape hell, which he painted in the most frightful way he could, and reach paradise, which he made desirable and charming. There was among the congregation a rich, retired merchant, somewhat of a usurer, who had acquired two million francs by manufacturing coarse cloths, serges, and caddis. In his whole life-time M. Géborand had never given alms to a beggar, but after this sermon it was remarked that he gave every Sunday a sou to the old women begging at the cathedral gate. There were six of them to share it. One day the Bishop saw him bestowing his charity, and said to his sister, with a smile, "Look at M. Géborand buying heaven for a sou."

When it was a question of charity he would not let himself be rebuffed even by a refusal, and at such times made remarks which caused people to reflect. Once he was collecting for the poor in a drawing-room of the town. The Marquis de Champtercier was present, a rich old avaricious man, who contrived to be at once ultra-Royalist and ultra-Voltairian. This variety has existed. The Bishop on reaching him touched his arm, "Monsieur le Marquis, you must give me something." The Marquis turned and answered dryly: "I have my own poor, Monseigneur." "Give them to me," said the Bishop. One day he delivered the following sermon at the cathedral:—

"My very dear brethren, my good friends, there are in France thirteen hundred and twenty thousand peasants' houses which have only three openings; eighteen hundred and seventeen thousand which have only two openings, the door and the window; and, lastly, three hundred and forty-six thousand cabins which have only one opening, the door, and this is because of a thing called the door and window tax. Just place poor families, aged women and little children, in these houses, and then see the fevers and maladies! Alas! God gives men fresh air, and the law sells it to them. I do not accuse the law, but I bless God. In the Isère, in the Var, in the two Alps, Upper and Lower, the peasants have not even trucks, but carry manure on their backs: they have no candles, and burn resinous logs and pieces of rope steeped in pitch. It is the same through all the high parts of Dauphiné. They make bread for six months, and bake it with dried cow-dung. In winter they break this bread with axes and steep it in water for four-and-twenty hours before they can eat it. Brethren, have pity, see how people suffer around you!"

A Provençal by birth, he easily accustomed himself to all the dialects of the South: this greatly pleased the people, and had done no little in securing him admission to all minds. He was, as it were, at home in the hut and on the mountain. He could say the grandest things in the most vulgar idioms, and as he spoke all languages he entered all hearts. However, he was the same to people of fashion as to the lower classes.

He never condemned anything hastily or without taking the circumstances into calculation. He would say, Let us look at the road by which the fault has come. Being, as he called himself with a smile, an ex-sinner, he had none of the intrenchments of rigorism, and, careless of the frowns of the unco' good, professed loudly a doctrine which might be summed up nearly as follows,—

"Man has upon him the flesh which is at once his burden and his temptation. He carries it with him and yields to it. He must watch, restrain, and repress it, and only obey it in the last extremity. In this obedience there may still be a fault: but the fault thus committed is venial. It is a fall, but a fall on the knees, which may end in prayer. To be a saint is the exception, to be a just man is the rule. Err, fail, sin, but be just. The least possible amount of sin is the law of man: no sin at all is the dream of angels. All that is earthly is subjected to sin, for sin is a gravitation."

When he saw everybody cry out and grow indignant, all of a sudden, he would say with a smile, "Oh! oh, it seems as if this is a great crime which all the world is committing. Look at the startled hypocrites, hastening to protest and place themselves under cover."

He was indulgent to the women and the poor on whom the weight of human society presses. He would say, "The faults of women, children, servants, the weak, the indigent, and the ignorant are the fault of husbands, fathers, masters, the strong, the rich, and the learned." He also said, "Teach the ignorant as much as you possibly can: society is culpable for not giving instruction gratis, and is responsible for the night it produces. This soul is full of darkness, and sin is committed, but the guilty person is not the man who commits the sin, but he who produces the darkness."

As we see, he had a strange manner, peculiarly his own, of judging things. I suspect that he obtained it from the Gospels. He one day heard in a drawing-room the story of a trial which was shortly to take place. A wretched man, through love of a woman and a child he had by her, having exhausted his resources, coined false money, which at that period was an offence punished by death. The woman was arrested while issuing the first false piece manufactured by the man. She was detained, but there was no proof against her. She alone could accuse her lover and ruin him by confessing. She denied. They pressed her, but she adhered to her denial. Upon this, the attorney for the crown had an idea: he feigned infidelity on the lover's part, and contrived, by cleverly presenting the woman with fragments of letters, to persuade her that she had a rival, and that the man was deceiving her. Then, exasperated by jealousy, she denounced her lover, confessed everything, proved everything. The man was ruined, and would shortly be tried with his accomplice at Aix. The story was told, and everybody was delighted at the magistrate's cleverness. By bringing jealousy into play he brought out the truth through passion, and obtained justice through revenge. The Bishop listened to all this in silence, and when it was ended he asked: "Where will this man and woman

13

be tried?" "At the assizes." Then he continued, "And where will the attorney for the crown be tried?"

A tragical event occurred at D——. A man was condemned to death for murder. He was a wretched fellow, not exactly educated, not exactly ignorant, who had been a mountebank at fairs and a public writer. The trial attracted the attention of the towns-people. On the eve of the day fixed for the execution the prison chaplain was taken ill, and a priest was wanted to assist the sufferer in his last moments. The Curé was sent for, and it seems that he refused, saying, "It is no business of mine, I have nothing to do with the mountebank, I am ill too, and besides, that is not my place." This answer was carried to the Bishop, who said, "The Curé is right, it is not his place, it is mine." He went straight to the prison, entered the mountebank's cell, called him by name, took his hand, and spoke to him. He spent the whole day with him, forgetting sleep and food while praying to God for the soul of the condemned man. He told him the best truths, which are the most simple. He was father, brother, friend —bishop only to bless. He taught him everything, while reassuring and consoling him. This man was about to die in desperation: death was to him like an abyss, and he shuddered as he stood on its gloomy brink. He was not ignorant enough to be completely indifferent, and his condemnation, which was a profound shock, had here and there broken through that partition which separates us from the mystery of things, and which we call life. He peered incessantly out of this world through these crevices, and only saw darkness; but the Bishop showed him a light.

On the morrow, when they came to fetch the condemned man, the Bishop was with him. He followed him, and showed himself to the mob in his purple cassock, and with the episcopal cross round his neck, side by side with this rope-bound wretch. He entered the cart with him, he mounted the scaffold with him. The sufferer, so gloomy and crushed on the previous day, was radiant; he felt that his soul was reconciled, and he hoped for heaven. The Bishop embraced him, and at the moment when the knife was about to fall, said: "The man whom his fellow-men kill, God resuscitates. He whom his brothers expel finds the Father again. Pray, believe, enter into life! The Father is there!" When he descended from the scaffold there was something in his glance which made the people open a path for him; it was impossible to say whether his pallor or his serenity were the more admirable. On returning to the humble abode, which he called smilingly his palace, he said to his sister: "I have just been officiating pontifically."

As the most sublime things are often those least understood, there were persons in the town who said, in commenting on the Bishop's conduct, "It is affectation." This, however, was only the talk of drawing-rooms; the people who do not regard holy actions with suspicion were affected, and admired. As for the Bishop, the sight of the guillotine was a shock to him, and it was long ere he recovered from it.

The scaffold, in fact, when it stands erect before you, has something about it that hallucinates. We may feel a certain amount of indifference about the punishment of death, not express an opinion, and say yes or no, so long as we have never seen a guillotine; but when we have come across one the shock is violent, and we must decide either for or against. Some admire it, like De Maistre, others execrate it, like Beccaria. The guillotine is the concretion of the law, it calls itself *vindicta*; it is not neutral, and does not allow you to remain neutral. The person who perceives it shudders with the most mysterious of shudders. All the social questions raise their notes of interrogation round this cutter. The scaffold is a vision, it is not carpenter's work, it is not a machine, it is not a lifeless mechanism made of wood, steel, and ropes. It seems to be a species of being possessing a gloomy intuition; you might say that the wood-work lives, that the machine hears, that the mechanism understands, that the wood, the steel, and the ropes, have a volition. In the frightful reverie into which its presence casts the mind the scaffold appears terrible, and mixed up with what it does. The scaffold is the accomplice of the executioner; it devours, it eats flesh and drinks blood. The scaffold is a species of monster, manufactured by the judge and the carpenter, a spectre that seems to live a sort of horrible life made up of all the death it has produced. Hence the impression was terrible and deep; on the day after the execution, and for many days beyond, the Bishop appeared crushed. The almost violent serenity of the mournful moment had departed; the phantom of social justice haunted him. He who usually returned from all his duties with such radiant satisfaction seemed to be reproaching himself. At times he soliloquized, and stammered unconnected sentences in a low voice. Here is one which his sister overheard and treasured up: "I did not believe that it was so monstrous. It is wrong to absorb oneself in the divine law so greatly as no longer to perceive the human law. Death belongs to God alone. By what right do men touch that unknown thing?"

With time these impressions were attenuated, and perhaps effaced. Still it was noticed that from this period the Bishop avoided crossing the execution square.

M. Myriel might be called at any hour to the bedside of the sick and the dying. He was not ignorant that his greatest duty and greatest labor lay there. Widowed or orphaned families had no occasion to send for him, for he came of himself. He had the art of sitting down and holding his tongue for hours by the side of a man who had lost the wife he loved, or of a mother bereaved of her child. As he knew the time to be silent, he also knew the time to speak. What an admirable consoler he was! he did not try to efface grief by oblivion, but to aggrandize and dignify it by hope. He would say: "Take care of the way in which you turn to the dead. Do not think of that which perishes. Look fixedly, and you will perceive the living light of your beloved dead in heaven." He knew that belief is healthy, and he sought to counsel and calm the desperate man by pointing out to him the resigned man, and to transform the grief that gazes at a grave by showing it the grief that looks at a star.

CHAPTER V.

MONSEIGNEUR'S CASSOCKS LAST TOO LONG.

M. Myriel's domestic life was full of the same thoughts as his public life. To any one who could inspect it closely, the voluntary poverty in which the Bishop lived would have been a solemn and charming spectacle. Like all old men, and like most thinkers, he slept little, but that short sleep was deep. In the morning he remained in contemplation for an hour, and then read mass either at the cathedral or in his house. Mass over, he breakfasted on rye bread dipped in the milk of his own cows. Then he set to work.

A bishop is a very busy man. He must daily receive the secretary to the bishopric, who is generally a canon, and almost every day his grand vicars. He has congregations to control, permissions to grant, a whole ecclesiastical library to examine, in the shape of diocesan catechisms, books of hours, etc.; mandates to write, sermons to authorize, curés and mayors to reconcile, a clerical correspondence, an administrative correspondence, on one side the State, on the other the Holy See; in a word, a thousand tasks. The time which these thousand tasks, his offices, and his breviary left him, he gave first to the needy, the sick, and the afflicted; the time which the afflicted, the sick, and the needy left him he gave to work. Sometimes he hoed in his garden, at others he read and wrote. He had only one name for both sorts of labor, he called them gardening. "The mind is a garden," he would say.

Toward mid-day, when the weather was fine, he went out and walked in the country or the town, frequently entering the cottages. He could be seen walking alone in deep thought, looking down, leaning on his long cane, dressed in his violet wadded and warm great coat, with his violet stockings thrust into clumsy shoes, and wearing his flat hat, through each corner of which were passed three golden acorns as tassels. It was a festival wherever he appeared, it seemed as if his passing had something warming and luminous about it; old men and children came to the door to greet the Bishop as they did the sun. He blessed them and they blessed him, and his house was pointed out to anybody who was in want of anything. Now and then he stopped, spoke to the little boys and girls, and smiled on their mothers. He visited the poor so long as he had any money; when he had none he visited the rich. As he made his cassocks last a long time, and he did not wish the fact to be noticed, he never went into town save in his wadded violet coat. This was rather tiresome in summer.

On returning home he dined. The dinner resembled the breakfast. At half-past eight in the evening he supped with his sister, Madame Magloire standing behind them and waiting on them. Nothing could be more frugal than this meal; but if the Bishop had a curé to supper, Madame Magloire would take advantage of it to serve Monseigneur with some excellent fish from the lake, or famous game from the mountain. Every curé was the excuse for a good meal, and the Bishop held his tongue. On other occasions his repast only consisted of vegetables boiled in water and soup made with oil. Hence it was said in the town: "When the Bishop does not fare like a curé he fares like a trappist."

After supper he conversed for half an hour with Mlle. Baptistine and Madame Magloire; then he returned to his room and began writing again, either on loose leaves or on the margin of some folio. He was well read, and a bit of a *savant*, and has left five or six curious MSS. on theological subjects, among others a dissertation on the verse from Genesis, "In the beginning the Spirit of God moved upon the face of the waters." He compared this verse with three texts,—the Arabic, which says, "The winds of God breathed;" Flavius Josephus, who said, "A wind from on high fell upon the earth;" and lastly the Chaldaic of Onkelos, "A wind coming from God breathed on the face of the waters." In another dissertation he examines the works of Hugo, Bishop of Ptolemaïs, great-grand-uncle of him who writes this book, and he proves that to this bishop must be attributed the various opuscules published in the last century under the pseudonym of Barleycourt. At times, in the midst of his reading, no matter what book he held in his hands, he would suddenly fall into a deep meditation, from which he only emerged to write a few lines on the pages of the book. These lines have frequently no connection with the book that contains them. We have before us a note written by him on the margin of a quarto entitled, "Correspondence of Lord Germain with Generals Clinton and Cornwallis, and the Admirals of the American Station. Versailles, Prinçot; and Paris, Pissot, Quai des Augustins." Here is the note.

"O thou who art! Ecclesiastes calls you Omnipotence; the Maccabees call you

Creator; the Epistle to the Ephesians calls you Liberty; Baruch calls you Immensity; the Psalms call you Wisdom and Truth; St. John calls you Light; the Book of Kings calls you Lord; Exodus calls you Providence; Leviticus, Holiness; Esdras, Justice; Creation calls you God; man calls you the Father; but Solomon calls you Mercy, and that is the fairest of all your names."

About nine o'clock the two females withdrew and went up to their bed-rooms on the first floor, leaving him alone till morning on the ground floor. Here it is necessary that we should give an exact idea of the Bishop's residence.

CHAPTER VI

BY WHOM THE HOUSE WAS GUARDED.

The house the Bishop resided in consisted, as we have said, of a ground floor and one above it, three rooms on the ground, three bed-rooms on the first floor, and above them a store-room. Behind the house was a quarter of an acre of garden. The two females occupied the first floor, and the Bishop lodged below. The first room, which opened on the street, served him as dining-room, the second as bed-room, the third as oratory. You could not get out of the oratory without passing through the bed-room, or out of the bed-room without passing through the sitting-room. At the end of the oratory was a closed alcove with a bed, for any one who stayed the night, and the Bishop offered this bed to country curés whom business or the calls of their parish brought to D——.

The hospital surgery, a small building added to the house and built on a part of the garden, had been transformed into kitchen and cellar. There was also in the garden a stable, which had been the old hospital kitchen, and in which the Bishop kept two cows. Whatever the quantity of milk they yielded, he invariably sent one half every morning to the hospital patients. "I am paying my tithes," he was wont to say.

His room was rather spacious, and very difficult to heat in the cold weather. As wood is excessively dear at D——, he hit on the idea of partitioning off with planks a portion of the cow-house. Here he spent his evenings during the great frosts, and called it his "winter drawing-room." In this room, as in the dining-room, there was no other furniture but a square deal table and four straw chairs. The dining-room was also adorned with an old buffet stained to imitate rosewood. The Bishop had made the altar which decorated his oratory out of a similar buffet, suitably covered with white cloths and imitation lace.

His rich penitents and the religious ladies of D—— had often subscribed to pay for a handsome new altar for Monseigneur's oratory; each time he took the money and gave it to the poor. "The finest of all altars," he would say, "is the soul of an unhappy man who is consoled and thanks God."

There were in his oratory two straw priedieus, and an arm-chair, also of straw, in his bed-room. When he by chance received seven or eight persons at the same time, the Prefect, the General, the staff of the regiment quartered in the town, or some pupils of the Lower Seminary, it was necessary to fetch the chairs from the winter drawing-room, the priedieus from the oratory, and the easy chair from the bed-room: in this way as many as eleven seats could be collected for the visitors. At each new visit a room was unfurnished. It happened at times that there would be twelve; in such a case the Bishop concealed the embarrassing nature of the situation by standing before the chimney if it were winter, or walking up and down the room were it summer.

There was also another chair in the alcove, but it was half robbed of the straw, and had only three legs to stand on, so that it could only be used when resting against a wall. Mlle. Baptistine also had in her bed-room a very large settee of wood, which had once been gilt and covered with flowered chintz, but it had been necessary to raise this settee to the first floor through the window, owing to the narrowness of the stairs: and hence it could not be reckoned on in any emergency. It had been Mlle. Baptistine's ambition to buy drawing-room furniture of mahogany and covered with yellow Utrecht velvet, but this would have cost at least 500 francs, and seeing that she had only succeeded in saving for this object 42 francs 5 sous in five years, she gave up the idea. Besides, who is there that ever attains his ideal?

Nothing more simple can be imagined than the Bishop's bed-room. A long window opening on the garden; opposite the bed, an iron hospital bed with a canopy of green serge; in the shadow of the bed, behind a curtain, toilet articles, still revealing the old elegant habits of the man of fashion; two doors, one near the chimney leading to the oratory, the other near the library leading to the dining-room. The library was a large glass case full of books; the chimney of wood, painted to imitate marble, was habitually fireless; in the chimney were a pair of iron andirons ornamented with two vases, displaying garlands and grooves which had once been silvered, which was a species of episcopal luxury; over the chimney a crucifix of unsilvered copper fastened to threadbare black velvet, in a frame which had lost its gilding; near the window was a large table with an inkstand, loaded with irregularly arranged papers and heavy tomes; before the table the straw arm-chair; in front of the bed a priedieu borrowed from the oratory.

Two portraits, in oval frames, hung on the wall on either side of the bed.

Small gilded inscriptions on the neutral tinted ground of the canvas by the side of the figures indicated that the portraits represented, one the Abbé de Chaliot, Bishop of St. Claude; the other the Abbé Tourteau, Vicar-general of Agde, and Abbé of Grand Champs, belonging to the Cistertian order in the diocese of Chartres. The Bishop, on succeeding to the hospital infirmary, found the pictures there and left them. They were priests, probably donors,— two motives for him to respect them. All he knew of the two personages was that they had been nominated by the King, the one to his bishopric, the other to his benefice, on the same day, April 27, 1785. Madame Magloire having unhooked the portraits to remove the dust, the Bishop found this circumstance recorded in faded ink on a small square of paper which time had turned yellow, and fastened by four wafers behind the portrait of the Abbé of Grand Champs.

He had at his window an antique curtain of heavy woollen stuff, which had grown so old that Madame Magloire, in order to avoid the expense of a new one, was obliged to make a large seam in the very middle of it. The seam formed a cross, and the Bishop often drew attention to it. "How pleasant that is," he would say. All the rooms in the house, ground floor and first floor, were white-washed, which is a barrack and hospital fashion. Still, some years later, Madame Magloire discovered, as we shall see further on, paintings under the white-washed paper, in Mlle. Baptistine's bed-room. The rooms were paved with red bricks which were washed every week, and there were straw mats in front of all the beds. This house, moreover, managed by two females, was exquisitely clean from top to bottom. This was the only luxury the Bishop allowed himself, for, as he said, "It takes nothing from the poor." We must allow, however, that of the old property there still remained six silver spoons and forks and a soup-ladle, which Madame Magloire daily saw with delight shining splendidly on the coarse white table-cloth. And as we are here depicting the Bishop of D—— as he was, we must add that he had said, more than once, "I do not think I could give up eating with silver." To this plate must be added two heavy candlesticks of massive silver, which the Bishop inherited from a great-aunt. These branched candlesticks each held two wax candles, and usually figured on the Bishop's chimney. When he had any one to dinner, Madame Magloire lit the candles and placed the two candlesticks on the table. There was in the Bishop's bed-room, at the head of his bed, a small cupboard in the wall, in which Madame Magloire each night placed the plate and the large ladle. I am bound to add that the key was never taken out.

The garden, spoiled to some extent by the ugly buildings to which we have referred, was composed of four walks, radiating round a cesspool; another walk ran all round the garden close to the surrounding white wall. Between these walks were four box-bordered squares. In three of them Madame Magloire grew vegetables; in the fourth the Bishop had placed flowers; here and there were a few fruit-trees. Once Madame Magloire had said, with a sort of gentle malice, "Monseigneur, although you turn everything to use, here is an unemployed plot. It would be better to have lettuces there than bouquets." "Madame Magloire," the Bishop answered, "you are mistaken; the beautiful is as useful as the useful." He added, after a moment's silence, "More so, perhaps."

This square, composed of three or four borders, occupied the Bishop almost as much as his books did. He liked to spend an hour or two there, cutting, raking, and digging holes in which he placed seeds. He was not so hostile to insects as a gardener would have liked. However, he made no pretensions to botany; he was ignorant of groups and solidism; he did not make the slightest attempt to decide between Tournefort and the natural method; he was not a partisan either of Jussieu or Linnæus. He did not study plants, but he loved flowers. He greatly respected the professors, but he respected the ignorant even more; and without ever failing in this respect, he watered his borders every summer evening with a green-painted tin pot.

The house had not a single door that locked. The door of the dining-room, which, as we said, opened right on the cathedral square, had formerly been adorned with bolts and locks like a prison gate. The Bishop had all this iron removed, and the door was only hasped either night or day: the first passer-by, no matter the hour, had only to push it. At the outset the two females had been greatly alarmed by this never-closed door; but the Bishop said to them, "Have bolts placed on the doors of your rooms if you like." In the end they shared his confidence, or at least affected to do so: Madame Magloire alone was from time to time alarmed. As regards the Bishop, his idea is explained, or at least indicated, by these three lines, which he wrote on the margin of a Bible: "This is the distinction: the physician's doors must never be closed, the priest's door must always be open." On another book, entitled "Philosophy of Medical Science," he wrote this other note: "Am I not a physician like them? I also have my patients: in the first place, I have theirs, whom they call the sick, and then I have my own, whom I call the unhappy." Elsewhere he also wrote: "Do not ask the name of the man who seeks a bed from you, for it is before all the man whom his name embarrasses that needs an asylum."

It came about that a worthy curé—I forget whether it were he of Couloubroux or he of Pompierry—thought proper to ask him one day, probably at the instigation of Madame Magloire, whether Monseigneur was quite certain that he was not acting to some extent imprudently by leaving his door open day and night for any who liked to enter, and if he did not fear lest some misfortune might happen in a house so poorly guarded. The Bishop tapped his shoulder with gentle gravity, and said to him, "Nisi Dominus custodierit domum, in vanum vigilant qui custodiunt eam."

Then he spoke of something else. He was fond of saying too, "There is the Priest's bravery as well as that of the Colonel of Dragoons. The only thing is that ours must be quiet."

CHAPTER VII

CRAVATTE.

Here naturally comes a fact which we must not omit, for it is one of those which will enable us to see what manner of man the Bishop of D—— was. After the destruction of the band of Gaspard Bès, which had infested the gorges of Ollioules, Cravatte, one of his lieutenants, took refuge in the mountains. He concealed himself for a while with his brigands, the remnant of Bès' band, in the county of Nice, then went to Piedmont, and suddenly re-appeared in France, via Barcelonnette. He was seen first at Jauziers, and next at Tuiles; he concealed himself in the caverns of the Joug de l'Aigle, and descended thence on the hamlets and villages by the ravines of the Ubaye. He pushed on even as far as Embrun, entered the church one night and plundered the sacristy. His brigandage desolated the country, and the gendarmes were in vain placed on his track. He constantly escaped, and at times even offered resistance, for he was a bold scoundrel. In the midst of all this terror the Bishop arrived on his visitation, and the Mayor came to him and urged him to turn back. Cravatte held the mountain as far as Arche and beyond, and there was danger, even with an escort. It would be uselessly exposing three or four unhappy gendarmes.

"For that reason," said the Bishop, "I intend to go without escort."

"Can you mean it, Monseigneur?" the Mayor exclaimed.

"I mean it so fully that I absolutely refuse gendarmes, and intend to start in an hour."

"Monseigneur, you will not do that!"

"There is in the mountain," the Bishop continued, "a humble little parish, which I have not visited for three years. They are good friends of mine, and quiet and honest shepherds. They are the owners of one goat out of every thirty they guard; they make very pretty woollen ropes of different colors, and they play mountain airs on small six-holed flutes. They want to hear about heaven every now and then, and what would they think of a bishop who was afraid? What would they say if I did not go?"

"But, Monseigneur, the brigands."

"Ah," said the Bishop, "you are right; I may meet them. They too must want to hear about heaven."

"But this band is a flock of wolves."

"Monsieur Mayor, it may be that this is precisely the flock of which Christ has made me the shepherd. Who knows the ways of Providence?"

"Monseigneur, they will plunder you."

"I have nothing."

"They will kill you."

"A poor old priest who passes by, muttering his mummery? Nonsense, what good would that do them?"

"Oh, good gracious, if you were to meet them!"

"I would ask them for alms for my poor."

"Monseigneur, do not go. In Heaven's name do not, for you expose your life."

"My good sir," said the Bishop, "is that all? I am not in this world to save my life, but to save souls."

There was no help for it, and he set out only accompanied by a lad, who offered to act as his guide. His obstinacy created a sensation in the country, and caused considerable alarm. He would not take either his sister or Madame Magloire with him. He crossed the mountain on a mule, met nobody, and reached his good friends the goat-herds safe and sound. He remained with them a fortnight, preaching, administering the sacraments, teaching, and moralizing. When he was ready to start for home he resolved to sing a Te Deum pontifically, and spoke about it to the Curé. But what was to be done? There were no episcopal ornaments. All that could be placed at his disposal was a poor village sacristy, with a few old faded and pinchbeck covered chasubles.

"Pooh!" said the Bishop; "announce the Te Deum in your sermon for all that. It will come right in the end."

Inquiries were made in the surrounding churches: but all the magnificence of these united humble parishes would not have been sufficient decently to equip a cathedral chorister. While they were in this embarrassment a large chest was brought and left at the curacy for the Bishop by two strange horse-men, who started again at once. The chest was opened and found to contain a cope of cloth of gold, a mitre adorned with diamonds, an archiepiscopal cross, a magnificent crozier, and all the pontifical robes stolen a month back from the treasury of our Lady of Embrun. In the chest was a paper on which were written these words: "Cravatte to Monseigneur Welcome."

"Did I not tell you that it would be all right?" the Bishop said; then he added with a smile, "God sends an archbishop's cope to a man who is contented with a curé's surplice."

"Monseigneur," the Curé muttered, with a gentle shake of his head, "God—or the devil."

The Bishop looked fixedly at the Curé and repeated authoritatively, "God!"

When he returned to Chastelon, and all along the road, he was regarded curiously. He found at the Presbytery of that town Mlle. Baptistine and Madame Magloire waiting for him, and he said to his sister, "Well, was I right? The poor priest went among these poor mountaineers with empty hands, and returns with his hands full. I started only taking with me my confidence in Heaven, and I bring back the treasures of a cathedral."

The same evening before retiring he said too, "Never let us fear robbers or murderers. These are external and small dangers; let us fear ourselves; prejudices are the real robbers, vices the true murderers. The great dangers are within ourselves. Let us not trouble about what threatens our head or purse, and only think of what threatens our soul." Then, turning to his sister, he added, "Sister, a priest ought never to take precautions against his neighbor. What his neighbor does God permits, so let us confine ourselves to praying to God when we believe that a danger is impending over us. Let us pray, not for ourselves, but that our brother may not fall into error on our account."

Events, however, were rare in his existence. We relate those we know, but ordinarily he spent his life in always doing the same things at the same moment. A month of his year resembled an hour of his day. As to what became of the treasure of Embrun Cathedral, we should be greatly embarrassed if questioned on that head. There were many fine things, very tempting and famous to steal on behalf of the poor. Stolen they were already, one moiety of the adventure was accomplished: the only thing left to do was to change the direction of the robbery, and make it turn slightly towards the poor. Still, we affirm nothing on the subject; we merely mention that among the Bishop's papers a rather obscure note was found, which probably refers to this question, and was thus conceived: "The question is to know whether it ought to go to the cathedral or the hospital."

CHAPTER VIII.

PHILOSOPHY AFTER DRINKING.

The Senator, to whom we have already alluded, was a skilful man, who had made his way with a rectitude that paid no attention to all those things which constitute obstacles, and are called conscience, plighted word, right, and duty: he had gone straight to his object without once swerving from the line of his promotions and his interest. He was an ex-procureur, softened by success, anything but a wicked man, doing all the little services in his power for his sons, his sons-in-law, his relatives, and even his friends: he had selected the best opportunities, and the rest seemed to him something absurd. He was witty, and just sufficiently lettered to believe himself a disciple of Epicurus, while probably only a product of Pigault Lebrun. He was fond of laughing pleasantly at things infinite and eternal, and at the crotchets "of our worthy Bishop." He even laughed at them with amiable authority in M. Myriel's presence. On some semi-official occasion the Count—(this Senator) and M. Myriel met at the Prefect's table. At the dessert the Senator, who was merry but quite sober, said,—

"Come, Bishop, let us have a chat. A senator and a bishop can hardly meet without winking at each other, for we are two augurs, and I am about to make a confession to you. I have my system of philosophy."

"And you are right," the Bishop answered; "as you make your philosophy, so you must lie on it. You are on the bed of purple."

The Senator, thus encouraged, continued,—"Let us be candid."

"Decidedly."

"I declare to you," the Senator went on, "that the Marquis d'Argens, Pyrrho, Hobbes, and Naigeon are no impostors. I have in my library all my philosophers with gilt backs."

"Like yourself, Count," the Bishop interrupted him.

The Senator proceeded,—

"I hate Diderot; he is an ideologist, a declaimer, and a revolutionist, believing in his heart in Deity, and more bigoted than Voltaire. The latter ridiculed Needham, and was wrong, for Needham's eels prove that God is unnecessary. A drop of vinegar in a spoonful of flour supplies the *fiat lux*; suppose the drop larger, and the spoonful bigger, and you have the world. Man is the eel; then, of what use is the Eternal Father? My dear Bishop, the Jehovah hypothesis wearies me; it is only fitted to produce thin people who think hollow. Down with the great All which annoys me! Long live Zero, who leaves me at peace! Between ourselves, and in order to confess to my pastor, as is right and proper, I confess to you that I possess common sense. I am not wild about your Saviour, who continually preaches abnegation and sacrifice. It is advice offered by a miser to beggars. Abnegation, why? Sacrifice, for what object? I do not see that one wolf sacrifices itself to cause the happiness of another wolf. Let us, therefore, remain in nature. We are at the summit, so let us have the supreme philosophy. What is the use of being at the top, if you cannot see further than the end of other people's noses? Let us live gayly, for life is all in all. As for man having a future elsewhere, up there, down there, somewhere, I do not believe a syllable of it. Oh yes! recommend sacrifices and abnegation to me. I must take care of all I do. I must rack my brains about good and evil, justice and injustice, fas et nefas. Why so? because I shall have to give account for my actions. When? after my death. What a fine dream! after death! He will be a clever fellow who catches me. Just think of a lump of ashes seized by a shadowy hand. Let us speak the truth, we who are initiated and have raised the skirt of Isis; there is no good, no evil, but there is vegetation. Let us seek reality and go to the bottom; hang it all, we must scent the truth, dig into the ground for it and seize it. Then it offers you exquisite delights; then you become strong and laugh. I am square at the base, my dear Bishop, and human immortality is a thing which anybody who likes may listen to. Oh! what a charming prospect! What a fine billet Adam has! You are a soul, you will be an angel, and have blue wings on your shoulder-blades. Come, help me, is it not Tertullian who says that the blessed will go from one planet to the other? Very good; they will be the grasshoppers of the planets. And then they will see God; Ta, ta, ta. These paradises are all nonsense, and God is a monstrous fable. I would not say so in the *Moniteur*, of course, but I whisper it between friends, *inter pocula*. Sacrificing the earth for paradise is giving up the substance for the shadow. I am not such an ass as to be the dupe of the Infinite. I am nothing, my name is Count Nothing, Senator. Did I exist before my birth? no; shall I exist after my death? no. What am I? a little dust aggregated by an organism. What have I to do on this earth? I have the choice between suffering and enjoyment. To what will suffering lead me? to nothingness, but I shall have suffered. To what will enjoyment lead me? to nothingness, but I shall have enjoyed. My choice is made; a man must either eat or be eaten, and so I eat, for it is better to be the tooth than the grass. That is my wisdom; after which go on as I impel you; the grave-digger is there, the Pantheon for such as us, and all fall into the large hole. *Finis*, and total liquidation, that is the vanishing point Death is dead, take my word for it; and I laugh at the idea of any one present affirming the contrary. It is an invention of nurses, old Bogey for children, Jehovah for men. No, our morrow is night; behind the tomb there is nothing but equal nothings. You may have been Sardanapalus, you may have been St. Vincent de Paul: it all comes to the same—nothing. That is the truth, so live above all else; make use of your *me*, so long as you hold it. In truth, I tell you, my dear Bishop, I have my philosophy, and I have my philosophers, and I do not let myself be deluded by fables. After all, something must be offered persons who are down in the world,—the barefooted, the strugglers for existence and the wretched: and so they are offered pure legends—chimeras—the soul—immortality—paradise —the stars—to swallow. They chew that and put it on their dry bread. The man who has nothing has God, and that is something at any rate. I do not oppose it, but I keep M. Naigeon for myself; God is good for the plebs."

The Bishop clapped his hands.

"That is what I call speaking," he exclaimed. "Ah, what an excellent and truly wonderful thing this materialism is! it is not every man who wishes that can have it. Ah! when a man has reached that point, he is no longer a dupe; he does not let himself be stupidly exiled, like Cato; or stoned, like St. Stephen; or burnt, like Joan of Arc. Those who have succeeded in acquiring this materialism have the joy of feeling themselves irresponsible, and thinking that they can devour everything without anxiety, places, sinecures, power well or badly gained, dignities, lucrative tergiversations, useful treachery, folly, capitulations with their consciences, and that they will go down to the tomb after digesting it all properly. How agreeable this is! I am not referring to you, my dear Senator, still I cannot refrain from congratulating you. You great gentlemen have, as you say, a philosophy of your own, and for yourselves, exquisite, refined, accessible to the rich alone, good with any sauce, and admirably seasoning the joys of life. This philosophy is drawn from the profundities, and dug up by special searchers. But you are kind fellows, and think it no harm that belief in God should be the philosophy of the populace, much in the same way as a goose stuffed with chestnuts is the truffled turkey of the poor."

CHAPTER IX

THE BROTHER DESCRIBED BY THE SISTER.

To give an idea of the domestic life of the Bishop of D——, and the manner in which these two saintly women subordinated their actions, their thoughts, even their feminine instincts, which were easily startled, to the habits and intentions of the Bishop, before he required to express them in words, we cannot do better than copy here a letter from Mlle Baptistine to the Viscountess de Boischevron, her friend of childhood. This letter is in our possession.

"D——, 16th Dec., 18——.

"MY DEAR MADAME,—Not a day passes in which we do not talk about you.

That is our general habit, but there is an extra reason at present. Just imagine that, in washing and dusting the ceilings and walls, Madame Magloire has made a discovery, and now our two rooms papered with old white-washed paper would not disgrace a chateau like yours. Madame Magloire has torn down all the paper, and there are things under it. My sitting-room, in which there was no furniture, and in which we used to hang up the linen to dry, is fifteen feet in height, eighteen wide, and has a ceiling which was once gilded, and rafters, as in your house. It was covered with canvas during the time this mansion was an hospital. But it is my bed-room, you should see; Madame Magloire has discovered, under at least ten layers of paper, paintings which, though not excellent, are endurable. There is Telemachus dubbed a knight by Minerva; and there he is again in the gardens: I forget their names, but where the Roman ladies only went for a single night. What can I tell you? I have Roman ladies (*here an illegible word*), and so on. Madame Magloire has got it all straight. This summer she intends to repair a little damage, re-varnish it all, and my bed-room will be a real museum. She has also found in a corner of the garret two consoles in the old fashion; they want twelve francs to regild them, but it is better to give that sum to the poor: besides, they are frightfully ugly, and I should prefer a round mahogany table.

"I am very happy, for my brother is so good; he gives all he has to the sick and the poor, and we are often greatly pressed. The country is hard in winter, and something must be done for those who are in want. We are almost lighted and warmed, and, as you can see, that is a great comfort. My brother has peculiar habits; when he does talk, he says 'that a bishop should be so.' Just imagine that the house door is never closed: any one who likes can come in, and is at once in my brother's presence. He fears nothing, not even night; and he says that is his way of showing his bravery. He does not wish me to feel alarmed for him, or for Madame Magloire to do so; he exposes himself to all dangers, and does not wish us to appear as if we even noticed it. We must understand him. He goes out in the rain, he wades through the water, and travels in winter. He is not afraid of the night, suspicious roads, or encounters. Last year he went all alone into a country of robbers, for he would not take us with him. He stayed away a whole fortnight, and folk thought him dead, but he came back all right, and said, 'Here's the way in which I was robbed,' and he opened a chest full of all the treasures of Embrun Cathedral, which the robbers had given him. That time I could not refrain from scolding him a little, but was careful only to speak when the wheels made a noise, so that no one could hear me.

"At first I said to myself; there is no danger that checks him, and he is terrible; but at present I have grown accustomed to it. I make Madame Magloire a sign not to annoy him, and he risks his life as he pleases. I carry off Magloire, go to my bed-room, pray for him, and fall asleep. I am tranquil because I know that if any harm happened to him it would be the death of me. I shall go to heaven with my brother and my bishop. Madame Magloire has had greater difficulty than myself in accustoming herself to what she calls his imprudence, but at present she has learned to put up with it. We both pray; we are terrified together, and fall asleep. If the Fiend were to enter the house no one would try to stop him, and after all what have we to fear in this house? There is always some one with us who is the stronger, the demon may pass by, but our Lord lives in it. That is enough for me, and my brother no longer requires to say a word to me. I understand him without his speaking, and we leave ourselves in the hands of Providence, for that is the way in which you must behave to a man who has grandeur in his soul.

"I have questioned my brother about the information you require concerning the De Faux family. You are aware that he knows everything, and what a memory he has, for he is still a good Royalist. It is really a very old Norman family belonging to the Generalty of Caen. Five hundred years ago there were a Raoul, a John, and a Thomas de Faux, who were gentlemen, and one of them Seigneur of Rochefort. The last was Guy Stephen Alexander, who was Major-general, and something in the Brittany Light Horse: his daughter, Maria Louisa, married Adrian Charles de Gramont, son of Duke Louis de Gramont, Peer of France, Colonel of the French Guards, and Lieutenant-general in the army. The name is written Faux, Fauq, and Faouq.

"My dear madam, recommend us to the prayers of your holy relative the Cardinal. As for your dear Sylvanie, she has done well in not wasting the few moments she passes by your side in writing to me. She is well, works according to your wishes, and loves me still: that is all I desire. Her souvenir sent me through you safely reached me, and I am delighted at it. My health is not bad, and yet I grow thinner every day. Good-by, my paper is running out and compels me to break off. A thousand kind regards from your Baptistine.

"p.s. Your little nephew is delightful: do you know that he is nearly five years of age? Yesterday he saw a horse pass with knee-caps on, and he said, 'What has he got on his knees?' He is such a dear child. His little brother drags an old broom about the room like a coach, and cries, 'Hu!'"

As may be seen from this letter, the two women managed to yield to the Bishop's ways, with the genius peculiar to woman, who comprehends a man better than he does himself. The Bishop of D——, beneath the candid, gentle air which never broke down, at times did grand, bold, and magnificent things, without even appearing to suspect the fact. They trembled, but let him alone. At times Madame Magloire would hazard a remonstrance beforehand, but never during or after the deed. They never troubled him either by word or sign when he had once begun an affair. At certain moments, without his needing to mention the fact, or perhaps when he was not conscious of it, so perfect was his simplicity, they vaguely felt that he was acting episcopally, and at such times they were only two shadows in the house. They served him passively, and if disappearance were obedience, they disappeared. They knew, with an admirable intuitive delicacy, that certain attentions might vex him, and hence, though they might believe him in peril, they understood, I will not say his thoughts, but his nature, and no longer watched over him. They intrusted him to God. Moreover, Baptistine said, as we have just read, that her brother's death would be her death. Madame Magloire did not say so, but she knew it.

CHAPTER X

THE BISHOP FACES A NEW LIGHT.

At a period rather later than the date of the letter just quoted he did a thing which the whole town declared to be even more venturesome than his trip in the mountains among the bandits. A man lived alone in the country near D——: this man, let us out with the great word at once, was an ex-conventionalist, of the name of G——. People talked about him in the little world of D—— with a species of horror. A conventionalist, only think of that! Those men existed at the time when people "thou-ed" one another and were called citizens. This man was almost a monster: he had not voted for the King's death, but had done all but that, and was a quasi-regicide. How was it that this man had not been tried by court-martial, on the return of the legitimate princes? They need not have cut his head off, for clemency is all right and proper, but banishment for life would have been an example, and so on. Moreover, he was an atheist, like all those men. It was the gossip of geese round a vulture.

And was this G—— a vulture? Yes, if he might be judged by his ferocious solitude. As he had not voted the King's death, he was not comprised in the decree of exile, and was enabled to remain in France. He lived about three miles from the town, far from every village, every road, in a nook of a very wild valley. He had there, so it was said, a field, a hut, a den. He had no neighbors, not even passers-by; since he had lived in the valley the path leading to it had become overgrown with grass. People talked of the spot as of the hangman's house. Yet the Bishop thought of it, and from time to time gazed at a spot on the horizon where a clump of trees pointed out the old conventionalist's valley, and said "There is a soul there alone," and he added to himself, "I owe him a visit."

But, let us confess it, this idea, which at the first blush was natural, seemed to him after a moment's reflection strange and impossible, almost repulsive. For, in his heart, he shared the general impression, and the conventionalist inspired him, without his being able to account for it, with that feeling which is the border line of hatred, and which is so well expressed by the word "estrangement."

Still the shepherd ought not to keep aloof from a scabby sheep; but then what a sheep it was! The good Bishop was perplexed; at times he started in that direction, but turned back. One day a rumor spread in the town, that a shepherd boy who waited on G—— in his den, had come to fetch a doctor: the old villain was dying, paralysis was overpowering him, and he could not last out the night. Happy release! some added.

The Bishop took his stick, put on his overcoat to hide his well-worn cassock, as well as to protect him against the night breeze which would soon rise, and set out. The sun had almost attained the horizon when the Bishop reached the excommunicated spot. He perceived with a certain heart-beating that he was close to the wild beast's den. He strode across a ditch, clambered over a hedge, entered a neglected garden, and suddenly perceived the cavern behind some shrubs. It was a low, poor-looking hut, small and clean, with a vine nailed over the front.

In front of the door an old white-haired man, seated in a worn-out wheel-chair, was smiling in the sun. By his side stood a boy, who handed him a pot of milk. While the Bishop was looking at him the old man uplifted his voice. "Thanks," he said, "I want nothing further," and his smile was turned from the sun to rest on the boy.

The Bishop stepped forward, and at the noise of his footsteps the seated man turned his head, and his face expressed all the surprise it is possible to feel after a long life.

"Since I have lived here," he said, "you are the first person who has come to me. Who may you be, sir?"

The Bishop answered, "My name is Bienvenu Myriel."

"I have heard that name uttered. Are you not he whom the peasants call Monseigneur Welcome?"

"I am."

The old man continued, with a half-smile, "In that case you are my Bishop?"

"A little."

"Come in, sir."

The conventionalist offered his hand to the Bishop, but the Bishop did not take it—he confined himself to saying,—

"I am pleased to see that I was deceived. You certainly do not look ill."

"I am about to be cured, sir," the old man said; then after a pause he added, "I shall be dead in three hours. I am a bit of a physician, and know in what way the last hour comes. Yesterday only my feet were cold; to-day the chill reached my knees; now I can feel it ascending to my waist, and when it reaches the heart I shall stop. The sun is glorious, is it not? I had myself wheeled out in order to take a farewell glance at things. You can talk to me, for it does not weary me. You have done well to come and look at a dying man, for it is proper that there should be witnesses. People have their fancies, and I should have liked to go on till dawn. But I know that I can hardly last three hours. It will be night, but, after all, what matter? Finishing is a simple affair, and daylight is not necessary for it. Be it so, I will die by star-light."

Then he turned to the lad:

"Go to bed. You sat up the other night, and must be tired."

The boy went into the cabin; the old man looked after him, and added, as if speaking to himself,—

"While he is sleeping I shall die; the two slumbers can keep each other company."

The Bishop was not so moved as we might imagine he would be. He did not think that he saw God in this way of dying: and—let us out with it, as the small contradictions of great hearts must also be indicated—he, who at times laughed so heartily at his grandeur, was somewhat annoyed at not being called Monseigneur, and was almost tempted to reply, Citizen. He felt an inclination for coarse familiarity, common enough with doctors and priests, but to which he was not accustomed. This man after all, this conventionalist, this representative of the people, had been a mighty one of the earth: for the first time in his life, perhaps, the Bishop felt disposed to sternness.

The Republican, in the mean while, regarded him with modest cordiality, in which, perhaps, could be traced that humility which is so becoming in a man who is on the point of returning to the dust. The Bishop, on his side, though he generally guarded against curiosity, which according to him was akin to insult, could not refrain from examining the conventionalist with an attention which, as it did not emanate from sympathy, would have pricked his conscience in the case of any other man. The conventionalist produced the effect upon him of being beyond the pale of the law, even the law of charity.

G——, calm, almost upright, and possessing a sonorous voice, was one of those grand octogenarians who are the amazement of the physiologist. The Revolution possessed many such men, proportioned to the age. The thoroughly tried man could be seen in him, and, though so near his end, he had retained all the signs of health. There was something which would disconcert death in his bright glance, his firm accent, and the robust movement of his shoulders: Azrael, the Mohammedan angel of the tomb, would have turned back fancying that he had mistaken the door. G—— seemed to be dying because he wished to do so; there was liberty in his agony, and his legs alone, by which the shadows clutched him, were motionless. While the feet were dead and cold, the head lived with all the power of life and appeared in full light. G—— at this awful moment resembled the king in the Oriental legend, flesh above and marble below. The Bishop sat down on a stone and began rather abruptly:—

"I congratulate you," he said, in the tone people employ to reprimand; "*at least* you did not vote the King's death."

The Republican did not seem to notice the covert bitterness of this remark, *at least*; he replied, without a smile on his face,—

"Do not congratulate me, sir: I voted the death of the tyrant." It was the accent of austerity opposed to that of sternness.

"What do you mean?" the Bishop continued.

"I mean that man has a tyrant, Ignorance, and I voted for the end of that tyrant which engendered royalty, which is the false authority, while knowledge is the true authority. Man must only be governed by knowledge."

"And by his conscience," the Bishop added.

"That is the same thing. Conscience is the amount of innate knowledge we have in us."

Monseigneur Welcome listened in some surprise to this language, which was very novel to him. The Republican continued,—

"As for Louis XVI. I said No. I do not believe that I have the right to kill a man, but I feel the duty of exterminating a tyrant, and I voted for the end of the tyrant. That is to say, for the end of prostitution for women; the end of slavery for men; and the end of night for children. In voting for the Republic I voted for all this: I voted for fraternity, concord, the Dawn! I aided in the overthrow of errors and prejudices, and such an overthrow produces light; we hurled down the old world, and that vase of wretchedness, by being poured over the human race, became an urn of joy."

"Mingled joy," said the Bishop.

"You might call it a troubled joy, and now, after that fatal return of the past which is called 1814, a departed joy. Alas! the work was incomplete, I grant; we demolished the ancient régime in facts, but were not able to suppress it completely in ideas. It is not sufficient to destroy abuses, but morals must also be modified. Though the mill no longer exists, the wind still blows."

"You demolished: it may be useful, but I distrust a demolition complicated with passion."

"Right has its passion, Sir Bishop, and that passion is an element of progress. No matter what may be said, the French Revolution is the most powerful step taken by the human race since the advent of Christ. It may be incomplete, but it was sublime. It softened minds, it calmed, appeased, and enlightened, and it spread civilization over the world. The French Revolution was good, for it was the consecration of humanity."

The Bishop could not refrain from muttering,—"Yes? '93!"

The Republican drew himself up with almost mournful solemnity, and shouted, as well as a dying man could shout,—

"Ah! there we have it! I have been waiting for that. A cloud had been collecting for fifteen hundred years, and at the end of that period it burst: you are condemning the thunder-clap."

The Bishop, without perhaps confessing it to himself, felt that the blow had gone home; still he kept a good countenance, and answered,—

"The judge speaks in the name of justice; the priest speaks in that of pity, which is only a higher form of justice. A thunder-clap must not deceive itself."

And he added as he looked fixedly at the conventionalist,—

"And Louis XVII.?"

The Republican stretched forth his hand and seized the Bishop's arm.

"Louis XVII. Let us consider. Whom do you weep for? Is it the innocent child? in that case I weep with you. Is it the royal child? in that case I must ask leave to reflect. For me, the thought of the brother of Cartouche, an innocent lad, hung up under the armpits in the Place de Grève until death ensued, for the sole crime of being Cartouche's brother, is not less painful than the grandson of Louis XV., the innocent boy martyrized in the Temple Tower for the sole crime of being the grandson of Louis XV."

"I do not like such an association of names, sir," said the Bishop.

"Louis XV.? Cartouche? On behalf of which do you protest?"

There was a moment's silence; the Bishop almost regretted having come, and yet felt himself vaguely and strangely shaken. The conventionalist continued, —

"Ah! sir priest, you do not like the crudities of truth, but Christ loved them; he took a scourge and swept the temple. His lightning lash was a rough discourser of truths. When he exclaimed, 'Suffer little children to come unto me,' he made no distinction among them. He made no difference between the dauphin of Barabbas and the dauphin of Herod. Innocence is its own crown, and does not require to be a Highness; it is as august in rags as when crowned with *fleurs de lis*."

"That is true," said the Bishop in a low voice.

"You have named Louis XVII.," the conventionalist continued; "let us understand each other. Shall we weep for all the innocents, martyrs, and children of the lowest as of the highest rank? I am with you there, but as I said, in that case we must go back beyond '93, and begin our tears before Louis XVII. I will weep over the children of the kings with you, provided that you weep with me over the children of the people."

"I weep for all," said the Bishop.

"Equally!" G—— exclaimed; "and if the balance must be uneven, let it be on the side of the people, as they have suffered the longest."

There was again a silence, which the Republican broke. He rose on his elbow, held his chin with his thumb and forefinger, as a man does mechanically when he is interrogating and judging, and fixed on the Bishop a glance full of all the energy of approaching death. It was almost an explosion.

"Yes, sir; the people have suffered for a long time. But let me ask why you have come to question and speak to me about Louis XVII.? I do not know you. Ever since I have been in this country I have lived here alone, never setting my foot across the threshold, and seeing no one but the boy who attends to me. Your name, it is true, has vaguely reached me, and I am bound to say that it was pronounced affectionately, but that means nothing, for clever people have so many ways of making the worthy, simple folk believe in them. By the bye, I did not hear the sound of your coach; you doubtless left it down there behind that clump of trees at the cross roads. I do not know you, I tell you; you have informed me that you are the Bishop, but that teaches me nothing as to your moral character. In a word—I repeat my question, Who are you? You are a bishop, that is to say, a prince of the Church, one of those gilded, escutcheoned annuitants who have fat prebends—the Bishopric of D

——, with 15,000 francs income, 10,000 francs fees, or a total of 25,000 francs,—who have kitchens, liveries, keep a good table, and eat water-fowl on a Friday; who go about, with lackeys before and behind, in a gilded coach, in the name of the Saviour who walked barefoot! You are a prelate; you have, like all the rest, income, palace, horses, valets, a good table, and like all the rest you enjoy them: that is all very well, but it says either too much or too little; it does not enlighten me as to your intrinsic and essential value when you come with the probable intention of bringing me wisdom. To whom am I speaking—who are you?"

The Bishop bowed his head, and answered, "I am a worm."

"A worm in a carriage!" the Republican growled.

It was his turn to be haughty, the Bishop's to be humble; the latter continued gently,—

"Be it so, sir. But explain to me how my coach, which is a little way off behind the trees, my good table, and the water-fowl I eat on Friday, my palace, my income, and my footmen, prove that pity is not a virtue, that clemency is not a duty, and that '93 was not inexorable."

The Republican passed his hand over his forehead, as if to remove a cloud.

"Before answering you," he said, "I must ask you to forgive me. I was in the wrong, sir, for you are in my house and my guest. You discuss my ideas, and I must restrict myself to combating your reasoning. Your wealth and enjoyments are advantages which I have over you in the debate, but courtesy bids me not employ them. I promise not to do so again."

"I thank you," said the Bishop.

G—— continued: "Let us return to the explanation you asked of me. Where were we? What was it you said, that '93 was inexorable?"

"Yes, inexorable," the Bishop said; "what do you think of Marat clapping his hands at the guillotine?"

"What do you think of Bossuet singing a Te Deum over the Dragonnades?"

The response was harsh, but went to its mark with the rigidity of a Minié bullet. The Bishop started, and could not parry it, but he was hurt by this way of mentioning Bossuet. The best minds have their fetishes, and at times feel vaguely wounded by any want of respect on the part of logic. The conventionalist was beginning to gasp; that asthma which is mingled with the last breath affected his voice; still he retained perfect mental clearness in his eyes. He continued,—

"Let us say a few words more on this head. Beyond the Revolution, which, taken in its entirety, is an immense human affirmation, '93, alas, is a reply. You consider it inexorable, but what was the whole monarchy? Carrier is a bandit, but what name do you give to Montrevel? Fouquier Tainville is a scoundrel, but what is your opinion about Lamoignon-Bâville? Maillard is frightful, but what of Saulx-Tavannes, if you please? Father Duchêne is ferocious, but what epithet will you allow me for Père Letellier? Jourdan Coupe-Tête is a monster, but less so than the Marquis de Louvois. I pity Marie Antoinette, Archduchess and Queen, but I also pity the poor Huguenot woman who, in 1685, while suckling her child, was fastened, naked to the waist, to a stake, while her infant was held at a distance. Her breast was swollen with milk, her heart with agony; the babe, hungry and pale, saw that breast and screamed for it, and the hangman said to the wife, mother, and nurse, 'Abjure!' giving her the choice between the death of her infant and the death of her conscience. What do you say of this punishment of Tantalus adapted to a woman? Remember this carefully, sir, the French Revolution had its reasons, and its wrath will be absolved by the future. Its result is a better world; and a caress for the human race issues from its most terrible blows. I must stop, for the game is all in my favor—besides, I am dying."

And ceasing to regard the Bishop, the Republican finished his thought with the following few calm words,—

"Yes, the brutalities of progress are called revolutions, but when they are ended, this fact is recognized; the human race has been chastised, but it has moved onwards."

The Republican did not suspect that he had carried in turn every one of the Bishop's internal intrenchments. One still remained, however, and from this, the last resource of Monseigneur's resistance, came this remark, in which all the roughness of the commencement was perceptible.

"Progress must believe in God, and the good cannot have impious servants. A man who is an atheist is a bad guide for the human race."

The ex-representative of the people did not reply. He trembled, looked up to the sky, and a tear slowly collected in his eye. When the lid was full the tear ran down his livid cheek, and he said in a low, shaking voice, as if speaking to himself,—

"Oh thou! oh ideal! thou alone existest!"

The Bishop had a sort of inexpressible commotion; after a silence the old man raised a finger to heaven and said,—

"The infinite is. It is there. If the infinite had not a me, the I would be its limit; it would not be infinite; in other words, it would not be. But it is. Hence it has a me. This I of the infinite is God."

The dying man uttered these words in a loud voice, and with a shudder of ecstasy as if he saw some one. When he had spoken his eyes closed, for the effort had exhausted him. It was evident that he had lived in one minute the few hours left him. The supreme moment was at hand. The Bishop understood it; he had come here as a priest, and had gradually passed from extreme coldness to extreme emotion; he looked at these closed eyes, he took this wrinkled and chilly hand and bent down over the dying man.

"This hour is God's. Would you not consider it matter of regret if we had met in vain?"

The Republican opened his eyes again; a gravity which suggested the shadow of death was imprinted on his countenance.

"YOUR BLESSING!" SAID THE BISHOP, AND KNELT DOWN.

"Monsieur le Bishop," he said, with a slowness produced perhaps more by the dignity of the soul than by failing of his strength, "I have spent my life in meditation, contemplation, and study. I was sixty years of age when my country summoned me and ordered me to interfere in its affairs. I obeyed. There were abuses, and I combated them; tyranny, and I destroyed it; rights and principles, and I proclaimed and confessed them; the territory was invaded, and I defended it; France was menaced, and I offered her my chest; I was not rich, and I am poor. I was one of the masters of the State; the bank cellars were so filled with specie that it was necessary to prop up the walls, which were ready to burst through the weight of gold and silver, but I dined in the Rue de l'Arbre Sec, at two-and-twenty sous a head. I succored the oppressed. I relieved the suffering. I tore up the altar cloth, it is true, but it was to stanch the wounds of the country. I ever supported the onward march of the human race towards light, and I at times resisted pitiless progress. When opportunity served, I protected my adversaries, men of your class. And there is at Peteghem in Flanders, on the same site where the Merovingian Kings had their summer palace, a monastery of Urbanists, the Abbey of St. Claire en Beaulieu, which I saved in 1793. I did my duty according to my strength, and what good I could. After which I was driven out, tracked, pursued, persecuted, maligned, mocked, spat upon, accursed, and proscribed. For many years I have felt that persons believed they had a right to despise me. My face has been held accursed by the poor ignorant mob, and, while hating no one, I accepted the isolation of hatred. Now, I am eighty-six years of age and on the point of death; what have you come to ask of me?"

"Your blessing!" said the Bishop, and knelt down. When the Bishop raised his head again, the conventionalist's countenance had become august: he had just expired. The Bishop returned home absorbed in the strangest thoughts, and spent the whole night in prayer. On the morrow curious worthies tried to make him talk about G—— the Republican, but he only pointed to heaven. From this moment he redoubled his tenderness and fraternity for the little ones and the suffering.

Any allusion to "that old villain of a G——" made him fall into a singular reverie; no one could say that the passing of that mind before his, and the reflection that great conscience cast upon his, had not something to do with this approach to perfection. This "pastoral visit" nearly created a stir among the small local coteries.

"Was it a bishop's place to visit the death-bed of such a man? It was plain that he had no conversion to hope for, for all these Revolutionists are relapsed! Then why go? what had he to see there? He must have been very curious to see the fiend carry off a soul."

One day a Dowager, of the impertinent breed which believes itself witty, asked him this question, "Monseigneur, people are asking when your Grandeur will have the red cap?" "Oh, oh!" the Bishop answered, "that is an ominous color. Fortunately those who despise it in a cap venerate it in a hat."

CHAPTER XI

A RESTRICTION.

We should run a strong risk of making a mistake were we to conclude from this that Monseigneur Welcome was "a philosophic bishop," or "a patriotic curé." His meeting, which might almost be called his conjunction, with the conventionalist G—— produced in him a sort of amazement, which rendered him more gentle than ever. That was all.

Though Monseigneur was anything rather than a politician, this is perhaps the place to indicate briefly what was his attitude in the events of that period, supposing that Monseigneur ever dreamed of having an attitude. We will, therefore, go back for a few years. A short time after M. Myriel's elevation to the Episcopate, the Emperor made him a Baron, simultaneously with some other bishops. The arrest of the Pope took place, as is well known, on the night of July 5, 1809, at which time M. Myriel was called by Napoleon to the Synod of French and Italian Bishops convened at Paris. This Synod was held at Notre Dame and assembled for the first time on June 15, 1811, under the Presidency of Cardinal Fesch. M. Myriel was one of the ninety-five bishops convened, but he was only present at one session and three or four private conferences. As bishop of a mountain diocese, living so near to nature in rusticity and poverty, it seems that he introduced among these eminent personages ideas which changed the temperature of the assembly. He went back very soon to D——, and when questioned about this hurried return, he replied, "I was troublesome to them. The external air came in with me and I produced the effect of an open door upon them." Another time he said, "What would you have? those Messeigneurs are princes, while I am only a poor peasant bishop."

The fact is, that he displeased: among other strange things he let the following remarks slip out, one evening when he was visiting one of his most influential colleagues: "What fine clocks! What splendid carpets! What magnificent liveries! You must find all that very troublesome? Oh! I should not like to have such superfluities to yell incessantly in my ears: there are people who are hungry; there are people who are cold; there are poor, there are poor."

Let us remark parenthetically, that a hatred of luxury would not be an intelligent hatred, for it would imply a hatred of the arts. Still in churchmen any luxury beyond that connected with their sacred office is wrong, for it seems to reveal habits which are not truly charitable. An opulent priest is a paradox, for he is bound to live with the poor. Now, can a man incessantly both night and day come in contact with distress, misfortune, and want, without having about him a little of that holy wretchedness, like the dust of toil? Can we imagine a man sitting close to a stove and not feeling hot? Can we imagine a workman constantly toiling at a furnace, and have neither a hair burned, a nail blackened, nor a drop of perspiration, nor grain of soot on his face? The first proof of charity in a priest, in a bishop especially, is poverty. This was doubtless the opinion of the Bishop of D——.

We must not believe either that he shared what we might call the "ideas of the age" on certain delicate, points; he mingled but slightly in the theological questions of the moment, in which Church and State are compromised; but had he been greatly pressed we fancy he would have been found to be Ultramontane rather than Gallican. As we are drawing a portrait, and do not wish to conceal anything, we are forced to add that he was frigid toward the setting Napoleon. From 1813 he adhered to or applauded all hostile demonstrations, he refused to see him when he passed through on his return from Elba, and abstained from ordering public prayers for the Emperor during the Hundred Days.

Besides his sister, Mlle. Baptistine, he had two brothers, one a general, the other a prefect. He wrote very frequently to both of them. For some time he owed the former a grudge, because the General, who at the time of the landing at Cannes held a command in Provence, put himself at the head of twelve hundred men and pursued the Emperor as if he wished to let him escape. His correspondence was more affectionate with the other brother, the ex-prefect, a worthy, honest man, who lived retired at Paris.

Monseigneur Welcome, therefore, also had his hour of partisan spirit, his hour of bitterness, his cloud. The shadow of the passions of the moment fell athwart this gentle and great mind, which was occupied by things eternal. Certainly such a man would have deserved to have no political opinions. Pray let there be no mistake as to our meaning: we do not confound what are called "political opinions" with the grand aspiration for progress, with that sublime, patriotic, democratic and human faith, which in our days must be the foundation of all generous intelligence. Without entering into questions which only indirectly affect the subject of this book, we say, it would have been better had Monseigneur Welcome not been a Royalist, and if his eye had not turned away, even for a moment, from that serene contemplation, in which the three pure lights of Truth, Justice, and Charity are seen beaming above the fictions and hatreds of this world, and above the stormy ebb and flow of human affairs.

While allowing that GOD had not created Monseigneur Welcome for political functions, we could have understood and admired a protest in the name of justice and liberty, a proud opposition, a perilous and just resistance offered to

Napoleon, all-powerful. But conduct which pleases us towards those who are rising, pleases us less towards those who are falling. We only like the contest so long as there is danger; and, in any case, only the combatants from the beginning have a right to be the exterminators at the end. A man who has not been an obstinate accuser during prosperity must be silent when the crash comes; the denouncer of success is the sole legitimate judge of the fell. For our part, when Providence interferes and strikes we let it do so. 1812 begins to disarm us; in 1813 the cowardly rupture of silence by the taciturn legislative corps, emboldened by catastrophes, could only arouse indignation; in 1814, in the presence of the traitor Marshals, in the presence of that senate, passing from one atrocity to another, and insulting after deifying, and before the idolaters kicking their idol and spitting on it, it was a duty to turn one's head away; in 1815, as supreme disasters were in the air, as France had a shudder of their sinister approach, as Waterloo, already open before Napoleon could be vaguely distinguished, the dolorous acclamation offered by the army and the people had nothing laughable about it, and—leaving the despot out of the question—a heart like the Bishop of D——'s ought not to have misunderstood how much there was august and affecting in this close embrace between a great nation and a great man on the verge of an abyss.

With this exception, the Bishop was in all things just, true, equitable, intelligent, humble, and worthy; beneficent, and benevolent, which is another form of beneficence. He was a priest, a sage, and a man. Even in the political opinions with which we have reproached him, and which we are inclined to judge almost severely, we are bound to add that he was tolerant and facile, more so perhaps than the writer of these lines. The porter of the Town Hall had been appointed by the Emperor; he was an ex-non-commissioned officer of the old guard, a legionary of Austerlitz, and as Bonapartist as the eagle. This poor fellow now and then made thoughtless remarks, which the law of that day qualified as seditious. From the moment when the Imperial profile disappeared from the Legion of Honor, he never put on his uniform again, that he might not be obliged, as he said, to bear his cross. He had himself devotedly removed the Imperial effigy from the cross which Napoleon had given him with his own hands, and though this made a hole he would not let anything be put in its place. "Sooner die," he would say, "than wear the three frogs on my heart." He was fond of ridiculing Louis XVIII. aloud. "The old gouty fellow with his English gaiters, let him be off to Prussia with his salsifies." It delighted him thus to combine in one imprecation the two things he hated most, England and Prussia. He went on thus till he lost his place, and then he was starving in the street with wife and children. The Bishop sent for him, gave him a gentle lecturing, and appointed him Beadle to the cathedral.

In nine years, through his good deeds and gentle manners, Monseigneur

Welcome had filled the town of D—— with a sort of tender and filial veneration. Even his conduct to Napoleon had been accepted, and, as it were, tacitly pardoned, by the people, an honest weak flock of sheep, who adored their Emperor but loved their Bishop.

CHAPTER XII.

MONSEIGNEUR'S SOLITUDE.

There is nearly always round a bishop a squad of little abbés, as there is a swarm of young officers round a general. They are what that delightful St. Francis de Sales calls somewhere "sucking priests." Every career has its aspirants, who pay their respects to those who have reached the goal; there is not a power without its following, not a fortune without its court. The seekers for a future buzz round the splendid present. Every metropolitan has his staff: every bishop who is at all influential has his patrol of Seminarist Cherubim, who go the rounds, maintain order in the episcopal palace, and mount guard round Monseigneur's smile. Pleasing a bishop is a foot in the stirrup for a sub-deaconry; after all, a man must make his way, and apostles do not despise canonries.

In the same way as there are "gros bonnets," otherwise, there are large mitres in the Church. They are bishops who stand well with the Court, well endowed, clever, favorites of society, who doubtless know how to pray, but also how to solicit, not scrupulous about having a whole diocese waiting in their ante-rooms, connecting links between the sacristy and diplomacy, more abbés than priests, rather prelates than bishops. Happy the man who approaches them! As they stand in good credit they shower around them, on the obsequious and their favored, and on all the youth who know the art of pleasing, fat livings, prebends, archdeaconries, chaplaincies, and cathedral appointments, while waiting for episcopal dignities. While themselves advancing, they cause their satellites to progress, and it is an entire solar system moving onwards. Their beams throw a purple hue over their suite, and their prosperity is showered over the actors behind the scenes in nice little bits of promotions. The larger the patron's diocese, the larger the favorite's living. And then there is Rome. A bishop who contrives to become an archbishop, an archbishop who manages to become a cardinal, takes you with him as a Conclavist; you enter the rota, you have the pallium, you are an auditor, a chamberlain, a Monsignore, and from Grandeur to Eminence there is but a step, and between Eminence and Holiness there is only the smoke of the balloting tickets. Every cassock can dream of the tiara. The priest is in our days the only man who can regularly become a king, and what a king! The supreme king! Hence what a hotbed of longings is a seminary! How many blushing choristers, how many young abbés, have on their head Perrette's milk-jar! how easily ambition calls itself a profession! and perhaps it does so in good faith and in self-deception, for it is so unworldly.

Monseigneur Welcome, humble, poor, and out of the world, was not counted among the large mitres. This was visible in the utter absence of young priests around him. We have seen that at Paris "he did not take," and not an aspirant tried to cling to this solitary old man; not the most youthful ambition tried to flourish in his shade. His canons and vicars were good old men, walled up like him in this diocese which had no issue to the Cardinal's hat, and who resembled their bishop with this difference, that they were finished while he was completed. The impossibility of growing up near Monseigneur Welcome was so well felt, that young priests whom he ordained at once obtained letters commendatory to the Archbishop of Aix, or Auch, and went off at score. For, after all, we repeat, men wish to be pushed upward. A saint who lives in a state of excessive self-denial is a dangerous neighbor, he might possibly communicate to you by contagion an incurable poverty, a stiffening of the joints useful for advancement, and, in a word, more renunciation than you care for: and such scabby virtue is shunned. Hence came the isolation of Monseigneur Welcome. We live in the midst of a gloomy society. Succeed,— such is the teaching which falls drop by drop from the corruption hanging over us.

Success is a very hideous thing, and its resemblance with merit deceives men. For the herd, success has nearly the same profile as supremacy. Success, that twin brother of talent, has a dupe,—history. Tacitus and Juvenal alone grumble at it. In our days an almost official philosophy wears the livery of success, and waits in its ante-room. Succeed, that is the theory, for prosperity presupposes capacity. Win in the lottery and you are a clever man, for he who triumphs is revered. All you want is to be born under a fortunate star. Have luck and you will have the rest, be fortunate and you will be thought a great man; leaving out five or six immense exceptions, which form the lustre of an age, contemporary admiration is blear-eyedness. Gilding is gold, and it does you no harm to be any one so long as you are the parvenu. The mob is an old Narcissus, adoring itself and applauding the mob. That enormous faculty by which a man is a Moses, Æschylus, Dante, Michael Angelo, or Napoleon, the multitude decrees broadcast and by acclamation to any one who attains his object, no matter in what. Let a notary transfigure himself into a deputy; a false Corneille produce Tiridates; an eunuch contrive to possess a harem; a military Prudhomme accidentally gain the decisive battle of an age; an apothecary invent cardboard soles for the army of the Sambre-et-Meuse, and make out of the cardboard sold for leather an income of 400,000 francs a year; a pedler espouse usury and put it to bed with seven or eight millions, of which he is the father and she the mother; a preacher become a bishop by his nasal twang; let the steward of a good family be so rich on leaving service that he is made Chancellor of the Exchequer—and men will call it genius, in the same way as they call Mousqueton's face beauty and Claude's mien majesty. They confound with the constellations of profundity the stars which the duck's feet make in the soft mud of the pond.

CHAPTER XIII

WHAT HE BELIEVED.

It is not our business to gauge the Bishop of D—— from an orthodox point of view. In the presence of such a soul we only feel inclined to respect. The conscience of the just man must be believed on its word; besides, certain natures granted, we admit the possibility of the development of all the beauties of human virtue in a creed differing from our own. What did he think of this dogma or that mystery? These heart-secrets are only known to the tomb which souls enter in a state of nudity. What we are certain of is, that he never solved difficulties of faith by hypocrisy. It is impossible for the diamond to rot. He believed as much as he possibly could, and would frequently exclaim, "I believe in the Father." He also derived from his good deeds that amount of satisfaction which suffices the conscience, and which whispers to you, "You are with God."

What we think it our duty to note is that, beyond his faith, he had an excess of love. It was through this, *quia multum amavit*, that he was considered vulnerable by "serious men," "grave persons," and "reasonable people," those favorite phrases of our melancholy world in which selfishness is under the guidance of pedantry. What was this excess of love. It was a serene benevolence, spreading over men, as we have already indicated, and on occasion extending even to things. He loved without disdain, and was indulgent to God's creation. Every man, even the best, has in him an unreflecting harshness, which he reserves for animals, but the Bishop of D —— had not this harshness, which is, however, peculiar to many priests. He did not go so far as the Brahmin, but seemed to have meditated on the words of Ecclesiastes—"Who knoweth the spirit of the beast that goeth downward to the earth?" An ugly appearance, a deformity of instinct, did not trouble him or render him indignant; he was moved, almost softened, by them. It seemed as if he thoughtfully sought, beyond apparent life, for the cause, the explanation, or the excuse. He examined without anger, and with the eye of a linguist deciphering a palimpsest, the amount of chaos which still exists in nature. This reverie at times caused strange remarks to escape from him. One morning he was in his garden and fancied himself alone; but his sister was walking behind, though unseen by him. He stopped and looked at something on the ground. It was a large black, hairy, horrible spider. His sister heard him mutter, "Poor brute, it is not thy fault." Why should we not repeat this almost divine childishness of goodness? It may be puerile, but of such were the puerilities of St. Francis d'Assisi and Marcus Aurelius. One day he sprained himself because he did not wish to crush an ant.

Such was the way in which this just man lived: at times he fell asleep in his garden, and then nothing could be more venerable. Monseigneur Welcome had been formerly, if we may believe the stories about his youth and even his manhood, a passionate, perhaps violent man. His universal mansuetude was less a natural instinct than the result of a grand conviction, which had filtered through life into his heart, and slowly dropped into it thought by thought, for in a character, as in a rock, there may be waterholes. Such hollows, however, are ineffaceable, such formations indestructible. In 1815, as we think we have said, he reached his seventy-fifth year, but did not seem sixty. He was not tall, and had a tendency to stoutness, which he strove to combat by long walks; he stood firmly, and was but very slightly built. But these are details from which we will not attempt to draw any conclusion, for Gregory XVI. at the age of eighty was erect and smiling, which did not prevent him being a bad priest. Monseigneur Welcome had what people call "a fine head," which was so amiable that its beauty was forgotten. When he talked with that infantine gayety which was one of his graces you felt at your ease by his side, and joy seemed to emanate from his whole person. His fresh, ruddy complexion, and all his white teeth, which he had preserved and displayed when he laughed, gave him that open facile air which makes you say of an aged man, "He is a worthy person." That, it will be remembered, was the effect he produced on Napoleon. At the first glance, and when you saw him for the first time, he was in reality only a worthy man, but if you remained some hours in his company, and saw him in thought, he became gradually transfigured and assumed something imposing; his wide and serious brow, already august through the white hair, became also august through meditation; majesty was evolved from the goodness; though the latter did not cease to gleam, you felt the same sort of emotion as you would if you saw a smiling angel slowly unfold his wings without ceasing to smile. An inexpressible respect gradually penetrated you and ascended to your head, and you felt that you had before you one of those powerful, well-bred, and indulgent souls whose thoughts are so great that they cannot but be gentle.

As we have seen, prayer, celebration of the Mass, almsgiving, consoling the afflicted, tilling a patch of ground, frugality, hospitality, self-denial, confidence, study, and labor, filled every day of his life. *Filled* is the exact word, and certainly the Bishop's day was full of good thoughts, good words, and good actions. Still, it was not complete. If cold or wet weather prevented him from spending an hour or two in the garden before going to bed after the two females had retired, it seemed as it were a species of rite of his to prepare himself for sleep by meditation, in the presence of the grand spectacle of the heavens by night. At times, even at an advanced hour of night, if the women were not asleep, they heard him slowly pacing the walks. He was then alone with himself, contemplative, peaceful, adoring, comparing the serenity of his heart with that of ether, affected in the darkness by the visible splendor of the constellations, and the invisible splendor of God, and opening his soul to thoughts which fall from the unknown. At such moments, offering up his heart at the hour when the nocturnal flowers offer up their perfumes, he could not have said himself, possibly, what was passing in his mind; but he felt something fly out of him and something descend into him.

He dreamed of the grandeur and presence of God; of future eternity, that strange mystery; of past eternity, that even stranger mystery; of all the infinities which buried themselves before his eyes in all directions: and without seeking to comprehend the incomprehensible, he gazed at it. He did not study God; he was dazzled by Him. He considered this magnificent concourse of atoms which reveals forces, creates individualities in unity, proportions in space, innumerability in the Infinite, and through light produces beauty. Such a concourse incessantly takes place, and is dissolved again, and hence come life and death.

He would sit down on a wood bench with his back against a rickety trellis, and gaze at the stars through the stunted sickly profiles of his fruit trees. This quarter of an acre, so poorly planted, and so encumbered with sheds and out-houses, was dear to him, and was sufficient for him. What more was wanting to this aged man, who divided the leisure of his life, which knew so little leisure, between gardening by day and contemplation by night? Was not this limited enclosure with the sky for its roof sufficient for him to be able to adore God by turns in His most delicious and most sublime works? Was not this everything, in fact? and what could be desired beyond? A small garden to walk about in, and immensity to dream in; at his feet, what can be cultivated and gathered; over his head, what can be studied and meditated; a few flowers on the earth, and all the stars in the heavens.

CHAPTER XIV.

WHAT HE THOUGHT.

One last word.

As these details might, especially at the present day, and to employ an expression which is now fashionable, give the Bishop of D—— a certain "Pantheistic" physiognomy, and cause it to be believed, either to his praise or blame, that he had in him one of those personal philosophies peculiar to our age, which germinate sometimes in solitary minds, and grow until they take the place of religion, we must lay stress on the fact that not one of the persons who knew Monseigneur Welcome believed himself authorized in thinking anything of the sort. What enlightened this man was his heart, and his wisdom was the product of the light which emanates from it.

He had no systems, but abundance of deeds. Abstruse speculations contain vertigo, and nothing indicates that he ventured his mind amid the Apocalypses. The apostle may be bold, but the bishop must be timid. He probably refrained from going too deep into certain problems reserved to some extent for great and terrible minds. There is a sacred horror beneath the portals of the enigma; the dark chasms gape before you, but something tells you that you must not enter: woe to him who penetrates. Geniuses, in the profundities of abstraction and pure speculation, being situated, so to speak, above dogmas, propose their ideas to God; their prayer audaciously offers a discussion, and their adoration interrogates. This is direct religion, full of anxiety and responsibility for the man who attempts to carry the escarpment by storm.

Human meditation has no limits; at its own risk and peril it analyzes and produces its own bedazzlement; we might almost say that, through a species of splendid reaction, it dazzles nature with it. The mysterious world around us gives back what it receives, and it is probable that the contemplators are contemplated. However this may be, there are in the world men—are they men?—who distinctly perceive on the horizon of dreamland the heights of the Absolute, and have the terrible vision of the mountain of the Infinite. Monseigneur Welcome was not one of these men, for he was not a genius. He would have feared these sublimities, on which even very great men, like Swedenborg and Pascal, fell in their insanity. Assuredly, such powerful reveries have their utility, and by these arduous routes ideal perfection is approached, but he took a short-cut,—the Gospel. He did not attempt to convert his chasuble into Elijah's cloak, he cast no beam of the future over the gloomy heaving of events; there was nothing of the prophet or the Magus about him. This humble soul loved, that was all.

It is probable that he expanded prayer into a superhuman aspiration; but a man can no more pray too much than he can love too much, and if it were a heresy to pray further than the text, St Theresa and St Jérôme would be heretics. He bent down over all that groaned and all that expiated; the universe appeared to him an immense malady; he felt a fever everywhere; he heard the panting of suffering all around him, and without trying to solve the enigma, he sought to heal the wound. The formidable spectacle of created things developed tenderness in him; he was solely engaged in finding for himself and arousing in others the best way of pitying and relieving. Existence was to this good and rare priest a permanent subject of sorrow seeking for consolation.

There are some men who toil to extract gold, but he labored to extract pity; the universal wretchedness was his mine. Sorrow all around was only an opportunity for constant kindness. "Love one another" he declared to be complete; he wished for nothing more, and that was his entire doctrine. One day the Senator, who believed himself a "philosopher," said to the Bishop: "Just look at the spectacle of the world; all are fighting, and the strongest man is the cleverest. Your 'love one another' is nonsense." "Well," Monseigneur Welcome replied, without discussion, "if it be nonsense, the soul must shut itself up in it like the pearl in the oyster." He consequently shut himself up in it, lived in it, was absolutely satisfied with it, leaving on one side those prodigious questions which attract and terrify, the unfathomable perspectives of the abstract, the precipices of metaphysics, all those depths which for the apostle converge in God, for the atheist in nothingness: destiny, good, and evil, the war of being against being, human consciousness, the pensive somnambulism of the animal, transformation through death, the recapitulation of existences which the grave contains, the incomprehensible grafting of successive loves on the enduring Me, essence, substance, the Nil and Ens nature, liberty, necessity; in a word, he avoided all the gloomy precipices over which the gigantic archangels of the human mind bend, the formidable abysses which Lucretius, Manou, St. Paul, and Dante contemplate with that flashing eye which seems, in regarding Infinity, to make stars sparkle in it.

Monseigneur Welcome was simply a man who accepted mysterious questions without scrutinizing, disturbing them, or troubling his own mind, and who had in his soul a grave respect for the shadow.

BOOK II

THE FALL.

CHAPTER I

THE CLOSE OF A DAY'S MARCH.

At the beginning of October, 1815, and about an hour before sunset, a man travelling on foot entered the little town of D——. The few inhabitants, who were at the moment at their windows or doors, regarded this traveller with a species of inquietude. It would be difficult to meet a wayfarer of more wretched appearance; he was a man of middle height, muscular and robust, and in the full vigor of life. He might be forty-six to forty-eight years of age. A cap with a leather peak partly concealed his sunburnt face, down which the perspiration streamed. His shirt of coarse yellow calico, fastened at the neck by a small silver anchor, allowed his hairy chest to be seen; he had on a neck-cloth twisted like a rope, trousers of blue ticking worn and threadbare, white at one knee and torn at the other; an old gray ragged blouse patched at one elbow with a rag of green cloth; on his back a large new well-filled and well-buckled knapsack, and a large knotty stick in his hand. His stockingless feet were thrust into iron-shod shoes, his hair was clipped, and his beard long. Perspiration, heat, travelling on foot, and the dust, added something sordid to his wretched appearance. His hair was cut close and yet was bristling, for it was beginning to grow a little, and did not seem to have been cut for some time.

No one knew him; he was evidently passing through the town. Where did he come from? The South perhaps, the sea-board, for he made his entrance into D—— by the same road Napoleon had driven along seven months previously when going from Cannes to Paris. The man must have been walking all day, for he seemed very tired. Some women in the old suburb at the lower part of the town had seen him halt under the trees on the Gassendi Boulevard, and drink from the fountain at the end of the walk. He must have been very thirsty, for the children that followed him saw him stop and drink again at the fountain on the Market-place. On reaching the corner of the Rue Poichevert, he turned to the left and proceeded to the Mayor's office. He went in and came out again a quarter of an hour after. A gendarme was sitting on the stone bench near the door, on which General Drouot had mounted on March 4th, to read to the startled town-folk of D—— the proclamation of the gulf of Juan.

The man doffed his cap and bowed humbly to the gendarme; the latter, without returning his salute, looked at him attentively, and then entered the office.

There was at that time at D—— a capital inn, with the sign of the Cross of Colbas. This inn was kept by a certain Jacquin Labarre, a man highly respected in the town for his relationship to another Labarre, who kept the Three Dolphins at Grenoble, and had served in the Guides. When the Emperor landed, many rumors were current in the country about the Three Dolphins; it was said that General Bertrand, in the disguise of a wagoner, had stopped there several times in the month of January, and distributed crosses of honor to the soldiers, and handsful of napoleons to the towns-people. The fact was that the Emperor on entering Grenoble refused to take up his quarters at the Prefecture; he thanked the Mayor, and said, "I am going to a worthy man whom I know," and he went to the Three Dolphins. The glory of the Grenoble Labarre was reflected for a distance of five-and-twenty leagues on the Labarre of the Cross of Colbas. The towns-people said of him, "He is cousin to the one at Grenoble."

The man proceeded to this inn, which was the best in the town, and entered the kitchen, the door of which opened on the street. All the ovens were heated, and a large fire blazed cheerily in the chimney. The host, who was at the same time head-cook, went from the hearth to the stew-pans, very busy in attending to a dinner intended for the carriers, who could be heard singing and talking noisily in an adjoining room. Any one who has travelled knows that no people feed so well as carriers. A fat marmot, flanked by white-legged partridges and grouse, was turning on a long spit before the fire; while two large carp from Lake Lauzet and an Alloz trout were baking in the ovens. The landlord, on hearing the door open and a stranger enter, said, without raising his eyes from his stew-pans,—

"What do you want, sir?"

"Supper and a bed," the man replied.

"Nothing easier," said mine host. At this moment he looked up, took in the stranger's appearance at a glance, and added, "On paying."

The man drew a heavy leathern purse from the pocket of his blouse, and replied,—

"I have money."

"In that case I am at your service," said the host.

The man returned the purse to his pocket, took off his knapsack, placed it on the ground near the door, kept his stick in his hand, and sat down on a low stool near the fire. D—— is in the mountains, and the evenings there are cold in October. While going backwards and forwards the landlord still inspected his guest.

"Will supper be ready soon?" the man asked.

"Directly."

While the new-comer had his back turned to warm himself, the worthy landlord took a pencil from his pocket, and then tore off the corner of an old newspaper which lay on a small table near the window. On the white margin he wrote a line or two, folded up the paper, and handed it to a lad who seemed to serve both as turnspit and page. The landlord whispered a word in the boy's ear, and he ran off in the direction of the Mayor's house. The traveller had seen nothing of all this, and he asked again whether supper would be ready soon. The boy came back with the paper in his hand, and the landlord eagerly unfolded it, like a man who is expecting an answer. He read it carefully, then shook his head, and remained thoughtful for a moment. At last he walked up to the traveller, who seemed plunged in anything but a pleasant reverie.

"I cannot make room for you, sir," he said.

The man half turned on his stool.

"What do you mean? Are you afraid I shall bilk you? Do you want me to pay you in advance? I have money, I tell you."

"It is not that"

"What is it, then?"

"You have money."

"Yes," said the man.

"But I have not a spare bed-room."

The man continued quietly: "Put me in the stables."

"I cannot."

"Why?"

"The horses take up all the room."

"Well," the man continued, "a corner in the loft and a truss of straw: we will see to that after supper."

"I cannot give you any supper."

This declaration, made in a measured but firm tone, seemed to the stranger serious. He rose.

"Nonsense, I am dying of hunger. I have been on my legs since sunrise, and have walked twelve leagues. I can pay, and demand food."

"I have none," said the landlord.

The man burst into a laugh, and turned to the chimney and the oven.

"Nothing! Why, what is all this?"

"All this is ordered."

"By whom?"

"By the carriers."

"How many are there of them?"

"Twelve."

"There is enough food here for twenty."

The man sat down again, and said without raising his voice,—

"I am at an inn, I am hungry, and so shall remain."

The landlord then stooped down, and whispered with an accent which made him start, "Be off with you!"

The stranger at this moment was thrusting some logs into the fire with the ferule of his stick, but he turned quickly, and as he was opening his mouth to reply, the landlord continued in the same low voice: "Come, enough of this. Do you wish me to tell you your name? It is Jean Valjean. Now, do you wish me to tell you who you are? On seeing you come in I suspected something, so I sent to the police office, and this is the answer I received. Can you read?"

While saying this, he handed the stranger the paper which had travelled from the inn to the office and back again. The man took a glance at it, and mine host continued after a moment's silence,—

"I am accustomed to be polite with everybody. Be off."

The man stooped, picked up his knapsack, and went off. He walked along the high street hap-hazard, keeping close to the houses like a sad and humiliated man. He did not look back once; had he done so he would have seen the landlord of the Cross of Colbas in his doorway surrounded by all his guests and the passers-by, talking eagerly and pointing to him: and judging from the looks of suspicion and terror, he might have guessed that ere long his arrival would be the event of the whole town. He saw nothing of all this, for men who are oppressed do not look back, as they know only too well that an evil destiny is following them.

He walked on thus for a long time, turning down streets he did not know, and forgetting his fatigue, as happens in sorrow. All at once he was sharply assailed by hunger: night was approaching, and he looked round to see whether he could not discover a shelter. The best inn was closed against him, and he sought some very humble pot-house, some wretched den. At this moment a lamp was lit at the end of the street, and a fir-branch hanging from an iron bar stood out on the white twilight sky. He went towards it: it was really a pot-house. The stranger stopped for a moment and looked through the window into the low tap-room, which was lighted up by a small lamp on the table and a large fire on the hearth. Some men were drinking, and the landlord was warming himself; over the flames bubbled a caldron hanging from an iron hook. This pot-house, which is also a sort of inn, has two entrances, one on the street, the other opening on a small yard full of manure. The traveller did not dare enter by the street door: he slipped into the yard, stopped once again, and then timidly raised the latch and opened the door.

"Who's there?" the landlord asked.

"Some one who wants a supper and bed."

"Very good. They are to be had here."

He went in, and all the topers turned to look at him; they examined him for some time while he was taking off his knapsack. Said the landlord to him, "Here is a fire; supper is boiling in the pot: come and warm yourself, comrade."

He sat down in the ingle and stretched out his feet, which were swollen with fatigue. A pleasant smell issued from the caldron. All that could be distinguished of his face under his cap-peak assumed a vague appearance of comfort blended with the other wretched appearance which the habit of suffering produces. It was, moreover, a firm, energetic, and sad profile; the face was strangely composed, for it began by appearing humble and ended by becoming severe. His eyes gleamed under his brows, like a fire under brushwood. One of the men seated at the table was a fishmonger, who, before entering the pot-house, had gone to put up his horse in Labarre's stables. Accident willed it, that on the same morning he had met this ill-looking stranger walking between Bras d'Asse and—(I have forgotten the name, but I fancy it is Escoublon). Now, on meeting him, the man, who appeared very fatigued, had asked the fishmonger to give him a lift, which had only made him go the faster. This fishmonger had been half an hour previously one of the party surrounding Jacquin Labarre, and had told his unpleasant encounter in the morning to the people at the Cross of Colbas. He made an imperceptible sign to the landlord from his seat, and the latter went up to him, and they exchanged a few whispered words. The man had fallen back into his reverie.

The landlord went up to the chimney, laid his hand sharply on the man's shoulder, and said to him,—

"You must be off from here."

The stranger turned and replied gently, "Ah, you know?"

"Yes."

"I was turned out of the other inn."

"And so you will be out of this."

"Where would you have me go?"

"Somewhere else."

The man took his knapsack and stick and went away. As he stepped out, some boys who had followed him from the Cross of Colbas, and seemed to have been waiting for him, threw stones at him. He turned savagely, and threatened them with his stick, and the boys dispersed like a flock of birds. He passed in front of the prison, and pulled the iron bell-handle; a wicket was opened.

"Mr. Jailer," he said, as he humbly doffed his cap, "would you be kind enough to open the door and give me a nights lodging?"

A voice answered, "A prison is not an inn; get yourself arrested, and then I will open the door."

The man entered a small street, in which there are numerous gardens, some of them being merely enclosed with hedges, which enliven the street. Among these gardens and hedges he saw a single-storeyed house, whose window was illuminated, and he looked through the panes as he had done at the pot-house. It was a large white-washed room, with a bed with printed chintz curtains, and a cradle in a corner, a few chairs, and a double-barrelled gun hanging on the wall. A table was laid for supper in the middle of the room; a copper lamp lit up the coarse white cloth, the tin mug glistening like silver and full of wine, and the brown smoking soup-tureen. At this table was seated a man of about forty years of age, with a hearty, open face, who was riding a child on his knee. By his side a woman, still young, was suckling another child. The father was laughing, the children were laughing, and the mother was smiling. The stranger stood for a moment pensively before this gentle and calming spectacle; what was going on within him? It would be impossible to say, but it is probable that he thought that this joyous house would prove hospitable, and that where he saw so much happiness he might find a little pity. He tapped very slightly on a window pane, but was not heard; he tapped a second time, and he heard the woman say, "Husband, I fancy I can hear some one knocking."

"No," the husband answered.

He tapped a third time. The husband rose, took the lamp, and walked to the front door. He was a tall man, half peasant, half artisan; he wore a huge, leathern apron, which came up to his left shoulder, and on which he carried a hammer, a red handkerchief, a powder-flask, and all sorts of things, which his belt held like a pocket. As he threw back his head, his turned-down shirt-collar displayed his full neck, white and bare. He had thick eye-brows, enormous black whiskers, eyes flush with his head, a bull-dog lower jaw, and over all this that air of being at home, which is inexpressible.

"I beg your pardon, sir," the traveller said, "but would you, for payment, give me a plateful of soup and a corner to sleep in in your garden outhouse?"

"Who are you?" the owner of the cottage asked.

The man answered, "I have come from Puy Moisson, I have walked the whole day. Could you do it,—for payment of course?"

"I would not refuse," the peasant answered, "to lodge any respectable person who paid. But why do you not go to the inn?"

"There is no room there."

"Nonsense! that is impossible; it is neither market nor fair day. Have you been to Labarre's?"

"Yes."

"Well?"

The traveller continued, with some hesitation, "I do not know why, but he refused to take me in."

"Have you been to what is his name, in the Rue de Chauffaut?"

The stranger's embarrassment increased; he stammered, "He would not take me in either."

The peasant's face assumed a suspicious look, he surveyed the new comer from head to foot, and all at once exclaimed with a sort of shudder,—

"Can you be the man?…"

He took another look at the stranger, placed the lamp on the table, and took down his gun. On hearing the peasant say "Can you be the man?" his wife had risen, taken her two children in her arms, and hurriedly sought refuge behind her husband, and looked in horror at the stranger as she muttered, "The villain!" All this took place in less time than is needed to imagine it.

58

After examining the man for some minutes as if he had been a viper, the peasant returned to the door and said: "Be off!"

"For mercy's sake," the man continued,—"a glass of water."

"A charge of shot!" the peasant said.

Then he violently closed the door, and the stranger heard two bolts fastened. A moment after the window shutters were closed, and the sound of the iron bar being put in reached his ear. Night was coming on apace: the cold wind of the Alps was blowing. By the light of the expiring day the stranger noticed in one of the gardens a sort of hut which seemed to him to be made of sods of turf. He boldly clambered over a railing and found himself in the garden; he approached the hut, which had as entrance a narrow, extremely low door, and resembled the tenements which road-menders construct by the side of the highway. He doubtless thought it was such: he was suffering from cold and hunger, and though he had made up his mind to starve, it was at any rate a shelter against the cold. As this sort of residence is not usually occupied at night, he lay down on his stomach and crawled into the hut: it was warm, and he found a rather good straw litter in it. He lay for a moment motionless on this bed as his fatigue was so great: but as his knapsack hurt his back and was a ready-made pillow, he began unbuckling one of the thongs. At this moment a hoarse growl was audible: he raised his eyes, and the head of an enormous mastiff stood out in the shadow at the opening of the hut, which was its kennel. The dog itself was strong and formidable, hence he raised his stick, employed his knapsack as a shield, and left the kennel as he best could, though not without enlarging the rents in his rags.

He also left the garden, but backwards, and compelled to twirl his stick in order to keep the dog at a respectful distance. When he, not without difficulty, had leaped the fence again, and found himself once more in the street, alone, without a bed, roof, or shelter, and expelled even from the bed of straw and the kennel, he fell rather than sat on a stone, and a passer-by heard him exclaim, "I am not even a dog." He soon rose and recommenced his walk. He left the town hoping to find some tree or mill in the fields which would afford him shelter. He walked on thus for some time with hanging head; when he found himself far from all human habitations, he raised his eyes and looked around him. He was in a field, and had in front of him one of those low hills with close-cut stubble, which after harvest resemble cropped heads. The horizon was perfectly black, but it was not solely the gloom of night, but low clouds, which seemed to be resting on the hill itself, rose and filled the whole sky. Still, as the moon was about to rise shortly, and a remnant of twilight still hovered in the zenith, these clouds formed a species of whitish vault whence a gleam of light was thrown on the earth.

The ground was therefore more illumined than the sky, which produces a peculiarly sinister effect, and the hill with its paltry outlines stood out vaguely and dully on the gloomy horizon. The whole scene was hideous, mean, mournful, and confined; there was nothing in the field or on the hill but a stunted tree, which writhed and trembled a few yards from the traveller. This man was evidently far from possessing those delicate habits of mind which render persons sensible of the mysterious aspects of things, still there was in the sky, this hill, this plain, and this tree, something so profoundly desolate, that after standing motionless and thoughtful for a while he suddenly turned back. There are instants in which nature seems to be hostile.

He went back and found the gates of the town closed. D——, which sustained sieges in the religious wars, was still begirt in 1815 by old walls flanked by square towers, which have since been demolished. He passed through a breach, and re-entered the town. It might be about eight o'clock in the evening, and as he did not know the streets he wandered about without purpose. He thus reached the prefecture and then the seminary; on passing through the Cathedral Square he shook his fist at the church. There is at the corner of this Square a printing-office, where the proclamations of the Emperor and the Imperial Guard to the army, brought from Elba, and drawn up by Napoleon himself, were first printed. Worn out with fatigue, and hopeless, he sat down on the stone bench at the door of this printing-office. An old lady who was leaving the church at the moment saw the man stretched out in the darkness.

"What are you doing there, my friend?" she said.

He answered, harshly and savagely, "You can see, my good woman, that I am going to sleep."

The good woman, who was really worthy of the name, was the Marchioness de R——.

"On that bench?" she continued.

"I have had for nineteen years a wooden mattress," the man said, "and now I have a stone one."

"Have you been a soldier?"

"Yes, my good woman."

"Why do you not go to the inn?"

"Because I have no money."

"Alas!" said Madame de R——, "I have only two-pence in my purse."

"You can give them to me all the same."

The man took the money, and Madame de R—— continued, "You cannot lodge at an inn for so small a sum, still you should make the attempt, for you cannot possibly spend the night here. Doubtless you are cold and hungry, and some one might take you in for charity."

"I have knocked at every door."

"Well?"

"And was turned away at all."

The "good woman" touched the man's arm and pointed to a small house next to the Bishop's Palace.

"You have," she continued, "knocked at every door. Have you done so there?"

"No."

"Then do it."

<hr />

CHAPTER II.

PRUDENCE RECOMMENDED TO WISDOM.

On this evening, the Bishop of D——, after his walk in the town, had remained in his bed-room till a late hour. He was engaged on a heavy work on the "duties," which he unfortunately has left incomplete. He was still working at eight o'clock, writing rather uncomfortably on small squares of paper, with a large book open on his knees, when Madame Magloire came in as usual to fetch the plate from the wall-cupboard near the bed. A moment after, the Bishop, feeling that supper was ready, and that his sister might be waiting, closed his book, rose from the table, and walked into the dining-room. It was an oblong apartment, as we have said, with a door opening on the street, and a window looking on the garden. Madame Magloire had laid the table, and while attending to her duties, was chatting with Mademoiselle Baptistine. A lamp was on the table, which was close to the chimney, in which a tolerable fire was lighted.

We can easily figure to ourselves the two females, who had both passed their sixtieth year: Madame Magloire, short, stout, and quick: Mademoiselle Baptistine, gentle, thin, and frail, somewhat taller than her brother, dressed in a puce-colored silk gown, the fashionable color in 1806, which she had bought in Paris in that year and which still held out. Madame Magloire wore a white cap, on her neck a gold *jeannette,* the only piece of feminine jewelry in the house, a very white handkerchief emerging from a black stuff gown with wide and short sleeves, a calico red and puce checked apron, fastened round the waist with a green ribbon, with a stomacher of the same stuff fastened with two pins at the top corners, heavy shoes and yellow stockings, like the Marseilles women. Mademoiselle Baptistine's gown was cut after the fashion of 1806, short-waisted, with epaulettes on the sleeves, flaps and buttons, and she concealed her gray hair by a curling front called *à l'enfant.* Madame Magloire had an intelligent, quick, and kindly air, though the unevenly raised corners of her mouth and the upper lip, thicker than the lower, gave her a somewhat rough and imperious air. So long as Monseigneur was silent, she spoke to him boldly with a mingled respect and liberty, but so soon as he spoke she passively obeyed, like Mademoiselle, who no longer replied, but restricted herself to obeying and enduring. Even when she was young the latter was not pretty; she had large blue eyes, flush with her head, and a long peaked nose; but all her face, all her person, as we said at the outset, breathed ineffable kindness. She had always been predestined to gentleness, but faith, hope, and charity, those three virtues that softly warm the soul, had gradually elevated that gentleness to sanctity. Nature had only made her a lamb, and religion had made her an angel. Poor holy woman! sweet departed recollection!

Mademoiselle afterwards narrated so many times what took place at the Bishopric on this evening that several persons still living remember the slightest details. At the moment when the Bishop entered Madame Magloire was talking with some vivacity; she was conversing with Mademoiselle on a subject that was familiar to her, and to which the Bishop was accustomed—it was the matter of the frontdoor latch. It appears that while going to purchase something for supper, Madame Magloire had heard things spoken of in certain quarters; people were talking of an ill-looking prowler, that a suspicious vagabond had arrived, who must be somewhere in the town, and that it would possibly be an unpleasant thing for any one out late to meet him. The police were very badly managed because the Prefect and the Mayor were not friendly, and tried to injure each other by allowing things to happen. Hence wise people would be their own police, and be careful to close their houses *and lock their doors.*

Madame Magloire italicized the last sentence, but the Bishop had come from his room where it was rather cold, and was warming himself at the fire while thinking of other matters; in fact, he did not pick up the words which Madame Magloire had just let drop. She repeated them, and then Mademoiselle, who wished to satisfy Madame Magloire without displeasing her brother, ventured to say timidly,—

"Brother, do you hear what Madame Magloire is saying?"

"I vaguely heard something," the Bishop answered; then he half turned his chair, placed his hand on his knees, and looked up at the old servant with his cordial and easily-pleased face, which the fire illumined from below: "Well, what is it? what is it? are we in any great danger?"

Then Madame Magloire told her story over again, while exaggerating it slightly, though unsuspicious of the fact. It would seem that a gypsy, a barefooted fellow, a sort of dangerous beggar, was in the town at the moment. He had tried to get a lodging at Jacquin Labarre's, who had refused to take him in. He had been seen prowling about the streets at nightfall, and was evidently a gallows bird, with his frightful face.

"Is he really?" said the Bishop.

This cross-questioning encouraged Madame Magloire; it seemed to indicate that the Bishop was beginning to grow alarmed, and hence she continued triumphantly,—

"Yes, Monseigneur, it is so, and some misfortune will occur in the town this night: everybody says so, and then the police are so badly managed [useful repetition]. Fancy living in a mountain town, and not even having lanterns in the streets at nights! You go out and find yourself in pitch darkness. I say, Monseigneur, and Mademoiselle says—"

"I," the sister interrupted, "say nothing; whatever my brother does is right."

Madame Magloire continued, as if no protest had been made,—

"We say that this house is not at all safe, and that if Monseigneur permits I will go to Paulin Musebois, the locksmith, and tell him to put the old bolts on the door again; I have them by me, and it will not take a minute; and I say, Monseigneur, that we ought to have bolts if it were only for this night, for I say that a door which can be opened from the outside by the first passer-by is most terrible: besides, Monseigneur is always accustomed to say "Come in," and in the middle of the night, oh, my gracious! there is no occasion to ask for permission."

At this moment there was a rather loud rap at the front door.

"Come in," said the Bishop.

CHAPTER III.

THE HEROISM OF PASSIVE OBEDIENCE.

The door was thrown open wide, as if some one were pushing it energetically and resolutely. A man entered whom we already know; it was the traveller whom we saw just now wandering about in search of a shelter. He entered and stopped, leaving the door open behind him. He had his knapsack on his shoulder, his stick in his hand, and a rough, bold, wearied, and violent expression in his eyes. The fire-light fell on him; he was hideous; it was a sinister apparition.

Madame Magloire had not even the strength to utter a cry, she shivered and stood with widely-open mouth. Mademoiselle Baptistine turned, perceived the man who entered, and half started up in terror; then, gradually turning her head to the chimney, she began looking at her brother, and her face became again calm and serene. The Bishop fixed a quiet eye on the man, as he opened his mouth, doubtless to ask the new-comer what he wanted. The man leaned both his hands on his stick, looked in turn at the two aged females and the old man, and, not waiting for the Bishop to speak, said in a loud voice,—

"Look here! My name is Jean Valjean. I am a galley-slave, and have spent nineteen years in the bagne. I was liberated four days ago, and started for Pontarlier, which is my destination. I have been walking for four days since I left Toulon, and to-day I have marched twelve leagues. This evening on coming into the town I went to the inn, but was sent away in consequence of my yellow passport, which I had shown at the police office. I went to another inn, and the landlord said to me, "Be off!" It was the same everywhere, and no one would have any dealings with me. I went to the prison, but the jailer would not take me in. I got into a dogs kennel, but the dog bit me and drove me off, as if it had been a man; it seemed to know who I was. I went into the fields to sleep in the star-light, but there were no stars. I thought it would rain, and as there was no God to prevent it from raining, I came back to the town to sleep in a doorway. I was lying down on a stone in the square, when a good woman pointed to your house, and said, "Go and knock there." What sort of a house is this? Do you keep an inn? I have money, 109 francs 15 sous, which I earned at the bagne by my nineteen years' toil. I will pay, for what do I care for that, as I have money! I am very tired and frightfully hungry; will you let me stay here?"

"Madame Magloire," said the Bishop, "you will lay another knife and fork."

The man advanced three paces, and approached the lamp which was on the table. "Wait a minute," he continued, as if he had not comprehended, "that will not do. Did you not hear me say that I was a galley-slave, a convict, and have just come from the bagne?" He took from his pocket a large yellow paper, which he unfolded. "Here is my passport, yellow as you see, which turns me out wherever I go. Will you read it? I can read it, for I learned to do so at the bagne, where there is a school for those who like to attend it. This is what is written in my passport: 'Jean Valjean, a liberated convict, native of'— but that does not concern you—'has remained nineteen years at the galleys. Five years for robbery with house-breaking, fourteen years for having tried to escape four times. The man is very dangerous.' All the world has turned me out, and are you willing to receive me? Is this an inn? Will you give me some food and a bed? Have you a stable?"

"Madame Magloire," said the Bishop, "you will put clean sheets on the bed in the alcove."

We have already explained of what nature was the obedience of the two females. Madame Magloire left the room to carry out the orders. The Bishop turned to the man.

"Sit down and warm yourself, sir. We shall sup directly, and your bed will be got ready while we are supping."

The man understood this at once. The expression of his face, which had hitherto been gloomy and harsh, was marked with stupefaction, joy, doubt, and became extraordinary. He began stammering like a lunatic.

"Is it true? what? You will let me stay, you will not turn me out, a convict? You call me *Sir,* you do not 'thou' me. 'Get out, dog!' that is what is always said to me; I really believed that you would turn me out, and hence told you at once who I am. Oh! what a worthy woman she was who sent me here! I shall have supper, a bed with mattresses and sheets, like everybody else. For nineteen years I have not slept in a bed! You really mean that I am to stay. You are worthy people; besides, I have money, and will pay handsomely. By the way, what is your name, Mr. Landlord? I will pay anything you please, for you are a worthy man. You keep an inn, do you not?"

"I am," said the Bishop, "a priest living in this house."

"A priest!" the man continued. "Oh! what a worthy priest! I suppose you will not ask me for money. The Curé, I suppose,—the Curé of that big church? Oh yes, what an ass I am! I did not notice your cassock."

While speaking he deposited his knapsack and stick in a corner, returned his passport to his pocket, and sat down. While Mademoiselle Baptistine regarded him gently, he went on,—

"You are humane, sir, and do not feel contempt. A good priest is very good. Then you do not want me to pay?"

"No," said the Bishop, "keep your money. How long did you take in earning these 109 francs?"

"Nineteen years."

"Nineteen years!" The Bishop gave a deep sigh.

The man went on: "I have all my money still; in four days I have only spent 25 sous, which I earned by helping to unload carts at Grasse. As you are an abbé I will tell you: we had a chaplain at the bagne, and one day I saw a bishop, Monseigneur, as they call him. He is the curé over the curés, you know. Pardon, I express it badly; but it is so far above me, a poor convict, you see. He said mass in the middle of the bagne at an altar, and had a pointed gold thing on his head, which glistened in the bright sunshine; we were drawn up on three sides of a square, with guns and lighted matches facing us. He spoke, but was too far off, and we did not hear him. That is what a bishop is."

While he was speaking the Bishop had gone to close the door, which had been left open. Madame Magloire came in, bringing a silver spoon and fork, which she placed on the table.

"Madame Magloire," said the Bishop, "lay them as near as you can to the fire;" and turning to his guest, he said, "The night breeze is sharp on the Alps, and you must be cold, sir."

Each time he said the word *Sir* with his gentle grave voice the man's face was illumined. *Sir* to a convict is the glass of water to the shipwrecked sailor of the Méduse. Ignominy thirsts for respect.

"This lamp gives a very bad light," the Bishop continued. Madame Magloire understood, and fetched from the chimney of Monseigneur's bed-room the two silver candlesticks, which she placed on the table ready lighted.

"Monsieur le Curé," said the man, "you are good, and do not despise me. You receive me as a friend and light your wax candles for me, and yet I have not hidden from you whence I come, and that I am an unfortunate fellow."

The Bishop, who was seated by his side, gently touched his hand. "You need not have told me who you were; this is not my house, but the house of Christ. This door does not ask a man who enters whether he has a name, but if he has a sorrow; you are suffering, you are hungry and thirsty, and so be welcome. And do not thank me, or say that I am receiving you in my house, for no one is at home here excepting the man who has need of an asylum. I tell you, who are a passer-by, that you are more at home here than I am myself, and all there is here is yours. Why do I want to know your name? besides, before you told it to me you had one which I knew."

The man opened his eyes in amazement.

"Is that true? you know my name?"

"Yes," the Bishop answered, "you are my brother."

"Monsieur le Curé," the man exclaimed, "I was very hungry when I came in, but you are so kind that I do not know at present what I feel; it has passed over."

The Bishop looked at him and said,—

"You have suffered greatly?"

"Oh! the red jacket, the cannon ball on your foot, a plank to sleep on, heat, cold, labor, the set of men, the blows, the double chain for a nothing, a dungeon for a word, even when you are ill in bed, and the chain-gang. The very dogs are happier. Nineteen years! and now I am forty-six; and at present, the yellow passport! There it is!"

"Yes," said the Bishop, "you have come from a place of sorrow. Listen to me; there will be more joy in heaven over the tearful face of a repentant sinner than over the white robes of one hundred just men. If you leave that mournful place with thoughts of hatred and anger against your fellow-men you are worthy of pity; if you leave it with thoughts of kindliness, gentleness, and peace, you are worth more than any of us."

In the meanwhile Madame Magloire had served the soup: it was made of water, oil, bread, and salt, and a little bacon, and the rest of the supper consisted of a piece of mutton, figs, a fresh cheese, and a loaf of rye bread. She had herself added a bottle of old Mauves wine. The Bishop's face suddenly assumed the expression of gayety peculiar to hospitable natures. "To table," he said eagerly, as he was wont to do when any stranger supped with him; and he bade the man sit down on his right hand, while Mlle. Baptistine, perfectly peaceful and natural, took her seat on his left. The Bishop said grace, and then served the soup himself, according to his wont. The man began eating greedily. All at once the Bishop said,—

"It strikes me that there is something wanting on the table."

Madame Magloire, truth to tell, had only laid the absolutely necessary silver. Now it was the custom in this house, when the Bishop had any one to supper, to arrange the whole stock of plate on the table, as an innocent display. This graceful semblance of luxury was a species of childishness full of charm in this gentle and strict house, which elevated poverty to dignity. Madame Magloire took the hint, went out without a word, and a moment after the remaining spoons and forks glittered on the cloth, symmetrically arranged before each of the guests.

CHAPTER IV

CHEESEMAKING AT PONTARLIER.

And now, in order to give an idea of what took place at table, we cannot do better than transcribe a passage of a letter written by Mademoiselle Baptistine to Madame Boischevron, in which the conversation between the convict and the Bishop is recorded with simple minuteness.

"The man paid no attention to any one; he ate with frightful voracity, but after supper he said,—

"Monsieur le Curé, all this is much too good for me; but I am bound to say that the carriers who would not let me sup with them have better cheer than you."

"Between ourselves, this remark slightly offended me, but my brother answered,—

"They are harder worked than I am."

"No," the man continued, "they have more money. You are poor, as I can plainly see; perhaps you are not even curé. Ah, if Heaven were just you ought to be a curé."

"Heaven is more than just," said my brother. A moment after he added,—

"Monsieur Jean Valjean, I think you said you were going to Pontarlier?"

"I am compelled to go there." Then he continued, "I must be off by sunrise to-morrow morning; it is a tough journey, for if the nights are cold the days are hot."

"You are going to an excellent part of the country," my brother resumed. "When the Revolution ruined my family I sought shelter first in Franche Comté, and lived there for some time by the labor of my arms. I had a good will, and found plenty to do, as I need only choose. There are paper-mills, tanneries, distilleries, oil-mills, wholesale manufactories of clocks, steel works, copper works, and at least twenty iron foundries, of which the four at Lods, Chatillon, Audincourt, and Beure are very large."

"I am pretty sure I am not mistaken, and that they are the names my brother mentioned; then he broke off and addressed me.

"My dear sister, have we not some relatives in those parts?"

"My answer was, 'We used to have some; among others Monsieur de Lucinet, who was Captain of the gates at Pontarlier, under the ancient régime."

"Yes," my brother continued, "but in '93 people had no relatives, but only their arms, and so I worked. In the country to which you are going, Monsieur Valjean, there is a truly patriarchal and pleasing trade. My dear sister, I mean their cheese manufactures, which they call *fruitières*."

"Then my brother, while pressing this man to eat, explained in their fullest details the *fruitières* of Pontarlier, which were divided into two classes—the large farms which belong to the rich, and where there are forty or fifty cows, which produce seven to eight thousand cheeses in the summer, and the partnership *fruitières*, which belong to the poor. The peasants of the central mountain district keep their cows in common and divide the produce. They have a cheese-maker, who is called the *grurin*; he receives the milk from the partners thrice a day, and enters the quantities in a book. The cheese-making begins about the middle of April, and the dairy farmers lead their cows to the mountains toward midsummer.

"The man grew animated while eating, and my brother made him drink that excellent Mauves wine, which he does not drink himself because he says that it is expensive. My brother gave him all these details with that easy gayety of his which you know, mingling his remarks with graceful appeals to myself. He dwelt a good deal on the comfortable position of the *grurin*, as if wishful that this man should understand, without advising him directly and harshly, that it would be a refuge for him. One thing struck me: the man was as I have described him to you; well, my brother, during the whole of supper, and indeed of the evening, did not utter a word which could remind this man of what he was, or tell him who my brother was. It was apparently a good opportunity to give him a little lecture, and let the Bishop produce a permanent effect on the galley-slave. It might have seemed to any one else that having this wretched man in hand it would be right to feed his mind at the same time as his body, and address to him some reproaches seasoned with morality and advice, or at any rate a little commiseration, with an exhortation to behave better in future. My brother did not even ask him where he came from, or his history, for his fault is contained in his history, and my brother appeared to avoid everything which might call it to his mind. This was carried to such a point that at a certain moment, when my brother was talking about the mountaineers of Pontarlier, 'who had a pleasant task near heaven,' and who, he added, 'are happy because they are innocent,' he stopped short, fearing lest there might be in the remark something which might unpleasantly affect this man. After considerable reflection, I believe I can understand what was going on in my brother's heart: he doubtless thought that this Jean Valjean had his misery ever present to his mind, that the best thing was to distract his attention, and make him believe, were it only momentarily, that he was a man like the rest, by behaving to him as he would to others. Was not this really charity? Is there not, my dear lady, something truly evangelical in this delicacy, which abstains from all lecturing and allusions, and is it not the best pity, when a man has a sore point, not to touch it at all? It seemed to me that this might be my brother's innermost thought: in any case, what I can safely say is, that if he had all these ideas, he did not let any of them be visible, even to me; he was from beginning to end the same man he is every night, and he supped with Jean Valjean with the same air and in the same way as if he had been supping with M. Gedeon le Prevost, or with the parish curate.

"Toward the end, when we had come to the figs, there was a knock at the door. It was Mother Gerbaud with her little baby in her arms. My brother kissed the child's forehead, and borrowed from me 15 sous which I happened to have about me, to give them to the mother. The man, while this was going on, did not seem to pay great attention: he said nothing, and seemed very tired. When poor old Mother Gerbaud left, my brother said grace, and then said to this man: 'You must need your bed.' Madame Magloire hastily removed the plate. I understood that we must retire in order to let this traveller sleep, and we both went up-stairs. I, however, sent Madame Magloire to lay on the man's bed a roebuck's hide from the Black Forest, which was in my room, for the nights are very cold, and that keeps you warn. It is a pity that this skin is old and the hair is wearing off. My brother bought it when he was in Germany, at Tottlingen, near the source of the Danube, as well as the small ivory-handled knife which I use at meals.

"Madame Magloire came up again almost immediately. We said our prayers in the room where the clothes are hung up to dry, and then retired to our bedrooms without saying a word to each other."

CHAPTER V

TRANQUILLITY.

After bidding his sister good-night, Monseigneur Welcome took up one of the silver candlesticks, handed the other to his guest, and said,—

"I will lead you to your room, sir."

The man followed him. The reader will remember, from our description, that the rooms were so arranged that in order to reach the oratory where the alcove was it was necessary to pass through the Bishop's bed-room. At the moment when he went through this room Madame Magloire was putting away the plate in the cupboard over the bed-head: it was the last job she did every night before retiring. The Bishop led his guest to the alcove, where a clean bed was prepared for him; the man placed the branched candlestick on a small table.

"I trust you will pass a good night," said the Bishop. "To-morrow morning, before starting, you will drink a glass of milk fresh from our cows."

"Thank you, Monsieur l'Abbé," the man said. He had hardly uttered these peaceful words when, suddenly and without any transition, he had a strange emotion, which would have frightened the two old females to death had they witnessed it. Even at the present day it is difficult to account for what urged him at the moment. Did he wish to warn or to threaten? was he simply obeying a species of instinctive impulse which was obscure to himself? He suddenly turned to the old gentleman, folded his arms, and, fixing on him a savage glance, he exclaimed hoarsely,—

"What! you really lodge me so close to you as that?" He broke off and added with a laugh, in which there was something monstrous,—

"Have you reflected fully? who tells you that I have not committed a murder?"

The Bishop answered: "That concerns God."

Then gravely moving his lips, like a man who is praying and speaking to himself, he stretched out two fingers of his right hand and blessed the man, who did not bow his head, and returned to his bed-room, without turning his head or looking behind him. When the alcove was occupied, a large serge curtain drawn right across the oratory concealed the altar. The Bishop knelt down as he passed before this curtain, and offered up a short prayer; a moment after he was in his garden, walking, dreaming, contemplating, his soul and thoughts entirely occupied by those grand mysteries which God displays at night to eyes that remain open.

As for the man, he was really so wearied that he did not even take advantage of the nice white sheets. He blew out the candle with his nostrils, after the fashion of convicts, and threw himself in his clothes upon the bed, where he at once fell into a deep sleep. Midnight was striking as the Bishop returned from the garden to his room, and a few minutes later everybody was asleep in the small house.

CHAPTER VI

JEAN VALJEAN.

Toward the middle of the night Jean Valjean awoke. He belonged to a poor peasant family of La Brie. In his childhood he had not been taught to read, and when he was of man's age he was a wood-lopper at Faverolles. His mother's name was Jeanne Mathieu, his father's Jean Valjean or Vlajean, probably a sobriquet and a contraction of *Voilà Jean*. Jean Valjean possessed a pensive but not melancholy character, which is peculiar to affectionate natures; but altogether he was a dull, insignificant fellow, at least apparently. He had lost father and mother when still very young: the latter died of a badly-managed milk fever; the former, a pruner like himself, was killed by a fall from a tree. All that was left Jean Valjean was a sister older than himself, a widow with seven children, boys and girls. This sister brought Jean Valjean up, and so long as her husband was alive she supported her brother. When the husband died, the oldest of the seven children was eight years of age, the youngest, one, while Jean Valjean had just reached his twenty-fifth year; he took the place of the father, and in his turn supported the sister who had reared him. This was done simply as a duty, and even rather roughly by Jean Valjean; and his youth was thus expended in hard and ill-paid toil. He was never known to have had a sweetheart, for he had no time for love-making.

At night he came home tired, and ate his soup without saying a word. His sister, mother Jeanne, while he was eating, often took out of his porringer the best part of his meal, the piece of meat, the slice of bacon, or the heart of the cabbage, to give it to one of her children; he, still eating, bent over the table with his head almost in the soup, and his long hair falling round his porringer and hiding his eyes, pretended not to see it, and let her do as she pleased. There was at Faverolles, not far from the Valjeans' cottage, on the other side of the lane, a farmer's wife called Marie Claude. The young Valjeans, who were habitually starving, would go at times and borrow in their mother's name a pint of milk from Marie Claude, which they drank behind a hedge or in some corner, tearing the vessel from each other so eagerly that the little girls spilt the milk over their aprons. Their mother, had she been aware of this fraud, would have severely corrected the delinquents, but Jean Valjean, coarse and rough though he was, paid Marie Claude for the milk behind his sister's back, and the children were not punished.

He earned in the pruning season eighteen sous a day, and besides hired himself out as reaper, laborer, neat-herd, and odd man. He did what he could; his sister worked too, but what could she do with seven children? It was a sad group, which wretchedness gradually enveloped and choked. One winter was hard, and Jean had no work to do, and the family had no bread. No bread, literally none, and seven children!

One Sunday evening, Maubert Isabeau, the baker in the church square at Faverolles, was just going to bed when he heard a violent blow dealt the grating in front of his shop. He arrived in time to see an arm passed through a hole made by a fist through the grating and window pane; the arm seized a loaf, and carried it off. Isabeau ran out hastily; the thief ran away at his hardest, but the baker caught him and stopped him. The thief had thrown away the loaf, but his arm was still bleeding; it was Jean Valjean.

This took place in 1795. Jean Valjean was brought before the courts of the day, charged "with burglary committed with violence at night, in an inhabited house." He had a gun, was a splendid shot, and a bit of a poacher, and this injured him. There is a legitimate prejudice against poachers, for, like smugglers, they trench very closely on brigandage. Still we must remark that there is an abyss between these classes and the hideous assassins of our cities: the poacher lives in the forest; the smuggler in the mountains and on the sea. Cities produce ferocious men, because they produce corrupted men; the forest, the mountain, and the sea produce savage men, but while they develop their ferocious side, they do not always destroy their human part. Jean Valjean was found guilty, and the terms of the code were precise. There are in our civilization formidable hours; they are those moments in which penal justice pronounces a shipwreck. What a mournful minute is that in which society withdraws and consummates the irreparable abandonment of a thinking being! Jean Valjean was sentenced to five years at the galleys.

On April 22d, 1796, men were crying in the streets of Paris the victory of Montenotte, gained by the General-in-chief of the army of Italy, whom the message of the Directory to the Five Hundred, of the 2 Floréal, year IV., calls Buona-Parte; and on the same day a heavy gang was put in chains at Bicetre, and Jean Valjean formed part of the chain. An ex-jailer of the prison, who is now nearly ninety years of age, perfectly remembers the wretched man, who was chained at the end of the fourth cordon, in the north angle of the courtyard. He was seated on the ground like the rest, and seemed not at all to understand his position, except that it was horrible. It is probable that he also saw something excessive through the vague ideas of an utterly ignorant man. While the bolt of his iron collar was being riveted with heavy hammer-blows behind his head, he wept, tears choked him, and prevented him from speaking, and he could only manage to say from time to time: "I was a wood-cutter at Faverolles." Then, while still continuing to sob, he raised his right hand, and lowered it gradually seven times, as if touching seven uneven heads in turn, and from this gesture it could be guessed that whatever the crime he had committed, he had done it to feed and clothe seven children.

He started for Toulon, and arrived there after a journey of twenty-seven days in a cart, with the chain on his neck. At Toulon he was dressed in the red jacket. All that had hitherto been his life, even to his name, was effaced. He was no longer Jean Valjean, but No. 24,601. What became of his sister? What became of the seven children? Who troubles himself about that? What becomes of the spray of leaves when the stem of the young tree has been cut at the foot? It is always the same story. These poor living beings, these creatures of God, henceforth without support, guide, or shelter, went off haphazard, and gradually buried themselves in that cold fog in which solitary destinies are swallowed up, that mournful gloom in which so many unfortunates disappear during the sullen progress of the human race. They left their country; what had once been their steeple forgot them; what had once been their hedge-row forgot them; and after a few years' stay in the bagne, Jean Valjean himself forgot them. In that heart where there had once been a wound there was now a scar: that was all. He only heard about his sister once during the whole time he spent at Toulon; it was, I believe, toward the end of the fourth year of his captivity, though I have forgotten in what way the information reached him. She was in Paris, living in the Rue du Geindre, a poor street, near St. Sulpice, and had only one child with her, the youngest, a boy. Where were the other six? Perhaps she did not know herself. Every morning she went to a printing-office, No. 3, Rue du Sabot, where she was a folder and stitcher; she had to be there at six in the morning, long before daylight in winter. In the same house as the printing-office there was a day-school, to which she took the little boy, who was seven years of age, but as she went to work at six and the school did not open till seven o'clock, the boy was compelled to wait in the yard for an hour, in winter,—an hour of night in the open air. The boy was not allowed to enter the printing-office, because it was said that he would be in the way. The workmen as they passed in the morning saw the poor little fellow seated on the pavement, and often sleeping in the darkness, with his head on his satchel. When it rained, an old woman, the portress, took pity on him; she invited him into her den, where there were only a bed, a spinning-wheel, and two chairs, when the little fellow fell asleep in a corner, clinging to the cat, to keep him warm. This is what Jean Valjean was told; it was a momentary flash, as it were a window suddenly opened in the destiny of the beings he had loved, and then all was closed again; he never heard about them more. Nothing reached him from them; he never saw them again, never met them, and we shall not come across them in the course of this melancholy narrative.

Toward the end of this fourth year, Jean Valjean's turn to escape arrived, and his comrades aided him as they always do in this sorrowful place. He escaped and wandered about the fields at liberty for two days: if it is liberty to be hunted down; to turn ones head at every moment; to start at the slightest sound; to be afraid of everything,—of a chimney that smokes, a man who passes, a barking dog, a galloping horse, the striking of the hour, of day because people see, of night because they do not see, of the highway, the path, the thicket, and even sleep. On the evening of the second day he was recaptured; he had not eaten or slept for six-and-thirty hours. The maritime tribunal added three years to his sentence for his crime, which made it eight years. In the sixth year, it was again his turn to escape; he tried, but could not succeed. He was missing at roll-call, the gun was fired, and at night the watchman found him hidden under the keel of a ship that was building, and he resisted the *garde chiourme*, who seized him. Escape and rebellion: this fact, foreseen by the special code, was punished by an addition of five years, of which two would be spent in double chains. Thirteen years. In his tenth year his turn came again, and he took advantage of it, but succeeded no better: three years for this new attempt, or sixteen years in all. Finally, I think it was during his thirteenth year that he made a last attempt, and only succeeded so far as to be recaptured in four hours: three years for these four hours, and a total of nineteen years. In October, 1815, he was liberated; he had gone in in 1796 for breaking a window and stealing a loaf.

Let us make room for a short parenthesis. This is the second time that, during his essays on the penal question and condemnation by the law, the author of this book has come across a loaf as the starting point of the disaster of a destiny. Claude Gueux stole a loaf, and so did Jean Valjean, and English statistics prove that in London four robberies out of five have hunger as their immediate cause. Jean Valjean entered the bagne sobbing and shuddering: he left it stoically. He entered it in despair: he came out of it gloomy. What had taken place in this soul?

CHAPTER VII.

A DESPERATE MAN'S HEART.

Society must necessarily look at these things, because they are created by it. He was, as we have said, an ignorant man, but he was not weak-minded. The natural light was kindled within him, and misfortune, which also has its brightness, increased the little daylight there was in this mind. Under the stick and the chain in the dungeon, when at work, beneath the torrid sun of the bagne, or when lying on the convict's plank, he reflected. He constituted himself a court, and began by trying himself. He recognized that he was not an innocent man unjustly punished; he confessed to himself that he had committed an extreme and blamable action; that the loaf would probably not have been refused him had he asked for it; that in any case it would have been better to wait for it, either from pity or from labor, and that it was not a thoroughly unanswerable argument to say, "Can a man wait when he is hungry?" That, in the first place, it is very rare for a man to die literally of hunger; next, that, unhappily or happily, man is so made that he can suffer for a long time and severely, morally and physically, without dying; that hence he should have been patient; that it would have been better for the poor little children; that it was an act of madness for him, a wretched weak man, violently to collar society and to imagine that a man can escape from wretchedness by theft; that in any case the door by which a man enters infamy is a bad one by which to escape from wretchedness; and, in short, that he had been in the wrong.

Then he asked himself if he were the only person who had been in the wrong in his fatal history? whether, in the first place, it was not a serious thing that he, a workman, should want for work; that he, laborious as he was, should want for bread? whether, next, when the fault was committed and confessed, the punishment had not been ferocious and excessive, and whether there were not more abuse on the side of the law in the penalty than there was on the side of the culprit in the crime? whether there had not been an excessive weight in one of the scales, that one in which expiation lies? whether the excess of punishment were not the effacement of the crime, and led to the result of making a victim of the culprit, a creditor of the debtor, and definitively placing the right on the side of the man who had violated it? whether this penalty, complicated by excessive aggravations for attempted escapes, did not eventually become a sort of attack made by the stronger on the weaker, a crime of society committed on the individual, a crime which was renewed every day, and had lasted for nineteen years? He asked himself if human society could have the right to make its members equally undergo, on one side, its unreasonable improvidence, on the other its pitiless foresight, and to hold a man eternally between a want and an excess, want of work and excess of punishment? whether it were not exorbitant that society should treat thus its members who were worst endowed in that division of property which is made by chance, and consequently the most worthy of indulgence?

These questions asked and solved, he passed sentence on society and condemned it—to his hatred. He made it responsible for the fate he underwent, and said to himself that he would not hesitate to call it to account some day. He declared that there was no equilibrium between the damage he had caused and the damage caused him; and he came to the conclusion that his punishment was not an injustice, but most assuredly an iniquity. Wrath may be wild and absurd; a man may be wrongly irritated; but he is only indignant when he has some show of reason somewhere. Jean Valjean felt indignant. And then, again, human society had never done him aught but harm, he had only seen its wrathful face, which is called its justice, and shows itself to those whom it strikes. Men had only laid hands on him to injure him, and any contact with them had been a blow to him. Never, since his infancy, since his mother and his sister, had he heard a kind word or met a friendly look. From suffering after suffering, he gradually attained the conviction that life was war, and that in this war he was the vanquished. As he had no other weapon but his hatred, he resolved to sharpen it in the bagne and take it with him when he left.

There was at Toulon a school for the chain-gang, kept by the Ignorantin Brethren, who imparted elementary instruction to those wretches who were willing to learn. He was one of the number, and went to school at the age of forty, where he learned reading, writing, and arithmetic; he felt that strengthening his mind was strengthening his hatred. In certain cases, instruction and education may serve as allies to evil. It is sad to say, that after trying society which had caused his misfortunes, he tried Providence, who had made society, and condemned it also. Hence, during these nineteen years of torture and slavery, this soul ascended and descended at the same time; light entered on one side and darkness on the other. As we have seen, Jean Valjean was not naturally bad, he was still good when he arrived at the bagne. He condemned society then, and felt that he was growing wicked; he condemned Providence, and felt that he was growing impious.

Here it is difficult not to meditate for a moment. Is human nature thus utterly transformed? Can man, who is created good by God, be made bad by man? Can the soul be entirely remade by destiny, and become evil if the destiny be evil? Can the heart be deformed, and contract incurable ugliness and infirmity under the pressure of disproportionate misfortune, like the spine beneath too low a vault? Is there not in every human soul, was there not in that of Jean Valjean especially, a primary spark, a divine element, incorruptible in this world, and immortal for the other, which good can develop, illumine, and cause to glisten splendidly, and which evil can never entirely extinguish?

These are grave and obscure questions, the last of which every physiologist would unhesitatingly have answered in the negative, had he seen at Toulon, in those hours of repose which were for Jean Valjean hours of reverie, this gloomy, stern, silent, and pensive galley-slave—the pariah of the law which regarded men passionately—the condemned of civilization, who regarded Heaven with severity—seated with folded arms on a capstan bar, with the end of his chain thrust into his pocket to prevent it from dragging. We assuredly do not deny that the physiological observer would have seen there an irremediable misery; he would probably have pitied this patient of the law, but he would not have even attempted a cure: he would have turned away from the caverns he noticed in this soul, and, like Dante at the gates of the Inferno, he would have effaced from this existence that word which GOD, however, has written on the brow of every man: *hope!*

Was this state of his soul, which we have attempted to analyze, as perfectly clear to Jean Valjean as we have tried to render it to our readers? Did Jean Valjean see after their formation, and had he seen distinctly as they were formed, all the elements of which his moral wretchedness was composed? Had this rude and unlettered man clearly comprehended the succession of ideas by which he had step by step ascended and descended to the gloomy views which had for so many years been the inner horizon of his mind? Was he really conscious of all that had taken place in him and all that was stirring in him? This we should not like to assert, and, indeed, we are not inclined to believe it. There was too much ignorance in Jean Valjean for a considerable amount of vagueness not to remain, even after so much misfortune; at times he did not even know exactly what he experienced. Jean Valjean was in darkness; he suffered in darkness, and he hated in darkness. He lived habitually in this shadow, groping like a blind man and a dreamer; at times he was attacked, both internally and externally, by a shock of passion, a surcharge of suffering, a pale and rapid flash which illumined his whole soul, and suddenly made him see all around, both before and behind him, in the glare of a frightful light, the hideous precipices and gloomy perspective of his destiny. When the flash had passed, night encompassed him again, and where was he? He no longer knew.

The peculiarity of punishments of this nature, in which nought but what is pitiless, that is to say brutalizing, prevails, is gradually, and by a species of stupid transfiguration, to transform a man into a wild beast, at times a ferocious beast. Jean Valjean's attempted escapes, successive and obstinate, would be sufficient to prove the strange work carried on by the law upon a human soul; he would have renewed these attempts, so utterly useless and mad, as many times as the opportunity offered itself, without dreaming for a moment of the result, or the experiments already made. He escaped impetuously like the wolf that finds its cage open. Instinct said to him, "Run away;" reasoning would have said to him, "Remain;" but in the presence of so violent a temptation, reason disappeared and instinct alone was left. The brute alone acted, and when he was recaptured the new severities inflicted on him only served to render him more wild.

One fact we must not omit mentioning is that he possessed a physical strength with which no one in the bagne could compete. In turning a capstan, Jean Valjean was equal to four men; he frequently raised and held on his back enormous weights, and took the place at times of that instrument which is called a jack, and was formerly called *orgueil*, from which, by the way, the Rue Montorgueil derived its name. His comrades surnamed him Jean the Jack. Once when the balcony of the Town Hall at Toulon was being repaired, one of those admirable caryatides of Puget's which support the balcony, became loose and almost fell. Jean Valjean, who was on the spot, supported the statue with his shoulder, and thus gave the workmen time to come up.

His suppleness even exceeded his vigor. Some convicts, who perpetually dream of escaping, eventually make a real science of combined skill and strength; it is the science of the muscles. A full course of mysterious statics is daily practised by the prisoners, those eternal enviers of flies and birds. Swarming up a perpendicular, and finding a resting-place where a projection is scarcely visible, was child's play for Jean Valjean. Given a corner of a wall, with the tension of his back and hams, with his elbows and heels clinging to the rough stone, he would hoist himself as if by magic to a third story, and at times would ascend to the very roof of the bagne. He spoke little and never laughed; it needed some extreme emotion to draw from him, once or twice a year, that mournful convict laugh, which is, as it were, the echo of fiendish laughter. To look at him, he seemed engaged in continually gazing at something terrible. He was, in fact, absorbed. Through the sickly perceptions of an incomplete nature and a crushed intellect, he saw confusedly that a monstrous thing was hanging over him. In this obscure and dull gloom through which he crawled, wherever he turned his head and essayed to raise his eye, he saw, with a terror blended with rage, built up above him, with frightfully scarped sides, a species of terrific pile of things, laws, prejudices, men, and facts, whose outline escaped him, whose mass terrified him, and which was nothing else but that prodigious pyramid which we call civilization. He distinguished here and there in this heaving and shapeless conglomeration—at one moment close to him, at another on distant and inaccessible plateaux—some highly illumined group;—here the jailer and his stick, there the gendarme and his sabre, down below the mitred archbishop, and on the summit, in a species of sun, the crowned and dazzling Emperor. It seemed to him as if this distant splendor, far from dissipating his night, only rendered it more gloomy and black. All these laws, prejudices, facts, men, and things, came and went above him, in accordance with the complicated and mysterious movement which God imprints on civilization, marching over him, and crushing him with something painful in its cruelty and inexorable in its indifférence. Souls which have fallen into the abyss of possible misfortune, hapless men lost in the depths of those limbos into which people no longer look, and the reprobates of the law, feel on their heads the whole weight of the human society which is so formidable for those outside it, so terrific for those beneath it.

In this situation, Jean Valjean thought, and what could be the nature of his reverie? If the grain of corn had its thoughts, when ground by the mill-stone, it would doubtless think as did Jean Valjean. All these things, realities full of spectres, phantasmagorias full of reality, ended by creating for him a sort of internal condition which is almost inexpressible. At times, in the midst of his galley-slave toil, he stopped and began thinking; his reason, at once riper and more troubled than of yore, revolted. All that had happened appeared to him absurd; all that surrounded him seemed to him impossible. He said to himself that it was a dream; he looked at the overseer standing a few yards from him, and he appeared to him a phantom, until the phantom suddenly dealt him a blow with a stick. Visible nature scarce existed for him; we might almost say with truth, that for Jean Valjean there was no sun, no glorious summer-day, no brilliant sky, no fresh April dawn; we cannot describe the gloomy light which illumined his soul.

In conclusion, to sum up all that can be summed up in what we have indicated, we will confine ourselves to establishing the fact that in nineteen years, Jean Valjean, the inoffensive wood-cutter of Faverolles, and the formidable galley-slave of Toulon, had become, thanks to the manner in which the bagne had fashioned him, capable of two sorts of bad actions: first, a rapid, unreflecting bad deed, entirely instinctive, and a species of reprisal for the evil he had suffered; and, secondly, of a grave, serious evil deed, discussed conscientiously and meditated with the false ideas which such a misfortune can produce. His premeditations passed through the three successive phases which natures of a certain temperament can alone undergo, —reasoning, will, and obstinacy. He had for his motives habitual indignation, bitterness of soul, the profound feeling of iniquities endured, and reaction even against the good, the innocent, and the just, if such exist. The starting-point, like the goal, of all his thoughts, was hatred of human law; that hatred, which, if it be not arrested in its development by some providential incident, becomes within a given time a hatred of society, then a hatred of the human race, next a hatred of creation, and which is expressed by a vague, incessant, and brutal desire to injure some one, no matter whom. As we see, it was not unfairly that the passport described Jean Valjean as a highly dangerous man. Year by year this soul had become more and more withered, slowly but fatally. A dry soul must have a dry eye, and on leaving the bagne, nineteen years had elapsed since he had shed a tear.

CHAPTER VIII.

THE WAVE AND THE DARKNESS.

Man overboard!

What of it? The ship does not stop. The wind is blowing, and this dark ship has a course which she must keep. She goes right on.

The man disappears, then appears again. He goes down and again comes up to the surface; he shouts, he holds up his arms, but they do not hear him. The ship, shivering under the storm, has all she can do to take care of herself. The sailors and the passengers can no longer even see the drowning man; his luckless head is only a speck in the vastness of the waves.

His cries of despair sound through the depths. What a phantom that is,—that sail, fast disappearing from view! He gazes after it; his eyes are fixed upon it with frenzy. It is disappearing, it is fading from sight, it is growing smaller and smaller. Only just now he was there; he was one of the crew; he was going and coming on the deck with the rest; he had his share of air and sun; he was a living man. What, then, has happened? He has slipped, he has fallen; it is all over with him.

He is in the huge waves. There is nothing now under his feet but death and sinking. The fearful waves, torn and frayed by the wind, surround him; the swells of the abyss sweep him along; all the crests of the waves are blown about his head; a crowd of waves spit upon him; uncertain gulfs half swallow him; every time he plunges down he catches a glimpse of precipices black as night; frightful, unknown seaweeds seize him, tie his feet, drag him down to them. He feels that he is becoming a part of the abyss, of the foam; the waves throw him from one to another; he tastes the bitterness; the cowardly ocean has given itself up to drowning him; the vastness sports with his agony. All this water seems to be hate.

Still he struggles.

He tries to save himself, to keep himself up; he strikes out, he swims. He, this pitiful force, at once exhausted, is matched against the inexhaustible.

Where is the ship now? Way down there, barely visible in the pale obscurity of the horizon. The squalls hum about him, the wave-crests wash over him. He raises his eyes, and sees only the lividness of the clouds. In his death struggle he takes part in the madness of the sea. He is tortured by this madness. He hears sounds, strange to man, which seem to come from beyond the earth, and from some terrible world outside.

There are birds in the clouds, just as there are angels above human griefs, but what can they do for him? There is one, flying, singing, and hovering, while he has the death-rattle in his throat.

He feels himself buried at the same time by these two Infinites, the ocean and the heavens; the one a tomb, the other a shroud.

Night falls; he has been swimming now for hours; his strength has reached its end; this ship, this far-off thing where there were men, is blotted from his sight; he is alone in the fearful gulf of twilight; he sinks, he braces himself, he writhes, he feels below him the roving monsters of the invisible. He cries aloud.

"There are no longer any men here." "Where is God?"

He calls "Somebody!" "Somebody!" He keeps on calling.

Nothing on the horizon; nothing in heaven.

He implores the waste of waters, the wave, the seaweed, the rock; it is deaf. He supplicates the tempest; the pitiless tempest obeys only the Infinite.

Around him is darkness, mist, solitude, the stormy and unreasoning tumult, the boundless rolling of the wild waters. In him is horror and weariness. Under him the abyss. There is nothing to rest on. He thinks of what will happen to his body in the boundless shades. The infinite cold benumbs him. His hands shrivel; they clutch and find nothing. Winds, clouds, whirlwinds, puffs, useless stars. What is he to do? In despair, he gives up. Worn out as he is, he makes up his mind to die, he abandons himself, he lets himself go, he relaxes himself, and there he is rolling forever into the dismal depths in which he is swallowed up.

Oh, implacable course of human society! What a loss of men and of souls on the way! Ocean into which falls all that the law lets fall. Wicked vanishing of help! Oh, moral death!

The sea is the pitiless social night into which the penal law thrusts its condemned; the sea is boundless wretchedness.

The soul, swept with the stream into this gulf, may be drowned. Who will bring it to life again?

CHAPTER IX

NEW WRONGS.

When the hour for quitting the bagne arrived, when Jean Valjean heard in his ear the unfamiliar words "You are free," the moment seemed improbable and extraordinary, and a ray of bright light, of the light of the living, penetrated to him; but it soon grew pale. Jean Valjean had been dazzled by the idea of liberty, and had believed in a new life, but he soon saw that it is a liberty to which a yellow passport is granted. And around this there was much bitterness; he had calculated that his earnings, during his stay at the bagne, should have amounted to 171 francs. We are bound to add that he had omitted to take into his calculations the forced rest of Sundays and holidays, which, during nineteen years, entailed a diminution of about 24 francs. However this might be, the sum was reduced, through various local stoppages, to 109 francs, 15 sous, which were paid to him when he left the bagne. He did not understand it all, and fancied that he had been robbed.

On the day after his liberation, he saw at Grasse men in front of a distillery of orange-flower water,—men unloading bales; he offered his services, and as the work was of a pressing nature, they were accepted. He set to work; he was intelligent, powerful, and skilful, and his master appeared satisfied. While he was at work a gendarme passed, noticed him, asked for his paper, and he was compelled to show his yellow pass. This done, Jean Valjean resumed his toil. A little while previously he had asked one of the workmen what he earned for his day's work, and the answer was 30 sous. At night, as he was compelled to start again the next morning, he went to the master of the distillery and asked for payment; the master did not say a word, but gave him 15 sous, and when he protested, the answer was, "That is enough for you." He became pressing, the master looked him in the face and said, "Mind you don't get into prison."

Here again he regarded himself as robbed; society, the state, by diminishing his earnings, had robbed him wholesale; now it was the turn of the individual to commit retail robbery. Liberation is not deliverance; a man may leave the bagne, but not condemnation. We have seen what happened to him at Grasse, and we know how he was treated at D——.

CHAPTER X

THE MAN AWAKE.

As two o'clock pealed from the cathedral bell, Jean Valjean awoke. What aroused him was that the bed was too comfortable, for close on twenty years he had not slept in a bed, and though he had not undressed, the sensation was too novel not to disturb his sleep. He had been asleep for more than four hours, and his weariness had worn off; and he was accustomed not to grant many hours to repose. He opened his eyes and looked into the surrounding darkness, and then he closed them again to go to sleep once more. When many diverse sensations have agitated a day, and when matters preoccupy the mind, a man may sleep, but he cannot go to sleep again. Sleep comes more easily than it returns, and this happened to Jean Valjean. As he could not go to sleep again, he began thinking.

It was one of those moments in which the ideas that occupy the mind are troubled, and there was a species of obscure oscillation in his brain. His old recollections and immediate recollections crossed each other, and floated confusedly, losing their shape, growing enormously, and then disappearing suddenly, as if in troubled and muddy water. Many thoughts occurred to him, but there was one which constantly reverted and expelled all the rest. This thought we will at once describe; he had noticed the six silver forks and spoons and the great ladle which Madame Magloire put on the table. This plate overwhelmed him; it was there, a few yards from him. When he crossed the adjoining room to reach the one in which he now was, the old servant was putting it in a small cupboard at the bed-head,—he had carefully noticed this cupboard; it was on the right as you came in from the dining-room. The plate was heavy and old, the big soup-ladle was worth at least 200 francs, or double what he had earned in nineteen years, though it was true that he would have earned more had not the officials robbed him.

His mind oscillated for a good hour, in these fluctuations with which a struggle was most assuredly blended. When three o'clock struck he opened his eyes, suddenly sat up, stretched out his arms, and felt for his knapsack which he had thrown into a corner of the alcove, then let his legs hang, and felt himself seated on the bed-side almost without knowing how. He remained for a while thoughtfully in this attitude, which would have had something sinister about it, for any one who had seen him, the only wakeful person in the house. All at once he stooped, took off his shoes, then resumed his thoughtful posture, and remained motionless. In the midst of this hideous meditation, the ideas which we have indicated incessantly crossed his brain, entered, went out, returned, and weighed upon him; and then he thought, without knowing why, and with the mechanical obstinacy of reverie, of a convict he had known at the bagne, of the name of Brevet, whose trousers were only held up by a single knitted brace. The draught-board design of that brace incessantly returned to his mind. He remained in this situation, and would have probably remained so till sunrise, had not the clock struck the quarter or the half-hour. It seemed as if this stroke said to him, To work! He rose, hesitated for a moment and listened; all was silent in the house, and he went on tip-toe to the window, through which he peered. The night was not very dark; there was a full moon, across which heavy clouds were chased by the wind. This produced alternations of light and shade, and a species of twilight in the room; this twilight, sufficient to guide him, but intermittent in consequence of the clouds, resembled that livid hue produced by the grating of a cellar over which people are continually passing. On reaching the window, Jean Valjean examined it; it was without bars, looked on the garden, and was only closed, according to the fashion of the country, by a small peg. He opened it, but as a cold sharp breeze suddenly entered the room, he closed it again directly. He gazed into the garden with that attentive glance which studies rather than looks, and found that it was enclosed by a white-washed wall, easy to climb over. Beyond it he noticed the tops of trees standing at regular distances, which proved that this wall separated the garden from a public walk.

After taking this glance, he walked boldly to the alcove, opened his knapsack, took out something which he laid on the bed, put his shoes in one of the pouches, placed the knapsack on his shoulders, put on his cap, the peak of which he pulled over his eyes, groped for his stick, which he placed in the window nook, and then returned to the bed, and took up the object he had laid on it. It resembled a short iron bar, sharpened at one of its ends. It would have been difficult to distinguish in the darkness for what purpose this piece of iron had been fashioned; perhaps it was a lever, perhaps it was a club. By daylight it could have been seen that it was nothing but a miners candlestick. The convicts at that day were sometimes employed in extracting rock from the lofty hills that surround Toulon, and it was not infrequent for them to have mining tools at their disposal. The miner's candlesticks are made of massive steel, and have a point at the lower end, by which they are dug into the rock. He took the bar in his right hand, and holding his breath and deadening his footsteps he walked towards the door of the adjoining room, the Bishop's as we know. On reaching this door he found it ajar—the Bishop had not shut it.

CHAPTER XI

WHAT HE DID.

Jean Valjean listened, but there was not a sound; he pushed the door with the tip of his finger lightly, and with the furtive restless gentleness of a cat that wants to get in. The door yielded to the pressure, and made an almost imperceptible and silent movement, which slightly widened the opening. He waited for a moment, and then pushed the door again more boldly. It continued to yield silently, and the opening was soon large enough for him to pass through. But there was near the door a small table which formed an awkward angle with it, and barred the entrance.

Jean Valjean noticed the difficulty: the opening must be increased at all hazards. He made up his mind, and pushed the door a third time, more energetically still. This time there was a badly-oiled hinge, which suddenly uttered a hoarse prolonged cry in the darkness. Jean Valjean started; the sound of the hinge smote his ear startlingly and formidably, as if it had been the trumpet of the day of judgment. In the fantastic exaggerations of the first minute, he almost imagined that this hinge had become animated, and suddenly obtained a terrible vitality and barked like a dog to warn and awaken the sleepers. He stopped, shuddering and dismayed, and fell back from tip-toes on his heels. He felt the arteries in his temples beat like two forge hammers, and it seemed to him that his breath issued from his lungs with the noise of the wind roaring out of a cavern. He fancied that the horrible clamor of this irritated hinge must have startled the whole house like the shock of an earthquake; the door he opened had been alarmed and cried for help; the old man would rise, the two aged females would shriek, and assistance would arrive within a quarter of an hour, the town would be astir, and the gendarmerie turned out. For a moment he believed himself lost.

He remained where he was, petrified like the pillar of salt, and not daring to make a movement. A few minutes passed, during which the door remained wide open. He ventured to look into the room, and found that nothing had stirred. He listened; no one was moving in the house, the creaking of the rusty hinge had not awakened any one. The first danger had passed, but still there was fearful tumult within him. But he did not recoil, he had not done so even when he thought himself lost; he only thought of finishing the job as speedily as possible, and entered the bed-room. The room was in a state of perfect calmness; here and there might be distinguished confused and vague forms, which by day were papers scattered over the table, open folios, books piled on a sofa, an easy-chair covered with clothes, and a priedieu, all of which were at this moment only dark nooks and patches of white. Jean Valjean advanced cautiously and carefully, and avoided coming into collision with the furniture. He heard from the end of the room the calm and regular breathing of the sleeping Bishop. Suddenly he stopped, for he was close to the bed; he had reached it sooner than he anticipated.

Nature at times blends her effects and scenes with our actions, with a species of gloomy and intelligent design, as if wishing to make us reflect. For nearly half an hour a heavy cloud had covered the sky, but at the moment when Jean Valjean stopped at the foot of the bed, this cloud was rent asunder as if expressly, and a moonbeam passing through the tall window suddenly illumined the Bishop's pale face. He was sleeping peacefully, and was wrapped up in a long garment of brown wool, which covered his arms down to the wrists. His head was thrown back on the pillow in the easy attitude of repose, and his hand, adorned with the pastoral ring, and which had done so many good deeds, hung out of bed. His entire face was lit up by a vague expression of satisfaction, hope, and beatitude—it was more than a smile and almost a radiance. He had on his forehead the inexpressible reflection of an invisible light, for the soul of a just man contemplates a mysterious heaven during sleep. A reflection of this heaven was cast over the Bishop, but it was at the same time a luminous transparency, for the heaven was within him, and was conscience.

At the moment when the moonbeam was cast over this internal light, the sleeping Bishop seemed to be surrounded by a glory, which was veiled, however, by an ineffable semi-light. The moon in the heavens, the slumbering landscape, the quiet house, the hour, the silence, the moment, added something solemn and indescribable to this man's venerable repose, and cast a majestic and serene halo round his white hair and closed eyes, his face in which all was hope and confidence, his aged head, and his infantine slumbers. There was almost a divinity in this unconsciously august man. Jean Valjean was standing in the shadow with his crow-bar in his hand, motionless and terrified by this luminous old man. He had never seen anything like this before, and such confidence horrified him. The moral world has no greater spectacle than this,—a troubled, restless conscience, which is on the point of committing a bad action, contemplating the sleep of a just man.

This sleep in such isolation, and with a neighbor like himself, possessed a species of sublimity which he felt vaguely, but imperiously. No one could have said what was going on within him, not even himself. In order to form any idea of it we must imagine what is the most violent in the presence of what is gentlest. Even in his face nothing could have been distinguished with certainty, for it displayed a sort of haggard astonishment. He looked at the Bishop, that was all, but what his thoughts were it would be impossible to divine; what was evident was, that he was moved and shaken, but of what nature was this emotion? His eye was not once removed from the old man, and the only thing clearly revealed by his attitude and countenance was a strange indecision. It seemed as if he were hesitating between two abysses, the one that saves and the one that destroys; he was ready to dash out the Bishop's brains or kiss his hand. At the expiration of a few minutes his left arm slowly rose to his cap, which he took off; then his arm fell again with the same slowness, and Jean Valjean recommenced his contemplation, with his cap in his left hand, his crow-bar in his right, and his hair standing erect on his savage head.

The Bishop continued to sleep peacefully beneath this terrific glance. A moonbeam rendered the crucifix over the mantel-piece dimly visible, which seemed to open its arms for both, with a blessing for one and a pardon for the other. All at once Jean Valjean put on his cap again, then walked rapidly along the bed, without looking at the Bishop, and went straight to the cupboard. He raised his crow-bar to force the lock, but as the key was in it, he opened it, and the first thing he saw was the plate-basket, which he seized. He hurried across the room, not caring for the noise he made, re-entered the oratory, opened the window, seized his stick, put the silver in his pocket, threw away the basket, leaped into the garden, bounded over the wall like a tiger, and fled.

CHAPTER XII.

THE BISHOP AT WORK.

The next morning at sunrise Monseigneur Welcome was walking about the garden, when Madame Magloire came running toward him in a state of great alarm.

"Monseigneur, Monseigneur!" she screamed, "does your Grandeur know where the plate-basket is?"

"Yes," said the Bishop.

"The Lord be praised," she continued; "I did not know what had become of it."

The Bishop had just picked up the basket in a flower-bed, and now handed it to Madame Magloire. "Here it is," he said.

"Well!" she said, "there is nothing in it; where is the plate?"

"Ah!" the Bishop replied, "it is the plate that troubles your mind. Well, I do not know where that is."

"Good Lord! it is stolen, and that man who came last night is the robber."

In a twinkling Madame Magloire had run to the oratory, entered the alcove, and returned to the Bishop. He was stooping down and looking sorrowfully at a cochlearia, whose stem the basket had broken. He raised himself on hearing Madame Magloire scream,—

"Monseigneur, the man has gone! the plate is stolen!"

While uttering this exclamation her eyes fell on a corner of the garden, where there were signs of climbing; the coping of the wall had been torn away.

"That is the way he went! He leaped into Cochefilet lane. Oh, what an outrage! He has stolen our plate."

The Bishop remained silent for a moment, then raised his earnest eyes, and said gently to Madame Magloire,—

"By the way, was that plate ours?"

Madame Magloire was speechless; there was another interval of silence, after which the Bishop continued,—

"Madame Magloire, I had wrongfully held back this silver, which belonged to the poor. Who was this person? Evidently a poor man."

"Good gracious!" Madame Magloire continued; "I do not care for it, nor does Mademoiselle, but we feel for Monseigneur. With what will Monseigneur eat now?"

The Bishop looked at her in amazement. "Why, are there not pewter forks to be had?"

Madame Magloire shrugged her shoulders. "Pewter smells!"

"Then iron!"

Madame Magloire made an expressive grimace. "Iron tastes."

"Well, then," said the Bishop, "wood!"

A few minutes later he was breakfasting at the same table at which Jean Valjean sat on the previous evening. While breakfasting Monseigneur Welcome gayly remarked to his sister, who said nothing, and to Madame Magloire, who growled in a low voice, that spoon and fork, even of wood, are not required to dip a piece of bread in a cup of milk.

"What an idea!" Madame Magloire said, as she went backwards and forwards, "to receive a man like that, and lodge him by one's side. And what a blessing it is that he only stole! Oh, Lord! the mere thought makes a body shudder."

As the brother and sister were leaving the table there was a knock at the door.

"Come in," said the Bishop.

The door opened, and a strange and violent group appeared on the threshold. Three men were holding a fourth by the collar. The three men were gendarmes, the fourth was Jean Valjean. A corporal, who apparently commanded the party, came in and walked up to the Bishop with a military salute.

"Monseigneur," he said.

At this word Jean Valjean, who was gloomy and crushed, raised his head with a stupefied air.

"'Monseigneur,'" he muttered; "then he is not the Curé."

"Silence!" said a gendarme. "This gentleman is Monseigneur the Bishop."

In the mean while Monseigneur Welcome had advanced as rapidly as his great age permitted.

"Ah! there you are," he said, looking at Jean Valjean. "I am glad to see you. Why, I gave you the candlesticks too, which are also silver, and will fetch you 200 francs. Why did you not take them away with the rest of the plate?"

Jean Valjean opened his eyes, and looked at the Bishop with an expression which no human language could render.

"Monseigneur," the corporal said; "what this man told us was true then? We met him, and as he looked as if he were running away, we arrested him. He had this plate—"

"And he told you," the Bishop interrupted, with a smile, "that it was given to him by an old priest at whose house he passed the night? I see it all. And you brought him back here? That is a mistake."

"In that case," the corporal continued, "we can let him go?"

"Of course," the Bishop answered.

The gendarmes loosed their hold of Jean Valjean, who tottered back.

"Is it true that I am at liberty?" he said, in an almost inarticulate voice, and as if speaking in his sleep.

"Yes, you are let go; don't you understand?" said a gendarme.

"My friend," the Bishop continued, "before you go take your candlesticks."

He went to the mantel-piece, fetched the two candlesticks, and handed them to Jean Valjean. The two females watched him do so without a word, without a sign, without a look that could disturb the Bishop. Jean Valjean was trembling in all his limbs; he took the candlesticks mechanically, and with wandering looks.

"Now," said the Bishop, "go in peace. By the bye, when you return, my friend, it is unnecessary to pass through the garden, for you can always enter, day and night, by the front door, which is only latched."

Then, turning to the gendarmes, he said,—

"Gentlemen, you can retire."

They did so. Jean Valjean looked as if he were on the point of fainting; the Bishop walked up to him, and said in a low voice,—

"Never forget that you have promised me to employ this money in becoming an honest man."

Jean Valjean, who had no recollection of having promised anything, stood silent. The Bishop, who had laid a stress on these words, continued solemnly, —

"Jean Valjean, my brother, you no longer belong to evil, but to good. I have bought your soul of you. I withdraw it from black thoughts and the spirit of perdition, and give it to God."

<hr />

CHAPTER XIII.

LITTLE GERVAIS.

Jean Valjean left the town as if running away; he walked hastily across the fields, taking the roads and paths that offered themselves, without perceiving that he was going round and round. He wandered thus the entire morning, and though he had eaten nothing, he did not feel hungry. He was attacked by a multitude of novel sensations; he felt a sort of passion, but he did not know with whom. He could not have said whether he was affected or humiliated; at times a strange softening came over him, against which he strove, and to which he opposed the hardening of the last twenty years. This condition offended him, and he saw with alarm that the species of frightful calmness, which the injustice of his misfortune had produced, was shaken within him. He asked himself what would take its place; at times he would have preferred being in prison and with the gendarmes, and that things had not happened thus; for that would have agitated him less. Although the season was advanced, there were still here and there in the hedges a few laggard flowers, whose smell recalled childhood's memories as he passed them. These recollections were almost unendurable, for it was so long since they had recurred to him.

Indescribable thoughts were thus congregated within him the whole day through. When the sun was setting, and lengthening on the ground the shadow of the smallest pebble, Jean Valjean was sitting behind a bush in a large tawny and utterly-deserted plain. There were only the Alps on the horizon, there was not even the steeple of a distant village. Jean Valjean might be about three leagues from D——, and a path that crossed the plain ran a few paces from the bushes. In the midst of this meditation, which would have contributed no little in rendering his rags startling to any one who saw him, he heard a sound of mirth. He turned his head and saw a little Savoyard about ten years of age coming along the path, with his hurdy-gurdy at his side and his dormouse-box on his back. He was one of those gentle, merry lads who go about from place to place, displaying their knees through the holes in their trousers.

While singing the lad stopped every now and then to play at pitch and toss with some coins he held in his hand, which were probably his entire fortune. Among these coins was a two-franc piece. The lad stopped by the side of the bushes without seeing Jean Valjean, and threw up the handful of sous, all of which he had hitherto always caught on the back of his hand. This time the two-franc piece fell, and rolled up to Jean Valjean, who placed his foot upon it. But the boy had looked after the coin, and seen him do it; he did not seem surprised, but walked straight up to the man. It was an utterly deserted spot; as far as eye could extend there was no one on the plain or the path. Nothing was audible, save the faint cries of a swarm of birds of passage passing through the sky, at an immense height. The boy had his back turned to the sun, which wove golden threads in his hair, and suffused Jean Valjean's face with a purpled, blood-red hue.

"Sir," the little Savoyard said, with that childish confidence which is composed of ignorance and innocence, "my coin?"

"What is your name?" Jean Valjean said.

"Little Gervais, sir."

"Be off," said Jean Valjean.

"Give me my coin, if you please, sir."

Jean Valjean hung his head, but said nothing.

The boy began again,—

"My two-franc piece, sir."

Jean Valjean's eye remained fixed on the ground.

"My coin," the boy cried, "my silver piece, my money."

It seemed as if Jean Valjean did not hear him, for the boy seized the collar of his blouse and shook him, and at the same time made an effort to remove the iron-shod shoe placed on his coin.

"I want my money, my forty-sous piece."

The boy began crying, and Jean Valjean raised his head. He was still sitting on the ground, and his eyes were misty. He looked at the lad with a sort of amazement, then stretched forth his hand to his stick, and shouted in a terrible voice, "Who is there?"

"I, sir," the boy replied. "Little Gervais; give me back my two francs, if you please. Take away your foot, sir, if you please." Then he grew irritated, though so little, and almost threatening.

"Come, will you lift your foot? Lift it, I say!"

"Ah, it is you still," said Jean Valjean, and springing up, with his foot still held on the coin, he added, "Will you be off or not?"

The startled boy looked at him, then began trembling from head to foot, and after a few moments of stupor ran off at full speed, without daring to look back or utter a cry. Still, when he had got a certain distance, want of breath forced him to stop, and Jean Valjean could hear him sobbing. In a few minutes the boy had disappeared. The sun had set, and darkness collected around Jean Valjean. He had eaten nothing all day, and was probably in a fever. He had remained standing and not changed his attitude since the boy ran off. His breath heaved his chest at long and unequal intervals, his eye, fixed ten or twelve yards ahead, seemed to be studying with profound attention the shape of an old fragment of blue earthenware which had fallen in the grass. Suddenly he started, for he felt the night chill; he pulled his cap over his forehead, mechanically tried to cross and button his blouse, made a step, and stooped to pick up his stick.

At this moment he perceived the two-franc piece, which his foot had half buried in the turf, and which glistened among the pebbles. It had the effect of a galvanic shock upon him. "What is this?" he muttered. He fell back three paces, then stopped, unable to take his eye from the spot his foot had trodden a moment before, as if the thing glistening there in the darkness had an open eye fixed upon him. In a few moments he dashed convulsively at the coin, picked it up, and began looking out into the plain, while shuddering like a straying wild beast which is seeking shelter.

He saw nothing, night was falling, the plain was cold and indistinct, and heavy purple mists rose in the twilight. He set out rapidly in a certain direction, the one in which the lad had gone. After going some thirty yards he stopped, looked and saw nothing; then he shouted with all his strength, "little Gervais, Little Gervais!" He was silent, and waited, but there was no response. The country was deserted and gloomy, and he was surrounded by space. There was nothing but a gloom in which his gaze was lost, and a stillness in which his voice was lost. An icy breeze was blowing, and imparted to things around a sort of mournful life. The bushes shook their little thin arms with incredible fury; they seemed to be threatening and pursuing some one.

He walked onwards and then began running, but from time to time he stopped, and shouted in the solitude with a voice the most formidable and agonizing that can be imagined: "Little Gervais, Little Gervais!" Assuredly, if the boy had heard him, he would have felt frightened, and not have shown himself; but the lad was doubtless a long way off by this time. The convict met a priest on horseback, to whom he went up and said,—

"Monsieur le Curé, have you seen a lad pass?"

"No," the priest replied.

"A lad of the name of 'Little Gervais?'"

"I have seen nobody."

The convict took two five-franc pieces from his pouch and handed them to the Priest.

"Monsieur le Curé, this is for your poor. He was a boy of about ten years of age, with a dormouse, I think, and a hurdy-gurdy,—a Savoyard, you know."

"I did not see him."

"Can you tell me if there is any one of the name of Little Gervais in the villages about here?"

"If it is as you say, my good fellow, the lad is a stranger. Many of them pass this way."

Jean Valjean violently took out two other five-franc pieces, which he gave the priest.

"For your poor," he said; then added wildly, "Monsieur l'Abbé, have me arrested: I am a robber."

The priest urged on his horse, and rode away in great alarm, while Jean Valjean set off running in the direction he had first taken. He went on for a long distance, looking, calling, and shouting, but he met no one else. Twice or thrice he ran across the plain to something that appeared to him to be a person lying or sitting down; but he only found heather, or rocks level with the ground. At last he stopped at a spot where three paths met; the moon had risen; he gazed afar, and called out for the last time, "Little Gervais, Little Gervais, Little Gervais!" His shout died away in the mist, without even awakening an echo. He muttered again, "Little Gervais," in a weak and almost inarticulate voice, but it was his last effort. His knees suddenly gave way under him as if an invisible power were crushing him beneath the weight of a bad conscience. He fell exhausted on a large stone, with his hand tearing his hair, his face between his knees, and shrieked: "I am a scoundrel!" Then his heart melted, and he began to weep; it was the first time for nineteen years.

When Jean Valjean quitted the Bishop's house he was lifted out of his former thoughts, and could not account for what was going on within him. He stiffened himself against the angelic deeds and gentle words of the old man: "You have promised me to become an honest man. I purchase your soul; I withdraw it from the spirit of perverseness and give it to God." This incessantly recurred to him, and he opposed to this celestial indulgence that pride which is within us as the fortress of evil. He felt indistinctly that this priest's forgiveness was the greatest and most formidable assault by which he had yet been shaken; that his hardening would be permanent if he resisted this clemency; that if he yielded he must renounce that hatred with which the actions of other men had filled his soul during so many years, and which pleased him; that this time he must either conquer or be vanquished, and that the struggle, a colossal and final struggle, had begun between his wickedness and that man's goodness.

In the presence of all these gleams he walked on like a drunken man. While he went on thus with haggard eye, had he any distinct perception of what the result of his adventure at D—— might be? Did he hear all that mysterious buzzing which warns or disturbs the mind at certain moments of life? Did a voice whisper in his ear that he had just gone through the solemn hour of his destiny, that no middle way was now left him, and that if he were not henceforth the best of men he would be the worst; that he must now ascend higher than the bishop, or sink lower than the galley-slave; that if he wished to be good he must become an angel, and if he wished to remain wicked that he must become a monster?

Here we must ask again the question we previously asked, Did he confusedly receive any shadow of all this into his mind? Assuredly, as we said, misfortune educates the intellect, still it is doubtful whether Jean Valjean was in a state to draw the conclusions we have formed. If these ideas reached him, he had a glimpse of them rather than saw them, and they only succeeded in throwing him into an indescribable and almost painful trouble. On leaving that shapeless black thing which is called the bagne the Bishop had hurt his soul, in the same way as a too brilliant light would have hurt his eyes on coming out of darkness. The future life, the possible life, which presented itself to him, all pure and radiant, filled him with tremor and anxiety, and he really no longer knew how matters were. Like an owl that suddenly witnessed a sunrise the convict had been dazzled and, as it were, blinded by virtue.

One thing which he did not suspect is certain, however, that he was no longer the same man; all was changed in him, and it was no longer in his power to get rid of the fact that the Bishop had spoken to him and taken his hand. While in this mental condition he met Little Gervais, and robbed him of his two francs: why did he so? Assuredly he could not explain it. Was it a final, and as it were supreme, effort of the evil thought he had brought from the bagne, a remainder of impulse, a result of what is called in Statics "acquired force"? It was so, and was perhaps also even less than that. Let us say it simply, it was not he who robbed, it was not the man, but the brute beast that through habit and instinct stupidly placed its foot on the coin, while the intellect was struggling with such novel and extraordinary sensations. When the intellect woke again and saw this brutish action, Jean Valjean recoiled with agony and uttered a cry of horror. It was a curious phenomenon, and one only possible in his situation, that, in robbing the boy of that money, he committed a deed of which he was no longer capable.

However this may be, this last bad action had a decisive effect upon him: it suddenly darted through the chaos which filled his mind and dissipated it, placed on one side the dark mists, on the other the light, and acted on his soul, in its present condition, as certain chemical re-agents act upon a troubled mixture, by precipitating one element and clarifying another. At first, before even examining himself or reflecting, he wildly strove to find the boy again and return him his money; then, when he perceived that this was useless and impossible, he stopped in despair. At the moment when he exclaimed, "I am a scoundrel!" he had seen himself as he really was, and was already so separated from himself that he fancied himself merely a phantom, and that he had there before him, in flesh and blood, his blouse fastened round his hips, his knapsack full of stolen objects on his back, with his resolute and gloomy face and his mind full of hideous schemes, the frightful galley-slave, Jean Valjean.

As we have remarked, excessive misfortune had made him to some extent a visionary, and this therefore was a species of vision. He really saw that Jean Valjean with his sinister face before him, and almost asked himself who this man who so horrified him was. His brain was in that violent and yet frightfully calm stage when the reverie is so deep that it absorbs reality. He contemplated himself, so to speak, face to face, and at the same time he saw through this hallucination a species of light which he at first took for a torch. On looking more attentively at this light which appeared to his conscience, he perceived that it had a human shape and was the Bishop. His conscience examined in turn the two men standing before him, the Bishop and Jean Valjean. By one of those singular effects peculiar to an ecstasy of this nature, the more his reverie was prolonged, the taller and more brilliant the Bishop appeared, while Jean Valjean grew less and faded out of sight. At length he disappeared and the Bishop alone remained, who filled the wretched man's soul with a magnificent radiance.

Jean Valjean wept for a long time, and sobbed with more weakness than a woman, more terror than a child. While he wept the light grew brighter in his brain,—an extraordinary light, at once ravishing and terrible. His past life, his first fault, his long expiation, his external brutalization, his internal hardening, his liberation, accompanied by so many plans of vengeance, what had happened at the Bishop's, the last thing he had done, the robbery of the boy, a crime the more cowardly and monstrous because it took place after the Bishop's forgiveness, —all this recurred to him, but in a light which he had never before seen. He looked at his life, and it appeared to him horrible; at his soul, and it appeared to him frightful. Still a soft light was shed over both, and he fancied that he saw Satan by the light of Paradise.

How many hours did he weep thus? what did he do afterwards? whither did he go? No one ever knew. It was stated, however, that on this very night the mail carrier from Grenoble, who arrived at D—— at about three o'clock in the morning, while passing through the street where the Bishop's Palace stood, saw a man kneeling on the pavement in the attitude of prayer in front of Monseigneur Welcome's door.

BOOK III

IN THE YEAR 1817.

CHAPTER I.

THE YEAR 1817.

1817 is the year which Louis XVIII., with a certain royal coolness which was not deficient in pride, entitled the twenty-second of his reign. It is the year in which M. Bruguière de Sorsum was celebrated. All the wig-makers' shops, hoping for powder and the return of the royal bird, were covered with azure and fleurs de lys. It was the candid time when Count Lynch sat every Sunday as churchwarden at St. Germain-des-Près in the coat of a peer of France, with his red ribbon, his long nose, and that majestic profile peculiar to a man who has done a brilliant deed. The brilliant deed done by M. Lynch was having, when Mayor of Bordeaux, surrendered the town rather prematurely on March 12, 1814, to the Duc d'Angoulême; hence his peerage. In 1817 fashion buried little boys of the age of six and seven beneath vast morocco leather caps with earflaps, much resembling Esquimaux fur-bonnets. The French army was dressed in white, like the Austrian; the regiments were called Legions, and bore the names of the departments instead of numbers. Napoleon was at St Helena, and as England refused him green cloth he had his old coats turned. In 1817 Pellegrini sang, and Mlle. Bigottini danced, Potier reigned, and Odry was not as yet. Madame Saqui succeeded Forioso. There were still Prussians in France. M. Delalot was a personage. Legitimacy had just strengthened itself by cutting off the hand and then the head of Pleignier, Carbonneau, and Tolleron. Prince de Talleyrand, Lord High Chamberlain, and the Abbé Louis, Minister Designate of Finance, looked at each other with the laugh of two augurs. Both had celebrated on July 14, 1790, the Mass of the confederation in the Champ de Mars. Talleyrand had read it as bishop, Louis had served it as deacon. In 1817, in the side walks of the same Champ de Mars, could be seen large wooden cylinders, lying in the wet and rotting in the grass, painted blue, with traces of eagles and bees which had lost their gilding. These were the columns which two years previously supported the Emperor's balcony at the Champ de Mai. They were partly blackened by the bivouac fires of the Austrians encamped near Gros Caillou, and two or three of the columns had disappeared in the bivouac fires, and warmed the coarse hands of the Kaiserlichs. The Champ de Mai had this remarkable thing about it, that it was held in the month of June, and on the Champ de Mars. In this year, 1817, two things were popular,—the Voltaire Touquet and the snuff-box *à la charte*. The latest Parisian sensation was the crime of Dautun, who threw his brother's head into the basin on the Flower Market. People were beginning to grow anxious at the Admiralty that no news arrived about that fatal frigate *la Méduse*, which was destined to cover Chaumareix with shame and Géricault with glory. Colonel Selves proceeded to Egypt to become Soliman Pacha there. The palace of the Thermes, in the Rue de la Harpe, served as a shop for a cooper. On the platform of the octagonal tower of the Hotel de Cluny, could still be seen the little wooden house, which had served as an observatory for Messier, astronomer to the Admiralty under Louis XVI. The Duchesse de Duras was reading to three or four friends in her boudoir furnished with sky-blue satin X's, her unpublished romance of *Ourika*. The N's were scratched off the Louvre. The Austerlitz bridge was forsworn, and called the Kings' Gardens' bridge,—a double enigma which at once disguised the Austerlitz bridge and the Jardin des Plantes. Louis XVIII., while annotating Horace with his nail, was troubled by heroes who make themselves emperors and cobblers who make themselves dauphins; he had two objects of anxiety,—Napoleon and Mathurin Bruneau. The French Academy offered as subject for the prize essay the happiness produced by study. M. Billart was officially eloquent; and in his shadow could be seen growing up that future Advocate-General de Broë, promised to the sarcasms of Paul Louis Courier. There was a false Châteaubriand called Marchangy, while waiting till there should be a false Marchangy, called d'Arlincourt. "Claire d'Albe" and "Malek-Adel" were master-pieces; and Madame Cottin was declared the first writer of the age. The Institute erased from its lists the Academician Napoleon Bonaparte. A royal decree constituted Angoulême a naval school, for, as the Duc d'Angoulême was Lord High Admiral, it was evident that the city from which he derived his title possessed *de jure* all the qualifications of a seaport; if not, the monarchical principle would be encroached on. In the cabinet-council the question was discussed whether the wood-cuts representing tumblers, which seasoned Franconi's bills and caused the street scamps to congregate, should be tolerated. M. Paër, author of l'Agnese, a square-faced man with a carbuncle on his chin, directed the private concerts of the Marchioness de Sassenaye in the Rue de la Ville'd'Evêque. All the young ladies were singing, "L'ermite de Saint Avelle," words by Edmond Géraud. The Yellow Dwarf was transformed into the Mirror. The Café Lemblin stood up for the Emperor against the Café Valois, which supported the Bourbons. The Duc de Berry, whom Louvel was already gazing at from the darkness, had just been married to a princess of Sicily. It was a year since Madame de Staël had died. The Life Guards hissed Mademoiselle Mars. The large papers were all small; their size was limited, but the liberty was great. The *Constitutionnel* was constitutional, and the *Minerva* called Châteaubriand, Châteaubriant; this *t* made the city laugh heartily, at the expense of the great writer. Prostituted journalists insulted in sold journals the proscripts of 1815. David had no longer talent, Arnault wit, Carnot probity. Soult never had won a battle. It is true that Napoleon no longer had genius. Everybody knows that it is rare for letters sent by post to reach an exile, for the police make it a religious duty to intercept them. The fact is not new, for Descartes when banished complained of it. David having displayed some temper in a Belgian paper at not receiving letters written to him, this appeared very amusing to the Royalist journals, which ridiculed the proscribed man. The use of the words regicides or voters, enemies or allies, Napoleon or Buonaparte, separated two men more than an abyss. All persons of common sense were agreed that the era of revolutions was eternally closed by Louis XVIII., surnamed "the immortal author of the Charter." On the platform of the Pont Neuf the word "Redivivus" was carved on the pedestal which was awaiting the statue of Henri IV. M. Piet was excogitating at No. 4 Rue Thérèse his council to consolidate the monarchy. The leaders of the Right said in grave complications, "Bacot must be written to." Messieurs Canuel, O'Mahony, and de Chappedelaine, were sketching under the covert approval of Monsieur what was destined to be at a later date "the conspiracy du Bord de l'eau." The "Black Pin" was plotting on its side. Delaverderie was coming to an understanding with Trogoff. M. Decazes, a rather liberally-minded man, was in the ascendant. Châteaubriand, standing each morning at his No. 27 Rue Saint Dominique, in trousers and slippers, with his gray hair fastened by a handkerchief, with his eyes fixed on a mirror, and a case of dentist's instruments open before him,—was cleaning his teeth, which were splendid, while dictating "the Monarchy according to the Charter" to M. Pilorge, his secretary. Authoritative critics preferred Lafon to Talma. M. de Feletz signed A; M. Hoffman signed Z. Charles Nodier was writing "Thérèse Aubert." Divorce was abolished. The lyceums were called colleges. The collegians, with a gold fleur de lys on their collar, were fighting about the King of Rome. The counter-police of the Château denounced to her Royal Highness Madame, the universally exposed portrait of the Duc d'Orléans, who looked much handsomer in his uniform of Colonel General of Hussars than the Duc de Berry did in his uniform as Colonel General of Dragoons, which was a serious annoyance. The city of Paris was having the dome of the Invalides regilt at its own cost. Serious-minded men asked themselves what M. de Trinquelague would do in such and such a case. M. Clausel de Montais diverged on certain points from M. Clausel de Coussergues; M. de Salaberry was not satisfied. Picard the comedian, who belonged to the Academy of which Molière was not a member, was playing the two Philiberts at the Odéon, on the façade of which could still be distinctly read: THÉÂTRE DE L'IMPÉRATRICE, although the letters had been torn down. People were taking sides for or against Cugnet de Montarlot. Fabvier was factious; Bavoux was revolutionary; Pelicier the publisher brought out an edition of Voltaire with the title "The Works of Voltaire, of the Académie Française." "That catches purchasers," the simple publisher said. It was the general opinion that M. Charles Loyson would be the genius of the age; envy was beginning to snap at him, which is a sign of glory, and the following line was written about him.

"Même quand Loyson vole, on sent qu'il a des pattes."

As Cardinal Fesch refused to resign, M. de Pins, Archbishop of Amasia, was administering the diocese of Lyons. The quarrel about the Dappes valley began between Switzerland and France, through a memorial of Captain Dufour, who has since become a general. Saint Simon, utterly ignored, was building up his sublime dream. There were in the Academy of Sciences a celebrated Fourier whom posterity has forgotten, and in some obscure garret a Fourier whom the future will remember. Lord Byron was beginning to culminate; a note to a poem of Millevoye's announced him to France in these terms, "un certain Lord Baron." David d'Angers was trying to mould marble. The Abbé Caron spoke in terms of praise to a select audience in the Alley of the Feuillantines of an unknown priest called Félicité Robert, who was at a later date Lamennais. A thing that smoked and plashed on the Seine with the noise of a swimming dog, went under the Tuileries windows from the Pont Royal to the Pont Louis XV.; it was a mechanism not worth much, a sort of plaything, a reverie of a dreamy inventor, an Utopia: a steamboat. The Parisians looked at this useless thing with indifference. M. de Vaublanc, reformer of the Institute by coup d'état, and distinguished author of several academicians, after making them, could not succeed in becoming one himself. The Faubourg St Germain and the Pavilion Marson desired to have M. Delvau as Prefect of police on account of his devotion. Dupuytren and Récamier quarrelled in the theatre of the School of Medicine, and were going to fight about the divinity of the Saviour. Cuvier, with one eye on Genesis and the other on nature, was striving to please the bigoted reaction by placing forms in harmony with texts, and letting Moses be flattered by the Mastodons. M. François de Neufchâteau, the praiseworthy cultivator of the memory of Parmentier, was making a thousand efforts to have "pommes de terre" pronounced "parmentière," but did not succeed. The Abbé Grégoire, ex-bishop, ex-conventionalist, and ex-senator, had reached in the royal polemics the state of the "infamous Grégoire," which was denounced as a neologism by M. Royer-Collard. In the third arch of the Pont de Jéna, the new stone could still be distinguished through its whiteness, with which two years previously the mine formed by Blucher to blow up the bridge was stopped up. Justice summoned to her bar a man who, on seeing the Comte d'Artois enter Notre Dame, said aloud: "Sapristi! I regret the days when I saw Napoleon and Talma enter the Bal Sauvage arm in arm," seditious remarks punished with six months' imprisonment.

Traitors displayed themselves unblushingly; some, who had passed over to the enemy on the eve of a battle, did not conceal their reward, but walked immodestly in the sunshine with the cynicism of wealth and dignities; the deserters at Ligny and Quatre Bras, well rewarded for their turpitude, openly displayed their monarchical devotion.

Such are a few recollections of the year 1817, which is now forgotten. History neglects nearly all these details, and cannot do otherwise, as the infinity would crush it. Still these details, wrongly called little,—there are no little facts in humanity or little leaves in vegetation,—are useful, for the face of ages is composed of the physiognomy of years.

In this year 1817 four young Parisians played a capital joke.

CHAPTER II.

A DOUBLE QUARTETTE.

These Parisians came, one from Toulouse, the second from Limoges, the third from Cahors, the fourth from Montauban, but they were students, and thus Parisians; for studying in Paris is being born in Paris. These young men were insignificant, four every-day specimens, neither good nor bad, wise nor ignorant, geniuses nor idiots, and handsome with that charming Aprilia which is called twenty years. They were four Oscars, for at that period Arthurs did not yet exist. "Burn for him the perfumes of Arabia," the romance said; "Oscar is advancing, I am about to see him." People had just emerged from Ossian: the elegant world was Scandinavian and Caledonian, the English style was not destined to prevail till a later date, and the first of the Arthurs, Wellington, had only just won the battle of Waterloo.

The names of these Oscars were Félix Tholomyès, of Toulouse; Listolier, of Cahors; Fameuil, of Limoges; and Blachevelle, of Montauban. Of course each had a mistress; Blachevelle loved Favourite, so called because she had been to England; Listolier adored Dahlia, who had taken the name of a flower for her *nom de guerre*; Fameuil idolized Zéphine, an abridgment of Josephine; while Tholomyès had Fantine, called the Blonde, owing to her magnificent suncolored hair. Favourite, Dahlia, Zéphine, and Fantine were four exquisitely pretty girls, still to some extent workwomen. They had not entirely laid down the needle, and though unsettled by their amourettes, they still had in their faces a remnant of the serenity of toil, and in their souls that flower of honesty, which in a woman survives the first fall. One of the four was called the young one, because she was the youngest, and one called the old one, who was only three-and-twenty. To conceal nothing, the three first were more experienced, more reckless, and had flown further into the noise of life than Fantine the Blonde, who was still occupied with her first illusion.

Dahlia, Zéphine, and especially Favourite, could not have said the same. There was already more than one episode in their scarce-begun romance, and the lover who was called Adolphe in the first chapter, became Alphonse in the second, and Gustave in the third. Poverty and coquettishness are two fatal counsellors: one scolds, the other flatters, and the poor girls of the lower classes have them whispering in both ears. Badly-guarded souls listen, and hence come the falls they make, and the stones hurled at them. They are crushed with the splendor of all that is immaculate and inaccessible. Alas! what if the Jungfrau had hunger? Favourite, who had been to England, was admired by Zéphine and Dahlia. She had a home of her own from an early age. Her father was an old brutal and boasting professor of mathematics, unmarried, and still giving lessons in spite of his age. This professor, when a young man, had one day seen a lady's maid's gown caught in a fender; he fell in love with this accident, and Favourite was the result. She met her father from time to time, and he bowed to her. One morning, an old woman with a hypocritical look came into her room and said, "Do you not know me, Miss?" "No." "I am your mother." Then the old woman opened the cupboard, ate and drank, sent for a mattress she had, and installed herself. This mother, who was grumbling and proud, never spoke to Favourite, sat for hours without saying a word, breakfasted, dined, and supped for half a dozen, and spent her evenings in the porter's lodge, where she abused her daughter. What drew Dahlia toward Listolier, towards others perhaps, towards idleness, was having too pretty pink nails. How could she employ such nails in working? A girl who wishes to remain virtuous must not have pity on her hands. As for Zéphine, she had conquered Fameuil by her little saucy and coaxing way of saying "Yes, Sir." The young men were comrades, the girls friends. Such amours are always doubled by such friendships.

A sage and a philosopher are two persons; and what proves it is that, after making all reservations for these little irregular households, Favourite, Zéphine, and Dahlia were philosophic girls, and Fantine a prudent girl. Prudent, it will be said, and Tholomyès? Solomon would reply, that love forms part of wisdom. We confine ourselves to saying that Fantine's love was a first love, a single love, a faithful love. She was the only one of the four who was addressed familiarly by one man alone.

Fantine was one of those beings who spring up from the dregs of the people; issuing from the lowest depths of the social darkness, she had on her forehead the stamp of the anonymous and the unknown. She was born at M. sur M.; of what parents, who could say? She had never known either father or mother. She called herself Fantine, and why Fantine? She was never known by any other name. At the period of her birth, the Directory was still in existence. She had no family name, as she had no family; and no Christian name, as the Church was abolished. She accepted the name given her by the first passer-by, who saw her running barefooted about the streets. She was called little Fantine, and no one knew any more. This human creature came into the world in that way. At the age of ten, Fantine left the town, and went into service with farmers in the neighborhood. At the age of fifteen she went to Paris, "to seek her fortune." Fantine was pretty and remained pure as long as she could. She was a charming blonde, with handsome teeth; she had gold and pearls for her dower, but the gold was on her head, and the pearls in her mouth.

She worked for a livelihood; and then she loved, still for the sake of living, for the heart is hungry too. She loved Tholomyès; it was a pastime for him, but a passion with her. The streets of the Quartier Latin, which are thronged with students and grisettes, saw the beginning of this dream. Fantine, in the labyrinth of the Pantheon Hill, where so many adventures are fastened and unfastened, long shunned Tholomyès, but in such a way as to meet him constantly. There is a manner of avoiding which resembles seeking,—in a word, the eclogue was played.

Blachevelle, Listolier, and Fameuil formed a sort of group, of which Tholomyès was the head, for it was he who had the wit. Tholomyès was the antique old student; he was rich, for he had an income of 4000 francs a year, a splendid scandal on the Montagne St. Geneviève. Tholomyès was a man of the world, thirty years of age, and in a bad state of preservation. He was wrinkled and had lost teeth, and he had an incipient baldness, of which he himself said without sorrow: "The skull at thirty, the knee at forty." He had but a poor digestion, and one of his eyes was permanently watery. But in proportion as his youth was extinguished, his gayety became brighter; he substituted jests for his teeth, joy for his hair, irony for his health, and his weeping eye laughed incessantly. He was battered, but still flowering. His youth had beaten an orderly retreat, and only the fire was visible. He had had a piece refused at the Vaudeville Theatre, and wrote occasional verses now and then. In addition, he doubted everything in a superior way, which is a great strength in the eyes of the weak. Hence, being ironical and bald, he was the leader. We wonder whether irony, is derived from the English word "iron"? One day Tholomyès took the other three aside, made an oracular gesture, and said,—

"It is nearly a year that Fantine, Dahlia, Zéphine, and Favorite have been asking us to give them a surprise, and we promised solemnly to do so. They are always talking about it, especially to me. In the same way as the old women of Naples cry to Saint Januarius, "Yellow face, perform your miracle!" our beauties incessantly say to me, "Tholomyès, when will you be delivered of your surprise?" At the same time our parents are writing to us, so let us kill two birds with one stone. The moment appears to me to have arrived, so let us talk it over."

Upon this, Tholomyès lowered his voice, and mysteriously uttered something so amusing that a mighty and enthusiastic laugh burst from four mouths simultaneously, and Blacheville exclaimed "That is an idea!" An *estaminet* full of smoke presenting itself, they went in, and the remainder of their conference was lost in the tobacco clouds. The result of the gloom was a brilliant pleasure excursion, that took place on the following Sunday, to which the four young men invited the girls.

CHAPTER III

FOUR TO FOUR.

It is difficult to form an idea at the present day of what a pleasure party of students and grisettes was four-and-forty years ago. Paris has no longer the same environs; the face of what may be termed circum-Parisian life has completely changed during half a century; where there was the old-fashioned coach, there is a railway-carriage; where there was the fly-boat, there is now the steamer; people talk of Fécamp as people did in those days of St. Cloud. Paris of 1862 is a city which has France for its suburbs.

The four couples conscientiously accomplished all the rustic follies possible at that day. It was a bright warm summer day; they rose at five o'clock; then they went to St. Cloud in the stage-coach, looked at the dry cascade, and exclaimed, "That must be grand when there is water;" breakfasted at the Tête Noire, where Castaing had not yet put up, ran at the ring in the Quincunx of the great basin, ascended into the Diogenes lantern, gambled for macaroons at the roulette board by the Sêvres bridge, culled posies at Puteaux, bought reed-pipes at Neuilly, ate apple tarts everywhere, and were perfectly happy. The girls prattled and chattered like escaped linnets; they were quite wild, and every now and then gave the young men little taps. Oh, youthful intoxication of life! adorable years! the wing of the dragon-fly rustles. Oh, whoever you may be, do you remember? have you ever walked in the woods, removing the branches for the sake of the pretty head that comes behind you? have you laughingly stepped on a damp slope, with a beloved woman who holds your hand, and cries, "Oh, my boots, what a state they are in!" Let us say at once, that the merry annoyance of a shower was spared the happy party, although Favourite had said on starting, with a magisterial and maternal air, "The slugs are walking about the paths; that is a sign of rain, children."

All four were pretty madcaps. A good old classic poet, then renowned, M. le Chevalier de Labouisse, a worthy man who had an Eléanore, wandering that day under the chestnut-trees of St. Cloud, saw them pass at about ten in the morning, and exclaimed, "There is one too many," thinking of the Graces. Favourite, the girl who was three-and-twenty and the old one, ran in front under the large green branches, leaped over ditches, strode madly across bushes, and presided over the gayety with the spirit of a young fawn. Zéphine and Dahlia, whom accident had created as a couple necessary to enhance each other's beauty by contrast, did not separate, though more through a coquettish instinct than through friendship, and leaning on one another, assumed English attitudes; the first "Keepsakes" had just come out, melancholy was culminating for women, as Byronism did at a later date for men, and the hair of the tender sex was beginning to become dishevelled. Zéphine and Dahlia had their hair in rolls. Listolier and Fameuil, who were engaged in a discussion about their professors, were explaining to Fantine the difference there was between M. Delvincourt and M. Blondeau. Blachevelle seemed to have been created expressly to carry Favourite's faded shabby shawl on Sundays.

Tholomyès came last; he was very gay, but there was something commanding in his joviality; his principal ornament was nankeen trousers, cut in the shape of elephant's legs, with leathern straps; he had a mighty rattan worth 200 francs in his hand, and, as he was quite reckless, a strange thing called a cigar in his mouth; nothing being sacred to him, he smoked. "That Tholomyès is astounding," the others were wont to say with veneration. "What trousers! what energy!"

As for Fantine she was the personification of joy. Her splendid teeth had evidently been made for laughter by nature. She carried in her hand, more willingly than on her head, her little straw bonnet, with its long streamers. Her thick, light hair, inclined to float, and which had to be done up continually, seemed made for the flight of Galatea under the willows. Her rosy lips prattled enchantingly; the corners of her mouth voluptuously raised, as in the antique masks of Erigone, seemed to encourage boldness; but her long eyelashes, full of shade, were discreetly lowered upon the seductiveness of the lower part of the face, as if to command respect. Her whole toilet had something of song and sunshine about it; she had on a dress of mauve barége, little buskin slippers, whose strings formed an X on her fine, open-worked stockings, and that sort of muslin spencer, a Marseillais invention, whose name of canezou, a corrupted pronunciation of *quinze Août* at the Cannebière, signifies fine weather and heat. The three others, who were less timid, as we said, bravely wore low-necked dresses, which in summer are very graceful and attractive, under bonnets covered with flowers; but by the side of this bold dress, Fantine's canezou, with its transparency, indiscretion, and reticences, at once concealing and displaying, seemed a provocative invention of decency; and the famous Court of Love, presided over by the Vicomtesse de Cette with the sea-green eyes, would have probably bestowed the prize for coquettishness on this canezou, which competed for that of chastity. The simplest things are frequently the cleverest.

Dazzling from a front view, delicate from a side view, with dark blue eyes, heavy eye-lids, arched and small feet, wrists and ankles admirably set on, the white skin displaying here and there the azure arborescences of the veins, with a childish fresh cheek, the robust neck of the Æginetan Juno shoulders, apparently modelled by Couston, and having in their centre a voluptuous dimple, visible through the muslin; a gayety tempered by reverie; a sculptural and exquisite being,—such was Fantine; you could trace beneath the ribbons and finery a statue, and inside the statue a soul. Fantine was beautiful, without being exactly conscious of it. Those rare dreamers, the mysterious priests of the beautiful, who silently confront everything with perfection, would have seen in this little work-girl the ancient sacred euphony, through the transparency of Parisian grace! This girl had blood in her, and had those two descriptions of beauty which are the style and the rhythm. The style is the form of the ideal; the rhythm is its movement.

We have said that Fantine was joy itself; she was also modesty. Any one who watched her closely would have seen through all this intoxication of youth, the season, and love, an invincible expression of restraint and modesty. She remained slightly astonished, and this chaste astonishment distinguishes Psyche from Venus. Fantine had the long white delicate fingers of the Vestal, who stirs up the sacred fire with a golden bodkin. Though she had refused nothing, as we shall soon see, to Tholomyès, her face, when in repose, was supremely virginal; a species of stern and almost austere dignity suddenly invaded it at certain hours, and nothing was so singular and affecting as to see gayety so rapidly extinguished on it, and contemplation succeed cheerfulness without any transition. This sudden gravity, which was at times sternly marked, resembled the disdain of a goddess. Her forehead, nose, and chin offered that equilibrium of outline which is very distinct from the equilibrium of proportion, and produces the harmony of the face; in the characteristic space between the base of the nose and the upper lip, she had that imperceptible and charming curve, that mysterious sign of chastity, which made Barbarossa fall in love with a Diana found in the ruins of Iconium. Love is a fault; be it so; but Fantine was innocence floating on the surface of the fault.

CHAPTER IV

THOLOMYÈS SINGS A SPANISH SONG.

The whole of this day seemed to be composed of dawn; all nature seemed to be having a holiday, and laughing. The pastures of St. Cloud exhaled perfumes; the breeze from the Seine vaguely stirred the leaves; the branches gesticulated in the wind; the bees were plundering the jessamine; a madcap swarm of butterflies settled down on the ragwort, the clover, and the wild oats; there was in the august park of the King of France a pack of vagabonds, the birds. The four happy couples enjoyed the sun, the fields, the flowers, and the trees. And in this community of Paradise, the girls, singing, talking, dancing, chasing butterflies, picking bind-weed, wetting their stockings in the tall grass, fresh, madcap, not bad, all received kisses from all the men, every now and then, save Fantine, enveloped in her vague resistance, dreamy and shy, and who was in love. "You always look strange," Favourite said to her.

Such passings-by of happy couples are a profound appeal to life and nature, and bring caresses and light out of everything. Once upon a time there was a fairy, who made fields and trees expressly for lovers; hence the eternal hedge-school of lovers, which incessantly recommences, and will last so long as there are bushes and scholars. Hence the popularity of spring among thinkers;

the patrician and the knifegrinder, the duke and the limb of the law, people of the court and people of the city, as they were called formerly, are all subjects of this fairy. People laugh and seek each other; there is the brilliancy of an apotheosis in the air, for what a transfiguration is loving! Notary's clerks are gods. And then the little shrieks, pursuits in the grass, waists caught hold of, that chattering which is so melodious, that adoration which breaks out in the way of uttering a word, cherries torn from lips,—all this is glorious! People believe that it will never end; philosophers, poets, artists, regard these ecstasies, and know not what to do, as they are so dazzled by them. The departure for Cythera! exclaims Watteau; Lancret, the painter of the middle classes, regards his cits flying away in the blue sky; Diderot stretches out his arms to all these amourettes, and d'Urfé mixes up Druids with them.

After breakfast the four couples went to see, in what was then called the King's Square, a plant newly arrived from the Indies, whose name we have forgotten, but which at that time attracted all Paris to St. Cloud; it was a strange and pretty shrub, whose numerous branches, fine as threads and leafless, were covered with a million of small white flowers giving it the appearance of a head of hair swarming with flowers; there was always a crowd round it, admiring it. After inspecting the shrub, Tholomyès exclaimed, "I will pay for donkeys;" and after making a bargain with the donkey-man, they returned by Vauvres and Issy. At the latter place an incident occurred; the park, a national estate held at this time by Bourguin the contractor, was accidentally open. They passed through the gates, visited the wax hermit in his grotto, and tried the mysterious effect of the famous cabinet of mirrors, a lascivious trap, worthy of a satyr who had become a millionnaire. They bravely pulled the large swing, fastened to the two chestnut-trees celebrated by the Abbé de Bernis. While swinging the ladies in turn, which produced, amid general laughter, a flying of skirts by which Greuze would have profited, the Toulousian Tholomyès, who was somewhat of a Spaniard, as Toulouse is the cousin of Tolosa, sang to a melancholy tune the old gallega, which was probably inspired by the sight of a pretty girl swinging between two trees,—

> "Soy tie Badajoz
> Amor me llama
> Toda mi alma
> Es en mis ojos
> Porque enseflas
> A tus piernas."

Fantine alone declined to swing.

"I do not like people to be so affected," Favourite muttered rather sharply.

On giving up the donkeys there was fresh pleasure; the Seine was crossed in a boat, and from Passy they walked to the Barrière de l'Étoile. They had been afoot since five in the morning; but no matter! "There is no such thing as weariness on Sunday," said Favourite; "on Sundays fatigue does not work." At about three o'clock, the four couples, wild with delight, turned into the Montagnes Busses, a singular building, which at that time occupied the heights of Beaujon, and whose winding line could be seen over the trees of the Champs Élysées. From time to time Favourite exclaimed,—

"Where's the surprise? I insist on the surprise."

"Have patience," Tholomyès answered.

CHAPTER V

AT BOMBARDA'S.

The Russian mountain exhausted, they thought about dinner, and the radiant eight, at length somewhat weary, put into the Cabaret Bombarda, an offshoot established in the Champs Élysées by that famous restaurateur Bombarda, whose sign could be seen at that time at the Rue de Rivoli by the side of the Delorme passage.

A large but ugly room, with an alcove and a bed at the end (owing to the crowded state of the houses on Sundays they were compelled to put up with it); two windows from which the quay and river could be contemplated through the elm-trees; a magnificent autumn sun illumining the windows; two tables, on one of them a triumphal mountain of bottles, mixed up with hats and bonnets, at the other four couples joyously seated round a mass of dishes, plates, bottles, and glasses, pitchers of beer, mingled with wine-bottles; but little order on the table, and some amount of disorder under it.

> "Ils faisaient sous la table
> Un bruit, un trique-trac de pieds épouvantable,"

as Molière says. Such was the state of the pastoral which began at 5 A.M.; at half-past 4 P.M. the sun was declining and appetite was satisfied.

The Champs Élysées, full of sunshine and crowd, were nought but light and dust, two things of which glory is composed. The horses of Marly, those neighing marbles, reared amid a golden cloud. Carriages continually passed along; a squadron of splendid guards, with the trumpeter at their head, rode down the Neuilly avenue; the white flag, tinged with pink by the setting sun, floated above the dome of the Tuileries. The Place de la Concorde, which had again become the Place Louis XV., was crowded with merry promenaders. Many wore a silver *fleur de lys* hanging from a black moiré ribbon, which, in 1817, had not entirely disappeared from the buttonholes. Here and there, in the midst of applauding crowds, little girls were singing a royalist *bourrée,* very celebrated at that time, intended to crush the hundred days, and which had a chorus of,—

> "Rendez nous notre père de Gand,
> Rendez vous notre père."

Heaps of suburbans, dressed in their Sunday clothes, and some wearing *fleur de lys* like the cits, were scattered over the squares, playing at quintain or riding in roundabouts; others were drinking; some who were printers' apprentices wore paper caps, and their laughter was the loudest. All was radiant; it was a time of undeniable peace, and of profound royalist security; it was a period when a private and special report of Anglès, prefect of police to the King, terminated with these lines: "All things duly considered, Sire, there is nothing to fear from these people. They are as careless and indolent as cats, and though the lower classes in the provinces are stirring, those in Paris are not so. They are all little men, Sire, and it would take two of them to make one of your grenadiers. There is nothing to fear from the populace of the capital. It is remarkable that their height has decreased during the last fifty years, and the people of the suburbs of Paris are shorter than they were before the Revolution. They are not dangerous, and, in a word, are good-tempered *canaille.*"

Prefects of police do not believe it possible that a cat can be changed into a lion; it is so, however, and that is the miracle of the people of Paris. The cat, so despised by Count Anglès, possessed the esteem of the old Republics; it was the incarnation of liberty in their eyes, and as if to serve as a pendant to the Minerva Apteros of the Piræus, there was on the public square of Corinth a colossal bronze statue of a cat. The simple police of the restoration had too favorable an opinion of the people of Paris, and they were not such good-tempered *canaille* as they were supposed to be. The Parisian is to the French-man what the Athenian is to the Greek; no one sleeps sounder than he; no one is more frankly frivolous and idle than he; no one can pretend to forget so well as he,—but he must not be trusted; he is suited for every species of nonchalance, but when there is a glory as the result, he is admirable for every sort of fury. Give him a pike and he will make August 10; give him a musket, and you will have Austerlitz. He is the support of Napoleon, and the resource of Danton. If the country is in danger, he enlists; if liberty is imperilled, he tears up the pavement. His hair, full of wrath, is epical, his blouse assumes the folds of a chlamys. Take care; for of the first Rue Grenétat he comes to be will make Caudine forks. If the hour strikes, this suburban grows, the little man looks in a terrible manner, his breath becomes a tempest, and from his weak chest issues a blast strong enough to uproot the Alps. It was through the Parisian suburban that the Revolution, joined with armies, conquered Europe. He sings, and that forms his delight; proportion his song to his nature, and you shall see! So long as he has no burden but the Carmagnole, he will merely overthrow Louis XVI.; but make him sing the Marseillaise, and he will deliver the world.

After writing this note on the margin of Count Anglès' report, we will return to our four couples. The dinner, as we said, was drawing to a close.

CHAPTER VI

IN WHICH PEOPLE ADORE EACH OTHER.

Love talk and table talk are equally indescribable, for the first is a cloud, the second smoke. Fantine and Dahlia were humming a tune, Tholomyès was drinking, Zéphine laughing, Fantine smiling, Listolier was blowing a penny trumpet bought at St. Cloud, Favourite was looking tenderly at Blachevelle and saying,—

"Blachevelle, I adore you."

This led to Blachevelle asking,—

"What would you do, Favourite, if I ceased to love you?"

"I?" Favourite exclaimed, "oh, do not say that, even in fun! If you ceased to love me I would run after you, claw you, throw water over you, and have you arrested."

Blachevelle smiled with the voluptuous fatuity of a man whose self-esteem is tickled. Dahlia, while still eating, whispered to Favourite through the noise,—

"You seem to be very fond of your Blachevelle?"

"I detest him," Favourite answered in the same key, as she seized her fork again. "He is miserly, and I prefer the little fellow who lives opposite to me. He is a very good-looking young man; do you know him? It is easy to see that he wants to be an actor, and I am fond of actors. So soon as he comes in, his mother says,—'Oh, good heavens! my tranquillity is destroyed: he is going to begin to shout; my dear boy, you give me a headache;' because he goes about the house, into the garrets as high as he can get, and sings and declaims, so that he can be heard from the streets! He already earns 20 sous a day in a lawyer's office. He is the son of an ex-chorister at St. Jacques du Haut Pas. Ah! he adores me to such a pitch that one day when he saw me making batter for pancakes, he said to me, 'Mamselle, make fritters of your gloves, and I will eat them.' Only artists are able to say things like that. Ah! he is very good-looking, and I feel as if I am about to fall madly in love with the little fellow. No matter, I tell Blachevelle that I adore him: what a falsehood, eh, what a falsehood!"

After a pause, Favourite continued,—

"Dahlia, look you, I am sad. It has done nothing but rain all the summer: the wind annoys me, Blachevelle is excessively mean, there are hardly any green peas in the market, one does not know what to eat; I have the spleen, as the English say, for butter is so dear; and then it is horrifying that we are dining in a room with a bed in it, and that disgusts me with life."

CHAPTER VII

THE WISDOM OF THOLOMYÈS.

At length, when all were singing noisily, or talking all together, Tholomyès interfered.

"Let us not talk hap-hazard or too quickly," he exclaimed; "we must meditate if we desire to be striking; too much improvisation stupidly empties the mind. Gentlemen, no haste; let us mingle majesty with our gayety, eat contemplatively, and let *festina lente* be our rule. We must not hurry. Look at the Spring; if it goes ahead too fast it is floored, that is to say, nipped by frost. Excessive zeal ruins the peach and apricot trees; excessive zeal kills the grace and joy of good dinners. No zeal, gentlemen; Grimaud de la Reynière is of the same opinion as Talleyrand."

A dull rebellion broke out in the party.

"Tholomyès, leave us at peace," said Blachevelle.

"Down with the tyrant!" said Fameuil.

"Sunday exists," Listolier added.

"We are sober," Fameuil remarked again.

"Tholomyès," said Blachevelle, "contemplate my calmness" (*mon calme.*)

"You are the Marquis of that ilk," Tholomyès replied. This poor pun produced the effect of a stone thrown into a pond. The Marquis de Montcalm was a celebrated Royalist at that day. All the frogs were silent.

"My friends," Tholomyès shouted with the accent of a man who is recapturing his empire, "recover yourselves: too great stupor should not greet this pun which has fallen from the clouds, for everything that falls in such a manner is not necessarily worthy of enthusiasm and respect. Far be from me to insult puns: I honor them according to their deserts, and no more. All the most august, sublime, and charming in humanity and perhaps beyond humanity have played upon words. Christ made a pun on Saint Peter, Moses on Isaac, Æschylus on Polynices, and Cleopatra on Octavius. And note the fact that Cleopatra's pun preceded the battle of Actium, and that, were it not for that pun, no one would know the town of Toryne, a Greek word signifying a potladle. This granted, I return to my exhortation. Brethren, I repeat, no zeal, no row, no excess, even in witticisms, gayeties, merriments, and playing upon words. Listen to me, for I possess the prudence of Amphiaralis and the baldness of Cæsar; there should be a limit even to the rebus. *Est modus in rebus.* There should be a limit even to dinners; you are fond of apple-puffs, ladies, but no abuse; even in the matter of apple-puffs, good sense and art are needed. Gluttony chastises the glutton. *Gula punit gulax.* Indigestion was sent into the world to read a lecture to our stomachs; and, bear this in mind, each of our passions, even love, has a stomach which must not be filled too full. In all things, we must write betimes the word *finis*, we must restrain ourselves when it becomes urgent, put a bolt on our appetites, lock up our fancy, and place ourselves under arrest. The wise man is he who knows how, at a given moment, to arrest himself. Place some confidence in me: it does not follow because I know a little law, as my examinations prove; because I have supported a thesis in Latin as to the mode in which torture was applied at Rome at the time when Munatius Demens was *quæstor parricidæ*; and because I am going to be a Doctor at Law, as it seems,—it does not necessarily follow, I say, that I am an ass. I recommend to you moderation in your desires. As truly as my name is Félix Tholomyès, I am speaking the truth. Happy the man who, when the hour has struck, forms an heroic resolve, and abdicates like Sylla or Origen."

Favourite was listening with profound attention. "Félix!" she said, "what a pretty name; I like it. It is Latin, and means happy."

Tholomyès continued,—

"Gentlemen, be suspicious of women; woe to the man who surrenders himself to a woman's fickle heart; woman is perfidious and tortuous, and detests the serpent from professional jealousy. It is the shop opposite."

"Tholomyès," Blachevelle shouted, "you are drunk."

"I hope so!"

"Then be jolly."

"I am agreeable," Tholomyès answered. And filling his glass, he rose.

"Glory to wine! *nunc te, Bacche, canam*! Pardon, ladies, that is Spanish, and the proof, Señoras, is this: as the country is, so is the measure. The arroba of Castille contains sixteen quarts, the cantaro of Alicante twelve, the almuda of the Canary Isles twenty-five, the cuartino of the Balearic Isles twenty-six, and Czar Peter's boot thirty. Long live the Czar who was great, and his boot which was greater still! Ladies, take a friend's advice; deceive your neighbor, if you think proper. The peculiarity of love is to wander, and it is not made to crouch like an English servant girl who has stiff knees from scrubbing. It is said that error is human; but I say, error is amorous. Ladies, I idolize you all. O Zéphine, you with your seductive face, you would be charming were you not all askew; your face looks for all the world as if it had been sat upon by mistake. As for Favourite, O ye Nymphs and Muses! one day when Blachevelle was crossing the gutter in the Rue Guérin-Boisseau, he saw a pretty girl with white, well-drawn-up stockings, who displayed her legs. The prologue was pleasing, and Blachevelle fell in love; the girl he loved was Favourite. O Favourite, you have Ionian lips; there was a Greek painter of the name of Euphorion, who was christened the painter of lips, and this Greek alone would be worthy to paint your mouth. Listen to me: before you there was not a creature deserving of the name; you are made to receive the apple like Venus, or to eat it like Eve. Beauty begins with you, and you deserve a patent for inventing a pretty woman. You alluded to my name just now; it affected me deeply, but we must be distrustful of names, for they may be deceptive. My name is Félix, and yet I am not happy. Let us not blindly accept the indications they give us; it would be a mistake to write to Liège for corks, or to Pau for gloves.[1] Miss Dahlia, in your place I would call myself Rose, for a flower ought to smell agreeably, and a woman have spirit. I say nothing of Fantine, for she is a dreamer, pensive and sensitive; she is a phantom, having the form of a nymph, and the modesty of a nun, who has strayed into the life of a grisette, but takes shelter in illusions, and who sings, prays, and looks at the blue sky, without exactly knowing what she sees or what she does, and who, with her eyes fixed on heaven, wanders about a garden in which there are more birds than ever existed. O Fantine, be aware of this fact: I, Tholomyès, am an illusion—why, the fair girl of chimeræ is not even listening to me! All about her is freshness, suavity, youth, and sweet morning brightness. O Fantine, girl worthy to be called Margaret or Pearl, you are a woman of the fairest East. Ladies, here is a second piece of advice; do not marry, for marriage is a risk, and you had better shun it. But nonsense! I am wasting my words! girls are incurable about wedlock; and all that we sages may say will not prevent waistcoat-makers and shoebinders from dreaming of husbands loaded with diamonds. Well, beauties, be it so: but bear this in mind, you eat too much sugar. You have only one fault, O women, and that is nibbling sugar. O rodent sex, your pretty little white teeth adore sugar. Now, listen to this: sugar is a salt, and salts are of a drying nature, and sugar is the most drying of all salts. It pumps out the fluidity of the blood through the veins; this produces first coagulation and then solidifying of the blood; from this come tubercles in the lungs, and thence death. Hence do not nibble sugar, and you will live. I now turn to my male hearers: Gentlemen, make conquests. Rob one another of your well-beloved ones remorselessly; change partners, for, in love there are no friends. Whenever there is a pretty woman, hostilities are opened; there is no quarter, but war to the knife! a pretty woman is a *casus belli* and a flagrant offence. All the invasions of history were produced by petticoats; for woman is the lawful prey of man. Romulus carried off the Sabine women, William the Saxon women, and Cæsar the Roman women. A man who is not loved soars like a vulture over the mistresses of other men: and for my part, I offer all these unfortunate widowers, Bonaparte's sublime proclamation to the army of Italy: 'Soldiers, you want for everything; the enemy possesses it.'"

Here Tholomyès broke off.

"Take a breather, my boy," said Blachevelle.

At the same time the other three gentlemen struck up to a doleful air one of those studio-songs, as destitute of sense as the motion of a tree or the sound of the wind, which are composed extemporaneously, either in rhyme or prose, which spring up from the smoke of pipes, and fly away with it. The song was not adapted to calm Tholomyès' inspiration; hence he emptied his glass, filled it again, and began once more.

"Down with wisdom! forget all I have said to you. Be neither prudish, nor prudent, nor *prud'hommes.* I drink the health of jollity: so let us be jolly. Let us complete our legal studies by folly and good food, for indigestion should run in a curricle with digests. Let Justinian be the male and merriment the female! Live, O creation; the world is one large diamond; I am happy, and the birds are astounding. What a festival all around us; the nightingale is a gratis Elleviou. Summer, I salute thee. O Luxembourg! O ye Georgics of the Rue Madame and the Allée de l'Observatoire! O ye dreaming soldiers! O ye delicious nurses, who, while taking care of children, fancy what your own will be like! the Pampas of America would please me if I had not the arcades of the Odéon. My soul is flying away to the Virgin forests and the savannas. All is glorious: the flies are buzzing in the light; the sun has sneezed forth the humming-bird. Kiss me, Fantine!"

He made a mistake and kissed Favourite.

<hr>

CHAPTER VIII.

THE DEATH OF A HORSE.

"It is a better dinner at Édon's than at Bombarda's," Zéphine exclaimed.

"I prefer Bombarda," Blachevelle declared; "there is more luxury: it is more Asiatic. Just look at the dining-room with its mirrors: look at the knives, they are silver-handled here and bone at Édon's; now, silver is more precious than bone."

"Excepting for those persons who have a silver chin," Tholomyès observed.

He was looking at this moment at the dome of the Invalides which was visible from Bombardas window. There was a pause.

"Tholomyès," cried Fameuil, "just now, Listolier and I had a discussion."

"A discussion is good," replied Tholomyès; "a quarrel is better."

"We discussed philosophy; which do you prefer, Descartes or Spinoza?"

"Désangiers," said Tholomyès.

This judgment rendered, he continued,—

"I consent to live: all is not finished in the world. Since men can still be unreasonable, I return thanks to the immortal gods. Men lie, but they laugh: they affirm, but they doubt: and something unexpected issues from the syllogism. This is grand: there are still in the world human beings who can joyously open and shut the puzzle-box of paradox. This wine, ladies, which you are drinking so calmly, is Madeira, you must know, grown at Coural das Freiras, which is three hundred and seventeen *toises* above the sea level. Attention while drinking! three hundred and seventeen *toises*, and M. Bombarda, the magnificent restaurateur, lets you have these three hundred and seventeen *toises* for four francs, fifty centimes."

Tholomyès drained his glass and then continued:

"Honor to Bombarda! he would be equal to Memphis of Elephanta if he could ladle me up an Almeh, and to Thygelion of Cheronea if he could procure me an Hetæra! for, ladies, there were Bombardas in Greece and Egypt, as Apuleius teaches us. Alas! ever the same thing and nothing new: nothing is left unpublished in the creation of the Creator. 'Nothing new under the sun,' says Solomon: *amor omnibus idem*, and Carabine gets into the St. Cloud fly-boat with Carabin, just as Aspasia embarked with Pericles aboard the Samos fleet. One last word: Do you know who Aspasia was, ladies? Although she lived at a time when women had no soul, she was a soul: a soul of a pink and purple hue, hotter than fire, and fresher than the dawn. Aspasia was a creature in whom the two extremes of woman met. She was a prostituted goddess: Socrates *plus* Manon Lescaut."

Tholomyès, when started, would hardly have been checked, had not a horse fallen in the street at this very moment. Through the shock, cart and orator stopped short. It was a Beauce mare, old and lean and worthy of the knacker, dragging a very heavy cart. On getting in front of Bombarda's, the beast, exhausted and worn out, refused to go any further, and this incident produced a crowd. The carter, swearing and indignant, had scarce time to utter with the suitable energy the sacramental word, "Rascal!" backed up by a pitiless lash, ere the poor beast fell, never to rise again. Tholomyès' gay hearers turned their heads away on noticing the confusion, while he wound up his speech by the following sad strophe,—

> "Elle était de ce monde où coucous et carrosses,
> Ont le même destin,
> Et, rosse, elle a vécu ce que vivent les rosses,
> L'espace   d'un: Mâtin!"

"Poor horse!" Fantine said with a sigh; and Dahlia shouted,—

"Why, here is Fantine beginning to feel pity for horses: how can she be such a fool!"

At this moment, Favourite crossed her arms and threw her head back; she then looked boldly at Tholomyès, and said,—

"Well, how about the surprise?"

"That is true, the hour has arrived," Tholomyès answered. "Gentlemen, it is time to surprise the ladies. Pray wait for us a moment."

"It begins with a kiss," said Blacheve.

"On the forehead," Tholomyès added.

Each solemnly kissed the forehead of his mistress: then they proceeded to the door in Indian file, with a finger on their lip. Favourite clapped her hands as they went out.

"It is amusing already," she said.

"Do not be long," Fantine murmured, "we are waiting for you."

CHAPTER IX.

THE JOYOUS END OF JOY.

The girls, when left alone, leaned out of the windows, two by two, talking, looking out, and wondering. They watched the young men leave the Bombarda cabaret arm in arm; they turned round, made laughing signs, and disappeared in that dusty Sunday mob which once a week invaded the Champs Élysées.

"Do not be long," Fantine cried.

"What will they bring us?" said Zéphine.

"I am certain it will be pretty," said Dahlia.

"For my part," Favourite added, "I hope it will be set in gold."

They were soon distracted by the movement on the quay, which they could notice through the branches of the lofty trees, and which greatly amused them. It was the hour for the mail-carts and stages to start, and nearly all those bound for the South and West at that time passed through the Champs Élysées. Most of them followed the quay and went out by the Passy barrier. Every moment some heavy vehicle, painted yellow and black, heavily loaded and rendered shapeless by trunks and valises, dashed through the crowd with the sparks of a forge, the dust representing the smoke. This confusion amused the girls.

"What a racket!" exclaimed Favourite; "one might say a pile of chairs was flying about."

One of these vehicles, which could hardly be distinguished through the branches, stopped for a moment, and then started again at a gallop. This surprised Fantine.

"That is strange," she said; "I fancied that the diligence never stopped."

Favourite shrugged her shoulders.

"This Fantine is really amazing, and is surprised at the simplest things. Let us suppose that I am a traveller and say to the guard of the stage-coach, "I will walk on and you can pick me up on the quay as you pass." The coach passes, sees me, stops and takes me in. That is done every day; you are ignorant of life, my dear."

Some time elapsed; all at once Favourite started as if waking from sleep.

"Well," she said, "where is the surprise?"

"Oh yes," Dahlia continued, "the famous surprise."

"They are a long time," said Fantine.

Just as Fantine had ended this sigh, the waiter who had served the dinner came in; he held in his hand something that resembled a letter.

"What is that?" Favourite asked.

The waiter answered,—

"It is a paper which the gentlemen left for you, ladies."

"Why did you not bring it to us at once?"

"Because the gentlemen," the waiter went on, "ordered that it should not be delivered to you for an hour."

Favourite snatched the paper from the waiter's hands; it was really a letter.

"Stay," she said; "there is no address, but the following words are written on it: THIS IS THE SURPRISE." She quickly opened the letter and read (she could read):—

"WELL-BELOVED,—Know that we have relatives: perhaps you are not perfectly cognizant what they are; it means fathers and mothers in the civil, puerile, and honest code. Well, these relatives are groaning; these old people claim us as their own; these worthy men and women call us prodigal sons. They desire our return home, and offer to kill the fatted calf. We obey them, as we are virtuous; at the hour when you read this, five impetuous steeds will be conveying us back to our papas and mammas. 'We decamp,' as Bossuet said; "we are going, gone." We are flying away in the arms of Laffitte and on the wings of Gaillard. The Toulouse coach is dragging us away from the abyss, and that abyss is yourselves, pretty dears. We are re-entering society, duty, and order, at a sharp trot, and at the rate of nine miles an hour. It is important for our country that we should become, like everybody else, Prefects, fathers of a family, game-keepers, and councillors of state. Revere us, for we are sacrificing ourselves. Dry up your tears for us rapidly, and get a substitute speedily. If this letter lacerates your hearts, treat it in the same fashion. Good-by. For nearly two years we rendered you happy, so do not owe us any grudge.

(Signed)

BLACHEVELLE.
FAMEUIL.

121

"P.S. The dinner is paid for."

The four girls looked at each other, and Favourite was the first to break the silence.

"I don't care," she said, "it is a capital joke."

"It is very funny," Zéphine remarked.

"It must have been Blachevelle who had that idea," Favourite continued; "it makes me in love with him. So soon as he has left me I am beginning to grow fond of him; the old story."

"No," said Dahlia, "that is an idea of Tholomyès. That can be easily seen."

"In that case," Favourite retorted, "down with Blachevelle and long live Tholomyès!"

And they burst into a laugh, in which Fantine joined.

An hour later though, when she returned to her bed-room, she wept: this was, as we have said, her first love; she had yielded to Tholomyès as to a husband, and the poor girl had a child.

BOOK IV.

TO CONFIDE IS SOMETIMES TO ABANDON.

CHAPTER I.

TWO MOTHERS MEET.

There was in the first quarter of this century a sort of pot-house at Montfermeil, near Paris, which no longer exists. It was kept by a couple of the name of Thénardier, and was situated in the Rue du Boulanger. Over the door a board was nailed to the wall, and on this board was painted something resembling a man carrying on his back another man, who wore large gilt general's epaulettes with silver stars; red dabs represented blood, and the rest of the painting was smoke, probably representing a battle. At the bottom

122

could be read the inscription: THE SERGEANT OF WATERLOO.

Though nothing is more common than a cart at a pot-house door, the vehicle, or rather fragment of a vehicle, which blocked up the street in front of the Sergeant of Waterloo, one spring evening in 1818, would have certainly attracted the attention of any painter who had passed that way. It was the forepart of one of those wains used in wood countries for dragging planks and trunks of trees; it was composed of a massive iron axle-tree, in which a heavy pole was imbedded and supported by two enormous wheels. The whole thing was sturdy, crushing, and ugly, and it might have passed for the carriage of a monster gun. The ruts had given the wheels, felloes, spokes, axle-tree, and pole a coating of mud, a hideous yellow plaster, much like that with which cathedrals are so often adorned. The wood-work was hidden by mud and the iron by rust. Under the axle-tree was festooned a heavy chain suited for a convict Goliath. This chain made you think, not of the wood it was intended to secure, but of the mastodons and mammoths for which it would have served as harness; it had the air of a cyclopean and superhuman bagne, and seemed removed from some monster. Homer would have bound Polyphemus with it, and Shakespeare, Caliban.

Why was this thing at this place in the street? First, to block it up; secondly, to finish the rusting process. There is in the old social order a multitude of institutions which may be found in the same way in the open air, and which have no other reasons for being there. The centre of the chain hung rather close to the ground, and on the curve, as on the rope of a swing, two little girls were seated on this evening, in an exquisite embrace, one about two years and a half, the other eighteen months; the younger being in the arms of the elder. An artfully-tied handkerchief prevented them from falling, for a mother had seen this frightful chain, and said, "What a famous plaything for my children!" The two children, who were prettily dressed and with some taste, were radiant; they looked like two roses among old iron; their eyes were a triumph, their healthy cheeks laughed; one had auburn hair, the other was a brunette; their innocent faces had a look of surprise; a flowering shrub a little distance off sent to passers-by a perfume which seemed to come from them; and the younger displayed her nudity with the chaste indecency of childhood. Above and around their two delicate heads, moulded in happiness and bathed in light, the gigantic wheels, black with rust, almost terrible, and bristling with curves and savage angles, formed the porch of a cavern, as it were. A few yards off, and seated in the inn door, the mother, a woman of no very pleasing appearance, but touching at this moment, was swinging the children by the help of a long cord, and devouring them with her eyes, for fear of an accident, with that animal and heavenly expression peculiar to maternity. At each oscillation the hideous links produced a sharp sound, resembling a cry of anger. The little girls were delighted; the setting sun mingled with the joy, and nothing could be so charming as this caprice of accident which had made of a Titanic chain a cherub's swing. While playing with her little ones, the mother sang, terribly out of tune, a romance, very celebrated at that day,—

"Il le faut, disait un guerrier."

Her song and contemplation of her daughters prevented her hearing and seeing what took place in the street. Some one, however, had approached her, as she began the first couplets of the romance, and suddenly she heard a voice saying close to her ear,—

"You have two pretty children, Madame."

"—à la belle et tendre Imogène,"

the mother answered, continuing her song, and then turned her head. A woman was standing a few paces from her, who also had a child, which she was carrying in her arms. She also carried a heavy bag. This woman's child was one of the most divine creatures possible to behold; she was a girl between two and three years of age, and could have vied with the two other little ones in the coquettishness of her dress. She had on a hood of fine linen, ribbons at her shoulders, and Valenciennes lace in her cap. Her raised petticoats displayed her white, dimpled, fine thigh; it was admirably pink and healthy, and her cheeks made one long to bite them. Nothing could be said of her eyes, except that they were very large, and that she had magnificent lashes, for she was asleep. She was sleeping with the absolute confidence peculiar to her age; a mother's arms are made of tenderness, and children sleep soundly in them. As for the mother, she looked grave and sorrowful, and was dressed like a work-girl who was trying to become a country-woman again. She was young; was she pretty? Perhaps so; but in this dress she did not appear so. Her hair, a light lock of which peeped out, seemed very thick, but was completely hidden beneath a nun's hood; ugly, tight, and fastened under her chin. Laughter displays fine teeth, when a person happens to possess them; but she did not laugh. Her eyes looked as if they had not been dry for a long time; she had a fatigued and rather sickly air, and she looked at the child sleeping in her arms in the manner peculiar to a mother who has suckled her babe. A large blue handkerchief, like those served out to the invalids, folded like a shawl, clumsily hid her shape. Her hands were rough and covered with red spots, and her forefinger was hardened and torn by the needle. She had on a brown cloth cloak, a cotton gown, and heavy shoes. It was Fantine.

It was difficult to recognize her, but, after an attentive examination, she still possessed her beauty. As for her toilette,—that aerial toilette of muslin and ribbons which seemed made of gayety, folly, and music, to be full of bells, and perfumed with lilacs,—it had faded away like the dazzling hoar-frost which looks like diamonds in the sun; it melts, and leaves the branch quite black.

Ten months had elapsed Bince the "good joke." What had taken place during these ten months? We can guess. After desertion, want. Fantine at once lost sight of Favourite, Zéphine, and Dahlia, for this tie broken on the side of the men separated the women. They would have been greatly surprised a fortnight after had they been told that they were friends, for there was no reason for it. Fantine remained alone when the father of her child had gone away—alas! such ruptures are irrevocable. She found herself absolutely isolated; she had lost her habit of working, and had gained a taste for pleasure. Led away by her *liaison* with Tholomyès to despise the little trade she knew, she had neglected her connection, and it was lost. She had no resource. Fantine could hardly read, and could not write; she had been merely taught in childhood to sign her name, and she had sent a letter to Tholomyès, then a second, then a third, through a public writer, but Tholomyès did not answer one of them. One day Fantine heard the gossips say, while looking at her daughter, "Children like that are not regarded seriously, people shrug their shoulders at them." Then she thought of Tholomyès who shrugged his shoulders at her child, and did not regard the innocent creature seriously, and her heart turned away from this man. What was she to do now? She knew not where to turn. She had committed a fault, but the foundation of her nature, we must remember, was modesty and virtue. She felt vaguely that she was on the eve of falling into distress, and gliding into worse. She needed courage, and she had it. The idea occurred to her of returning to her native town M. sur M. There some one might know her, and give her work; but she must hide her fault. And she vaguely glimpsed at the possible necessity of a separation more painful still than the first; her heart was contracted, but she formed her resolution. Fantine, as we shall see, possessed the stern bravery of life. She had already valiantly given up dress; she dressed in calico, and had put all her silk ribbons and laces upon her daughter, the only vanity left her, and it was a holy one. She sold all she possessed, which brought her in 200 francs; and when she had paid her little debts, she had only about 80 francs left. At the age of two-and-twenty, on a fine Spring morning, she left Paris, carrying her child on her back. Any one who had seen them pass would have felt pity for them; the woman had nothing in the world but her child, and the child nothing but her mother in her world. Fantine had suckled her child; this had strained her chest, and she was coughing a little.

We shall have no further occasion to speak of M. Félix Tholomyès. We will merely say that twenty years later, in the reign of Louis Philippe, he was a stout country lawyer, influential and rich, a sensible elector, and a very strict juror, but always a man of pleasure.

About mid-day, after resting herself now and then by travelling from time to time, at the rate of three or four leagues an hour, in what were then called the "little vehicles of the suburbs of Paris," Fantine found herself at Montfermeil, in the Ruelle Boulanger. As she passed the Sergeant of Waterloo, the two little girls in their monster swing had dazzled her, and she stopped before this vision of joy. There are charms in life, and these two little girls were one for this mother. She looked at them with great emotion, for the presence of angels is an announcement of Paradise. She thought she saw over this inn the mysterious HERE of Providence. These two little creatures were evidently happy! She looked then, and admired them with such tenderness that at the moment when the mother was drawing breath between two verses of her song, she could not refrain from saying to her what we have already recorded.

"You have two pretty children, Madame."

The most ferocious creatures are disarmed by a caress given to their little ones. The mother raised her head, thanked her, and bade her sit down on the door bench. The two women began talking.

"My name is Madame Thénardier," the mother of the little ones said; "we keep this inn."

Then returning to her romance, she went on humming,—

> "Il le faut, je suis chevalier,
> Et je pars pour la Palestine."

This Madame Thénardier was a red-headed, thin, angular woman, the soldier's wife in all its ugliness, and, strange to say, with a languishing air which she owed to reading romances. She was a sort of lackadaisical male-woman. Old romances, working on the imaginations of landladies, produce that effect. She was still young, scarce thirty. If this woman, now sitting, had been standing up, perhaps her height and colossal proportions, fitting for a show, would have at once startled the traveller, destroyed her confidence, and prevented what we have to record. A person sitting instead of standing up— destinies hang on this.

The woman told her story with some modification. She was a work-girl, her husband was dead; she could get no work in Paris, and was going to seek it elsewhere, in her native town. She had left Paris that very morning on foot; as she felt tired from carrying her child, she had travelled by the stage-coach to Villemomble, from that place she walked to Montfermeil. The little one had walked a little, but not much, for she was so young, and so she had been obliged to cany her, and the darling had gone to sleep,—and as she said this she gave her daughter a passionate kiss, which awoke her. The babe opened her eyes, large blue eyes like her mother's, and gazed at what? Nothing, everything, with that serious and at times stern air of infants, which is a mystery of their luminous innocence in the presence of our twilight virtues. We might say that they feel themselves to be angels, and know us to be men. Then the child began laughing, and, though its mother had to check it, slipped down to the ground with the undauntable energy of a little creature wishing to run. All at once, she noticed the other two children in their swing, stopped short, and put out her tongue as a sign of admiration. Mother Thénardier unfastened her children, took them out of the swing, and said,—

"Play about, all three."

Children soon get familiar, and in a minute the little Thénardiers were playing with the new-comer at making holes in the ground, which was an immense pleasure. The stranger child was very merry; the goodness of the mother is written in the gayety of the baby. She had picked up a piece of wood which she used as a spade, and was energetically digging a grave large enough for a fly. The two went on talking.

"What 's the name of your bantling?"

"Cosette."

For Cosette read Euphrasie, for that was the child's real name; but the mother had converted Euphrasie into Cosette, through that gentle, graceful instinct peculiar to mothers and the people, which changes Josefa into Pépita, and Françoise into Sellette. It is a species of derivation which deranges and disconcerts the entire science of etymologists. We know a grandmother who contrived to make out of Theodore, Gnon.

"What is her age?"

"Going on to three."

"Just the same age as my eldest."

In the mean time the children were grouped in a posture of profound anxiety and blessedness; an event had occurred. A large worm crept out of the ground, and they were frightened, and were in ecstasy; their radiant brows touched each other; and they looked like three heads in a halo.

"How soon children get to know one another," Mother Thénardier exclaimed; "why, they might be taken for three sisters."

The word was probably the spark which the other mother had been waiting for; she seized the speaker's hand, looked at her fixedly, and said,—

"Will you take charge of my child for me?"

The woman gave one of those starts of surprise which are neither assent nor refusal. Fantine continued,—

"Look you, I cannot take the child with me to my town, for when a woman has a baby, it is a hard matter for her to get a situation. People are so foolish in our part. It was Heaven that made me pass in front of your inn; when I saw your little ones so pretty, so clean, so happy, it gave me a turn. I said to myself, "She is a kind mother." It is so; they will be three sisters. Then I shall not be long before I come back. Will you take care of my child?"

"We will see, said Mother Thénardier.

"I would pay six francs a month."

Here a man's voice cried from the back of the tap-room,—

"Can't be done under seven, and six months paid in advance."

"Six times seven are forty-two," said the landlady.

"I will pay it," said the mother.

"And seventeen francs in addition for extra expenses," the man's voice added.

"Total fifty-seven francs," said Madame Thénardier; and through these figures she sang vaguely,—

"Il le faut, disait un guerrier."

"I will pay it," the mother said; "I have eighty francs, and shall have enough left to get home on foot. I shall earn money there, and so soon as I have a little I will come and fetch my darling."

The man's voice continued,—

"Has the little one a stock of clothing?"

"It is my husband," said Mother Thénardier.

"Of course she has clothes, poor little treasure. I saw it was your husband; and a fine stock of clothes too, a wonderful stock, a dozen of everything, and silk frocks like a lady. The things are in my bag."

"They must be handed over," the man's voice remarked.

"Of course they must," said the mother; "it would be funny if I left my child naked."

The master's face appeared.

"All right," he said.

The bargain was concluded, the mother spent the night at the inn, paid her money and left her child, fastened up her bag, which was now light, and started the next morning with the intention of returning soon. Such departures are arranged calmly, but they entail despair. A neighbor's wife saw the mother going away, and went home saying,—

"I have just seen a woman crying in the street as if her heart was broken."

When Cosette's mother had gone, the man said to his wife,—

"That money will meet my bill for one hundred and ten francs, which falls due to-morrow, and I was fifty francs short. It would have been protested, and I should have had a bailiff put in. You set a famous mouse-trap with your young ones."

"Without suspecting it," said the woman.

CHAPTER II.

A SKETCH OF TWO UGLY FACES.

The captured mouse was very small, but the cat is pleased even with a thin mouse. Who were the Thénardiers? We will say one word about them for the present, and complete the sketch hereafter. These beings belonged to the bastard class, composed of coarse parvenus, and of degraded people of intellect, which stands between the classes called the middle and the lower, and combines some of the faults of the second with nearly all the vices of the first, though without possessing the generous impulse of the workingman or the honest regularity of the tradesman.

Theirs were those dwarf natures which easily become monstrous when any gloomy fire accidentally warms them. There was in the woman the basis of a witch, in the man the stuff for a beggar. Both were in the highest degree susceptible of that sort of hideous progress which is made in the direction of evil. There are crab-like souls which constantly recoil toward darkness, retrograde in life rather than advance, employ experience to augment their deformity, incessantly grow worse, and grow more and more covered with an increasing blackness. This man and this woman had souls of this sort.

Thénardier was peculiarly troublesome to the physiognomist: there are some men whom you need only look at to distrust them, for they are restless behind and threatening in front. There is something of the unknown in them. We can no more answer for what they have done than for what they will do. The shadow they have in their glance denounces them. Merely by hearing them say a word or seeing them make a gesture, we get a glimpse of dark secrets in their past, dark mysteries in their future. This Thénardier, could he be believed, had been a soldier—sergeant, he said; he had probably gone through the campaign of 1815, and had even behaved rather bravely, as it seems. We shall see presently how the matter really stood. The sign of his inn was an allusion to one of his exploits, and he had painted it himself, for he could do a little of everything—badly. It was the epoch when the old classical romance —which after being *Clélie*, had now become *Lodoiska*, and though still noble, was daily growing more vulgar, and had fallen from Mademoiselle de Scudéri to Madame Bournon Malarme, and from Madame de Lafayette to Madame Barthélémy Hadot—was inflaming the loving soul of the porters' wives in Paris, and even extended its ravages into the suburbs. Madame Thénardier was just intelligent enough to read books of this nature, and lived on them. She thus drowned any brains she possessed, and, so long as she remained young and a little beyond, it gave her a sort of pensive attitude by the side of her husband, who was a scamp of some depth, an almost grammatical ruffian, coarse and delicate at the same time, but who, in matters of sentimentalism, read Pigault Lebrun, and, in "all that concerned the sex," as he said in his jargon, was a correct and unadulterated booby. His wife was some twelve or fifteen years younger than he, and when her romantically flowing locks began to grow gray, when the Megæra was disengaged from the Pamela, she was only a stout wicked woman, who had been pampered with foolish romances. As such absurdities cannot be read with impunity, the result was that her eldest daughter was christened Éponine; as for the younger, the poor girl was all but named Gulnare, and owed it to a fortunate diversion made by a romance of Ducray Duminil's, that she was only christened Azelma.

By the way, all is not ridiculous and superficial in the curious epoch to which we are alluding, and which might be called the anarchy of baptismal names. By the side of the romantic element, which we have just pointed out, there was the social symptom. It is not rare at the present day for a drover's son to be called Arthur, Alfred, or Alphonse, and for the Viscount—if there are any Viscounts left—to be called Thomas, Pierre, or Jacques. This displacement which gives the "elegant" name to the plebeian, and the rustic name to the aristocrat, is nothing else than an eddy of equality. The irresistible penetration of the new breeze is visible in this as in everything else. Beneath this apparent discord there is a grand and deep thing, the French Revolution.

CHAPTER III.

THE LARK.

It is not enough to be bad in order to prosper: and the pot-house was a failure. Thanks to the fifty-seven francs, Thénardier had been able to avoid a protest, and honor his signature; but the next month they wanted money again, and his wife took Cosette's outfit to Paris and pledged it for sixty francs. So soon as this sum was spent, the Thénardiers grew accustomed to see in the little girl a child they had taken in through charity, and treated her accordingly. As she had no clothes, she was dressed in the left-off chemises and petticoats of the little Thénardiers, that is to say, in rags. She was fed on the leavings of everybody, a little better than the dog, and a little worse than the cat. Dog and cat were her usual company at dinner: for Cosette ate with them under the table off a wooden trencher like theirs.

The mother, who had settled, as we shall see hereafter, at M. sur M., wrote, or, to speak more correctly, had letters written every month to inquire after her child. The Thénardiers invariably replied that Cosette was getting on famously. When the first six months had passed, the mother sent seven francs for the seventh month, and continued to send the money punctually month by month. The year had not ended before Thénardier said, "A fine thing that! what does she expect us to do with seven francs!" and he wrote to demand twelve. The mother, whom they persuaded that her child was happy and healthy, submitted, and sent the twelve francs.

Some natures cannot love on one side without hating on the other. Mother Thénardier passionately loved her own two daughters, which made her detest the stranger. It is sad to think that a mother's love can look so ugly. Though Cosette occupied so little room, it seemed to her as if her children were robbed of it, and that the little one diminished the air her daughters breathed. This woman, like many women of her class, had a certain amount of caresses and another of blows and insults to expend daily. If she had not had Cosette, it is certain that her daughters, though they were idolized, would have received the entire amount; but the strange child did the service of diverting the blows on herself, while the daughters received only the caresses. Cosette did not make a movement that did not bring down on her head a hailstorm of violent and unmerited chastisement. The poor weak child, unnecessarily punished, scolded, cuffed, and beaten, saw by her side two little creatures like herself who lived in radiant happiness.

As Madame Thénardier was unkind to Cosette, Éponine and Azelma were the same; for children, at that age, are copies of their mother; the form is smaller, that is all. A year passed, then another, and people said in the village,—

"Those Thénardiers are worthy people. They are not well off, and yet they bring up a poor child left on their hands."

Cosette was supposed to be deserted by her mother; Thénardier, however, having learned in some obscure way that the child was probably illegitimate, and that the mother could not confess it, insisted on fifteen francs a month, saying that the creature was growing and eating, and threatening to send her back. "She must not play the fool with me," he shouted, "or I'll let her brat fall like a bomb-shell into her hiding-place. I must have an increase." The mother paid the fifteen francs. Year by year the child grew, and so did her wretchedness: so long as Cosette was little, she was the scape-goat of the two other children; so soon as she began to be developed a little, that is to say, even before she was five years old, she became the servant of the house. At five years, the reader will say, that is improbable; but, alas! it is true. Social suffering begins at any age. Have we not recently seen the trial of a certain Dumollard, an orphan, who turned bandit, and who from the age of five, as the official documents tell us, was alone in the world and "worked for a living and stole"? Cosette was made to go on messages, sweep the rooms, the yard, the street, wash the dishes, and even carry heavy bundles. The Thénardiers considered themselves the more justified in acting thus, because the mother, who was still at M. sur M., was beginning to pay badly, and was several months in arrear.

If the mother had returned to Montfermeil at the end of three years, she would not have recognized her child. Cosette, so pretty and ruddy on her arrival in this house, was now thin and sickly. She had a timid look about her; "It's cunning!" said the Thénardiers. Injustice had made her sulky and wretchedness had made her ugly. Nothing was left her but her fine eyes, which were painful to look at, because, as they were so large, it seemed as if a greater amount of sadness was visible in them. It was a heart-rending sight to see this poor child, scarce six years of age, shivering in winter under her calico rags, and sweeping the street before day-break, with an enormous broom in her small red hands and a tear in her large eyes.

The country people called her "the lark;" the lower classes, who are fond of metaphors, had given the name to the poor little creature, who was no larger than a bird, trembling, frightened, and starting, who was always the first awake in the house and the village, and ever in the street or the fields by day-break.

There was this difference, however,—this poor lark never sung.

BOOK V

THE DESCENT.

CHAPTER I

PROGRESS IN BLACK-BEAD MAKING.

What had become of the mother, who, according to the people of Montfermeil, appeared to have deserted her child? Where was she; what was she doing? After leaving her little Cosette with the Thénardiers, she had continued her journey and arrived at M. sur M. Fantine had been away from her province for ten years, and while she had been slowly descending from misery to misery, her native town had prospered. About two years before, one of those industrial facts which are the events of small towns had taken place. The details are important, and we think it useful to develop them; we might almost say, to understand them.

From time immemorial M. sur M. had as a special trade the imitation of English jet and German black beads. This trade had hitherto only vegetated, owing to the dearness of the material, which reacted on the artisan. At the moment when Fantine returned to M. sur M. an extraordinary transformation had taken place in the production of "black articles." Toward the close of 1815, a man, a stranger, had settled in the town, and had the idea of substituting in this trade gum lac for rosin, and in bracelets particularly, scraps of bent plate for welded plate. This slight change was a revolution: it prodigiously reduced the cost of the material, which, in the first place, allowed the wages to be raised, a benefit for the town; secondly, improved the manufacture, an advantage for the consumer; and, thirdly, allowed the goods to be sold cheap, while tripling them the profit, an advantage for the manufacturer.

In less than three years the inventor of the process had become rich, which is a good thing, and had made all rich about him, which is better. He was a stranger in the department; no one knew anything about his origin, and but little about his start. It was said that he had entered the town with but very little money, a few hundred francs at the most; but with this small capital, placed at the service of an ingenious idea, and fertilized by regularity and thought, he made his own fortune and that of the town. On his arrival at M. sur M. he had the dress, manners, and language of a workingman. It appears that on the very December night when he obscurely entered M. sur M. with his knapsack on his back, and a knotted stick in his hand, a great fire broke out in the Town Hall. This man rushed into the midst of the flames, and at the risk of his life saved two children who happened to belong to the captain of gendarmes; hence no one dreamed of asking for his passport. On this occasion his name was learned; he called himself Father Madeleine.

CHAPTER II

MADELEINE.

He was a man of about fifty, with a preoccupied air, and he was good-hearted. That was all that could be said of him.

Thanks to the rapid progress of this trade which he had so admirably remodelled, M. sur M. had become a place of considerable trade. Spain, which consumes an immense amount of jet, gave large orders for it annually, and in this trade M. sur M. almost rivalled London and Berlin. Father Madeleine's profits were so great, that after the second year he was able to build a large factory, in which were two spacious workshops, one for men, the other for women. Any one who was hungry need only to come, and was sure to find there employment and bread. Father Madeleine expected from the men good-will, from the women purity, and from all probity. He had divided the workshops in order to separate the sexes, and enable the women and girls to remain virtuous. On this point he was inflexible, and it was the only one in which he was at all intolerant. This sternness was the more justifiable because M. sur M. was a garrison town, and opportunities for corruption abounded. Altogether his arrival had been a benefit, and his presence was a providence. Before Father Madeleine came everything was languishing, and now all led the healthy life of work. A powerful circulation warmed and penetrated everything; stagnation and wretchedness were unknown. There was not a pocket, however obscure, in which there was not a little money, nor a lodging so poor in which there was not a little joy.

Father Madeleine employed every one. He only insisted on one thing,—be an honest man, a good girl!

As we have said, in the midst of this activity, of which he was the cause and the pivot, Father Madeleine made his fortune, but, singularly enough in a plain man of business, this did not appear to be his chief care; he seemed to think a great deal of others and but little of himself. In 1820, he was known to have a sum of 630,000 francs in Lafitte's bank; but before he put that amount on one side he had spent more than a million for the town and the poor. The hospital was badly endowed, and he added ten beds. M. sur M. is divided into an upper and a lower town; the latter, in which he lived, had only one school, a poor tenement falling in ruins, and he built two, one for boys and one for girls. He paid the two teachers double the amount of their poor official salary, and to some one who expressed surprise, he said, "The first two functionaries of the State are the nurse and the schoolmaster." He had established at his own charges an infant-school, a thing at that time almost unknown in France, and a charitable fund for old and infirm workmen. As his factory was a centre, a new district, in which there was a large number of indigent families, rapidly sprang up around it, and he opened there a free dispensary.

At the beginning, kind souls said, "He is a man who wants to grow rich:" when it was seen that he enriched the town before enriching himself, the same charitable souls said, "He is ambitious." This seemed the more likely because he was religious, and even practised to a certain extent a course which was admired in those days. He went regularly to hear Low Mass on Sundays, and the local deputy, who scented rivalry everywhere, soon became alarmed about this religion. This deputy, who had been a member of the legislative council of the Empire, shared the religious ideas of a Father of the Oratory, known by the name of Fouché, Duc d'Otranto, whose creature and friend he had been. But when he saw the rich manufacturer Madeleine go to seven o'clock Low Mass, he scented a possible candidate, and resolved to go beyond him; he chose a Jesuit confessor, and went to High Mass and vespers. Ambition at that time was, in the true sense of the term, a steeple-chase. The poor profited by the alarm, for the honorable deputy founded two beds at the hospital, which made twelve.

In 1819, the report spread one morning through the town that, on the recommendation of the Prefect, and in consideration of services rendered the town, Father Madeleine was about to be nominated by the king, Mayor of M——. Those who had declared the new-comer an ambitious man, eagerly seized this opportunity to exclaim: "Did we not say so?" All M—— was in an uproar; for the rumor was well founded. A few days after, the appointment appeared in the *Moniteur*, and the next day Father Madeleine declined the honor. In the same year, the new processes worked by him were shown at the Industrial Exhibition; and on the report of the jury, the King made the inventor a Chevalier of the Legion of Honor. There was a fresh commotion in the little town; "Well, it was the cross he wanted," but Father Madeleine declined the cross. Decidedly the man was an enigma, but charitable souls got out of the difficulty by saying, "After all, he is a sort of adventurer."

As we have seen, the country owed him much, and the poor owed him everything; he was so useful that he could not help being honored, and so gentle that people could not help loving him; his work-people especially adored him, and he bore this adoration with a sort of melancholy gravity. When he was known to be rich, "people in society" bowed to him, and he was called in the town Monsieur Madeleine; but his workmen and the children continued to call him Father Madeleine, and this caused him his happiest smile. In proportion as he ascended, invitations showered upon him; and society claimed him as its own. The little formal drawing-rooms, which had of course been at first closed to the artisan, opened their doors wide to the millionnaire. A thousand advances were made to him, but he refused them. This time again charitable souls were not thrown out: "He is an ignorant man of poor education. No one knows where he comes from. He could not pass muster in society, and it is doubtful whether he can read." When he was seen to be earning money, they said, "He is a tradesman;" when he scattered his money, they said, "He is ambitious;" when he rejected honor, they said, "He is an adventurer;" and when he repulsed society, they said, "He is a brute."

In 1820, five years after his arrival at M., the services he had rendered the town were so brilliant, the will of the whole country was so unanimous, that the King again nominated him Mayor of the Town. He refused again, but the Prefect would not accept his refusal; all the notables came to beg, the people supplicated him in the open streets, and the pressure was so great, that he eventually assented. It was noticed that what appeared specially to determine him was the almost angry remark of an old woman, who cried to him from her door: "A good Mayor is useful; a man should not recoil before the good he may be able to do." This was the third phase of his ascent; Father Madeleine had become Monsieur Madeleine, and Monsieur Madeleine became Monsieur le Maire.

<hr>

CHAPTER III.

SUMS LODGED AT LAFITTE'S.

Father Madeleine remained as simple as he had been on the first day: he had gray hair, a serious eye, the bronzed face of a workingman, and the thoughtful face of a philosopher. He habitually wore a broad-brimmed hat, and a long coat of coarse cloth buttoned up to the chin. He performed his duties as Mayor, but beyond that lived solitary; he spoke to few persons, shunned compliments, smiled to save himself from talking, and gave to save himself from smiling. The women said of him, "What a good bear!" and his great pleasure was to walk about the fields. He always took his meals with an open book before him, and he had a well-selected library. He was fond of books, for they are calm and sure friends. In proportion as leisure came with fortune, he seemed to employ it in cultivating his mind: it was noticed that with each year he spent in M—— his language became more polite, chosen, and gentle.

He was fond of taking a gun with him on his walks, but rarely fired; when he did so by accident, he had an infallible aim, which was almost terrific. He never killed an inoffensive animal or a small bird. Though he was no longer young, he was said to possess prodigious strength: he lent a hand to any one who needed it, raised a fallen horse, put his shoulder to a wheel stuck in the mud, or stopped a runaway bull by the horns. His pockets were always full of half-pence when he went out, and empty when he came home; whenever he passed through a village, the ragged children ran merrily after him, and surrounded him like a swarm of gnats. It was supposed that he must have formerly lived a rustic life, for he had all sorts of useful secrets which he taught the peasants. He showed them how to destroy blight in wheat by sprinkling the granary and pouring into the cracks of the boards a solution of common salt, and to get rid of weevils by hanging up everywhere, on the walls and roots, flowering orviot. He had recipes to extirpate from arable land tares and other parasitic plants which injure wheat, and would defend a rabbit hutch from rats by the mere smell of a little Guinea pig, which he placed in it.

One day he saw some countrymen very busy in tearing up nettles; he looked at the pile of uprooted and already withered plants and said: "They are dead, and yet they are good if you know how to use them. When nettles are young, the tops are an excellent vegetable. When they are old, they have threads and fibre like hemp and flax. When chopped up, nettles are good for fowls; when pounded, excellent for horned cattle. Nettle-seed mixed with the food renders the coats of cattle shining, and the root mixed with salt produces a fine yellow color. The nettle is also excellent hay, which can be mown twice; and what does it require? A little earth, no care, and no cultivation. The only thing is that the seed falls as it ripens, and is difficult to garner. If a little care were taken, the nettle would be useful; but, being neglected, it becomes injurious, and is then killed. How men resemble nettles!" He added after a moment's silence: "My friends, remember this,—there are no bad herbs or bad men; there are only bad cultivators."

The children also loved him, because he could make them pretty little toys of straw and cocoa-nut shells. When he saw a church door hung with black, he went in; he went after a funeral as other persons do after a christening. The misfortunes of others attracted him, owing to his great gentleness; he mingled with friends in mourning, and with the priests round a coffin. He seemed to be fond of hearing those mournful psalms which are full of the vision of another world. With his eye fixed on heaven, he listened, with a species of aspiration toward all the mysteries of Infinitude, to the sad voice singing on the brink of the obscure abyss of death. He did a number of good actions, while as careful to hide them as if they were bad. He would quietly at night enter houses, and furtively ascend the stairs. A poor fellow, on returning to his garret, would find that his door had been opened, at times forced, during his absence; the man would cry that a robber had been there, but when he entered, the first thing he saw was a gold coin left on the table. The robber who had been there was Father Madeleine.

He was affable and sad: people said, "There is a rich man who does not look proud: a lucky man who does not look happy." Some persons asserted that he was a mysterious character, and declared that no one ever entered his bed-room, which was a real anchorite's cell, furnished with winged hour-glasses and embellished with cross-bones and death's-heads. This was so often repeated that some elegant and spiteful ladies of M—— came to him one day, and said, "Monsieur le Maire, *do* show us your bed-room, for people say that it is a grotto." He smiled and led them straightway to the "grotto;" they were terribly punished for their curiosity, as it was a bed-room merely containing mahogany furniture as ugly as all furniture of that sort, and hung with a paper at twelve sous a roll. They could not notice anything but two double-branched candlesticks of an antiquated pattern, standing on the mantel-piece, and seeming to be silver, "because they were Hall-marked,"—a remark full of the wit of small towns. People did not the less continue to repeat, however, that no one ever entered this bed-room, and that it was a hermitage, a hole, a tomb. They also whispered that he had immense sums lodged with Lafitte, and with this peculiarity that things were always at his immediate disposal, "so that," they added, "M. Madeleine could go any morning to Lafitte's, sign a receipt, and carry off his two or three millions of francs in ten minutes." In reality, these "two or three millions" were reduced, as we have said, to six hundred and thirty or forty thousand francs.

CHAPTER IV

M. MADELEINE GOES INTO MOURNING.

At the beginning of 1821, the papers announced the decease of M. Myriel, Bishop of D——, "surnamed Monseigneur Welcome," who had died in the odor of sanctity at the age of eighty-two. The Bishop of D——, to add here a detail omitted by the papers, had been blind for several years, and was satisfied to be blind as his sister was by his side.

Let us say parenthetically that to be blind and to be loved is one of the most strangely exquisite forms of happiness upon this earth, where nothing is perfect. To have continually at your side a wife, a sister, a daughter, a charming being, who is there because you have need of her, and because she cannot do without you; to know yourself indispensable to a woman who is necessary to you; to be able constantly to gauge her affection by the amount of her presence which she gives you, and to say to yourself: "She devotes all her time to me because I possess her entire heart;" to see her thoughts in default of her face; to prove the fidelity of a being in the eclipse of the world; to catch the rustling of a dress like the sound of wings; to hear her come and go, leave the room, return, talk, sing, and then to dream that you are the centre of those steps, those words, those songs; to manifest at every moment your own attraction, and feel yourself powerful in proportion to your weakness; to become in darkness and through darkness the planet round which this angel gravitates,—but few felicities equal this. The supreme happiness of life is the conviction of being loved for yourself, or, more correctly speaking, loved in spite of yourself; and this conviction the blind man has. In this distress to be served is to be caressed. Does he want for anything? No. When you possess love, you have not lost the light. And what a love! a love entirely made of virtues. There is no blindness where there is certainty: the groping soul seeks a soul and finds it, and this found and tried soul is a woman. A hand supports you, it is hers; a mouth touches your forehead, it is hers; you hear a breathing close to you, it is she.

To have everything she has, from her worship to her pity, to be never left, to have this gentle weakness to succor you, to lean on this unbending reed, to touch providence with her hands, and be able to take her in your arms: oh! what heavenly rapture is this! The heart, that obscure celestial flower, begins to expand mysteriously, and you would not exchange this shadow for all the light! The angel soul is thus necessarily there; if she go away, it is to return; she disappears like a dream, and reappears like reality. You feel heat approaching you, it is she. You overflow with serenity, ecstasy, and gayety; you are a sunbeam in the night. And then the thousand little attentions, the nothings which are so enormous in this vacuum! The most ineffable accents of the human voice employed to lull you, and taking the place of the vanished universe. You are caressed with the soul: you see nothing, but you feel yourself adored; it is a paradise of darkness.

It was from this paradise that Monseigneur Welcome had passed to the other.

The announcement of his death was copied by the local paper of M——, and on the next day Monsieur Madeleine appeared dressed in black, with crape on his hat. The mourning was noticed in the town, and people gossiped about it, for it seemed to throw a gleam, over M. Madeleine's origin. It was concluded that he was somehow connected with the Bishop. "He is in mourning for the Bishop," was said in drawing-rooms; this added inches to M. Madeleine's stature, and suddenly gave him a certain consideration in the noble world of M——. The microscopic Faubourg St. Germain of the town thought about putting an end to the Coventry of M. Madeleine, the probable relation of a bishop, and M. Madeleine remarked the promotion he had obtained in the increased love of the old ladies, and the greater amount of smiles from the young. One evening a lady belonging to this little great world, curious by right of seniority, ventured to say, "M. le Maire is doubtless a cousin of the late Bishop of D——?"

He answered, "No, Madame."

"But," the dowager went on, "you wear mourning for him."

"In my youth I was a footman in his family," was the answer.

Another thing noticed was, that when a young Savoyard passed through the town, looking for chimneys to sweep, the Mayor sent for him, asked his name, and gave him money. The Savoyard boys told each other of this, and a great many passed through M——.

CHAPTER V.

VAGUE FLASHES ON THE HORIZON.

By degrees and with time all the opposition died out; at first there had been calumnies against M. Madeleine,—a species of law which all rising men undergo; then it was only backbiting; then it was only malice; and eventually all this faded away. The respect felt for him was complete, unanimous, and cordial, and the moment arrived in 1821 when the name of the Mayor was uttered at M—— with nearly the same accent as "Monseigneur the Bishop" had been said at D—— in 1815. People came for ten leagues round to consult M. Madeleine; he settled disputes, prevented lawsuits, and reconciled enemies. Everybody was willing to accept him as arbiter, and it seemed as if he had the book of natural law for his soul. It was a sort of contagious veneration, which in six or seven years spread all over the country-side.

Only one man in the town and bailiwick resisted this contagion, and whatever M. Madeleine might do, remained rebellious to it, as if a sort of incorruptible and imperturbable instinct kept him on his guard. It would appear, in fact, as if there is in certain men a veritable bestial instinct, though pure and honest as all instincts are, which creates sympathies and antipathies; which fatally separates one nature from another; which never hesitates; which is not troubled, is never silent, and never contradicts itself; which is clear in its obscurity, infallible, imperious; refractory to all the counsels of intelligence and all the solvents of the reason, and which, whatever the way in which destinies are made, surely warns the man-dog of the man-cat, and the man-fox of the presence of the man-lion. It often happened when M. Madeleine passed along a street, calmly, kindly, and greeted by the blessings of all, that a tall man, dressed in an iron-gray great-coat, armed with a thick cane, and wearing a hat with turned-down brim, turned suddenly and looked after him till he disappeared; folding his arms, shaking his head, and raising his upper lip with the lower as high as his nose, a sort of significant grimace, which may be translated,—"Who is that man? I am certain that I have seen him somewhere. At any rate, I am not his dupe."

This person, who was grave, with an almost menacing gravity, was one of those men who, though only noticed for a moment, preoccupy the observer. His name was Javert, and he belonged to the police, and performed at M—— the laborious but useful duties of an inspector. He had not seen Madeleine's beginning, for he was indebted for the post he occupied to the Secretary of Count Angle, at that time Prefect of Police at Paris. When Javert arrived at M ——, the great manufacturer's fortune was made, and Father Madeleine had become Monsieur Madeleine. Some police officers have a peculiar face, which is complicated by an air of baseness, blended with an air of authority. Javert had this face, less the baseness. In our conviction, if souls were visible, we should distinctly see the strange fact that every individual of the human species corresponds to some one of the species of animal creation; and we might occurred to the thinker, that, from the oyster to the eagle, from the hog to the tiger, all animals are in man, and that each of them is in a man; at times several of them at once. Animals are nothing else than the figures of our virtues and our vices, wandering before our eyes, the visible phantoms of our souls. God shows these to us in order to make us reflect; but, as animals are only shadows, God has not made them capable of education in the complete sense of the term, for of what use would it be? On the other hand, our souls being realities and having an end of their own, God has endowed them with intelligence; that is to say, possible education. Social education, properly carried out, can always draw out of a soul, no matter its nature, the utility which it contains.

Now, if the reader will admit with me for a moment that in every man there is one of the animal species of creation, it will be easy for us to say what Javert the policeman was. The Asturian peasants are convinced that in every litter of wolves there is a dog which is killed by the mother, for, otherwise, when it grew it would devour the other whelps. Give a human face to this dog-son of a she-wolf, and we shall have Javert. He was born in prison; his mother was a fortune-teller, whose husband was at the galleys. When he grew up he thought that he was beyond the pale of society, and despaired of ever entering it. He noticed that society inexorably keeps at bay two classes of men,—those who attack it, and those who guard it; he had only a choice between these two classes, and at the same time felt within him a rigidness, regularity, and probity, combined with an inexpressible hatred of the race of Bohemians to which he belonged. He entered the police, got on, and at the age of forty was an inspector. In his youth he was engaged in the Southern Bagnes.

Before going further, let us explain the words "human face" which we applied just now to Javert. His human face consisted of a stub-nose, with two enormous nostrils, toward which enormous whiskers mounted on his cheeks. You felt uncomfortable the first time that you saw these two forests and these two caverns. When Javert laughed, which was rare and terrible, his thin lips parted, and displayed, not only his teeth, but his gums, and a savage flat curl formed round his nose, such as is seen on the muzzle of a wild beast. Javert when serious was a bull-dog; when he laughed he was a tiger. To sum up, he had but little skull and plenty of jaw; his hair hid his forehead and fell over his brows; he had between his eyes a central and permanent frown, like a star of anger, an obscure glance, a pinched-up and formidable mouth, and an air of ferocious command.

This man was made up of two very simple and relatively excellent feelings, but which he almost rendered bad by exaggerating them,—respect for authority and hatred of rebellion; and in his eyes, robbery, murder, and every crime were only forms of rebellion. He enveloped in a species of blind faith everybody in the service of the State, from the Prime Minister down to the game-keeper. He covered with contempt, aversion, and disgust, every one who had once crossed the legal threshold of evil. He was absolute, and admitted of no exceptions; on one side he said: "A functionary cannot be mistaken, a magistrate can do no wrong;" on the other he said: "They are irremediably lost: no good can come of them." He fully shared the opinion of those extreme minds that attribute to the human law some power of making or verifying demons, and that place a Styx at the bottom of society. He was stoical, stern, and austere; a sad dreamer, and humble yet haughty, like all fanatics. His glance was a gimlet, for it was cold and piercing. His whole life was composed in the two words, watching and overlooking. He had introduced the straight line into what is the most tortuous thing in the world; he was conscious of his usefulness, had religious respect for his duties, and was a spy as well as another is a priest. Woe to the wretch who came into his clutches! he would have arrested his father if escaping from prison, and denounced his mother had she broken her ban. And he would have done it with that sort of inner satisfaction which virtue produces. With all this he spent a life of privation, isolation, self-denial, chastity. He was the implacable duty, the police comprehended as the Spartans comprehended Sparta, a pitiless watchman, a savage integrity, a marble-hearted spy, a Brutus contained in a Vidocq.

Javert's entire person expressed the man who spies and hides himself. The mystic school of Joseph de Maîstre, which at this epoch was seasoning with high cosmogony what were called the ultra journals, would not have failed to say that Javert was a symbol. His forehead could not be seen, for it was hidden by his hat; his eyes could not be seen, because they were lost under his eye-brows; his chin was plunged into his cravat, his hands were covered by his cuffs, and his cane was carried under his coat. But when the opportunity arrived, there could be seen suddenly emerging from all this shadow, as from an ambush, an angular, narrow forehead, a fatal glance, a menacing chin, enormous hands, and a monstrous rattan. In his leisure moments, which were few, he read, though he hated books, and this caused him not to be utterly ignorant, as could be noticed through a certain emphasis in his language. As we have said, he had no vice; when satisfied with himself, he indulged in a pinch of snuff, and that was his connecting link with humanity. Our readers will readily understand that Javert was the terror of all that class whom the yearly statistics of the minister of justice designate under the rubric—vagabonds. The name of Javert, if uttered, set them to flight; the face of Javert, if seen, petrified them. Such was this formidable man.

Javert was like an eye ever fixed on M. Madeleine, an eye fall of suspicion and conjectures. M. Madeleine noticed it in the end; but he considered it a matter of insignificance. He did not even ask Javert his motive, he neither sought nor shunned him, and endured his annoying glance without appearing to notice it. He treated Javert like every one else, easily and kindly. From some remarks that dropped from Javert, it was supposed that he had secretly sought, with that curiosity belonging to the breed, and in which there is as much instinct as will, all the previous traces which Father Madeleine might have left. He appeared to know, and sometimes said covertly, that some one had obtained certain information in a certain district about a certain family which had disappeared. Once he happened to say, talking to himself, "I believe that I have got him;" then he remained thoughtful for three days without saying a word. It seems that the thread which he fancied he held was broken. However, there cannot be any theory really infallible in a human creature, and it is the peculiarity of instinct that it can be troubled, thrown out, and routed. If not, it would be superior to intelligence, and the brute would have a better light than man. Javert was evidently somewhat disconcerted by M. Madeleine's complete naturalness and calmness. One day, however, his strange manner seemed to produce an impression on M. Madeleine. The occasion was as follows.

CHAPTER VI

FATHER FAUCHELEVENT.

When M. Madeleine was passing one morning through an unpaved lane in the town, he heard a noise and saw a group at some distance, to which he walked up. An old man, known as Father Fauchelevent, had fallen under his cart, and his horse was lying on the ground. This Fauchelevent was one of the few enemies M. Madeleine still had at this time. When Madeleine came to these parts, Fauchelevent, a tolerably well-educated peasant, was doing badly in business; and he saw the simple workman grow rich, while he, a master, was being ruined. This filled him with jealousy, and he had done all in his power, on every possible occasion, to injure Madeleine. Then bankruptcy came, and in his old days, having only a horse and cart left, and no family, he turned carter to earn a living.

The horse had both legs broken and could not get up, while the old man was entangled between the wheels. The fall had been so unfortunate, that the whole weight of the cart was pressing on his chest, and it was heavily loaded. Fauchelevent uttered lamentable groans, and attempts had been made, though in vain, to draw him out; any irregular effort, any clumsy help or shock, might kill him. It was impossible to extricate him except by raising the cart from below, and Javert, who came up at the moment of the accident, had sent to fetch a jack. When M. Madeleine approached, the mob made way respectfully.

"Help!" old Fauchelevent cried; "is there no good soul who will save an old man?"

M. Madeleine turned to the spectators.

"Have you a jack?"

"They have gone to fetch one," a peasant answered.

144

"How soon will it be here?"

"Well, the nearest is at Flachot the blacksmith's, but it cannot be brought here under a good quarter of an hour."

"A quarter of an hour!" Madeleine exclaimed.

It had rained on the previous night, the ground was soft, the cart sunk deeper into it every moment, and more and more pressed the old man's chest. It was evident that his ribs would be broken within five minutes.

"It is impossible to wait a quarter of an hour," said M. Madeleine to the peasants who were looking on.

"We must."

"But do you not see that the cart is sinking into the ground?"

"Hang it! so it is."

"Listen to me," Madeleine continued; "there is still room enough for a man to slip under the cart and raise it with his back. It will only take half a minute, and the poor man can be drawn out. Is there any one here who has strong loins? There are five louis to be earned."

No one stirred.

"Ten louis," Madeleine said.

His hearers looked down, and one of them muttered, "A man would have to be deucedly strong, and, besides, he would run a risk of being smashed."

"Come," Madeleine began again, "twenty louis." The same silence.

"It is not the good-will they are deficient in," a voice cried.

M. Madeleine turned and recognized Javert: he had noticed him when he came up. Javert continued,—

"It is the strength. A man would have to be tremendously strong to lift a cart like that with his back."

Then, looking fixedly at M. Madeleine, he continued, laying a marked stress on every word he uttered,—

"Monsieur Madeleine, I never knew but *one* man capable of doing what you ask."

Madeleine started, but Javert continued carelessly, though without taking his eyes off Madeleine,—

"He was a galley-slave."

"Indeed!" said Madeleine.

"At the Toulon Bagne."

Madeleine turned pale; all this while the cart was slowly settling down, and Father Fauchelevent was screaming,—

"I am choking: it is breaking my ribs: a jack! something—oh!"

Madeleine looked around him.

"Is there no one here willing to earn twenty louis and save this poor old man's life?"

No one stirred, and Javert repeated,—

"I never knew but one man capable of acting as a jack, and it was that convict."

"Oh, it is crushing me!" the old man yelled.

Madeleine raised his head, met Javert's falcon eye still fixed on him, gazed at the peasants, and sighed sorrowfully. Then, without saying a word, he fell on his knees, and, ere the crowd had time to utter a cry, was under the cart. There was a frightful moment of expectation and silence. Madeleine almost lying flat under the tremendous weight, twice tried in vain to bring his elbows up to his knees. The peasants shouted: "Father Madeleine, come out!" And old Fauchelevent himself said: "Monsieur Madeleine, go away! I must die, so leave me; you will be killed too."

Madeleine made no answer; the spectators gasped; the wheels had sunk deeper, and it was now almost impossible for him to get out from under the cart. All at once the enormous mass shook, the cart slowly rose, and the wheels half emerged from the rut. A stifled voice could be heard crying, "Make haste, help!" It was Madeleine, who had made a last effort. They rushed forward, for the devotion of one man had restored strength and courage to all. The cart was lifted by twenty arms, and old Fauchelevent was saved. Madeleine rose; he was livid, although dripping with perspiration: his clothes were torn and covered with mud. The old man kissed his knees, and called him his savior, while Madeleine had on his face a strange expression of happy and celestial suffering, and turned his placid eye on Javert, who was still looking at him.

FATHER FAUCHELEVENT.

CHAPTER VII.

FAUCHELEVENT BECOMES A GARDENER AT PARIS.

Fauchelevent had put out his knee-cap in his fall, and Father Madeleine had
him carried to an infirmary he had established for his workmen in his factory,

and which was managed by two sisters of charity. The next morning the old man found a thousand-franc note by his bed-side, with a line in M. Madeleine's handwriting, "Payment for your cart and horse, which I have bought:" the cart was smashed and the horse dead. Fauchelevent recovered, but his leg remained stiff, and, hence M. Madeleine, by the recommendation of the sisters and his curé, procured him a situation as gardener at a convent in the St. Antoine quarter of Paris.

Some time after, M. Madeleine was appointed Mayor; the first time Javert saw him wearing the scarf which gave him all authority in the town, he felt that sort of excitement a dog would feel that scented a wolf in its master's clothes. From this moment he avoided him as much as he could, and when duty imperiously compelled him, and he could not do otherwise than appear before the Mayor, he addressed him with profound respect.

The prosperity created in M—— by Father Madeleine had, in addition to the visible signs we have indicated, another symptom, which, though not visible, was not the less significant, for it is one that never deceives: when the population is suffering, when work is scarce and trade bad, tax-payers exhaust and exceed the time granted them, and the State spends a good deal of money in enforcing payment. When work abounds, when the country is happy and rich, the taxes are paid cheerfully, and cost the State little. We may say that wretchedness and the public exchequer have an infallible thermometer in the cost of collecting the taxes. In seven years these costs had been reduced three-fourths in the arrondissement of M——, which caused it to be frequently quoted by M. de Villele, at that time Minister of Finances.

Such was the state of the town when Fantine returned to it. No one remembered her, but luckily the door of M. Madeleine's factory was like a friendly face; she presented herself at it, and was admitted to the female shop. As the trade was quite new to Fantine, she was awkward at it and earned but small wages; but that was enough, for she had solved the problem,—she was earning her livelihood.

CHAPTER VIII.

MADAME VICTURNIEN SPENDS THIRTY FRANCS ON MORALITY.

When Fantine saw that she could earn her own living, she had a moment of joy. To live honestly by her own toil, what a favor of Heaven! A taste for work really came back to her: she bought a looking-glass, delighted in seeing in it her youth, her fine hair and fine teeth; forgot many things, only thought of Cosette, and her possible future, and was almost happy. She hired a small room and furnished it, on credit, to be paid for out of her future earnings,— this was a relic of her irregular habits.

Not being able to say that she was married, she was very careful not to drop a word about her child. At the outset, as we have seen, she punctually paid the Thénardiers; and as she could only sign her name, she was compelled to write to them through the agency of a public writer. It was noticed that she wrote frequently. It was beginning to be whispered in the shop that Fantine "wrote letters," and was "carrying on."

No one spies the actions of persons so much as those whom they do not concern. Why does this gentleman never come till nightfall? Why does So-and-So never hang up his key on Thursdays? Why does he always take back streets? Why does Madame always get out of her hackney coach before reaching her house? Why does she send out to buy a quire of note-paper, when she has a desk full? and so on. There are people who, in order to solve these inquiries, which are matters of utter indifference to them, spend more money, lavish more time, and take more trouble, than would be required for ten good deeds: and they do it gratuitously for the pleasure, and they are only paid for their curiosity with curiosity. They will follow a gentleman or a lady for whole days, will stand sentry at the corner of a street or in a gateway at night in the cold and rain; corrupt messengers, intoxicate hackney coachmen and footmen, buy a lady's-maid, and make a purchase of a porter,—why? For nothing; for a pure desire to see, know, and find out—it is a simple itch for talking. And frequently these secrets, when made known, these mysteries published, these enigmas brought to daylight, entail catastrophes, duels, bankruptcies, ruin of families, to the great delight of those who found it all out, without any personal motives, through pure instinct. It is a sad thing. Some persons are wicked solely through a desire to talk, and this conversation, which is gossip in the drawing-room, scandal in the ante-room, is like those chimneys which consume wood rapidly; they require a great deal of combustible, and this combustible is their neighbor.

Fantine was observed then, and besides, more than one girl was jealous of her light hair and white teeth. It was noticed that she often wiped away a tear in the shop; it was when she was thinking of her child, perhaps of the man she had loved. It is a painful labor to break off all the gloomy connecting links with the past. It was a fact that she wrote, at least twice a month, and always to the same address, and paid the postage. They managed to obtain the address: "Monsieur Thénardier, Publican, Montfermeil." The public writer, who could not fill his stomach with wine without emptying his pocket of secrets, was made to talk at the wine-shop; and, in short, it was known that Fantine had a child. A gossip undertook a journey to Montfermeil, spoke to the Thénardiers, and on her return said, "I do not begrudge my thirty francs, for I have seen the child."

The gossip who did this was a Gorgon of the name of Madame Victurnien, guardian and portress of everybody's virtue. She was fifty-six years of age, and covered the mask of ugliness with the mask of old age. Astounding to say, this old woman had once been young; in her youth, in '93, she had married a monk, who escaped from the cloisters in a red cap, and passed over from the Bernardines to the Jacobins. She was dry, crabbed, sharp, thorny, and almost venomous, while remembering the monk whose widow she was and who had considerably tamed her. At the Restoration she had turned bigot, and so energetically, that the priests forgave her her monk. She had a small estate which she left with considerable pallor to a religious community, and she was very welcome at the Episcopal Palace of Arras. This Madame Victurnien, then, went to Montfermeil, and when she returned, said, "I have seen the child."

All this took time, and Fantine had been more than a year at the factory, when one morning the forewoman handed her 50 francs in the Mayor's name, and told her that she was no longer engaged, and had better leave the town, so the Mayor said. It was in this very month that the Thénardiers, after asking for 12 francs instead of 7, raised a claim for 15 instead of 12. Fantine was startled; she could not leave the town, for she owed her rent and for her furniture, and 50 francs would not pay those debts. She stammered a few words of entreaty, but the forewoman intimated to her that she must leave the shop at once; moreover, Fantine was but an indifferent workwoman. Crushed by shame more than disgrace, she left the factory, and returned to her room: her fault then was now known to all! She did not feel the strength in her to say a word; she was advised to see the Mayor, but did not dare do so. The Mayor gave her 50 francs because he was kind, and discharged her because he was just; and she bowed her head to the sentence.

CHAPTER IX

SUCCESS OF MADAME VICTURNIEN.

The monk's widow, then, was good for something. M. Madeleine, however, knew nothing of all this; and they were combinations of events of which the world is fall. M. Madeleine made it a rule hardly, ever to enter the female work-room; he had placed at its head an old maid, whom the curé had given him, and he had entire confidence in her. She was really a respectable, firm, equitable, and just person, fall of that charity which consists in giving, but not possessing to the same extent the charity which comprehends and pardons. M. Madeleine trusted to her in everything, for the best men are often forced to delegate their authority, and it was with this fall power, and in the conviction she was acting rightly, that the forewoman tried, condemned, and executed Fantine. As for the 50 francs, she had given them out of a sum M. Madeleine had given her for alms and helping the workwomen, and which she did not account for.

Fantine tried to get a servant's place in the town, and went from house to house, but no one would have anything to do with her. She could not leave the town, for the broker to whom she was in debt for her furniture—what furniture!—said to her, "If you go away, I will have you arrested as a thief." The landlord to whom she owed her rent, said to her, "You are young and pretty, you can pay." She divided the 50 francs between the landlord and the broker, gave back to the latter three-fourths of the goods, only retaining what was absolutely necessary, and found herself without work, without a trade, with only a bed, and still owing about 100 francs. She set to work making coarse shirts for the troops, and earned at this sixpence a day, her daughter costing her fourpence. It was at this moment she began to fall in arrears with the Thénardiers. An old woman, however, who lit her candle for her when she came in at nights, taught her the way to live in wretchedness. Behind living on little, there is living on nothing: there are two chambers,—the first is obscure, the second quite dark.

Fantine learned how she could do entirely without fire in winter, how she must get rid of a bird that cost her a halfpenny every two days, how she could make a petticoat of her blanket and a blanket of her petticoat, and how candle can be saved by taking your meals by the light of the window opposite. We do not know all that certain weak beings, who have grown old in want and honesty, can get out of a halfpenny, and in the end it becomes a talent. Fantine acquired this sublime talent, and regained a little courage. At this period she said to a neighbor, "Nonsense, I say to myself; by only sleeping for five hours and working all the others at my needle, I shall always manage to earn bread, at any rate. And then, when you are sad, you eat less. Well! suffering, anxiety, a little bread on one side and sorrow on the other, all will support me."

In this distress, it would have been a strange happiness to have had her daughter with her, and she thought of sending for her. But, what! make her share her poverty? And then she owed money to the Thénardiers! how was she to pay it and the travelling expenses? The old woman who had given her lessons in what may be called indigent life, was a pious creature, poor, and charitable to the poor and even to the rich, who could just write her name, "Marguerite," and believed in God, which is knowledge. There are many such virtues down here, and one day they will be up above, for this life has a morrow.

At the beginning Fantine had been so ashamed that she did not dare go out. When she was in the streets, she perceived that people turned round to look at her and pointed to her. Every one stared at her, and no one bowed to her; the cold bitter contempt of the passers-by passed through her flesh and her mind like an east wind. In small towns an unhappy girl seems to be naked beneath the sarcasm and curiosity of all. In Paris, at least no one knows you, and that obscurity is a garment. Oh! how glad she would have been to be back in Paris. She must grow accustomed to disrespect, as she had done to poverty. Gradually she made up her mind, and after two or three months shook off her shame, and went as if nothing had occurred. "It is no matter to me," she said. She came and went, with head erect and with a bitter smile, and felt that she was growing impudent. Madame Victurnien sometimes saw her pass from her window; she noticed the distress of "the creature whom she had made know her place," and congratulated herself. The wicked have a black happiness. Excessive labor fatigued Fantine, and the little dry cough she had grew worse. She sometimes said to her neighbor, "Marguerite, just feel how hot my hands are!" Still, in the morning, when she passed an old broken comb through her glorious hair, which shone like floss silk, she had a minute of happy coquettishness.

CHAPTER X

RESULT OF HER SUCCESS.

She had been discharged toward the end of winter; the next summer passed away, and winter returned. Short days and less work; in winter there is no warmth, no light, no mid-day, for the evening is joined to the morning; there is fog, twilight, the window is gray, and you cannot see clearly. The sky is like a dark vault, and the sun has the look of a poor man. It is a frightful season; winter changes into stone the water of heaven and the heart of man. Her creditors pressed her, for Fantine was earning too little, and her debts had increased. The Thénardiers, being irregularly paid, constantly wrote her letters, whose contents afflicted her, and postage ruined her. One day they wrote her that little Cosette was quite naked, that she wanted a flannel skirt, and that the mother must send at least ten francs for the purpose. She crumpled the letter in her hands all day, and at nightfall went to a barber's at the corner of the street, and removed her comb. Her splendid light hair fell down to her hips.

"What fine hair!" the barber exclaimed.

"What will you give me for it?" she asked.

"Ten francs."

"Cut it off."

She bought a skirt and sent to the Thénardiers; it made them furious, for they wanted the money. They gave it to Éponine, and the poor lark continued to shiver. Fantine thought, "My child is no longer cold, for I have dressed her in my hair." She wore small round caps which hid her shorn head, and she still looked pretty in them.

A dark change took place in Fantine's heart. When she found that she could no longer dress her hair, she began to hate all around her. She had long shared the universal veneration for Father Madeleine: but, through the constant iteration that he had discharged her and was the cause of her misfortune, she grew to hate him too, and worse than the rest. When she passed the factory she pretended to laugh and sing. An old workwoman who once saw her doing so, said, "That's a girl who will come to a bad end." She took a lover, the first who offered, a man she did not love, through bravado and with rage in her heart. He was a scoundrel, a sort of mendicant musician, an idle scamp, who beat her, and left her, as she had chosen him, in disgust. She adored her child. The lower she sank, the darker the gloom became around her, the more did this sweet little angel gleam in her soul. She said: "When I am rich, I shall have my Cosette with me;" and she laughed. She did not get rid of her cough, and she felt a cold perspiration in her back. One day she received from the Thénardiers a letter to the following effect: "Cosette is ill with a complaint which is very prevalent in the country. It is called miliary fever. She must have expensive drugs, and that ruins us, and we cannot pay for them any longer. If you do not send us forty francs within a week, the little one will be dead." She burst into a loud laugh, and said to her old neighbor, "Oh, what funny people! they want forty francs; where do they expect me to get them? What fools those peasants are!" Still, she went to a staircase window and read the letter again; then she went out into the street, still laughing and singing. Some one who met her said, "What has made you so merry?" and she answered, "It is a piece of stupidity some country folk have written; they want forty francs of me—the asses."

As she passed across the market-place she saw a crowd surrounding a vehicle of a strange shape, on the box of which a man dressed in red was haranguing. He was a dentist going his rounds, who offered the public complete sets of teeth, opiates, powders, and elixirs. Fantine joined the crowd and began laughing like the rest at this harangue, in which there was slang for the mob, and scientific jargon for respectable persons. The extractor of teeth saw the pretty girl laughing, and suddenly exclaimed,—

"You have fine teeth, my laughing beauty. If you like to sell me your two top front teeth, I will give you a napoleon apiece for them."

"What a horrible idea!" Fantine exclaimed.

"Two napoleons!" an old toothless woman by her side grumbled; "there's a lucky girl."

Fantine ran away and stopped her ears not to hear the hoarse voice of the man, who shouted,—

"Think it over, my dear: two napoleons may be useful. If your heart says Yes, come to-night to the *Tillac d'Argent*, where you will find me."

Fantine, when she reached home, was furious, and told her good neighbor Marguerite what had happened. "Can you understand it? Is he not an abominable man? How can people like that be allowed to go about the country? Pull out my two front teeth! Why, I should look horrible; hair grows again, but teeth! oh, the monster! I would sooner throw myself head first out of a fifth-floor window on to the pavement."

"And what did he offer you?" Marguerite asked.

"Two napoleons."

"That makes forty francs."

"Yes," said Fantine, "that makes forty francs."

She became thoughtful and sat down to her work. At the end of a quarter of an hour, she left the room and read Thénardier's letter again on the staircase. When she returned, she said to Marguerite,—

"Do you know what a miliary fever is?"

"Yes," said the old woman, "it is an illness."

"Does it require much medicine?"

"Oh, an awful lot!"

"Does it attack children?"

"More than anybody."

"Do they die of it?"

"Plenty," said Marguerite.

Fantine went out and read the letter once again on the staircase. At night she went out, and could be seen proceeding in the direction of the Rue de Paris, where the inns are. The next morning, when Marguerite entered Fantine's room before day-break, for they worked together, and they made one candle do for them both, she found her sitting on her bed, pale and chill. Her cap had fallen on her knees, and the candle had been burning all night, and was nearly consumed. Marguerite stopped in the doorway, horrified by this enormous extravagance, and exclaimed,—

"Oh, Lord! the candle nearly burnt out! something must have happened."

Then she looked at Fantine, who turned her close-shaven head towards her, and seemed to have grown ten years older since the previous day.

"Gracious Heaven!" said Marguerite, "what is the matter with you, Fantine?"

"Nothing," the girl answered; "I am all right. My child will not die of that frightful disease for want of assistance, and I am satisfied."

As she said this, she pointed to two napoleons that glistened on the table.

"Oh, Lord!" said Marguerite; "why, 't is a fortune; where ever did you get them from?"

"I had them by me," Fantine answered.

At the same time she smiled, the candle lit up her face, and it was a fearful smile. A reddish saliva stained the corner of her lips, and she had a black hole in her mouth; the two teeth were pulled out. She sent the forty francs to Montfermeil. It had only been a trick of the Thénardiers to get money, for Cosette was not ill.

Fantine threw her looking-glass out of the window; she had long before left her cell on the second floor for a garret under the roof,—one of those tenements in which the ceiling forms an angle with the floor, and you knock your head at every step. The poor man can only go to the end of his room, as to the end of his destiny, by stooping more and more. She had no bed left; she had only a rag she called a blanket, a mattress on the ground, and a bottomless chair; a little rose-tree she had had withered away, forgotten in a corner. In another corner she had a pail to hold water, which froze in winter, and in which the different levels of the water remained marked for a long time by rings of ice. She had lost her shame, and now lost her coquetry; the last sign was, that she went out with dirty caps. Either through want of time or carelessness, she no longer mended her linen, and as the heels of her stockings wore out, she tucked them into her shoes. She mended her worn-out gown with rags of calico, which tore away at the slightest movement. The people to whom she owed money made "scenes," and allowed her no rest; she met them in the street, she met them again on the stairs. Her eyes were very bright, and she felt a settled pain at the top of her left shoulder-blade, while she coughed frequently. She deeply hated Father Madeleine, and sewed for seventeen hours a day; but a speculator hired all the female prisoners, and reduced the prices of the free workmen to nine sous a day. Seventeen hours' work for nine sous! Her creditors were more pitiless than ever, and the broker, who had got back nearly all her furniture, incessantly said to her, "When are you going to pay me, you cheat?" What did they want of her, good Heavens! She felt herself tracked, and something of the wild beast was aroused in her. About the same time Thénardier wrote to her, that he had decidedly waited too patiently, and that unless he received one hundred francs at once, he would turn poor Cosette, who had scarce recovered, out of doors into the cold, and she must do what she could or die. "One hundred francs!" Fantine thought; "but where is the trade in which I can earn one hundred sous a day? Well! I will sell all that is left!"

And the unfortunate girl went on the streets.

CHAPTER XI.

CHRISTUS NOS LIBERAVIT.

What is this story of Fantine? It is society buying a slave.

Of whom? Of misery, of hunger, of cold, of loneliness, of desertion, of destitution. Cursed bargain! A soul for a morsel of bread. Misery offers its wares, and society accepts.

The holy law of Jesus Christ governs our civilization, but it does not yet pervade it. They say that slavery has disappeared from European civilization. That's a mistake. It still exists; but it weighs now only on woman, and its name is prostitution.

It weighs on woman; that is, on grace, on helplessness, on beauty, on motherhood. This is not one of the least reproaches upon man.

At the point which we have reached in this painful drama, there is nothing left in Fantine of her former self. She became marble when she became mud. Whoever touches her is chilled. She is handed along, she submits to you, but she forgets your presence. She is the type of dishonor and rigidity. Life and social order have said to her their last word. Everything that can happen to her, has already happened. She has felt all, borne all, endured all, suffered all, lost all, wept for all. She is resigned with a resignation which is as like indifference as death is like sleep. She shuns nothing now. She fears nothing now. Let the whole sky fall on her, let the whole ocean pass over her! What does she care? She is a sponge soaked full.

At least she thinks so; but it is never safe to think that you have drained the cup of misfortune, or that you have reached the end of anything.

Alas! what are all these destinies driven along thus helter-skelter? Where are they going? Why are they what they are?

He who knows this sees the whole shadow. He is one alone. His name is God.

CHAPTER XII.

M. BAMATABOIS' IDLENESS.

There is in all small towns, and there was at M—— in particular, a class of young men, who squander fifteen hundred francs a year in the provinces with the same air as those of the same set in Paris devour two hundred thousand. They are beings of the great neutral species; geldings, parasites, nobodies, who possess a little land, a little folly, and a little wit, who would be rustics in a drawing-room, and believe themselves gentlemen in a pot-house. They talk about my fields, my woods, my peasants, horses, the actresses, to prove themselves men of taste; quarrel with the officers, to prove themselves men of war; shoot, smoke, yawn, drink, smell of tobacco, play at billiards, watch the travellers get out of the stage-coach, live at the café, dine at the inn, have a dog that gnaws bones under the table, and a mistress who places the dishes upon it; haggle over a son, exaggerate the fashions, admire tragedy, despise women, wear out their old boots, copy London through Paris, and Paris through Pont-à-Mousson; grow stupidly old, do not work, are of no use, and do no great harm. Had M. Félix Tholomyès remained in his province and not seen Paris, he would have been one of them. If they were richer, people would say they are dandies; if poorer, they are loafers; but they are simply men without occupation. Among them there are bores and bored, dreamers, and a few scamps.

At that day, a dandy was composed of a tall collar, a large cravat, a watch and seals, three waist-coats over one another, blue and red inside, a short-waisted olive-colored coat, with a swallow tail, and a double row of silver buttons, sewn on close together, and ascending to the shoulders, and trousers of a lighter olive, adorned on the seams with an undetermined but always uneven number of ribs, varying from one to eleven, a limit which was never exceeded. Add to this, slipper-boots with iron-capped heels, a tall, narrow-brimmed hat, hair in a tuft, an enormous cane, and a conversation improved by Potier's puns; over and above all these were spurs and moustachios, for at that period moustachios indicated the civilian, and spurs the pedestrian. The provincial dandy wore longer spurs and more ferocious moustachios. It was the period of the struggle of the South American Republics against the King of Spain, of Bolivar against Morillo. Narrow-brimmed hats were Royalist, and called Morillos, while the Liberals wore broad brims, which were called Bolivars.

Eight or ten months after the events we have described in the previous chapter, toward the beginning of January, and on a night when snow had fallen, one of these dandies—a man of "right sentiments," for he wore a Morillo, and was also warmly wrapped up in one of the large Spanish cloaks which at that time completed the fashionable costume in cold weather—was amusing himself by annoying a creature who was prowling about in a low-neck balldress, and with flowers in her hair, before the window of the officers' café. This dandy was smoking, as that was a decided mark of fashion. Each time this woman passed him, he made some remark to her, which he fancied witty and amusing, as: "How ugly you are!—Why don't you go to kennel?—You have no teeth," etc., etc. This gentleman's name was Monsieur Bamatabois. The woman, a sad-dressed phantom walking backwards and forwards in the snow, made him no answer, did not even look at him, but still continued silently and with a gloomy regularity her walk, which, every few minutes, brought her under his sarcasms, like the condemned soldier running the gauntlet. The slight effect produced doubtless annoyed the idler, for taking advantage of her back being turned, he crept up behind her, stooped to pick up a handful of snow, and suddenly plunged it between her bare shoulders. The girl uttered a yell, turned, leaped like a panther on the man, and dug her nails into his face with the most frightful language that could fall from a guard-room into the gutter. These insults, vomited by a voice rendered hoarse by brandy, hideously issued from a mouth in which the two front teeth were really missing. It was Fantine.

At the noise, the officers left the café in a throng, the passers-by stopped, and a laughing, yelling, applauding circle was made round these two beings, in whom it was difficult to recognize a man and a woman,—the man struggling, his hat on the ground, the woman striking with feet and fists, bareheaded, yelling, without teeth or hair, livid with passion, and horrible. All at once a tall man quickly broke through the crowd, seized the woman's satin dress, which was covered with mud, and said: "Follow me." The woman raised her hand, and her passionate voice suddenly died out. Her eyes were glassy, she grew pale instead of being livid, and trembled with fear. She had recognized Javert. The dandy profited by this incident to make his escape.

CHAPTER XIII

THE POLICE OFFICE.

Javert broke through the circle and began walking with long strides toward the police office, which is at the other end of the market-place, dragging the wretched girl after him. She allowed him to do so mechanically, and neither he nor she said a word. The crowd of spectators, in a paroxysm of delight, followed them with coarse jokes, for supreme misery is an occasion for obscenities. On reaching the police office, which was a low room, heated by a stove, and guarded by a sentry, and having a barred glass door opening on the street, Javert walked in with Fantine, and shut the door after him, to the great disappointment of the curious, who stood on tip-toe, and stretched out their necks in front of the dirty window trying to see. Curiosity is gluttony, and seeing is devouring.

On entering, Fantine crouched down motionless in a corner like a frightened dog. The sergeant on duty brought in a candle. Javert sat down at a table, took a sheet of stamped paper from his pocket, and began writing. Women of this class are by the French laws left entirely at the discretion of the police: they do what they like with them, punish them as they think proper, and confiscate the two sad things which they call their trade and their liberty. Javert was stoical: his grave face displayed no emotion, and yet he was seriously and deeply preoccupied. It was one of those moments in which he exercised without control, but with all the scruples of a strict conscience, his formidable discretionary power. At this instant he felt that his high stool was a tribunal, and himself the judge. He tried and he condemned: he summoned all the ideas he had in his mind round the great thing he was doing. The more he examined the girl's deed, the more outraged he felt: for it was evident that he had just seen a crime committed. He had seen in the street, society, represented by a householder and elector, insulted and attacked by a creature beyond the pale of everything. A prostitute had assaulted a citizen, and he, Javert, had witnessed it. He wrote on silently. When he had finished, he affixed his signature, folded up the paper, and said to the sergeant as he handed it to him: "Take these men and lead this girl to prison." Then he turned to Fantine, "You will have six months for it."

The wretched girl started.

"Six months, six months' imprisonment!" she cried; "six months! and only earn seven sous a day! Why, what will become of Cosette, my child, my child! Why, I owe more than one hundred francs to Thénardier, M. Inspector; do you know that?"

She dragged herself across the floor, dirtied by the muddy boots of all these men, without rising, with clasped hands and taking long strides with her knees.

"Monsieur Javert," she said, "I ask for mercy. I assure you that I was not in the wrong; if you had seen the beginning, you would say so; I swear by our Saviour that I was not to blame. That gentleman, who was a stranger to me, put snow down my back. Had he any right to do that when I was passing gently, and doing nobody a harm? It sent me wild, for you must know I am not very well, and besides he had been abusing me—"You are ugly, you have no teeth." I am well aware that I have lost my teeth. I did nothing, and said to myself, "This gentleman is amusing himself." I was civil to him, and said nothing, and it was at this moment he put the snow down my back. My good M. Javert, is there no one who saw it to tell you that this is the truth? I was, perhaps, wrong to get into a passion, but at the moment, as you are aware, people are not masters of themselves, and I am quick-tempered. And then, something so cold put down your back, at a moment when you are least expecting it! It was; wrong to destroy the gentleman's hat, but why has he gone away? I would ask his pardon. Oh! I would willingly do so. Let me off this time. M. Javert, perhaps you do not know that in prison you can only earn seven sous a day; it is not the fault of Government, but you only earn seven sous; and just fancy! I have one hundred francs to pay, or my child will be turned into the street. Oh! I cannot have her with me, for my mode of life is so bad! Oh, my Cosette, oh, my little angel, what ever will become of you, poor darling! I must tell you that the Thénardiers are inn-keepers, peasants, and unreasonable; they insist on having their money. Oh, do not send me to prison! Look you, the little thing will be turned into the streets in the middle of winter to go where she likes, and you must take pity on that, my kind M. Javert. If she were older she could earn her living, but at her age it is impossible. I am not a bad woman at heart, it is not cowardice and gluttony that have made me what I am. If I drink brandy, it is through wretchedness; I do not like it, but it makes me reckless. In happier times you need only have looked into my chest of drawers, and you would have seen that I was not a disorderly woman, for I had linen, plenty of linen. Take pity on me, M. Javert!"

She spoke thus, crushed, shaken by sobs, blinded by tears, wringing her hands, interrupted by a sharp dry cough, and stammering softly, with death imprinted on her voice. Great sorrow is a divine and terrible ray which transfigures the wretched, and at this moment Fantine became lovely again. From time to time she stopped, and tenderly kissed the skirt of the policeman's coat. She would have melted a heart of granite,—but a wooden heart cannot be moved.

"Well," said Javert, "I have listened to you. Have you said all? Be off now; you have six months. The Eternal Father in person could not alter it."

On hearing this solemn phrase, she understood that sentence was passed; she fell all of a heap, murmuring, "Mercy!" But Javert turned his back, and the soldiers seized her arm. Some minutes previously a man had entered unnoticed; he had closed the door, leaned against it, and heard Fantine's desperate entreaties. At the moment when the soldiers laid hold of the unhappy girl, who would not rise, he emerged from the gloom, and said,—

"Wait a minute, if you please."

Javert raised his eyes, and recognized M. Madeleine; he took off his hat, and bowed with a sort of vexed awkwardness.

"I beg your pardon, M. le Maire—"

The words "M. le Maire" produced a strange effect on Fantine; she sprang up like a spectre emerging from the ground, thrust back the soldiers, walked straight up to M. Madeleine before she could be prevented, and, looking at him wildly, she exclaimed,—

"So you are the Mayor?"

Then she burst into a laugh, and spat in his face. M. Madeleine wiped his face, and said,—

"Inspector Javert, set this woman at liberty."

Javert felt for a moment as if he were going mad; he experienced at this instant the most violent emotions he had ever felt in his life, following each other in rapid succession, and almost mingled. To see a girl of the town spit in the Mayor's face was so monstrous a thing that he would have regarded it as sacrilege even to believe it possible. On the other side, he confusedly made a hideous approximation in his mind between what this woman was and what this Mayor might be, and then he saw with horror something perfectly simple in this prodigious assault. But when he saw this Mayor, this magistrate, calmly wipe his face, and say, "Set this woman at liberty," he had a bedazzlement of stupor, so to speak; thought and language failed him equally, for he had passed the limits of possible amazement. He remained dumb. His sentence had produced an equally strange effect on Fantine; she raised her bare arm, and clung to the chimney-key of the stove like a tottering person. She looked around, and began saying in a low voice, as if speaking to herself, —

"At liberty! I am to be let go! I shall not be sent to prison for six months! Who said that? It is impossible that any one said it. I must have heard badly; it cannot be that monster of a Mayor. Was it you, my kind M. Javert, who said that I was to be set at liberty? Well, I will tell you all about it, and you will let me go. That monster of a Mayor, that old villain of a Mayor, is the cause of it all. Just imagine, M. Javert, he discharged me on account of a parcel of sluts gossiping in the shop. Was not that horrible,—to discharge a poor girl who is doing her work fairly! After that I did not earn enough, and all this misfortune came. In the first place, there is an improvement which the police gentry ought to make, and that is to prevent persons in prison injuring poor people. I will explain this to you; you earn twelve sous for making a shirt, but it falls to seven, and then you can no longer live, and are obliged to do what you can. As I had my little Cosette I was forced to become a bad woman. You can now understand how it was that beggar of a Mayor who did all the mischief. My present offence is that I trampled on the gentleman's hat before the officers' café, but he had ruined my dress with snow; and our sort have only one silk dress for night. Indeed, M. Javert, I never did any harm purposely, and I see everywhere much worse women than myself who are much more fortunate. Oh, Monsieur Javert, you said that I was to be set at liberty, did you not? Make inquiries, speak to my landlord; I pay my rent now, and you will hear that I am honest. Oh, good gracious! I ask your pardon, but I have touched the damper of the stove without noticing it, and made a smoke."

M. Madeleine listened to her with deep attention: while she was talking, he took out his purse, but as he found it empty on opening it, he returned it to his pocket. He now said to Fantine,—

"How much did you say that you owed?"

Fantine, who was looking at Javert, turned round to him,—

"Am I speaking to you?"

Then she said to the soldiers,—

"Tell me, men, did you see how I spat in his face? Ah, you old villain of a Mayor! you have come here to frighten me, but I am not afraid of you; I am only afraid of M. Javert, my kind Monsieur Javert."

While saying this, she turned again to the Inspector,—

"After all, people should be just. I can understand that you are a just man, M. Javert; in fact, it is quite simple; a man who played at putting snow down a woman's back, made the officers laugh; they must have some amusement, and we girls are sent into the world for them to make fun of. And then you came up: you are compelled to restore order; you remove the woman who was in the wrong, but, on reflection, as you are kind-hearted, you order me to be set at liberty, for the sake of my little girl, for six months' imprisonment would prevent my supporting her. Only don't come here again, fagot! Oh, I will not come here again, M. Javert; they can do what they like to me in future, and I will not stir. Still I cried out to-night because it hurt me; I did not at all expect that gentleman's snow; and then besides, as I told you; I am not very well,—I cough, I have something like a ball in my stomach which burns, and the doctor says: "Take care of yourself." Here, feel, give me your hand; do not be frightened."

She no longer cried, her voice was caressing; she laid Javert's large coarse hand on her white, delicate throat, and looked up at him smilingly. All at once she hurriedly repaired the disorder in her clothes, let the folds of her dress fall, which had been almost dragged up to her knee, and walked toward the door, saying to the soldiers with a friendly nod,—

"My lads, M. Javert says I may go, so I will be off."

She laid her hand on the hasp; one step further, and she would be in the street. Up to this moment Javert had stood motionless, with his eyes fixed on the ground, appearing in the centre of this scene like a statue waiting to be put up in its proper place. The sound of the hasp aroused him: he raised his head with an expression of sovereign authority,—an expression the more frightful, the lower the man in power stands; it is ferocity in the wild beast, atrocity in the nobody.

"Sergeant," he shouted, "do you not see that the wench is bolting? Who told you to let her go?"

"I did," said Madeleine.

Fantine, at the sound of Javert's voice, trembled, and let go the hasp, as a detected thief lets fall the stolen article. At Madeleine's voice she turned, and from this moment, without uttering a word, without even daring to breathe freely, her eye wandered from Madeleine to Javert, and from Javert to

Madeleine, according as each spoke. It was evident that Javert must have been "lifted off the hinges," as people say, when he ventured to address the sergeant as he had done, after the Mayor's request that Fantine should be set at liberty. Had he gone so far as to forget the Mayor's presence? Did he eventually declare to himself that it was impossible for "an authority" to have given such an order, and that the Mayor must certainly have said one thing for another without meaning it? Or was it that, in the presence of all the enormities he had witnessed during the last two hours, he said to himself that he must have recourse to a supreme resolution, that the little must become great, the detective be transformed into the magistrate, and that, in this prodigious extremity, order, law, morality, government, and society were personified in him, Javert? However this may be, when M. Madeleine said "I did," the Inspector of Police could be seen to turn to the Mayor, pale, cold, with blue lips, with a desperate glance, and an imperceptible tremor all over him, and—extraordinary circumstance!—to say to him, with downcast eye, but in a fierce voice,—

"Monsieur le Maire, that cannot be."

"Why so?"

"This creature has insulted a gentleman."

"Inspector Javert," M. Madeleine replied with a conciliating and calm accent, "listen to me. You are an honest man, and I shall have no difficulty in coming to an explanation with you. The truth is as follows: I was crossing the market-place at the time you were leading this girl away; a crowd was still assembled; I inquired, and know all. The man was in the wrong, and, in common justice, ought to have been arrested instead of her."

Javert objected,—

"The wretched creature has just insulted M. le Maire."

"That concerns myself," M. Madeleine said; "my insult is, perhaps, my own, and I can do what I like with it."

"I ask your pardon, sir; the insult does not belong to you, but to the Judicial Court."

"Inspector Javert," Madeleine replied, "conscience is the highest of all courts. I have heard the woman, and know what I am doing."

"And I, Monsieur le Maire, do not know what I am seeing."

"In that case, be content with obeying."

"I obey my duty; my duty orders that this woman should go to prison for six months."

M. Madeleine answered gently,—

"Listen to this carefully; she will not go for a single day."

On hearing these decided words, Javert ventured to look fixedly at the Mayor, and said to him, though still with a respectful accent,—

"I bitterly regret being compelled to resist you. Monsieur le Maire, it is the first time in my life, but you will deign to let me observe that I am within the limits of my authority. As you wish it, sir, I will confine myself to the affair with the gentleman. I was present; this girl attacked M. Bamatabois, who is an elector and owner of that fine three-storied house, built of hewn stone, which forms the corner of the Esplanade. Well, there are things in this world! However this may be, M. le Maire, this is a matter of the street police which concerns me, and I intend to punish the woman Fantine."

M. Madeleine upon this folded his arms, and said in a stern voice, which no one in the town had ever heard before,—

"The affair to which you allude belongs to the Borough police; and by the terms of articles nine, eleven, fifteen, and sixty-six of the Criminal Code, I try it. I order that this woman be set at liberty."

Javert tried a final effort.

"But, Monsieur le Maire—"

"I call your attention to article eighty-one of the law of Dec. 13th, 1799, upon arbitrary detention."

"Permit me, sir—"

"Not a word!" "Still—
"

"Leave the room!" said M. Madeleine.

Javert received the blow right in his chest like a Russian soldier; he bowed down to the ground to the Mayor, and went out. Fantine stood up against the door, and watched him pass by her in stupor. She too was suffering from a strange perturbation: for she had seen herself, so to speak, contended for by two opposite powers. She had seen two men struggling in her presence, who held in their hands her liberty, her life, her soul, her child. One of these men dragged her towards the gloom, the other restored her to the light. In this struggle, which she gazed at through the exaggeration of terror, the two men seemed to her giants,—one spoke like a demon, the other like her good angel. The angel had vanquished the demon, and the thing which made her shudder from head to foot was that this angel, this liberator, was the very man whom

165

she abhorred, the Mayor whom she had so long regarded as the cause of all her woes; and at the very moment when she had insulted him in such a hideous way, he saved her. Could she be mistaken? Must she change her whole soul? She did not know, but she trembled; she listened wildly, she looked on with terror, and at every word that M. Madeleine said, she felt the darkness of hatred fade away in her heart, and something glowing and ineffable spring up in its place, which was composed of joy, confidence, and love. When Javert had left the room, M. Madeleine turned to her, and said in a slow voice, like a serious man who is making an effort to restrain his tears,—

"I have heard your story. I knew nothing about what you have said, but I believe, I feel, that it is true. I was even ignorant that you had left the factory, but why did you not apply to me? This is what I will do for you; I will pay your debts and send for your child, or you can go to it. You can live here, in Paris, or wherever you please, and I will provide for your child and yourself. I will give you all the money you require, and you will become respectable again in becoming happy; and I will say more than that: if all be as you say, and I do not doubt it, you have never ceased to be virtuous and holy in the sight of God! Poor woman!"

This was more than poor Fantine could endure. To have her Cosette! to leave this infamous life! to live free, rich, happy, and respectable with Cosette! to see all these realities of Paradise suddenly burst into flower, in the midst of her wretchedness! She looked as if stunned at the person who was speaking, and could only sob two or three times: "Oh, oh, oh!" Her legs gave way, she fell on her knees before M. Madeleine, and before he could prevent it, he felt her seize his hand and press her lips to it.

Then she fainted.

BOOK VI.

JAVERT.

CHAPTER I.

THE COMMENCEMENT OF REPOSE.

M. Madeleine had Fantine conveyed to the infirmary he had established in his own house, and intrusted her to the sisters, who put her to bed. A violent fever had broken out; she spent a part of the night in raving and talking aloud, but at length fell asleep. On the morrow, at about mid-day, Fantine woke, and hearing a breathing close to her bed, she drew the curtain aside, and noticed M. Madeleine gazing at something above her head. His glance was full of pity and agony, and supplicated: she followed its direction, and saw that it was fixed on a crucifix nailed to the wall. M. Madeleine was now transfigured in Fantine's eyes, and seemed to her surrounded by light. He was absorbed in a species of prayer, and she looked at him for some time without daring to interrupt him, but at length said, timidly,—

"What are you doing there?"

M. Madeleine had been standing at this spot for an hour, waiting till Fantine should wake. He took her hand, felt her pulse, and answered,—

"How are you?"

"Very comfortable; I have slept, and fancy I am better. It will be nothing."

He continued answering the question she had asked him first, and as if he had only just heard it,—

"I was praying to the martyr up there;" and he mentally added, "for the martyr down here."

M. Madeleine had spent the night and morning in making inquiries, and had learned everything; he knew all the poignant details of Fantine's history. He continued,—

"You have suffered deeply, poor mother. Oh! do not complain, for you have at present the dowry of the elect: it is in this way that human beings become angels. It is not their fault; they do not know what to do otherwise. The hell you have now left is the ante-room to heaven, and you were obliged to begin with that."

He breathed a deep sigh, but she smiled upon him with the sublime smile in which two teeth were wanting. Javert had written a letter during the past night, and posted it himself the next morning. It was for Paris, and the address was: "Monsieur Chabouillet, Secretary to the Prefect of Police." As a rumor had spread about the affair in the police office, the lady-manager of the post, and some other persons who saw the letter before it was sent off and recognized Javert's handwriting, supposed that he was sending in his resignation. M. Madeleine hastened to write to the Thénardiers. Fantine owed them over 120 francs, and he sent them 300, bidding them pay themselves out of the amount, and bring the child at once to M——, where a sick mother was awaiting it. This dazzled Thénardier. "Hang it all!" he said to his wife, "we must not let the brat go, for the lark will become a milch cow for us. I see it all; some fellow has fallen in love with the mother." He replied by sending a bill for 500 and odd francs very well drawn up. In this bill two undeniable amounts figure, one from a physician, the other from an apothecary, who had attended Éponine and Azelma in a long illness. Cosette, as we said, had not been ill, and hence it was merely a little substitution of names. At the bottom of the bill Thénardier gave credit for 300 francs received on account. M. Madeleine at once sent 300 francs more, and wrote, "Make haste and bring Cosette."

"Christi!" said Thénardier, "we must not let the child go."

In the mean while Fantine did not recover, and still remained in the infirmary. The sisters had at first received and nursed "this girl" with some repugnance; any one who has seen the bas-relief at Rheims will remember the pouting lower lip of the wise virgins looking at the foolish virgins. This ancient contempt of Vestals for Ambubaïæ is one of the deepest instincts of the feminine dignity, and the sisters had experienced it, with the increased dislike which religion adds. But in a few days Fantine disarmed them; she had all sorts of humble and gentle words, and the mother within her was touching. One day the sisters heard her say in the paroxysm of fever, "I have been a sinner, but when I have my child by my side, that will show that God has forgiven me. While I was living badly, I should not have liked to have Cosette with me, for I could not have endured her sad and astonished eyes. And yet it was for her sake that I did wrong, and for that reason God pardons me. I shall feel the blessing of Heaven when Cosette is here; I shall look at her, and it will do me good to see the innocent creature. She knows nothing, as she is an angel. My sisters, at her age the wings have not yet dropped off."

M. Madeleine went to see her twice a day, and every time she asked him, "Shall I see my Cosette soon?"

He would answer,—

"To-morrow, perhaps; she may arrive at any moment, for I am expecting her."

And the mother's pale face would grow radiant.

"Oh!" she said, "how happy I shall be!"

We have said that she did not improve; on the contrary, her condition seemed to grow worse week by week. The handful of snow placed between her naked shoulder-blades produced a sudden check of perspiration, which caused the illness that had smouldered in her for years suddenly to break out. Larmier's fine method for studying and healing diseases of the lungs was just beginning to be employed; the physician placed the stethoscope to Fantine's chest, and shook his head. M. Madeleine said to him,—

"Well?"

"Has she not a child that she wishes to see?" asked the doctor.

"Yes."

"Well, make haste to send for her."

Madeleine gave a start, and Fantine asked him,—

"What did the doctor say to you?"

M. Madeleine forced a smile.

"He said that your child must come at once, for that would cure you."

"Oh," she replied, "he is right; but what do those Thénardiers mean by keeping my Cosette? Oh, she will come, and then I shall see happiness close to me."

Thénardier, however, would not let the child go, and alleged a hundred poor excuses. Cosette was ailing, and it would be dangerous for her to travel in winter; and then there were some small debts still to pay, which he was collecting, &c.

"I will send some one to fetch Cosette," said Father Madeleine; "if necessary, I will go myself."

He wrote to Fantine's dictation the following letter, which she signed.

"M. THÉNARDIER,—" You will hand over Cosette to the bearer, who will pay up all little matters. "Yours, FANTINE."

About this time a great incident happened. However cleverly we may have carved the mysterious block of which our life is made, the black vein of destiny ever reappears in it.

CHAPTER II.

HOW "JEAN" MAY BECOME "CHAMP."

One morning M. Madeleine was in his study, engaged in settling some pressing mayoralty matters, in case he decided on the journey to Montfermeil, when he was told that Inspector Javert wished to speak with him. On hearing this name pronounced, M. Madeleine could not refrain from a disagreeable impression. Since the guard-room adventure Javert had avoided him more than ever, and M. Madeleine had not seen him again.

"Show him in," he said.

Javert entered. M. Madeleine remained at his table near the fire-place with a pen in his hand and his eyes fixed on a bundle of papers, which he ran through and annotated. He did not put himself out of the way for Javert, for he could not refrain from thinking of poor Fantine. Javert bowed respectfully to the Mayor, who had his back turned to him; the Mayor did not look at him, but continued to make his notes. Javert walked a little way into the study, and then halted without a word. A physiognomist familiar with Javert's nature, and who had studied for any length of time this savage in the service of civilization,—this strange composite of the Roman, the Spartan, the monk, and the corporal, this spy incapable of falsehood, this virgin detective,—a physiognomist aware of his secret and old aversion to M. Madeleine, and his conflict with him about Fantine, and who regarded Javert at this moment, would have asked himself, What has happened? It was evident to any one who knew this upright, clear, sincere, honest, austere, and ferocious conscience, that Javert had just emerged from some great internal struggle. Javert had nothing in his mind which he did not also have in his face, and, like all violent men, he was subject to sudden changes. Never had his face been stranger or more surprising. On entering, he bowed to M. Madeleine with a look in which there was neither rancor, anger, nor suspicion; he had halted a few yards behind the Mayor's chair, and was now standing there in an almost military attitude, with the simple cold rudeness of a man who has never been gentle and has ever been patient. He was waiting, without saying a word, without making a movement, in a true humility and tranquil resignation, till the Mayor might think proper to turn round,—calm, serious, hat in hand, and with an expression which was half-way between the private before his officer and the culprit before the judge. All the feelings as well as all the resolutions he might be supposed to possess had disappeared: there was nothing but a gloomy sadness on this face, which was impenetrable and simple as granite. His whole person displayed humiliation and firmness, and a sort of courageous despondency. At length the Mayor laid down his pen and half turned round.

"Well, what is the matter, Javert?"

Javert remained silent for a moment, as if reflecting, and then raised his voice with a sad solemnity, which, however, did not exclude simplicity.

"A culpable deed has been committed, sir."

"What deed?"

"An inferior agent of authority has failed in his respect to a magistrate in the gravest matter. I have come, as is my duty, to bring the fact to your knowledge."

"Who is this agent?" M. Madeleine asked

"Myself."

"And who is the magistrate who has cause to complain of the agent?"

"You, Monsieur le Maire."

M. Madeleine sat up, and Javert continued with a stern air and still looking down,—

"Monsieur le Maire, I have come to request that you will procure my dismissal from the service."

M. Madeleine in his stupefaction opened his mouth, but Javert interrupted him,—

"You will say that I could have sent in my resignation, but that is not enough. Such a course is honorable, but I have done wrong, and deserve punishment. I must be dismissed."

And after a pause he added,—

"Monsieur le Maire, you were severe to me the other day unjustly, be so to-day justly."

"What is the meaning of all this nonsense?" M. Madeleine exclaimed. "What is the culpable act you have committed? What have you done to me? You accuse yourself, you wish to be removed—"

"Dismissed," said Javert.

"Very good, dismissed. I do not understand it."

"You shall do so, sir."

Javert heaved a deep sigh, and continued still coldly and sadly,—

"Six weeks ago, M. le Maire, after the scene about that girl, I was furious, and denounced you."

"Denounced me?"

"To the Prefect of Police at Paris."

M. Madeleine, who did not laugh much oftener than Javert, burst into a laugh.

"As a Mayor who had encroached on the police?"

"As an ex-galley slave."

The Mayor turned livid, but Javert, who had not raised his eyes, continued,—

"I thought you were so, and have had these notions for a long time. A resemblance, information you sought at Faverolles, the strength of your loins, the adventures with old Fauchelevent, your skill in firing, your leg which halts a little—and so on. It was very absurd, but I took you for a man of the name of Jean Valjean."

"What name did you say?"

"Jean Valjean; he is a convict I saw twenty years ago when I was assistant keeper at the Toulon bagne. On leaving the galley, this Valjean, as it appears, robbed a bishop, and then committed a highway robbery on a little Savoyard. For eight years he has been out of the way and could not be found, and I imagined—in a word, I did as I said. Passion decided me, and I denounced you to the Prefect."

M. Madeleine, who had taken up the charge-book again, said with a careless accent,—

"And what was the answer you received?"

"That I was mad!"

"Well?"

"They were right."

"It is fortunate that you allow it."

"I must do so, for the real Jean Valjean has been found."

The book M. Madeleine was holding fell from his grasp, he raised his head, looked searchingly at Javert, said with an indescribable accent,—

"Ah!"

Javert continued,—

"The facts are these, M. le Maire. It seems that there was over at Ailly le Haut Clocher, an old fellow who was called Father Champmathieu. He was very wretched, and no attention was paid to him, for no one knows how such people live. This autumn Father Champmathieu was arrested for stealing cider apples: there was a robbery, a wall climbed over, and branches broken. This Champmathieu was arrested with the branch still in his hand, and was locked up. Up to this point it is only a matter for a police court, but here Providence interposes. As the lock-up was under repair, the magistrates ordered that Champmathieu should be taken to the departmental prison at Arras. In this prison there is an ex-convict of the name of Brevet, under imprisonment for some offence, and he has been made room-turnkey for his good behavior. Champmathieu no sooner arrived than Brevet cries out, "Why, I know this man: he is an ex-convict. Look at me, old fellow: you are Jean Valjean." "What do you mean?" says Champmathieu, affecting surprise. "Don't play the humbug with me," says Brevet; "you are Jean Valjean. You were at the Toulon bagne twenty years ago, and I was there too." Champmathieu denied identity, and, as you may suppose, the affair was thoroughly investigated, with the following result. This Champmathieu about thirty years ago was a journeyman wood-cutter at several places, especially at Faverolles, where his trail is lost. A long time after he is found again in Auvergne, and then in Paris, where he says he was a blacksmith, and had a daughter a washer-woman,— though there is no evidence of this,—and lastly, he turned up in these parts. Now, before being sent to the galleys, what was Jean Valjean? A wood-cutter. Where? At Faverolles. And here is another fact: this Valjean's Christian name was Jean, and his mother's family name Mathieu. What is more natural to suppose than that on leaving the bagne he assumed his mother's name as a disguise, and called himself Jean Mathieu? He went to Auvergne, where Jean is pronounced Chan, and thus he was transformed into Champmathieu. You are following me, I suppose? Inquiries have been made at Faverolles, but Jean Valjean's family is no longer there, and no one knows where it has gone. As you are aware, in those places families frequently disappear in such a way; these people, if they are not mud, are dust. And then, again, as the beginning of this story dates back thirty years, there is no one in Faverolles who knew Jean Valjean: and beside Brevet, there are only two convicts who remember him. These two were brought from the bagne and confronted with the pretended Champmathieu, and they did not hesitate for a moment. The same age,— fifty-four,—the same height, the same look, the same man, in short. It was at this very moment that I sent my denunciation to Paris, and the answer I received was that I had lost my senses, for Jean Valjean was in the hands of justice at Arras. You can conceive that this surprised me, as I fancied that I held my Jean Valjean here. I wrote to the magistrates, who sent for me, and Champmathieu was brought in."

"Well?" M. Madeleine interrupted him.

Javert answered with his incorruptible and sad face,—

"Monsieur le Maire, truth is truth: I am sorry, but that man is Jean Valjean: I recognized him too."

M. Madeleine said in a very low voice,—

"Are you sure?"

Javert burst into that sorrowful laugh which escapes from a profound conviction,—

"Oh! certain."

He stood for a moment pensive, mechanically taking pinches of saw-dust out of the sprinkler in the inkstand, and added,—

"And now that I have seen the real Jean Valjean, I cannot understand how I could have believed anything else. I ask your pardon, M. le Maire."

While addressing these supplicating words to the person who six weeks previously had humiliated him so deeply and bidden him leave the room, this haughty man was unconsciously full of dignity and simplicity. M. Madeleine merely answered his entreaty with the hurried question,—

"And what does this man say?"

"Well, Monsieur le Maire, it is an ugly business, for if he is Jean Valjean, he is an escaped convict. Scaling a wall, breaking a branch, and stealing apples is a peccadillo with a child, an offence in a man, but a crime in a convict. It is no longer a matter for the police courts, but for the assizes; it is no longer imprisonment for a few days, but the galleys for life. And there is the matter with the Savoyard, which, I trust, will be brought up again. There is enough to settle a man, is there not? But Jean Valjean is artful, and in that I recognize him too. Any other man would find it warm; he would struggle, cry out, refuse to be Jean Valjean, and so on. He pretends though not to understand, and says, "I am Champmathieu, and I shall stick to it." He has a look of amazement, and plays the brute-beast, which is better. Oh! he is a clever scoundrel! But no matter, the proofs are ready to hand; he has been recognized by four persons, and the old scoundrel will be found guilty. He is to be tried at Arras assizes, and I have been summoned as a witness."

M. Madeleine had turned round to his desk again, taken up his papers, and was quietly turning over the leaves, and busily reading and writing in turn. He now said to the Inspector,—

"Enough, Javert; after all, these details interest me but very slightly; we are losing our time, and have a deal of work before us. Javert, you will go at one to Mother Busaupied, who sells vegetables at the corner of the Rue St. Saulve, and tell her to take out a summons against Pierre the carter; he is a brutal fellow, who almost drove over this woman and her child, and he must be punished. You will then go to M. Charcillay in the Rue Champigny; he complains that there is a gutter next door which leaks, and is shaking the foundation of his house. But I am giving you a deal to do, and I think you said you were going away. Did you not state you were going to Arras on this matter in a week or ten days?"

"Sooner than that, sir."

"On what day, then?"

"I fancied I told you that the trial comes off to-morrow, and that I should start by to-night's coach."

"And how long will the trial last?"

"A day at the most, and sentence will be passed to-morrow night at the latest. But I shall not wait for that, but return so soon as I have given my evidence."

"Very good," said M. Madeleine; and he dismissed Javert with a wave of his hand. But he did not go.

"I beg your pardon, M. le Maire," he said.

"What's the matter now?" M. Madeleine asked.

"I have one thing to remind you of, sir."

"What is it?"

"That I must be discharged."

M. Madeleine rose.

"Javert, you are a man of honor, and I esteem you; you exaggerate your fault, and besides, it is another insult which concerns me. Javert, you are worthy of rising, not of sinking, and I insist on your keeping your situation."

Javert looked at M. Madeleine with his bright eyes, in which it seemed as if his unenlightened but rigid and chaste conscience could be seen, and he said quietly,—

"M. le Maire, I cannot allow it."

"I repeat," M. Madeleine replied, "that the affair concerns myself."

But Javert, only attending to his own thoughts, continued,—

"As for exaggerating, I am not doing so, for this is how I reason. I suspected you unjustly; that is nothing: it is the duty of men like myself to suspect, though there is an abuse in suspecting those above us. But, without proofs, in a moment of passion and for the purpose of revenge, I denounced you, a respectable man, a mayor and a magistrate; this is serious, very serious,—I, an agent of the authority, insulted that authority in your person. Had any of my subordinates done what I have done, I should have declared him unworthy of the service and discharged him. Stay, Monsieur le Maire, one word more. I have often been severe in my life to others, for it was just, and I was doing my duty, and if I were not severe to myself now, all the justice I have done would become injustice. Ought I to spare myself more than others? No. What! I have been only good to punish others and not myself? Why, I should be a scoundrel, and the people who call me that rogue of a Javert, would be in the right! M. le Maire, I do not wish you to treat me with kindness, for your kindness caused me sufficient ill-blood when dealt to others, and I want none for myself. The kindness that consists in defending the street-walker against the gentleman, the police agent against the Mayor, the lower classes against the higher, is what I call bad kindness, and it is such kindness that disorganizes society. Good Lord! it is easy enough to be good, but the difficulty is to be just. Come! if you had been what I believed you, I should not have been kind to you, as you would have seen. M. le Maire, I am bound to treat myself as I would treat another man; when I repressed malefactors, when I was severe with scamps, I often said to myself, "If you ever catch yourself tripping, look out," I have tripped, I have committed a fault, and all the worse for me. I have strong arms and will turn laborer. M. le Maire, the good of the service requires an example. I simply demand the discharge of Inspector Javert."

All this was said with a humble, proud, despairing, and convinced accent, which gave a peculiar grandeur to this strangely honest man.

"We will see," said M. Madeleine, and he offered him his hand; but Javert fell back, and said sternly,—

"Pardon me, sir, but that must not be; a mayor ought not to give his hand to a spy."

He added between his teeth,—

"Yes, a spy; from the moment when I misused my authority, I have been only a spy."

Then he bowed deeply and walked to the door. When he reached it he turned round and said, with eyes still bent on the ground,—

"M. le Maire, I will continue on duty till my place is filled up."

He went out. M. Madeleine thoughtfully listened to his firm, sure step as he walked along the paved passage.

BOOK VII

THE CHAMPMATHIEU AFFAIR.

CHAPTER I.

SISTER SIMPLICE.

The incidents we are about to record were only partially known at M——, but the few which were known left such a memory in that town, that it would be a serious gap in this book if we did not tell them in their smallest details. In these details the reader will notice two or three improbable circumstances, which we retain through respect for truth. In the afternoon that followed

Javert's visit, M. Madeleine went to see Fantine as usual; but before going to her, he asked for Sister Simplice. The two nuns who managed the infirmary, who were Lazarets, like all sisters of charity, were known by the names of Sisters Perpetua and Simplice. Sister Perpetua was an ordinary village girl, a clumsy sister of charity, who had entered the service of Heaven just as she would have taken a cook's place. This type is not rare, for the monastic orders gladly accept this clumsy peasant clay, which can be easily fashioned into a Capuchin friar or an Ursuline nun; and these rusticities are employed in the heavy work of devotion. The transition from a drover to a Carmelite is no hard task; the common substratum of village and cloister ignorance is a ready-made preparation, and at once places the countryman on a level with the monk. Widen the blouse a little and you have a gown. Sister Perpetua was a strong nun belonging to Marnies near Pantoise, who talked with a country accent, sang psalms to match, sugared the *tisane* according to the bigotry or hypocrisy of the patient, was rough with the sick, and harsh with the dying, almost throwing God in their faces, and storming their last moments with angry prayer. Withal she was bold, honest, and red-faced.

Sister Simplice was pale, and looked like a wax taper by the side of Sister Perpetua, who was a tallow candle in comparison. St. Vincent de Paul has divinely described the sister of charity in those admirable words in which so much liberty is blended with slavery: "They will have no other convent but the hospital, no other cell but a hired room, no chapel but the parish church, no cloister beyond the streets or the hospital wards, no walls but obedience, no grating but the fear of God, and no veil but modesty." Sister Simplice was the living ideal of this: no one could have told her age, for she had never been young, and seemed as if she would never grow old. She was a gentle, austere, well-nurtured, cold person—we dare not say a woman—who had never told a falsehood; she was so gentle that she appeared fragile, but she was more solid than granite. She touched the wretched with her delicate and pure fingers. There was, so to speak, silence in her language; she only said what was necessary, and possessed an intonation of voice which would at once have edified a confessional and delighted a drawing-room. This delicacy harmonized with the rough gown, for it formed in this rough contact a continual reminder of heaven. Let us dwell on one detail; never to have told a falsehood, never to have said, for any advantage or even indifferently, a thing which was not the truth, the holy truth, was the characteristic feature of Sister Simplice. She was almost celebrated in the congregation for this imperturbable veracity, and the Abbé Suard alludes to Sister Simplice in a letter to the deaf, mute Massieu. However sincere and pure we may be, we have all the brand of a little white lie on our candor, but she had not. Can there be such a thing as a white lie, an innocent lie? Lying is the absolute of evil. Lying a little is not possible; the man who lies tells the whole lie; lying is the face of the fiend, and Satan has two names,—he is called Satan and Lying. That is what she thought, and she practised as she thought. The result was the whiteness to which we have alluded, a whiteness which even covered with its radiance her lips and eyes, for her smile was white, her glance was white. There was not a spider's web nor a grain of dust on the window of this conscience; on entering the obedience of St. Vincent de Paul she took the name of Simplice through special choice. Simplice of Sicily, our readers will remember, is the saint who sooner let her bosom be plucked out than say she was a native of Segeste, as she was born at Syracuse, though the falsehood would have saved her. Such a patron saint suited this soul.

Simplice on entering the order had two faults, of which she had gradually corrected herself; she had a taste for dainties and was fond of receiving letters. Now she never read anything but a Prayer-book in large type and in Latin; though she did not understand the language, she understood the book. This pious woman felt an affection for Fantine, as she probably noticed the latent virtue in her, and nearly entirely devoted herself to nursing her. M. Madeleine took Sister Simplice on one side and recommended Fantine to her with a singular accent, which the sister remembered afterwards. On leaving the sister he went to Fantine. The patient daily awaited the appearance of M. Madeleine, as if he brought her warmth and light; she said to the sisters, "I only live when M. le Maire is here." This day she was very feverish, and so soon as she saw M. Madeleine she asked him,—

"Where is Cosette?"

He replied with a smile, "She will be here soon."

M. Madeleine behaved to Fantine as usual, except that he remained with her an hour instead of half an hour, to her great delight. He pressed everybody not to allow the patient to want for anything, and it was noticed at one moment that his face became very dark, but this was explained when it was learned that the physician had bent down to his ear and said, "She is rapidly sinking." Then he returned to the Mayoralty, and the office clerk saw him attentively examining a road-map of France which hung in his room, and write a few figures in pencil on a piece of paper.

CHAPTER II

SCAUFFLAIRE'S PERSPICACITY.

From the Mayoralty M. Madeleine proceeded to the end of the town, to a Fleming called Master Scaufflaer, gallicized into Scaufflaire, who let out horses and gigs by the day. To reach his yard the nearest way was through an unfrequented street, in which stood the house of the parish priest. The Curé was said to be a worthy and respectable man, who gave good advice. At the moment when M. Madeleine came in front of his house there was only one person in the street, and he noticed the following circumstances: M. le Maire, after passing the house, stopped for a moment, then turned back and walked up to the Curé's door, which had an iron knocker. He quickly seized the knocker and lifted it; then he stopped again as if in deep thought, and, after a few seconds, instead of knocking, he softly let the knocker fall back in its place and continued his way with a haste which he had not displayed before.

M. Madeleine found Master Scaufflaire at home and engaged in mending a set of harness.

"Master Scaufflaire", he inquired, "have you a good horse?"

"M. le Maire," the Fleming replied, "all my horses are good. What do you mean by a good horse?"

"I mean a horse that can cover twenty leagues of ground in a day."

"Harnessed in a gig?"

"Yes."

"And how long will it rest after the journey?"

"It must be in a condition to start again the next morning if necessary."

"To return the same distance?"

"Yes."

"Hang it all! and it is twenty leagues?"

M. Madeleine took from his pocket the paper on which he had pencilled the figures; they were "5, 6, 8 1/2."

"You see," he said, "total, nineteen and a half, or call them twenty leagues."

"M. le Maire," the Fleming continued, "I can suit you. My little white horse— you may have seen it pass sometimes—is an animal from the Bas Boulonnais, and full of fire. They tried at first to make a saddle-horse of it, but it reared and threw everybody that got on its back. It was supposed to be vicious, and they did not know what to do with it; I bought it and put it in a gig. That was just what it wanted; it is as gentle as a maid and goes like the wind. But you must not try to get on its back, for it has no notion of being a saddle-horse. Everybody has his ambition, and it appears as if the horse had said to itself,—

Draw, yes; carry, no."

"And it will go the distance?"

"At a trot, and under eight hours, but on certain conditions."

"What are they?"

"In the first place, you will let it breathe for an hour half way; it will feed, and you must be present while it is doing so, to prevent the ostler stealing the oats, for I have noticed that at inns oats are more frequently drunk by the stable-boys than eaten by the horses."

"I will be there."

"In the next place, is the gig for yourself, sir?"

"Yes."

"Do you know how to drive?"

"Yes."

"Well, you must travel alone and without luggage, in order not to overweight the horse."

"Agreed."

"I shall expect thirty francs a day, and the days of rest paid for as well,—not a farthing less; and you will pay for the horse's keep."

M. Madeleine took three napoleons from his purse and laid them on the table.

"There are two days in advance."

"In the fourth place, a cabriolet would be too heavy for such a journey, and tire the horse. You must oblige me by travelling in a little tilbury I have."

"I consent."

"It is light, but it is open."

"I do not care."

"Have you thought, sir, that it is now winter?"

M. Madeleine made no answer, and the Fleming continued,—

"That it is very cold?"

Monsieur Madeleine was still silent.

"That it may rain?"

The Mayor raised his head and said,—

"The tilbury and the horse will be before my door at half-past four to-morrow morning."

"Very good, sir," Scaufflaire answered; then scratching with his thumb-nail a stain in the wood of his table, he continued, with that careless air with which the Flemings so cleverly conceal their craft,—

"Good gracious! I have not thought of asking where you are going? Be kind enough to tell me, sir."

He had thought of nothing else since the beginning of the conversation, but somehow he had not dared to ask the question.

"Has your horse good legs?" said M. Madeleine.

"Yes, M. le Maire; you will hold it up a little in going down-hill. Are there many hills between here and the place you are going to?"

"Do not forget to be at my door at half-past four exactly," M. Madeleine answered, and went away.

The Fleming stood "like a fool," as he said himself a little while after. M. le Maire had been gone some two or three minutes when the door opened again; it was M. le Maire. He still wore the same impassive and preoccupied air.

"M. Scaufflaire," he said, "at how much do you value the tilbury and horse you are going to let me, one with the other?"

"Do you wish to buy them of me, sir?"

"No, but I should like to guarantee them against any accident, and when I come back you can return me the amount. What is the estimated value?"

"Five hundred francs, M. le Maire."

"Here they are."

M. Madeleine laid a bank note on the table, then went out, and this time did not come back. Master Scaufflaire regretted frightfully that he had not said a thousand francs, though tilbury and horse, at a fair valuation, were worth just three hundred. The Fleming called his wife and told her what had occurred. "Where the deuce can the Mayor be going?" They held a council. "He is going to Paris," said the wife. "I don't believe it," said the husband. M. Madeleine had left on the table the paper on which he had written the figures; the Fleming took it up and examined it. "'5, 6, 8 1/2;' why, that must mean post stations." He turned to his wife: "I have found it out." "How?" "It is five leagues from here to Hesdin, six from there to St. Pol, and eight and a half from St. Pol to Arras. He is going to Arras."

In the mean while the Mayor had returned home, and had taken the longest road, as if the gate of the priest's house were a temptation to him which he wished to avoid. He went up to his bed-room and locked himself in, which was not unusual, for he was fond of going to bed at an early hour. Still the factory portress, who was at the same time M. Madeleine's only servant, remarked that his candle was extinguished at a quarter-past eight, and mentioned the fact to the cashier when he came in, adding,—

"Can master be ill? I thought he looked very strange to-day." The cashier occupied a room exactly under M. Madeleine's; he paid no attention to the remarks of the portress, but went to bed and fell asleep. About midnight he woke with a start, for he heard in his sleep a noise above his head. He listened; it was a footfall coming and going, as if some one were walking about the room above him. He listened more attentively, and recognized M. Madeleine's step; and this seemed to him strange, for usually no sound could be heard from the Mayor's room till he rose. A moment later the cashier heard something like a wardrobe open and shut; a piece of furniture was moved, there was a silence, and the walking began again. The cashier sat up in bed, wide awake, looked out, and through his window noticed on a wall opposite, the red reflection of a lighted window; from the direction of the rays it could only be the window of M. Madeleine's bed-room. The reflection flickered as if it came from a fire rather than a candle, while the shadow of the framework could not be traced, which proved that the window was wide open, and this was a curious fact, considering the cold. The cashier fell asleep and woke again some two hours after; the same slow and regular footfall was still audible above his head. The reflection was still cast on the wall, but was now pale and quiet, as if it came from a lamp or a candle. The window was still open. This is what was occurring in M. Madeleine's bed-room.

CHAPTER III.

A TEMPEST IN A BRAIN.

The reader has, of course, guessed that M. Madeleine is Jean Valjean. We have already looked into the depths of this conscience, and the moment has arrived to look into them again. We do not do this without emotion or tremor, for there is nothing more terrifying than this species of contemplation. The mental eye can nowhere find greater brilliancy or greater darkness than within man; it cannot dwell on anything which is more formidable, complicated, mysterious, or infinite. There is a spectacle grander than the sea, and that is the sky; there is a spectacle grander than the sky, and it is the interior of the soul. To write the poem of the human conscience, were the subject only one man, and he the lowest of men, would be to resolve all epic poems into one supreme and final epic. Conscience is the chaos of chimeras, envies, and attempts, the furnace of dreams, the lurking-place of ideas we are ashamed of; it is the pandemonium of sophistry, the battlefield of the passions. At certain hours look through the livid face of a reflecting man, look into his soul, peer into the darkness. Beneath the external silence, combats of giants are going on there, such as we read of in Homer; *mêlées* of dragons and hydras and clouds of phantoms, such as we find in Milton; and visionary spirals, as in Dante. A sombre thing is the infinitude which every man bears within him, and by which he desperately measures the volitions of his brain and the actions of his life. Alighieri one day came to a gloomy gate, before which he hesitated; we have one before us, on the threshold of which we also hesitate, but we will enter.

We have but little to add to what the reader already knows as having happened to Jean Valjean since his adventure with Little Gervais. From this moment, as we have seen, he became another man, and he made himself what the Bishop wished to make him. It was more than a transformation, it was a transfiguration. He succeeded in disappearing, sold the Bishop's plate, only keeping the candlesticks as a souvenir, passed through France, reached M——, had the idea we have described, accomplished what we have narrated, managed to make himself unseizable and inaccessible, and henceforth settled at M——, happy at feeling his conscience saddened by the past, and the first half of his existence contradicted by the last half; he lived peacefully, reassured and trusting, and having but two thoughts,—to hide his name and sanctify his life; escape from men and return to God. These two thoughts were so closely blended in his mind, that they only formed one; they were both equally absorbing and imperious, and governed his slightest actions. Usually they agreed to regulate the conduct of his life; they turned him toward the shadow; they rendered him beneficent and simple, and they counselled him the same things. At times, however, there was a conflict between them, and in such cases the man whom the whole town of M—— called Monsieur Madeleine did not hesitate to sacrifice the first to the second,—his security to his virtue. Hence, despite all his caution and prudence, he had kept the Bishop's candlesticks, worn mourning for him, questioned all the little Savoyards who passed through the town, inquired after the family at Faverolles, and saved the life of old Fauchelevent, in spite of the alarming insinuations of Javert. It seemed, as we have already remarked, that he thought, after the example of all those who have been wise, holy, and just, that his first duty was not toward himself.

Still, we are bound to say, nothing like the present had before occurred; never had the two ideas which governed the unhappy man whose sufferings we are describing, entered upon so serious a struggle. He comprehended confusedly, but deeply, from the first words which Javert uttered on entering his study. At the moment when the name which he had buried so deeply was so strangely pronounced, he was struck with stupor, and, as it were, intoxicated by the sinister peculiarity of his destiny. And through this stupor he felt that quivering which precedes great storms; he bowed like an oak at the approach of a storm, like a soldier before a coming assault. He felt the shadows full of thunder and lightning collecting over his head: while listening to Javert he had a thought of running off, denouncing himself, taking Champmathieu out of prison, and taking his place. This was painful, like an incision in the flesh; but it passed away, and he said to himself, "We will see!" he repressed this first generous movement, and recoiled before his heroism.

It would doubtless be grand if, after the Bishop's holy remarks, after so many years of repentance and self-denial, in the midst of a penitence so admirably commenced, this man, even in the presence of such a terrible conjuncture, had not failed for a moment, but continued to march at the same pace toward this open abyss, at the bottom of which heaven was: this would be grand, but it did not take place. We are bound to describe all the things that took place in this mind, and cannot say that this was one of them. What carried him away first was the instinct of self-preservation. He hastily collected his ideas, stifled his emotion, deferred any resolution with the firmness of terror, deadened himself against what he had to do, and resumed his calmness as a gladiator puts up his buckler. For the remainder of the day he was in the same state,—a hurricane within, a deep tranquillity outside,—and he only took what may be called "conservative measures." All was still confused and jumbled in his brain; the trouble in it was so great that he did not see distinctly the outline of any idea, and he could have said nothing about himself, save that he had received a heavy blow. He went as usual to Fantine's bed of pain, and prolonged his visit, with a kindly instinct, saying to himself that he must act thus, and recommend her to the sisters in the event of his being obliged to go away. He felt vaguely that he must perhaps go to Arras; and, though not the least in the world decided about the journey, he said to himself that, safe from suspicion as he was, there would be no harm in being witness of what might take place, and he hired Scaufflaire's tilbury, in order to be ready for any event.

He dined with considerable appetite, and, on returning to his bed-room, reflected. He examined his situation, and found it extraordinary,—so extraordinary that, in the midst of his reverie, through some almost inexplicable impulse of anxiety, he rose from his chair and bolted his door. He was afraid lest something might enter, and he barricaded himself against the possible. A moment after, he blew out his light, for it annoyed him, and he fancied that he might be overseen. By whom? Alas! what he wanted to keep out had entered; what he wished to blind was looking at him. It was his conscience, that is to say, God. Still, at the first moment, he deceived himself; he had a feeling of security and solitude. When he put in the bolt, he thought himself impregnable; when the candle was out, he felt himself invisible. He then regained his self-possession; and he put his elbows on the table, leaned his head on his hand, and began dreaming in the darkness.

"Where am I? Am I not dreaming? What was I told? Is it really true that I saw that Javert, and that he spoke to me so? Who can this Champmathieu be? It seems he resembles me. Is it possible? When I think that I was so tranquil yesterday, and so far from suspecting anything! What was I doing yesterday at this hour? What will be the result of this event? What am I to do?"

Such was the trouble he was in that his brain had not the strength to retain ideas. They passed like waves, and he clutched his forehead with both hands to stop them. From this tumult which overthrew his wits and reason, and from which he sought to draw an evidence and a resolution, nothing issued but agony. His head was burning; and he went by the window and threw it wide open. There were no stars in the heavens, and he went back to the table and sat down by it. The first hour passed away thus, but gradually vague features began to shape themselves, and become fixed in his thoughts, and he could observe with the precision of reality some details of the situation, if not its entirety. He began by noticing that however critical and extraordinary his situation might be, he was utterly the master of it, and his stupor was only augmented.

Independently of the stern and religious object he proposed to himself in his actions, all that he had done up to this day was only a hole he dug in which to bury his name. What he had always most feared, in his hours of reflection as in his sleepless nights, was ever to hear *that* name pronounced. He said to himself that this would be to him the end of everything; that on the day when that name re-appeared, it would cause his new life to fade away, and possibly the new soul he had within him. He shuddered at the mere thought that this could happen. Assuredly if any one had told him at such moments that the hour would arrive in which this name would echo in his ear, when the hideous name of Jean Valjean would suddenly emerge from the night and rise before him, when this formidable light which dissipated the mystery with which he surrounded himself would suddenly shine above his head, and that the name would no longer menace him; that the light would produce only a denser gloom; that this rent veil would increase the mystery; that the earthquake would consolidate his edifice; that this prodigious incident would have no other result, if he thought proper, but to render his existence clearer and yet more impenetrable, and that from his confrontation with the phantom of Jean Valjean, the good and worthy M. Madeleine would come forth more honored, more peaceful, and more respected than ever,—if any one had told him this, he would have shaken his head, and considered such talk insane. And yet all this had really happened, and this heap of impossibilities was a fact, and Heaven had permitted all these wild things to become real.

His reverie continued to grow clearer, and each moment he comprehended his position better. It seemed to him that he had just awakened from a dream, and that he was descending an incline in the middle of the night, shuddering and recoiling in vain from the brink of an abyss. He distinctly saw in the shadows an unknown man, a stranger, whom destiny took for him, and thrust into the gulf in his place. In order that the gulf should close, either he or another must fall in. He had no necessity to do anything, the clearness became complete, and he confessed to himself—that his place was vacant at the galleys; that, whatever he might do, it constantly expected him, that the robbery of Little Gervais led him back to it, that this vacant place would wait for him and attract him until he filled it, and that this was inevitable and fatal. And then he said to himself that at this moment he had a substitute,—that it seemed a man of the name of Champmathieu had this ill-luck; and that, in future, himself at the bagne in the person of this Champmathieu, and present in society under the name of M. Madeleine, would have nothing more to fear, provided that he did not prevent justice from laying over the head of this Champmathieu the stone of infamy which, like the tombstone, falls once and is never raised again.

All this was so violent and so strange, that he suddenly felt within him that species of indescribable movement which no man experiences more than twice or thrice in his life,—a sort of convulsion of the conscience, which disturbs everything doubtful in the heart, which is composed of irony, joy, and despair, and what might be called an internal burst of laughter. He suddenly relit his candle.

"Well, what am I afraid of?" he said to himself; "what reason have I to have such thoughts? I am saved, and all is settled. There was only one open door through which my past could burst in upon my life: and that door is now walled up forever. That Javert, who has so long annoyed me, the formidable instinct which seemed to have scented me, and by Heavens! had scented me, the frightful dog ever making a point at me, is routed, engaged elsewhere, and absolutely thrown out! He is henceforth satisfied, he will leave me at peace, for he has got his Jean Valjean! It is possible that he may wish to leave the town too. And all this has taken place without my interference, and so, what is there so unlucky in it all? On my word, any people who saw me would believe that a catastrophe had befallen me. After all, if some people are rendered unhappy, it is no fault of mine. Providence has done it all, and apparently decrees it. Have I the right to derange what He arranges? What is it that I am going to interfere in? It does not concern me. What! I am not satisfied? Why! what else can I want? I have attained the object to which I have been aspiring for so many years, the dream of my nights, the matter of my prayers,—security. It is Heaven that wills it, and I have done nothing contrary to God's desire. And why has Heaven decreed it? That I may continue what I have begun; that I may do good; that I may one day be a grand and encouraging example; that it may be said that there is after all a little happiness attaching to the penance I have undergone. I really cannot understand why I was so afraid just now about visiting that worthy Curé, telling all to him as to a confessor, and asking his advice, for this is certainly what he would have advised me. It is settled; I will let matters take their course, and leave the decision to Heaven."

He spoke this in the depths of his conscience, while leaning over what might be called his own abyss. He got up from his chair and walked about the room. "Come," he said, "I will think no more of it; I have made up my mind;" but he felt no joy. It is no more possible to prevent thought from reverting to an idea than the sea from returning to the shore. With the sailor this is called the tide, with the culprit it is called remorse; God heaves the soul like the ocean. After a few moments, whatever he might do, he resumed the gloomy dialogue in which it was he who spoke and he who listened, saying what he wished to be silent about, listening to what he did not desire to hear, and yielding to that mysterious power which said to him "Think," as it did, two thousand years ago, to another condemned man, "Go on."

Before going further, and in order to be fully understood, let us dwell on a necessary observation. It is certain that men talk to themselves; and there is not a thinking being who has not realized the fact. It is only in this sense that the words frequently employed in this chapter, *he said, he exclaimed,* must be understood; men talk to themselves, speak to themselves, cry out within themselves, but the external silence is not interrupted. There is a grand tumult; everything speaks to us, excepting the mouth. The realities of the soul, for all that they are not visible and palpable, are not the less realities. He asked himself then, what he had arrived at, and cross-questioned himself about the resolution he had formed. He confessed to himself that all he had arranged in his mind was monstrous, and that leaving "God to act" was simply horrible. To allow this mistake of destiny and of men to be accomplished, not to prevent it, to lend himself to it, do nothing, in short, was to do everything; it was the last stage of hypocritical indignity! It was a low, cowardly, cunning, abject, hideous crime. For the first time during eight years this hapless man had the taste of a bad thought and a bad action, and he spat it out in disgust.

He continued to cross-question himself. He asked himself what he had meant by the words, "my object is attained"? He allowed that his life had an object, but what was its nature?—Conceal his name! deceive the police. Was it for so paltry a thing that he had done all that he had effected? Had he not another object which was the great and true one,—to save not his person, but his soul; to become once again honest and good? To be a just man! was it not that he craved solely, and that the Bishop had ordered him? Close the door on his past? But, great Heaven, he opened it again by committing an infamous action. He was becoming a robber once more, and the most odious of robbers! He was robbing another man of his existence, his livelihood, his peace, and his place in the sunshine. He was becoming an assassin, he was killing, morally killing, a wretched man; he was inflicting on him the frightful living death, the open-air death, which is called the galleys. On the other hand, if he gave himself up, freed this man who was suffering from so grievous an error, resumed his name, became through duty the convict Jean Valjean, that would be really completing his resurrection, and eternally closing the hell from which he was emerging! Falling back into it apparently would be leaving it in reality! He must do this: he would have done nothing unless he did this; all his life would be useless, all his penitence wasted. He felt that the Bishop was here, that he was the more present because he was dead, that the Bishop was steadfastly looking at him, and that henceforth Madeleine the Mayor would be an abomination to him, and Jean Valjean the convict admirable and pure in his sight. Men saw his mask, but the Bishop saw his face; men saw his life, but the Bishop saw his conscience. He must consequently go to Arras, deliver the false Jean Valjean, and denounce the true one. Alas! this was the greatest of sacrifices, the most poignant of victories, the last step to take; but he must take it. Frightful destiny his! he could not obtain sanctity in the sight of Heaven unless he returned to infamy in the sight of man.

"Well," he said, "I will make up my mind to this. I will do my duty and save this man."

He uttered those words aloud without noticing he had raised his voice. He fetched his books, verified and put them in order. He threw into the fire a number of claims he had upon embarrassed tradesmen, and wrote a letter, which he addressed "To M. Lafitte, banker, Rue d'Artois, Paris." He then took from his desk a pocket-book, which contained a few bank-notes and the passport he had employed just previously to go to the elections. Any one who had seen him while he was accomplishing these various acts, with which such grave meditation was mingled, would not have suspected what was taking place in him. At moments his lips moved, at others he raised his head and looked at a part of the wall, as if there were something there which he desired to clear up or question.

When the letter to M. Lafitte was finished, he put it into his portfolio, and began his walk once more. His reverie had not deviated; he continued to see his duty clearly written in luminous letters which flashed before his eyes, and moved about with his glance, Name yourself, denounce yourself! He could also see the two ideas which had hitherto been the double rule of his life—to hide his name and sanctify his life—moving before him as it were in a tangible shape. For the first time they seemed to him absolutely distinct, and he saw the difference that separated them. He recognized that one of these ideas was necessarily good, while the other might become bad; that the former was self-sacrifice, the latter selfishness; that one said, "My neighbor," the other "Myself;" that one came from the light and the other from darkness. They strove with each other, and he could see them doing so. While he was thinking, they had grown before his mental eye, and they had now colossal forms, and he fancied he could see a god and a giant wrestling within him, in the infinitude to which we just now alluded, and in the midst of obscurity and flashes of light. It was a horrible sight, but it seemed to him as if the good thought gained the victory. He felt that he was approaching the second decisive moment of his life; that the Bishop marked the first phase of his new life, and that this Champmathieu marked the second; after the great crisis came the great trial.

The fever, appeased for a moment, gradually returned, however. A thousand thoughts crossed his mind, but they continued to strengthen him in his resolution. At one moment he said to himself that he perhaps regarded the matter too seriously; that, after all, this Champmathieu did not concern him, and in any case was a thief. He answered himself: If this man has really stolen apples, he will have a month's imprisonment, but that is a long way from the galleys. And then, again, is it proved that he has committed a robbery? The name of Jean Valjean is crushing him, and seems to dispense with proofs. Do not public prosecutors habitually act in this way? A man is believed to be a thief because he is known to be a convict. At another moment the idea occurred to him that, when he had denounced himself, the heroism of his deed might perhaps be taken into consideration, as well as his life of honesty during the last seven years, and the good he had done the town, and that he would be pardoned. But this supposition soon vanished, and he smiled bitterly at the thought that the robbery of the 40 sous from Gervais rendered him a relapsed convict; that this affair would certainly be brought forward, and, by the precise terms of the law, sentence him to the galleys for life.

He turned away from all illusions, detached himself more and more from earth, and sought consolation and strength elsewhere. He said to himself that he must do his duty: that, perhaps, he would not be more wretched after doing it than he would have been had he eluded it: that, if he let matters take their course and remained at M——, his good name, good deeds, charity, wealth, popularity, and virtue would be tainted by a crime; and what flavor would all these sacred things have, when attached to this hideous thought; while, if he accomplished his sacrifice, he would mingle a heavenly idea with the galleys, the chain, the green cap, the unrelaxing toil, and the pitiless shame. At last he said to himself that it was a necessity, that his destiny was thus shaped, that he had no power to derange the arrangements of Heaven, and that in any case he must choose either external virtue and internal abomination, or holiness within and infamy outside him. His courage did not fail him in revolving so many mournful ideas, but his brain grew weary. He began thinking involuntarily of other and indifferent matters. His arteries beat violently in his temples, and he was still walking up and down; midnight struck, first from the parish church, and then from the Town Hall: he counted the twelve strokes of the two clocks, and compared the sound of the two bells. They reminded him that a few days before he had seen an old bell at a marine store, on which was engraved the name Antoine Albier, Romainville.

As he felt cold, he lit a fire, but did not dream of closing the window. Then he fell back into his stupor, obliged to make a mighty effort to remember what he had been thinking of before midnight struck. At last he succeeded.

"Ah, yes," he said to himself, "I had formed the resolution to denounce myself."

And then he suddenly began thinking of Fantine.

"Stay," he said; "and that poor woman!"

Here a fresh crisis broke out: Fantine, suddenly appearing in the midst of his reverie, was like a ray of unexpected light. He fancied that all changed around him, and exclaimed,—

"Wait a minute! Hitherto, I have thought of myself and consulted my own convenience. Whether it suits me to be silent or denounce myself—hide my person or save my soul—be a contemptible and respected Magistrate, or an infamous and venerable convict—it is always self, nought but self. Good heavens! all this is egotism; under different shapes, 't is true, but still egotism. Suppose I were to think a little about others! It is the first duty of a Christian to think of his neighbor. Well, let me examine: when I am effaced and forgotten, what will become of all this? If I denounce myself, that Champmathieu will be set at liberty. I shall be sent back to the galleys, and what then? What will occur here? Here are a town, factories, a trade, work-people, men, women, old grandfathers, children, and poor people: I have created all this. I keep it all alive: wherever there is a chimney smoking, I placed the brand in the fire and the meat in the pot: I have produced easy circumstances, circulation, and credit. Before I came there was nothing of all this; I revived, animated, fertilized, stimulated, and enriched the whole district. When I am gone the soul will be gone; if I withdraw all will die; and then, this woman, who has suffered so greatly, who has so much merit in her fall, and whose misfortune I unwittingly caused, and the child which I intended to go and fetch, and restore to the mother—Do not I also owe something to this woman in reparation of the wrong which I have done her? If I disappear, what will happen? The mother dies, and the child will become what it can. This will happen if I denounce myself. If I do not denounce myself? Come, let me see."

After asking himself this question, he hesitated, and trembled slightly; but this emotion lasted but a short time, and he answered himself calmly:—

"Well, this man will go to the galleys, it is true, but, hang it all! he has stolen. Although I may say to myself that he has not stolen, he has done so! I remain here and continue my operations: in ten years I shall have gained ten millions. I spread them over the country. I keep nothing for myself; but what do I care? I am not doing this for myself. The prosperity of all is increased; trades are revived, factories and forges are multiplied, and thousands of families are happy; the district is populated; villages spring up where there are only farms, and farms where there is nothing; wretchedness disappears, and with it debauchery, prostitution, robbery, murder, all the vices, all the crimes—and this poor mother brings up her child. Why, I was mad, absurd, when I talked about denouncing myself, and I must guard against precipitation. What! because it pleases me to play the grand and the generous—it is pure melodrama after all—because I only thought of myself, and in order to save from a perhaps exaggerated though substantially just punishment a stranger, a thief, and an apparent scoundrel—a whole department must perish, a poor woman die in the hospital, and a poor child starve in the streets, like dogs! Why, it is abominable! without the mother seeing her child again, or the child knowing her mother! and all this on behalf of an old scamp of an apple-stealer, who has assuredly deserved the galleys for something else, if not for that. These are fine scruples that save a culprit and sacrifice the innocent; that save an old vagabond who has not many years to live, and will not be more unhappy at the galleys than in his hovel, and destroy an entire population,—mothers, wives, and children. That poor little Cosette, who has only me in the world, and is doubtless at this moment shivering with cold in the den of those Thénardiers. There is another pair of wretches. And I would fail in my duties to all these poor creatures, and commit such a folly as to denounce myself! Let us put things at the worst: suppose that I am committing a bad action in this, and that my conscience reproaches me with it some day; there will be devotion and virtue in accepting, for the good of my neighbor, these reproaches, which only weigh on me, and this bad action, which only compromises my own soul."

He got up and began walking up and down again: this time he seemed to be satisfied with himself. Diamonds are only found in the darkness of the earth; truths are only found in the depths of thought. It seemed to him that after descending into these depths, after groping for some time in the densest of this darkness, he had found one of these diamonds, one of these truths, which he held in his hand and which dazzled his eyes when he looked at it.

"Yes," he thought, "I am on the right track and hold the solution of the problem. A man must in the end hold on to something, and my mind is made up. I will let matters take their course, so no more vacillation or backsliding. It is for the interest of all, not of myself. I am Madeleine, and remain Madeleine, and woe to the man who is Jean Valjean. I am no longer he. I do not know that man, and if any one happen to be Jean Valjean at this moment, he must look out for himself, for it does not concern me. It is a fatal name that floats in the night, and if it stop and settle on a head, all the worse for that head."

He looked into the small looking-glass over the mantel-piece, and said to himself,—

"How greatly has forming a resolution relieved me! I am quite a different man at present."

He walked a little way and then stopped short. "Come," he said, "I must not hesitate before any of the consequences of the resolution I have formed. There are threads which still attach me to Jean Valjean which must be broken. There are in this very room objects which would accuse me,—dumb things which would serve as witnesses, and they must all disappear."

He took his purse from his pocket, and drew a small key out of it. He put this key in a lock, the hole of which could scarcely be seen, for it was hidden in the darkest part of the design on the paper that covered the walls. A sort of false cupboard made between the corner of the wall and the mantel-piece was visible. In this hiding-place there were only a few rags,—a blue blouse, worn trousers, an old knapsack, and a large thorn-stick shod with iron at both ends. Any one who saw Jean Valjean pass through D—— in October, 1815, would easily have recognized all these wretched articles. He had preserved them, as he had done the candlesticks, that they might constantly remind him of his starting-point; still he hid what came from the galleys, and displayed the candlesticks which came from the Bishop. He took a furtive glance at the door, as if afraid that it might open in spite of the bolt; and then with a rapid movement he made but one armful of the things he had so religiously and perilously kept for so many years, and threw them all—rags, stick, and knapsack—into the fire. He closed the cupboard, and, redoubling his precautions, which were now useless since it was empty, dragged a heavy piece of furniture in front of it. In a few seconds, the room and opposite wall were lit up with a large red and flickering glow; all was burning, and the thorn-stick crackled and threw out sparks into the middle of the room. From the knapsack, as it burned with all the rags it contained, fell something that glistened in the ashes. On stooping it could be easily recognized as a coin; it was doubtless the little Savoyard's two-franc piece. He did not look at the fire, and continued his walk backwards and forwards. All at once his eye fell on the two candlesticks which the fire-light caused to shine vaguely on the mantel-piece.

"Stay," he thought, "all Jean Valjean is in them, and they must be destroyed too."

He seized the candlesticks—there was a fire large enough to destroy their shape, and convert them into unrecognizable ingots. He leaned over the hearth and wanned his hands for a moment; it was a great comfort to him.

He stirred up the ashes with one of the candlesticks, and in a moment they were both in the fire. All at once he fancied he heard a voice cry within him, "Jean Valjean! Jean Valjean!" His hair stood erect, and he became like a man who is listening to a terrible thing.

"Yes, that is right; finish!" the voice said: "complete what you are about; destroy those candlesticks, annihilate that reminiscence! forget the Bishop! forget everything! rain that Champmathieu; that is right. Applaud yourself; come, all is settled and resolved on. This old man, who does not know what they want with him, who is perhaps innocent, whose whole misfortune your name causes, on whom your name weighs like a crime, is going to be taken for you, sentenced, and will end his days in abjectness and horror. That is excellent! Be an honest man yourself; remain Mayor, honorable and honored, enrich the town, assist the indigent, bring up orphans, live happy, virtuous, and applauded; and during this time, while you are here in joy and light, there will be somebody who wears your red jacket, bears your name in ignominy, and drags along your chain at the galleys. Yes, that is excellently arranged. Oh, you scoundrel!"

The perspiration beaded on his forehead, and he fixed his haggard eye upon the candlesticks. The voice within him, however, had not ended yet.

"Jean Valjean! there will be around you many voices making a great noise, speaking very loud and blessing you, and one which no one will hear, and which will curse you in the darkness. Well, listen, infamous man! all these blessings will fall back on the ground before reaching Heaven, and the curse alone will ascend to God!"

This voice, at first very faint, and which spoke from the obscurest nook of his conscience, had gradually become sonorous and formidable, and he now heard it in his ear. He fancied that it was not his own voice, and he seemed to hear the last words so distinctly that he looked round the room with a species of terror.

"Is there any one here?" he asked, in a loud voice and wildly.

Then he continued with a laugh, which seemed almost idiotic,—

"What a fool I am! there can be nobody."

There was somebody, but not of those whom the human eye can see. He placed the candlesticks on the mantel-piece, and then resumed that melancholy, mournful walk, which aroused the sleeper underneath him. This walking relieved him, and at the same time intoxicated him. It appears sometimes as if on supreme occasions people move about to ask advice of everything they pass. At the end of a few moments he no longer knew what result to arrive at. He now recoiled with equal horror from the two resolutions he had formed in turn; the two ideas that counselled him seemed each as desperate as the other. What a fatality that this Champmathieu should be taken for him! He was hurled down precisely by the means which Providence at first seemed to have employed to strengthen his position.

There was a moment during which he regarded his future. Denounce himself! great Heavens! give himself up! He thought with immense despair of all that he must give up, of all that he must resume. He would be forced to bid adieu to this good, pure, radiant life,—to the respect of all classes,—to honor, to liberty! He would no longer walk about the fields, he would no longer hear the birds sing in May, or give alms to the little children! He would no longer feel the sweetness of glances of gratitude and love fixed upon him! He would leave this little house, which he had built, and his little bed-room. All appeared charming to him at this moment. He would no longer read those books or write at the little deal table; his old servant would no longer bring up his coffee in the morning. Great God! instead of all this, there would be the gang, the red jacket, the chain on his foot, fatigue, the dungeon, the camp-bed, and all the horrors he knew! At his age, after all he had borne! It would be different were he still young. But to be old, coarsely addressed by anybody, searched by the jailer, and receive blows from the keeper's stick! to thrust his naked feet into iron-shod shoes! to offer his leg morning and night to the man who examines the fetters! to endure the curiosity of strangers who would be told, "That is the famous Jean Valjean, who was Mayor of M——!" at night, when pouring with perspiration, and crushed by fatigue, with a green cap on his head, to go up two by two, under the sergeants whip, the side ladder of the hulks! Oh, what misery! Destiny, then, can be as wicked as an intelligent being and prove as monstrous as the human heart!

And whatever he might do, he ever fell back into this crushing dilemma, which was the basis of his reverie,—remain in paradise, and become a demon there; or re-enter hell, and become an angel? What should he do? Great God! what should he do? The trouble, from which he had escaped with such difficulty, was again let loose on him, and his thoughts became composed once more. They assumed something stupefied and mechanical, which is peculiar to despair. The name of Romainville incessantly returned to his mind, with two lines of a song which he had formerly heard. He remembered that Romainville is a little wood, near Paris, where lovers go to pick lilac in April. He tottered both externally and internally; he walked like a little child allowed to go alone. At certain moments, he struggled against his lassitude, and tried to recapture his intelligence; he tried to set himself, for the last time, the problem over which he had fallen in a state of exhaustion,—must he denounce himself, or must he be silent? He could not succeed in seeing anything distinct, the vague outlines of all the reasonings sketched in by his reverie were dissipated in turn like smoke. Still, he felt that, however he resolved, and without any possibility of escape, something belonging to him was about to die; that he entered a sepulchre, whether on his right hand or his left, and that either his happiness or his virtue would be borne to the grave.

Alas! all his irresolution had seized him again, and he was no further advanced than at the beginning. Thus the wretched soul writhed in agony! Eighteen hundred years before this unhappy man, the mysterious being in whom are embodied all the sanctities and sufferings of humanity had also, while the olive-trees shuddered in the fierce wind of the infinite, long put away with his hand the awful cup which appeared to him, dripping with shadow and overflowing with darkness in the starry depths.

CHAPTER IV.

SUFFERINGS IN SLEEP.

Three A.M. had struck, and he had been walking about in this way for five hours without a break, when he fell into his chair. He fell asleep, and had a dream. This dream, like most dreams, was only connected with his situation by something poignant and mournful, but it made an impression on him. This nightmare struck him so much that he wrote it down at a later date, and we think we are bound to transcribe it verbatim; for whatever the history of this man may be, it would be incomplete if we omitted it. Here it is then; on the envelope we notice the line,—*The dream I had on that night.*

"I was upon a plain, a large mournful plain, on which no grass grew. It did not seem to me to be day, but it was not night. I was walking with my brother, the brother of my boyish years, of whom I am bound to say I never think, and whom I scarce remember. We were talking, and met travellers. We spoke about a woman, formerly a neighbor of ours, who had always worked with her window open, since she had occupied a front room. While talking, we felt cold on account of this open window. There were no trees on the plain. We saw a man pass close by us; he was a perfectly naked man, of the color of ashes, mounted on a horse of an earthen color. The man had no hair, and I could see his skull, and the veins on his skull. He held in his hand a wand, which was supple as a vine-twig and heavy as lead. This horseman passed and said nothing to us.

"My brother said to me: 'Let us turn into the hollow way.'

"It was a hollow way in which not a bramble or even a patch of moss could be seen; all was earth-colored, even the sky. After going a few yards, I received no answer when I spoke, and I noticed that my brother was no longer with me. I entered a village that I saw, and I fancied that it must be Romainville. The first street I entered was deserted; I entered a second street, and behind the angle formed by the two streets a man was standing against the wall. I asked this man, "What is this place? where am I?" but he gave me no answer. I saw the door of a house open, and walked in.

"The first room was deserted, and I entered a second. Behind the door of this room there was a man leaning against the wall. I asked him, "To whom does this house belong? where am I?" but the man gave me no answer. I went out into the garden of the house, and it was deserted. Behind the first tree I found a man standing; I said to the man, "Whose is this garden? where am I?" but he made me no answer.

"I wandered about this village and fancied that it was a town. All the streets were deserted, all the doors open. Not a living soul passed along the street, moved in the rooms, or walked in the gardens. But there was behind every corner, every door, and every tree, a man standing silently. I never saw more than one at a time, and these men looked at me as I passed.

"I left the village and began walking about the fields. At the end of some time I turned back and saw a great crowd coming after me. I recognized all the men whom I had seen in the town, and they had strange heads. They did not appear to be in a hurry, and yet they walked faster than I, and made no noise in walking. In an instant this crowd joined me and surrounded me. The faces of these men were earth-colored. Then the man I had seen first and questioned when I entered the town said to me, "Where are you going? do you not know that you have been dead for a long time?" I opened my mouth to answer, and I perceived that there was no one near me."

He woke up, chilled to the marrow, for a wind, cold as the morning breeze, was shaking the open window. The fire had died away, the candle was nearly burned out, and it was still black night. He rose and went to the window; there were still no stars in the sky. From his window he could see the yard and his street, and a dry sharp sound on the ground below him induced him to look out. He saw two red stars whose rays lengthened and shortened curiously in the gloom. As his mind was half submerged in the mist of dreams, he thought, "There are no stars in the sky: they are on the earth now." A second sound like the first completely woke him, and he perceived that those two stars were carriage lamps, and by the light which they projected he could distinguish the shape of the vehicle; it was a tilbury, in which a small white horse was harnessed. The sound he had heard was the pawing of the horse's hoof on the ground.

"What's the meaning of this conveyance?" he said to himself. "Who can have come at so early an hour?"

At this moment there was a gentle tap at his bed-room door; he shuddered from head to foot, and shouted in a terrible voice, "Who's there?"

Some one replied, "I, sir," and he recognized his old servant's voice.

"Well," he continued, "what is it?"

"It is getting on for four o'clock, sir."

"What has that to do with me?"

"The tilbury has come, sir."

"What tilbury?"

"Did you not order one?"

"No," he said.

"The ostler says that he has come to fetch M. le Maire."

"What ostler?"

"M. Scaufflaire's."

This name made him start as if a flash of lightning had passed before his eyes.

"Ah, yes," he repeated, "M. Scaufflaire."

Could the old woman have seen him at this moment, she would have been horrified. There was a lengthened silence, during which he stupidly examined the candle flame and rolled up some of the wax in his fingers. The old woman, who was waiting, at length mustered up courage to raise her voice again.

"M. le Maire, what answer am I to give?"

"Say it is quite right, and that I shall be down directly."

CHAPTER V

OBSTACLES.

The letter-bags between Arras and M—— were still carried in small mail-carts, dating from the Empire. They were two-wheeled vehicles, lined with tawny leather, hung on springs, and having only two seats, one for the driver, and another for a passenger. The wheels were armed with those long offensive axle-trees, which kept other carriages at a distance, and may still be seen on German roads. The compartment for the bags was an immense oblong box at the back; it was painted black, and the front part was yellow. These vehicles, like which we have nothing at the present day, had something ugly and humpbacked about them, and when you saw them pass at a distance or creeping up a hill on the horizon, they resembled those insects called, we think, termites, and which with a small body drag a heavy burden after them. They went very fast, however, and the mail which left Arras at one in the morning, after the Paris mail had arrived, reached M—— a little before five A.M.

On this morning, the mail-cart, just as it entered M——, and while turning a corner, ran into a tilbury drawn by a white horse, coming in the opposite direction, and in which there was only one sitter, a man wrapped in a cloak. The wheel of the tilbury received a rather heavy blow, and though the driver of the mail-cart shouted to the man to stop, he did not listen, but went on at a smart trot.

"The man is in a deuce of a hurry," said the courier.

The man in this hurry was he whom we have just seen struggling in convulsions, assuredly deserving of pity. Where was he going? He could not have told. Why was he hurrying? He did not know. He was going onwards unthinkingly. Where to? Doubtless to Arras; but he might also be going elsewhere.

He buried himself in the darkness as in a gulf. Something urged him on; something attracted him. What was going on in him no one could tell, but all will understand it,—for what man has not entered, at least once in his life, this obscure cavern of the unknown? However, he had settled, decided, and done nothing; not one of the acts of his conscience had been definitive, and he was still as unsettled as at the beginning.

Why was he going to Arras? He repeated what he had already said on hiring the gig of Scaufflaire—that, whatever the result might be, there would be no harm in seeing with his own eyes, and judging matters for himself—that this was prudent; and he was bound to know what was going on—that he could not decide anything till he had observed and examined—that, at a distance, a man made mountains of molehills—that after all, when he had seen this Champmathieu, his conscience would probably be quietly relieved, and he could let the scoundrel go to the galleys in his place: that Javert would be there and the three convicts who had known him,—but, nonsense! they would not recognize him, for all conjectures and suppositions were fixed on this Champmathieu, and there is nothing so obstinate as conjectures and suppositions,—and that hence he incurred no danger. It was doubtless a black moment, but he would emerge from it. After all, he held his destiny, however adverse it might try to be, in his own hands, and was master of it. He clung wildly to the latter thought.

Although, to tell the whole truth, he would have preferred not to go to Arras, yet he went. While reflecting he lashed the horse, which was going at that regular and certain trot which covers two leagues and a half in an hour; and as the gig advanced, he felt something within him recoil. At day-break he was in the open country, and the town of M—— was far behind him. He watched the horizon grow white; he looked, without seeing them, at all the cold figures of a winter dawn. Morning has its spectres like night. He did not see them, but unconsciously, and through a sort of almost physical penetration, these black outlines of trees and hills added something gloomy and sinister to the violent state of his soul. Each time that he passed one of those isolated houses which skirt high roads, he said to himself: "And yet there are people asleep in them." The trot of the horse, the bells on the harness, the wheels on the stones, produced a gentle and monotonous sound, which is delightful when you are merry, and mournful when you are sad.

It was broad daylight when he reached Hesdin, and he stopped at the inn to let the horse breathe and give it a feed. This horse, as Scaufflaire had said, belonged to that small Boulonnais breed, which has too large a head, too much stomach, and not enough neck, but which also has a wide crupper, lean, slender legs, and a solid hoof: it is an ugly but strong and healthy breed. The capital little beast had done five leagues in two hours, and had not turned a hair.

He did not get out of the tilbury; the ostler who brought the oats suddenly stooped down and examined the left wheel.

"Are you going far in this state?" the man said.

He answered almost without emerging from his reverie,—

"Why do you ask?"

"Have you come any distance?" the ostler continued.

"Five leagues."

"Ah!"

"Why do you say, 'Ah'?"

The ostler bent down again, remained silent for a moment, with his eye fixed on the wheel, and then said as he drew himself up,—

"Because this wheel, which may have gone five leagues, cannot possibly go another mile."

He jumped out of the tilbury.

"What are you saying, my friend?"

"I say that it is a miracle you and your horse did not roll into a ditch by the road-side. Just look."

The wheel was, in fact, seriously damaged. The blow dealt it by the mail-cart had broken two spokes, and almost carried away the axle-tree.

"My good fellow," he said to the ostler, "is there a wheelwright here?"

"Of course, sir."

"Be good enough to go and fetch him."

"He lives close by. Hilloh, Master Bourgaillard."

Master Bourgaillard was standing in his doorway: he examined the wheel, and made a face like a surgeon regarding a broken leg.

"Can you mend this wheel?"

"Yes, sir."

"When can I start again?"

"To-morrow: there is a good day's work. Are you in a hurry, sir?"

"In a great hurry: I must set out again in an hour at the latest."

"It is impossible, sir."

"I will pay anything you ask."

"Impossible."

"Well, in two hours?"

"It is impossible for to-day; you will not be able to go on till to-morrow."

"My business cannot wait till to-morrow. Suppose, instead of mending this wheel, you were to put another on?"

"How so?"

"You are a wheelwright, and have probably a wheel you can sell me, and then I could set out again directly."

"I have no ready-made wheel to suit your gig, for wheels are sold in pairs, and it is not easy to match one."

"In that case, sell me a pair of wheels."

"All wheels, sir, do not fit all axle-trees."

"At any rate try."

"It is useless, sir; I have only cart-wheels for sale, for ours is a small place."

"Have you a gig I can hire?"

The wheelwright had noticed at a glance that the tilbury was a hired vehicle; he shrugged his shoulders.

"You take such good care of gigs you hire, that if I had one I would not let it to you."

"Well, one to sell me?"

"I have not one."

"What, not a tax-cart? I am not particular, as you see."

"This is a small place. I have certainly," the wheelwright added, "an old calèche in my stable, which belongs to a person in the town, and who uses it on the thirty-sixth of every month. I could certainly let it out to you, for it is no concern of mine, but the owner must not see it pass; and besides, it is a calèche, and will want two horses."

"I will hire post-horses."

"Where are you going to, sir?"

"To Arras."

"And you wish to arrive to-day?"

"Certainly."

"By taking post-horses?"

"Why not?"

"Does it make any difference to you if you reach Arras at four o'clock to-morrow morning?"

"Of course it does."

"There is one thing to be said about hiring post-horses; have you your passport, sir?"

"Yes."

"Well, if you take post-horses, you will not reach Arras before to-morrow. We are on a cross-country road. The relays are badly served, and the horses are out at work. This is the ploughing season, and as strong teams are required, horses are taken anywhere, from the post-houses like the rest. You will have to wait three or four hours, sir, at each station, and only go at a foot-pace, for there are many hills to ascend."

"Well, I will ride. Take the horse out. I suppose I can purchase a saddle here?"

"Of course, but will this horse carry a saddle?"

"No, I remember now that it will not."

"In that case—"

"But surely I can hire a saddle-horse in the village?"

"What! to go to Arras without a break?"

"Yes."

"You would want a horse such as is not to be found in these parts. In the first place, you would have to buy it, as you are a stranger, but you would not find one to buy or hire for five hundred francs,—not for a thousand."

"What is to be done?"

"The best thing is to let me mend the wheel and put off your journey till to-morrow."

"To-morrow will be too late."

"Hang it!"

"Is there not the Arras mail-cart? When does that pass?"

"Not till to-night."

"What! you will take a whole day in mending that wheel?"

"An honest day."

"Suppose you employed two workmen?"

"Ay, if I had ten."

"Suppose the spokes were tied with cords?"

"What is to be done with the axle? Besides, the felloe is in a bad state."

"Is there any one who lets out vehicles in the town?"

"No."

"Is there another wheelwright?"

The ostler and the wheelwright replied simultaneously—,

"No."

He felt an immense joy, for it was evident that Providence was interfering. Providence had broken the tilbury wheel and stopped his journey. He had not yielded to this species of first summons; he had made every possible effort to continue his journey; he had loyally and scrupulously exhausted all resources; he had not recoiled before the season, fatigue, or expense; and he had nothing to reproach himself with. If he did not go farther, it did not concern him; it was not his fault, it was not the doing of his conscience, but of Providence. He breathed freely and fully for the first time since Javert's visit. He felt as if the iron hand which had been squeezing his heart for twenty hours had relaxed its grasp; God now appeared to be on his side, and declared Himself openly. He said to himself that he had done all in his power, and at present need only return home quietly.

Had the conversation with the wheelwright taken place in an inn-room, it would probably have not been heard by any one,—matters would have remained in this state, and we should probably not have had to record any of the following events; but the conversation took place in the street. Any colloquy in the street inevitably produces a crowd, for there are always people who only ask to be spectators. While he was questioning the wheelwright, some passers-by stopped around, and a lad to whom no one paid any attention, after listening for some moments, ran off. At the instant when the traveller made up his mind to turn back, this boy returned, accompanied by an old woman.

"Sir," the woman said, "my boy tells me that you wish to hire a conveyance?"

This simple remark, made by an old woman led by a child, made the perspiration pour down his back. He fancied he saw the hand which had let him loose reappear in the shadow behind him, ready to clutch him again. He replied,—

"Yes, my good woman, I want to hire a gig."

And he hastily added, "But there is not one in the town."

"Yes there is," said the old woman.

"Where?" the wheelwright remarked.

"At my house," the old crone answered.

He gave a start, for the fatal hand had seized him again. The poor woman really had a sort of wicker-cart under a shed. The wheelwright and the ostler, sorry to see the traveller escape them, interfered:—

"It was a frightful rattle-trap, and had no springs,—it is a fact that the inside seats were hung with leathern straps—the rain got into it—the wheels were rusty, and ready to fall to pieces—it would not go much farther than the tilbury—the gentleman had better not get into it,"—and so on.

All this was true; but the rattle-trap, whatever it might be, rolled on two wheels, and could go to Arras. He paid what was asked, left the tilbury to be repaired against his return, had the horse put into the cart, got in, and went his way. At the moment when the cart moved ahead, he confessed to himself that an instant before he had felt a sort of joy at the thought that he could not continue his journey. He examined this joy with a sort of passion, and found it absurd. Why did he feel joy at turning back? After all, he was making this journey of his free will, and no one forced him to do so. And assuredly nothing could happen, except what he liked. As he was leaving Hesdin, he heard a voice shouting to him, "Stop, stop!" He stopped the cart with a hurried movement in which there was something feverish and convulsive that resembled joy. It was the old woman's boy.

"Sir," he said, "it was I who got you the cart."

"Well?"

"You have given me nothing."

He who gave to all, and so easily, considered this demand exorbitant, and almost odious.

"Oh, it's you, scamp," he said; "well, you will not have anything."

He flogged his horse, which started again at a smart trot. He had lost much time at Hesdin, and would have liked to recover it. The little horse was courageous, and worked for two; but it was February, it had been raining, and the roads were bad. The cart too ran much more heavily than the tilbury, and there were numerous ascents. He took nearly four hours in going from Hesdin to St. Pol: four hours for five leagues! At St. Pol he pulled up at the first inn he came to, and had the horse put in a stable. As he had promised Scaufflaire, he stood near the crib while it was eating, and had troubled and confused thoughts. The landlady entered the stable.

"Do you not wish to breakfast, sir?"

"It is true," said he, "I am very hungry."

He followed the woman, who had a healthy, ruddy face; she led him to a ground-floor room, in which were tables covered with oil-cloth.

"Make haste," he remarked, "for I am in a great hurry."

A plump Flemish servant-girl hastened to lay the cloth, and he looked at her with a feeling of comfort.

"That was the trouble," he thought; "I had not breakfasted."

He pounced upon the bread, bit a mouthful, and then slowly laid it back on the table, and did not touch it again. A wagoner was sitting at another table, and he said to him,—

"Why is their bread so bitter?"

The wagoner was a German, and did not understand him; he returned to his horse. An hour later he had left St. Pol, and was proceeding toward Tinques, which is only five leagues from Arras. What did he do during the drive? What was he thinking of? As in the morning, he looked at the trees, the roofs, the ploughed fields, and the diversities of a landscape which every turn in the road changes, as he passed them. To see a thousand different objects for the first and last time is most melancholy! Travelling is birth and death at every moment. Perhaps in the vaguest region of his mind he made a comparison between the changing horizon and human existence, for everything in this life is continually flying before us. Shadow and light are blended; after a dazzling comes an eclipse; every event is a turn in the road, and all at once you are old.

You feel something like a shock, all is black, you distinguish an obscure door, and the gloomy horse of life which dragged you, stops, and you see a veiled, unknown form unharnessing it. Twilight was setting in at the moment when the school-boys, leaving school, saw this traveller enter Tinques. He did not halt there, but as he left the village, a road-mender, who was laying stones, raised his head, and said to him,—

"Your horse is very tired."

The poor brute, in fact, could not get beyond a walk.

"Are you going to Arras?" the road-mender continued.

"Yes."

"If you go at that pace, you will not reach it very soon."

He stopped his horse, and asked the road-mender—,

"How far is it from here to Arras?"

"Nearly seven long leagues."

"How so? The post-book says only five and a quarter leagues."

"Ah" the road-mender continued, "you do not know that the road is under repair; you will find it cut up about a mile farther on, and it is impossible to pass."

"Indeed!"

"You must take the road on the left, that runs to Carency, and cross the river; when you reach Camblin you will turn to the right, for it is the Mont St. Eloy road that runs to Arras."

"But I shall lose my way in the dark."

"You do not belong to these parts?"

"No."

"And it is a cross-road; stay, sir," the road-mender continued; "will you let me give you a piece of advice? Your horse is tired, so return to Tinques, where there is a good inn; sleep there, and go to Arras to-morrow."

"I must be there to-night."

"That is different. In that case go back to the inn all the same, and hire a second horse. The stable boy will act as your guide across the country."

He took the road-mender's advice, turned back, and half an hour after passed the same spot at a sharp trot with a strong second horse. A stable lad, who called himself a postilion, was sitting on the shafts of the cart. Still he felt that he had lost time, for it was now dark. They entered the cross-road, and it soon became frightful; the cart tumbled from one rut into another, but he said to the postilion,—

"Keep on at a trot, and I will give you a double fee."

In one of the jolts the whipple-tree broke.

"The whipple-tree is broken, sir," said the postilion, "and I do not know how to fasten my horse, and the road is very bad by night. If you will go back and sleep at Tinques, we can get to Arras at an early hour to-morrow."

He answered, "Have you a piece of rope and a knife?"

"Yes, sir."

He cut a branch and made a whipple-tree; it was a further loss of twenty minutes, but they started again at a gallop. The plain was dark, and a low, black fog was creeping over the hills. A heavy wind, which came from the sea, made in all the corners of the horizon a noise like that of furniture being moved. All that he could see had an attitude of terror, for how many things shudder beneath the mighty breath of night! The cold pierced him, for he had eaten nothing since the previous morning. He vaguely recalled his other night-excursion, on the great plain of D—— eight years before, and it seemed to him to be yesterday. A clock struck from a distant steeple, and he asked the lad,—

"What o'clock is that?"

"Seven, sir, and we shall be at Arras by eight, for we have only three leagues to go."

At this moment he made for the first time this reflection—and considered it strange that it had not occurred to him before—that all the trouble he was taking was perhaps thrown away; he did not even know the hour for the trial, and he might at least have asked about that; it was extravagant to go on thus, without knowing if it would be of any service. Then he made some mental calculations: usually the sittings of assize courts began at nine o'clock; this matter would not occupy much time, the theft of the apples would be easily proved, and then there would be merely the identification, four or five witnesses to hear, and little for counsel to say. He would arrive when it was all over.

The postilion flogged the horses; they had crossed the river and left Mont St Hoy behind them; the night was growing more and more dark.

CHAPTER VI.

SISTER SIMPLICE IS SORELY TRIED.

At this very moment Fantine was joyful. She had passed a very bad night, she had coughed fearfully, and her fever had become worse. In the morning, when the physician paid his visit, she was raving; he felt alarmed, and begged to be sent for so soon as M. Madeleine arrived. All the morning she was gloomy, said little, and made folds in sheets, while murmuring in a low voice, and calculating what seemed to be distances. Her eyes were hollow and fixed, they seemed almost extinct, and then, at moments, they were relit, and flashed like stars. It seems as if, on the approach of a certain dark hour, the brightness of heaven fills those whom the brightness of earth is quitting. Each time that Sister Simplice asked her how she was, she invariably answered, "Well, but I should like to see M. Madeleine."

A few months previously, at the time when Fantine lost her last modesty, her last shame, and her last joy, she was the shadow of herself: now she was the ghost. Physical suffering had completed the work of moral suffering. This creature of five-and-twenty years of age had a wrinkled forehead, sunken cheeks, a pinched nose, a leaden complexion, a bony neck, projecting shoulder-blades, thin limbs, an earthy skin, and white hairs were mingled with the auburn. Alas! how illness improvises old age! At mid-day, the physician returned, wrote a prescription, inquired whether M. Madeleine had been to the infirmary, and shook his head. M. Madeleine usually came at three o'clock, and as punctuality was kindness, he was punctual. At about half-past two Fantine began to grow agitated, and in the next twenty minutes asked the nun more than ten times, "What o'clock is it?"

Three o'clock struck: at the third stroke Fantine, who usually could scarce move in her bed, sat up; she clasped her thin yellow hands in a sort of convulsive grasp, and the nun heard one of those deep sighs, which seem to remove a crushing weight, burst from her chest. Then Fantine turned and looked at the door: but no one entered, and the door was not opened. She remained thus for a quarter of an hour, with her eyes fixed on the door, motionless, and holding her breath. The nun did not dare speak to her, and as the clock struck the quarter, Fantine fell back on her pillow. She said nothing, and began again making folds in the sheet. The half-hour passed, then the hour, and no one came. Each time the clock struck Fantine sat up, looked at the door, and then fell back again. Her thoughts could be clearly read, but she did not say a word, complain, or make any accusation: she merely coughed in a sad way. It seemed as if something dark was settling down on her, for she was livid and her lips were blue. She smiled every now and then.

When five o'clock struck, the nun heard her say very softly and sweetly, "As I am going away to-morrow, it was wrong of him not to come to-day." Sister Simplice herself was surprised at M. Madeleine's delay. In the mean while Fantine looked up at the top of her bed, and seemed to be trying to remember something: all at once she began singing in a voice faint as a sigh. It was an old cradle-song with which she had in former times lulled her little Cosette to sleep, and which had not once recurred to her during the five years she had been parted from her child. She sang with so sad a voice and to so soft an air, that it was enough to make any one weep, even a nun. The sister, who was accustomed to austere things, felt a tear in her eye. The clock struck, and Fantine did not seem to hear it: she appeared not to pay any attention to things around her. Sister Simplice sent a servant-girl to inquire of the portress of the factory whether M. Madeleine had returned and would be at the infirmary soon: the girl came back in a few minutes. Fantine was still motionless and apparently engaged with her own thoughts. The servant told Sister Simplice in a very low voice that the Mayor had set off before six o'clock that morning in a small tilbury; that he had gone alone, without a driver; that no one knew what direction he had taken, for while some said they had seen him going along the Arras road, others declared they had met him on the Paris road. He was, as usual, very gentle, and he had merely told his servant she need not expect him that night.

While the two women were whispering with their backs turned to Fantine, the sister questioning, and the servant conjecturing, Fantine, with the feverish vivacity of certain organic maladies which blend the free movements of health with the frightful weakness of death, had knelt in bed, with her two clenched hands supported by the pillow, and listened with her head thrust between the curtains. All at once she cried,—

"You are talking about M. Madeleine: why do you whisper? What is he doing, and why does he not come?"

Her voice was so loud and hoarse that the two women fancied it a man's voice, and they turned round in alarm.

"Answer!" Fantine cried.

The servant stammered,—

"The portress told me that he could not come to-day."

"My child," the sister said, "be calm and lie down again."

Fantine, without changing her attitude, went on in a loud voice and with an accent at once imperious and heart-rending,—

"He cannot come: why not? You know the reason. You were whispering it to one another, and I insist on knowing."

The servant hastily whispered in the nun's ear, "Tell her that he is engaged at the Municipal Council."

Sister Simplice blushed slightly, for it was a falsehood that the servant proposed to her. On the other hand it seemed to her that telling the patient the truth would doubtless deal her a terrible blow, and this was serious in Fantine's present condition. The blush lasted but a little while: the sister fixed her calm sad eye on Fantine, and said,—

"The Mayor is gone on a journey."

Fantine rose and sat up on her heels, her eyes sparkled, and an ineffable joy shone on her sad face.

"He has gone to fetch Cosette," she exclaimed.

Then she raised her hands to heaven, and her lips moved: she was praying. When she had finished she said, "My sister, I am willing to lie down again and do everything you wish: I was naughty just now. I ask your pardon for having spoken so loud, for I know that it was wrong, good sister; but, look you, I am so happy. God is good, and M. Madeleine is good: only think, he has gone to Montfermeil to fetch my little Cosette."

She lay down again, helped the nun to smooth her pillow, and kissed a little silver cross she wore on her neck, and which Sister Simplice had given her.

"My child," the sister said, "try to go to sleep now, and do not speak any more."

"He started this morning for Paris, and indeed had no occasion to go there; for Montfermeil is a little to the left before you get there. You remember how he said to me yesterday when I asked him about Cosette, "Soon, soon"? He wishes to offer me a surprise, for, do you know, he made me sign a letter to get her back from the Thénardiers. They cannot refuse to give up Cosette, can they? for they are paid; the authorities would not allow a child to be kept, for now there is nothing owing. Sister, do not make me signs that I must not speak, for I am extremely happy: I am going on very well, I feel no pain at all; I am going to see Cosette again, and I even feel very hungry. It is nearly five years since I saw her: you cannot imagine how a mother clings to her child,— and then she must be so pretty. She has such pretty pink fingers, and she will have beautiful hands. She must be a great girl now, for she is going on to seven. I call her Cosette, but her real name is Euphrasie. This morning I was looking at the dust on the mantel-piece, and I had a notion that I should soon see Cosette again. Good Lord! how wrong it is for a mother to be so many years without seeing her child! She ought to reflect that life is not eternal. Oh, how kind it is of the Mayor to go! Is it true that it is so cold? I hope he took his cloak. He will be here again to-morrow, will he not? and we will make a holiday of it. To-morrow morning, sister, you will remind me to put on my little cap with the lace border. Montfermeil is a great distance, and I came from there to this town on foot, and it took me a long time; but the stage-coaches travel so quickly! He will be here to-morrow with Cosette. How far is it to Montfermeil?"

The sister, who had no notion of distances, answered, "Oh, I believe he can be here to-morrow."

"To-morrow! to-morrow!" said Fantine; "I shall see Cosette to-morrow, my good sister! I am not ill now; I feel wild, and would dance if you permitted me."

Any one who had seen her a quarter of an hour before would not have understood it; she was now quite flushed, she spoke with an eager natural voice, and her whole face was a smile. At times she laughed while speaking to herself in a low voice. A mother's joy is almost a childish joy.

"Well!" the nun said, "you are now happy. So obey me and do not speak any more."

Fantine laid her head on the pillow, and said in a low voice, "Yes, lie down, behave yourself, as you are going to have your child. Sister Simplice is right: all in this place are right."

And then, without stirring, without moving her head, she began looking around with widely opened eyes and a joyous air, and said nothing more. The sister closed the curtains, hoping she would fall off to sleep. The physician arrived between seven and eight o'clock. Hearing no sound, he fancied Fantine asleep. He entered softly and walked up to the bed on tip-toe. He opened the curtains, and by the light of the lamp saw Fantine's large calm eyes fixed on him. She said to him,—

"Oh, sir, my child will be allowed to sleep in a little cot by my bed-side?"

The physician fancied she was delirious. She added,—

"Only look; there is exactly room."

The physician took Sister Simplice on one side who explained the matter to him: that M. Madeleine was absent for a day or two, and being in doubt they had not thought it right to undeceive the patient, who fancied that he had gone to Montfermeil, and she might possibly be in the right. The physician approved, and drew near to Fantine's bed. She said to him,—

"In the morning, when the poor darling wakes, I will say good-day to her, and at night I, who do not sleep, will listen to her sleeping. Her gentle little breathing will do me good."

"Give me your hand," said the physician.

"Oh yes, you do not know that I am cured. Cosette arrives to-morrow."

The physician was surprised to find her better: the oppression was slighter, her pulse had regained strength, and a sort of altogether unlooked-for life reanimated the poor exhausted being.

"Doctor," she continued, "has the sister told you that M. Madeleine has gone to fetch my darling?"

The physician recommended silence, and that any painful emotion should be avoided: he prescribed a dose of quinine, and if the fever returned in the night, a sedative; and as he went away, he said to the sister: "She is better. If the Mayor were to arrive with the child to-morrow, I do not know what would happen: there are such astounding crises; great joy has been known to check diseases; and though hers is an organic malady, and in an advanced stage, it is all a mystery;—we might perchance save her."

CHAPTER VII

THE TRAVELLER TAKES PRECAUTIONS FOR RETURNING.

It was nearly eight in the evening when the cart we left on the road drove under the archway of the post-house at Arras. The man whom we have followed up to this moment got out, discharged the second horse, and himself led the white pony to the stables; then he pushed open the door of a billiard room on the ground-floor, sat down, and rested his elbows on the table. He had taken fourteen hours in a journey for which he had allowed himself six. He did himself the justice that it was no fault of his, but in his heart he was not sorry at it. The landlady came in.

"Will you sleep here, sir?"

He nodded in the negative.

"The ostler says that your horse is extremely tired."

"Will it not be able to start again to-morrow morning?"

"Oh dear, no, sir; it requires at least two days' rest."

"Is not the postoffice in this house?"

"Yes, sir."

The landlady led him to the office, where he showed his passport, and inquired whether he could return to M—— the same night by the mail-cart. Only one seat was vacant, and he took it and paid for it. "Do not fail, sir," said the clerk, "to be here at one o'clock precisely."

This done, he left the hotel, and began walking about the streets. He was not acquainted with Arras, the streets were dark, and he walked about hap-hazard, but he seemed obstinately determined not to ask his way of passers-by. He crossed the little river Crinchon, and found himself in a labyrinth of narrow lanes, in which he lost his way. A citizen came toward him with a lantern, whom, after some hesitation, he resolved to address, though not till he had looked before and behind him, as if afraid lest anybody should overhear the question he was about to ask.

"Will you be kind enough to tell me the way to the courts of justice, sir?" he said.

"You do not belong to the town, sir?" replied the man, who was rather old; "well, follow me, I am going in the direction of the courts, that is to say, of the Prefecture, for the courts are under repair at present, and the sittings take place temporarily at the Prefecture."

"Are the assizes held there?" he asked.

"Of course, sir: you must know that what is now the Prefecture was the Bishop's palace before the Revolution. Monsieur de Conzié, who was Bishop in '92, had a large hall built there, and the trials take place in this hall."

On the road, the citizen said to him,—

"If you wish to witness a trial you are rather late, for the court usually closes at six o'clock."

However, when they arrived in the great square the old man showed him four lofty lighted windows in a vast gloomy building.

"On my word, sir," he said, "you have arrived in time, and are in luck's way. Do you see those four windows? They belong to the assize courts. As there are lights, it is not closed yet: there must have been a long trial, and they are having an evening session. Are you interested in the trial? Is it a criminal offence, or are you a witness?"

He answered,—

"I have not come for any trial: I only wish to speak to a solicitor."

"That is different. That is the door, sir, where the sentry is standing, and you have only to go up the large staircase."

He followed the old man's instructions, and a few minutes later was in a large hall, in which there were a good many people, and groups of robed barristers were gossiping together. It is always a thing that contracts the heart, to see these assemblies of men dressed in black, conversing in a low voice on the threshold of a court of justice. It is rare for charity and pity to be noticed in their remarks, for they generally express condemnations settled before trial. All such groups appear to the thoughtful observer so many gloomy hives, in which buzzing minds build in community all sorts of dark edifices. This hall, which was large and only lighted by one lamp, served as a waiting-room: and folding-doors, at this moment closed, separated it from the grand chamber in which the assizes were being held. The obscurity was so great, that he was not afraid of addressing the first barrister he came across.

"How is it going, sir?" he said.

"It is finished."

"Finished!" This word was repeated with such an accent, that the barrister turned round.

"I beg your pardon, sir, but perhaps you are a relative?"

"No, I know no one here. Was a verdict of guilty brought in?"

"Of course; it could not possibly be otherwise."

"The galleys?"

"For life."

He continued in a voice so faint that it was scarce audible,—

"Then, the identity was proved?"

"What identity?" the barrister retorted. "Nothing of the sort was required; the affair was simple,—the woman had killed her child, the infanticide was proved, the jury recommended her to mercy, and she was sentenced to imprisonment for life."

"You are alluding to a woman, then?"

"Why, of course; a girl of the name of Limosin. To whom were you referring, pray?"

"To nobody; but as the trial is over, how is it that the court is still lighted?"

"It is for the other trial, which began about two hours back."

"What other trial?"

"Oh, it is clear too; he is a sort of beggar, a relapsed galley slave, who has been robbing. I forget his name, but he has a regular bandit face, on the strength of which I would send him to the galleys if for nothing else."

"Is there any way of entering the court, sir?" he asked.

"I do not think so, for it is very full. Still, the trial is suspended, and some persons have gone out. When the court resumes, you can try."

"Which is the way in?"

"By that large door."

The barrister left him; in a few minutes he had experienced almost simultaneously, and confusedly blended, every emotion possible. The words of this indifferent person had by turns pierced his heart like needles of ice and like red-hot sword-blades. When he found that the trial was not over, he breathed again; but he could not have said whether what he felt were satisfaction or pain. He walked up to several groups and listened to what they were saying; as the trial list was very heavy, the President had selected for this day two simple and short cases. They had begun with the infanticide, and were now engaged with the relapsed convict, the "return horse." This man had stolen apples, but it was proved that he had already been at the Toulon galleys. It was this that made his case bad. His examination and the deposition of the witnesses were over; but there were still the speech for the defence and the summing up, and hence it would not be finished till midnight. The man would probably be condemned, for the public prosecutor was sharp, and did not let his accused escape; he was a witty fellow who wrote verses. An usher was standing near the door communicating with the court, and he asked him,
—

"Will this door be opened soon?"

"It will not be opened," said the usher.

"Will it not be opened when the court resumes its sitting?"

"It has resumed," the usher replied, "but the door will not be opened."

"Why not?"

"Because the hall is full."

"What! is there no room?"

"For not a soul more. The door is closed, and no one can go in."

The usher added after a pause,—"There are certainly two or three seats behind the President, but he only admits public officials to them."

After saying this, the usher turned his back on him. He withdrew with hanging head, crossed the waiting-room, and slowly went down the stairs, hesitating at every step. He was probably holding counsel with himself; the violent combat which had been going on in him since the previous day was not finished, and every moment he entered some new phase. On reaching the landing he leaned against the banisters and folded his arms; but all at once he took his pocket-book, tore a leaf from it, wrote in pencil upon it, "M. Madeleine, Mayor of M. sur M.;" then he hurried up the stairs, cleft the crowd, walked up to the usher, handed him the paper, and said to him with an air of authority,—"Hand this to the President." The usher took the paper, glanced at it, and obeyed.

CHAPTER VIII.

INSIDE THE COURT.

Without suspecting the fact, the Mayor of M—— enjoyed a species of celebrity. During the seven years that his reputation for virtue had filled the whole of the Bas Boulonnais, it had gradually crossed the border line into two or three adjoining departments. In addition to the considerable service he had done the chief town, by restoring the glass-bead trade, there was not one of the one hundred and forty parishes in the bailiwick of M—— which was not indebted to him for some kindness. He had ever assisted and promoted, when necessary, the trades of other departments: thus he had supported with his credit and funds, the tulle factory at Boulogne, the flax-spinning machine at Nivers, and the hydraulic manufacture of canvas at Bourbus sur Cauche. The name of M. Madeleine was everywhere pronounced with veneration, and Arras and Douai envied the fortunate little town of M—— its Mayor. The Councillor of the Royal Court of Douai, who presided at the present Arras assizes, like every one else, was acquainted with this deeply and universally honored name. When the usher discreetly opened the door of the judges' robing room, leaned over the President's chair, and handed him the paper, adding, "This gentleman wishes to hear the trial," the President made a deferential movement, took up a pen, wrote a few words at the foot of the paper, and returned it to the usher, saying,—"Show him in."

The unhappy man whose history we are recording had remained near the door of the court at the same spot and in the same attitude as when the usher left him. He heard through his reverie some one say to him, "Will you do me the honor of following me, sir?" It was the same usher who had turned his back on him just before, and who now bowed to the ground. At the same time the usher handed him the paper; he unfolded it, and as he happened to be near the lamps he was able to read, "The President of the Assize Court presents his respects to M. Madeleine." He crumpled the paper in his hands, as if the words had a strange and bitter after-taste for him. He followed the usher, and a few minutes later found himself alone in a room of severe appearance, lighted by two wax candles standing on a green-baize covered table. He still had in his ears the last words of the usher, who had just left him,— "You are in the judges' chamber; you have only to turn the handle of that door, and you will find yourself in court behind the President's chair." These words were mingled in his thoughts with a confused recollection of narrow passages and dark staircases, which he had just passed through. The usher had left him alone; the supreme moment had arrived. He tried to collect himself, but could not succeed; for it is especially in the hours when men have the most need of thought that all the threads are broken in the brain. He was at the actual spot where the judges deliberate and pass sentence. He gazed with stupid tranquillity at this peaceful and yet formidable room, in which so many existences had been broken, where his name would be echoed ere long, and which his destiny was traversing at this moment. He looked at the walls and then at himself, astonished that it was this room and that it was he. He had not eaten for more than twenty-four hours, he was exhausted by the jolting of the cart, but he did not feel it; it seemed to him that he did not feel anything. He walked up to a black frame hanging on the wall, and which contained under glass an autograph letter of Jean Nicolas Pache, Mayor of Paris, and Minister, dated, doubtless in error, Juin 9 an II., and in which Pache sent to the commune a list of the ministers and deputies under arrest at their own houses. Any who saw him at this moment would doubtless have imagined that this letter appeared to him very curious, for he did not remove his eyes from it, and read it two or three times. But he read it without paying attention; and unconsciously he was thinking of Fantine and Cosette.

While thinking, he turned, and his eyes met the brass handle of the door that separated him from the assize court. He had almost forgotten this door, but his eye, at first calm, rested on it, then became wild and fixed, and was gradually filled with terror. Drops of perspiration started out from his hair and streamed down his temples. At one moment he made with a species of authority blended with rebellion that indescribable gesture which means and says so well,—"By heaven, who forces me?" Then he turned hurriedly, saw before him the door by which he had entered, walked up, opened it, and went out. He was no longer in that room, but in a passage, a long narrow passage, cut up by steps and wickets, making all sorts of turns, lit up here and there by reflectors like the night-lamps for the sick,—the passage by which he had come. He breathed, he listened, not a sound behind him, not a sound before him, and he began to fly as if he were pursued. When he had passed several turnings, he listened again,—there was still the same silence and the same gloom around him. He panted, tottered, and leaned against the wall; the stone was cold, the perspiration was chilled on his forehead, and he drew himself up with a shudder. Then standing there alone, trembling from cold, and perhaps from something else, he thought. He had thought all night, he had thought all day; but he only heard within him a voice that said, Alas!

A quarter of an hour passed thus; at length he inclined his head, sighed with agony, let his arms droop, and turned back. He walked slowly and as if stunned; it looked as if he had been caught up in his flight, and was being brought back. He entered the judges chamber, and the first thing he saw was the handle of the door. This handle, which was round and made of polished brass, shone for him like a terrific star; he looked at it as a sheep would look at the eye of a tiger. His eyes would not leave it, and from time to time he took a step which brought him nearer to the door. Had he listened he would have heard, like a species of confused murmur, the noise in the adjoining court; but he did not listen and did not hear. All at once, and without knowing how, he found himself close to the door; he convulsively seized the handle, and the door opened. He was in the assize court.

<hr>

THE TRIAL.

He advanced a step, closed the door mechanically after him, and gazed at the scene before him. It was a dimly-lighted large hall, at one moment full of sounds, and at another of silence, in which all the machinery of a criminal trial was displayed, with its paltry and lugubrious gravity, in the midst of a crowd. At one of the ends of the hall, the one where he was, judges with a vacant look, in shabby gowns, biting their nails or shutting their eye-lids; barristers in all sorts of attitudes; soldiers with honest harsh faces; old stained wainscoting, a dirty ceiling; tables covered with baize, which was rather yellow than green; doors blackened by hands; pot-house sconces that produced more smoke than light, hanging from nails driven into the wall;

upon the tables brass candlesticks,—all was obscurity, ugliness, and sadness. But all this yet produced an austere and august impression, for the grand human thing called law, and the great divine thing called justice, could be felt in it.

No one in this crowd paid any attention to him, for all eyes converged on a single point,—a wooden bench placed against a little door, along the wall on the left of the President; on this bench, which was illumined by several candles, sat a man between two gendarmes. This man was the man; he did not seek him, he saw him; his eyes went there naturally, as if they had known beforehand where that face was. He fancied he saw himself, aged, not absolutely alike in face, but exactly similar in attitude and appearance, with his bristling hair, with his savage restless eyeballs, and the blouse, just as he was on the day when he entered D——, full of hatred, and concealing in his mind that hideous treasure of frightful thoughts which he had spent nineteen years in collecting on the pavement of the bagne. He said to himself with a shudder, "My God! shall I become again like that?" This being appeared to be at least sixty years of age; he had something about him rough, stupid, and startled. On hearing the sound of the door, persons made way for the new comer, the President had turned his head, and guessing that the gentleman who had just entered was the Mayor of M——, he bowed to him. The public prosecutor who had seen M. Madeleine at M——, whither his duties had more than once called him, recognized him and also bowed. He scarce noticed it, for he was under a species of hallucination; he was looking at a judge, a clerk, gendarmes, a number of cruelly curious faces,—he had seen all this once, formerly, seven-and-twenty years ago. These mournful things he found again,—they were there, stirring, existing; it was no longer an effort of his memory, a mirage of his mind; they were real gendarmes, real judges, a real crowd, and real men in flesh and bone. He saw all the monstrous aspect of his past reappear, and live again around him, with all the terror that reality possesses. All this was yawning before him; he felt terrified, closed his eyes, and exclaimed in the depths of his mind. Never! And by a tragic sport of fate which made all his ideas terrible and rendered him nearly mad, it was another himself who was there. This man who was being tried everybody called Jean Valjean. He had before him an unheard-of vision, a species of representation of the most horrible moment of his life played by his phantom. All was there, —it was the same machinery, the same hour of the night, almost the same faces of judges, soldiers, and spectators. The only difference was that there was a crucifix over the President's head, which had been removed from the courts at the time of his condemnation. When he was tried God was absent. There was a chair behind him, into which he fell, terrified by the idea that people could see him. When he was seated he took advantage of a pile of paste-board cases on the judges' desk to hide his face from the spectators. He could now see without being seen: he fully regained the feeling of the real, and gradually recovered. He attained that phase of calmness in which a man can listen. Monsieur Bamatabois was serving on the jury. He looked for Javert, but could not see him, for the witnesses' bench was hidden by the clerk's table, and then, as we have said, the court was hardly lighted.

At the moment when he came in, the counsel for the defence was ending his speech. The attention of all was excited to the highest pitch; for three hours they had seen a man, a stranger, a species of miserable being, deeply stupid or deeply clever, being gradually crushed by the weight of a terrible resemblance. This man, as we know already, was a vagabond who was found in a field, carrying a branch covered with ripe apples, which had been broken off a tree in a neighboring orchard. Who was this man? Inquiries had been made, and witnesses heard; they were unanimous, and light had flashed all through the trial. The accusation said,—"We have got hold not only of a fruit-stealer, a marauder, but we hold under our hand a bandit, a man who has broken his ban, an ex-convict, a most dangerous villain, a malefactor of the name of Jean Valjean, whom justice has been seeking for a long time, and who, eight years ago, on leaving Toulon, committed a highway robbery with violence on a Savoyard lad, called Little Gervais, a crime provided for by Article 383 of the penal code, for which we intend to prosecute him hereafter, when the identity has been judicially proved. He has just committed a fresh robbery, and that is a case of relapse. Find him guilty of the new offence, and he will be tried at a later date for the old one." The prisoner seemed highly amazed at this accusation and the unanimity of the witnesses; he made gestures and signs intended to deny, or else looked at the ceiling. He spoke with difficulty, answered with embarrassment, but from head to foot his whole person denied. He was like an idiot in the presence of all these intellects ranged in battle-array round him, and like a stranger in the midst of this society which seized him. Still, a most menacing future was hanging over him; the probability of his being Jean Valjean increased with each moment, and the entire crowd regarded with greater anxiety than himself the sentence full of calamity which was gradually settling down on him. An eventuality even offered a glimpse of a death-penalty, should the identity be proved, and he was hereafter found guilty of the attack on Little Gervais. Who was this man? Of what nature was his apathy? Was it imbecility or cunning? Did he understand too much, or did he understand nothing at all? These questions divided the crowd, and the jury seemed to share their opinion. There was in this trial something terrific and something puzzling; the drama was not only gloomy, but it was obscure.

The counsel for the defence had argued rather cleverly, in that provincial language which for a long time constituted the eloquence of the bar, and which all barristers formerly employed, not only at Paris but at Romorantin or Montbrison, and which at the present day, having become classical, is only spoken by public prosecutors, whom it suits through its serious sonorousness and majestic movements. It is the language in which a husband is called a "consort;" a wife, a "spouse;" Paris, "the centre of the arts and of civilization;" the king, "the Monarch;" the bishop, a "holy Pontiff;" the public prosecutor, the "eloquent interpreter of the majesty of the law;" the pleadings, the "accents which we have just heard;" the age of Louis XIV., "the great age;" a theatre, the "temple of Melpomene;" the reigning family, the "august blood of our kings;" a concert, "a musical solemnity;" the general commanding in the department, "the illustrious warrior who, etc.;" the pupils of the seminary, "those tender Levites;" the mistakes imputed to the newspapers, "the imposture which distils its venom in the columns of these organs," etc., etc. The barrister had, consequently, begun by explaining away the robbery of the apples,—rather a difficult thing in this grand style; but Bénigne Bossuet himself was obliged to allude to a fowl in the midst of a formal speech, and got out of the difficulty with glory. The barrister had established the fact that the apple robbery was not materially proved,—his client, whom, in his quality as defender, he persistently called Champmathieu, had not been seen by any one scaling a wall or breaking the branch; he had been arrested with the branch in his possession, but he declared that he found it on the ground and picked it up. Where was the proof of the contrary? This branch had been broken off and then thrown away by the frightened robber, for doubtless there was one. But where was the evidence that this Champmathieu was a robber? Only one thing, his being an ex-convict. The counsel did not deny that this fact seemed unluckily proved. The prisoner had lived at Faverolles; he had been a wood-cutter; the name of Champmathieu might possibly be derived from Jean Mathieu; lastly, four witnesses unhesitatingly recognized Champmathieu as the galley slave, Jean Valjean. To these indications, to this testimony, the counsel could only oppose his client's denial, which was certainly interested: but, even supposing that he was the convict Jean Mathieu, did that prove he was the apple-stealer? It was a presumption at the most, but not a proof. The accused, it was true,—and his counsel was obliged "in his good faith" to allow it,—had adopted a bad system of defence; he insisted in denying everything,—not merely the robbery, but his quality as convict. A confession on the latter point would have doubtless been better, and gained him the indulgence of his judges; the counsel had advised him to do so, but the prisoner had obstinately refused, probably in the belief that he would save everything by confessing nothing. This was wrong, but should not his scanty intellect be taken into consideration? This man was visibly stupid: a long misery at the galleys, a long wretchedness out of them, had brutalized him, etc., etc.; his defence was bad, but was that a reason to find him guilty? As for the offence on Little Gervais, the counsel need not argue that, as it was not included in the indictment. The counsel wound up by imploring the jury and the court, if the identity of Jean Valjean appeared to them proved, to punish him as a criminal who had broken his ban, and not apply the fearful chastisement which falls on the relapsed convict.

The public prosecutor replied. He was violent and flowery, as public prosecutors usually are. He congratulated the counsel for the defence on his "fairness," and cleverly took advantage of it; he attacked the prisoner with all the concessions which his counsel had made. He appeared to allow that the prisoner was Jean Valjean, and he therefore was so. This was so much gained for the prosecution, and could not be contested; and here, reverting cleverly to the sources and causes of criminality, the public prosecutor thundered against the immorality of the romantic school, at that time in its dawn under the name of the "Satanic school," which the critics of the *Quotidienne* and the *Oriflamme* had given it; and he attributed, not without some show of reason, the crime of Champmathieu, or to speak more correctly, of Jean Valjean, to this perverse literature. These reflections exhausted, he passed to Jean Valjean himself. Who was this Jean Valjean? Here came a description of Jean Valjean, a monster in human form, etc. The model of this sort of description will be found in the recitation of Théramène, which is not only useful to tragedy but daily renders great services to judicial eloquence. The audience and the jury "quivered," and when the description was ended, the public prosecutor went on, with an oratorical outburst intended to excite to the highest pitch the enthusiasm of the country papers which would appear the next morning. "And it is such a man, etc., etc., etc., a vagabond, a beggar, having no means of existence, etc., etc., etc., accustomed through his past life to culpable actions, and but little corrected by confinement in the bagne, as is proved by the crime committed on little Gervais, etc., etc., etc.,—it is such a man, who, found on the high road with the proof of robbery in his hand, and a few paces from the wall he had climbed over, denies the fact, the robbery, denies everything, even to his name and his identity. In addition to a hundred proofs to which we will not revert, four witnesses recognize him,—Javert, the upright Inspector of Police, and three of his old comrades in ignominy, the convicts Brevet, Chenildieu, and Cochepaille. And what does he oppose to this crushing unanimity? He denies. What hardness of heart! But you will do justice, gentlemen of the jury, etc., etc., etc."

While the public prosecutor was speaking, the prisoner listened with open mouth, and with a sort of amazement in which there was certainly some admiration. He was evidently surprised that a man could speak like this. From time to time, at the most energetic apostrophes, when eloquence, unable to restrain itself, overflows in a flux of branding epithets, and envelopes the prisoner in a tempest, he slowly moved his head from right to left, and from left to right, in a sort of dumb and melancholy protest, with which he had contented himself ever since the beginning of the trial. Twice or thrice the spectators standing nearest to him heard him say in a low voice: "All this comes from not asking Monsieur Baloup." The public prosecutor drew the attention of the jury to this dull attitude, which was evidently calculated, and which denoted, not imbecility, but skill, cunning, and the habit of deceiving justice, and which brought out in full light the "profound perverseness" of this man. He concluded by reserving the affair of Little Gervais, and by demanding a severe sentence. The counsel for the defence rose, began by complimenting the public prosecutor on his "admirable speech," and then replied as well as he could, but feebly; it was plain that the ground was giving way under him.

CHAPTER X

THE SYSTEM OF DENIAL.

The moment for closing the trial had arrived: the President ordered the prisoner to stand up, and asked him the usual question: "Have you anything to add to your defence?" The man, who was rolling in his hands his hideous cap, made no reply, and the President repeated his question. This time the man heard, and seemed to understand; he moved like a person who is waking up, looked around him, at the public, the gendarmes, his counsel, the jury, and the court, laid his monstrous fist on the wood-work in front of his bench, and, suddenly fixing his eyes on the public prosecutor, began to speak. It was an eruption; from the way in which the words escaped from his lips, incoherent, impetuous, and pell-mell, it seemed as if they were all striving to get out at the same time. He said:

"I have this to say: That I was a wheelwright in Paris, and worked for Master Baloup. It is a hard trade, is a wheelwright's; you always work in the open air, in yards, under sheds when you have a good master, but never in a room, because you want space, look you. In winter you are so cold that you swing your arms to warm you, but the masters don't like when there is ice between the stones, is rough work; it soon uses a man up. You are old when quite young in that trade. At forty a man is finished. I was fifty-three, and had hard lines of it. And then the workmen are so unkind. When a man is not so young as he was, they call him an old fool, an old brute! I only earned thirty sous a day, for the masters took advantage of my age, and paid me as little as they could. With that I had my daughter, who was a washer-woman in the river. She earned a little for her part, and the pair of us managed to live. She was bothered too. All day in a tub up to your waist, in the snow and rain, and with the wind that cuts your face. When it freezes, it is all the same, for you must wash; there are persons who have not much linen, and expect it home; if a woman did not wash, she would lose her customers. The planks are badly joined, and drops of water fall on you everywhere. Her petticoats were wet through, over and under. That penetrates. She also worked at the wash-house of the Enfants Rouges, where the water is got from taps. You are no longer in the tub; you wash at the tap before you, and rinse in the basin behind you. As it is shut up, you don't feel so cold. But there is a steam of hot water which ruins your sight. She came home at seven in the evening, and went to bed directly, for she was so tired. Her husband used to beat her. He is dead. We were not very happy. She was a good girl, who did not go to balls, and was very quiet. I remember a Mardi-gras, on which she went to bed at eight o'clock. I am telling the truth. You need only inquire. Oh yes, inquire! What an ass I am! Paris is a gulf. Who is there that knows Father Champmathieu? And yet, I tell you, Monsieur Baloup. Ask him. After all, I do not know what you want of me."

The man ceased speaking and remained standing; he had said all this in a loud, quick, hoarse, hard voice, with a sort of wretched and savage energy. Once he broke off to bow to somebody in the crowd. The affirmations which he seemed to throw out hap-hazard came from him in gasps, and he accompanied each by the gesture of a man who is chopping wood. When he had finished, his hearers burst into a laugh; he looked at the public, seeing they were laughing, and understanding nothing, he began to laugh himself. That did him mischief. The President, a grave and kind man, began speaking. He reminded the "gentlemen of the jury" that "Monsieur Baloup, formerly a wheelwright in whose service the accused declared that he had been, was a bankrupt, and had not been found when an attempt was made to serve him with a subpoena." Then, turning to the prisoner, he requested him to listen to what he was about to say, and added: "You are in a situation which should cause you to reflect. The heaviest presumptions are weighing upon you, and may entail capital punishment. Prisoner, I ask you for the last time to explain yourself clearly on the two following facts: In the first place, did you, yes or no, climb over the wall, break a branch, and steal apples, that is to say, commit a robbery with escalade? Secondly, yes or no, are you the liberated convict, Jean Valjean?"

The prisoner shook his head with a confident air, like a man who understands and knows what answer he is going to make. He opened his mouth, turned to the President, and said,—

"In the first place—"

Then he looked at his cap, looked at the ceiling, and held his tongue.

"Prisoner," the public prosecutor said in a stern voice, "pay attention. You make no answer to the questions that are asked you, and your confusion condemns you. It is evident that your name is not Champmathieu, but Jean Valjean, at first concealed under the name of Jean Mathieu, your mother's name; that you went to Auvergne; that your birth-place is Faverolles, and that you are a wood-cutter. It is evident that you stole ripe apples by clambering over a wall, and the gentlemen of the jury will appreciate the fact."

The prisoner had sat down again, but he hurriedly rose when the public prosecutor had finished, and exclaimed,—

"You are a wicked man. This is what I wanted to say, but I could not think of it at first. I have stolen nothing. I am a man who does not eat every day. I was coming from Ailly, and walking after a flood, which had made the whole country yellow; the very ponds had overflowed, and nothing grew in the sand except a few little blades of grass by the road-side. I found a branch with apples lying on the ground, and picked it up, little thinking that it would bring me into trouble. I have been in prison and bullied for three months, and after that people talk against me, I don't know why, and say to me, Answer. The gendarme, who is a good-hearted fellow, nudges me with his elbow, and says, Why don't you answer? I cannot explain myself, for I am no scholar, but only a poor man, and you are wrong not to see it. I have not stolen, I only picked up things lying on the ground. You talk about Jean Valjean and Jean Mathieu. I do not know these persons, they are countrymen. I used to work for Monsieur Baloup, Boulevard de l'Hôpital, and my name is Champmathieu. You are a very clever fellow to tell me where I was born, for I don't know. It is not everybody who has a house to come into the world in. That would be too comfortable. I believe that my father and mother were folks who went about on the roads, but I do not know it after all. When I was a boy I was called little, and now I am called old. Those are my Christian names, and you can take them as you please. I have been in Auvergne. I have been at Faverolles. Well, hang it! may not a man have been at those two places without having been to the galleys? I tell you that I have not stolen, and that my name is Champmathieu. I worked for M. Baloup, and kept house. You tire me with your foolishness. Why is everybody so spiteful against me?"

The public prosecutor, who had not sat down, here addressed the President.

"In the presence of these confused but very clear denials on the part of the prisoner, who would like to pass for an idiot, but will not succeed,—we warn him,—we request that it may please you, sir, and the court to recall the prisoners Brevet, Cochepaille, and Chenildieu, and Police Inspector Javert, and examine them again as to the identity of the prisoner with Jean Valjean."

"I must remark," said the President, "that Inspector Javert, having been recalled to his duties at a neighboring town, left the hall and the town immediately after giving his evidence; we authorized him to do so with the consent of the public prosecutor and the counsel for the defence."

"Perfectly correct, sir," the public prosecutor continued. "In the absence of Inspector Javert, I believe it my duty to remind the gentlemen of the jury of the statement he made here a few hours ago. Javert is a worthy man, who honors by his rigorous and strict probity inferior but important functions. His evidence is as follows: "I do not require moral presumptions and material proof to contradict the prisoner's assertions, for I recognize him perfectly. This man's name is not Champmathieu, he is Jean Valjean, an ex-convict of a very violent and formidable character. It was with great reluctance that he was liberated when he completed his time. He had nineteen years' hard labor for qualified robbery, and made five or six attempts to escape. In addition to the little Gervais robbery and the larceny of the apples, I also suspect him of a robbery committed in the house of his Grandeur the late Bishop of D——. I frequently saw him when I was assistant jailer at Toulon, and I repeat that I recognize him perfectly."

Such a precise declaration seemed to produce a lively effect on the audience and the jury, and the public prosecutor wound up by requesting that the other three witnesses should be brought in and reexamined. The President gave an order to an usher, and a moment after the door of the witness-room opened. The usher, accompanied by a gendarme, brought in the prisoner Brevet. The audience were all in suspense, and their chests heaved as if they had but one soul among them. The ex-convict Brevet wore the black and gray jacket of the central prisons; he was a man of about sixty years of age, who had the face of a business man and the look of a rogue,—these are sometimes seen together. He had become a sort of jailer in the prison to which new offences had brought him, and was a man of whom the officials said, "He tries to make himself useful." The chaplains bore good testimony to his religious habits, and it must not be forgotten that this trial took place under the Restoration.

"Brevet," said the President, "as you have undergone a degrading punishment, you cannot be sworn."

Brevet looked down humbly.

"Still," the President continued, "there may remain, by the permission of

Heaven, a feeling of honor and equity even in the man whom the law has degraded, and it is to that feeling I appeal in this decisive hour. If it still exist in you, as I hope, reflect before answering me; consider, on one hand, this man whom a word from you may ruin, on the other, the justice which a word from you may enlighten. The moment is a solemn one, and there is still time for you to retract, if you believe that you are mistaken. Prisoner, stand up. Brevet, look at the prisoner. Think over your past recollections, and tell us on your soul and conscience whether you still persist in recognizing this man as your old mate at the galleys, Jean Valjean."

Brevet looked at the prisoner, and then turned to the court.

"Yes, sir, I was the first who recognized him, and I adhere to it. This man is Jean Valjean, who came to Toulon in 1796 and left in 1815. I came out a year later. He looks like a brute now, but in that case age has brutalized him, for he was cunning at the hulks. I recognize him positively."

"Go and sit down," said the President. "Prisoner, remain standing."

Chenildieu was next brought in, a convict for life, as was shown by his red jacket and green cap. He was serving his time at Toulon, whence he had been fetched for this trial. He was a little man of about fifty years of age, quick, wrinkled, thin, yellow, bold, and feverish, who had in all his limbs and his whole person a sort of sickly weakness, and immense strength in his look. His mates at the galleys had surnamed him Je-nie-Dieu. The President addressed him much as he had done Brevet. At the moment when he reminded him that his degradation robbed him of the right of taking an oath, Chenildieu raised his head and looked boldly at the crowd. The President begged him to reflect, and asked him if he still persisted in recognizing the prisoner. Chenildieu burst into a laugh:—

"I should think I do! Why, we were fastened to the same chain for five years! So you are sulky, old fellow?"

"Go and sit down," said the President.

The usher brought in Cochepaille. This second convict for life, who had been fetched from the galleys and was dressed in red like Chenildieu, was a peasant of Lourdes and a half-bear of the Pyrenees. He had guarded sheep in the mountains, and had gradually drifted into brigandage. Cochepaille was no less savage, and appeared even more stupid, than the prisoner; he was one of those wretched men whom nature has outlined as wild beasts and whom society finishes as galley-slaves. The President tried to move him by a few grave and pathetic words, and asked him, like the two others, whether he still persisted, without any hesitation or trouble, in recognizing the man standing before him.

"It is Jean Valjean," said Cochepaille. "He was nicknamed Jean the Jack, because he was so strong."

Each of the affirmations of these three men, evidently sincere and made in good faith, had aroused in the audience a murmur of evil omen for the prisoner,—a murmur which grew louder and more prolonged each time that a new declaration was added to the preceding one. The prisoner himself listened to them with that amazed face which, according to the indictment, was his principal means of defence. At the first the gendarmes heard him mutter between his teeth, "Well, there's one!" after the second he said rather louder, and with an air of satisfaction, "Good!" at the third he exclaimed, "Famous!" The President addressed him,—

"You have heard the evidence, prisoner; have you any answer to make?"

He answered,—

"I say—famous!"

A laugh broke out in the audience and almost affected the jury. It was plain that the man was lost.

"Ushers," said the President, "produce silence in the court: I am about to sum up."

At this moment there was a movement by the President's side: and a voice could be heard exclaiming,—

"Brevet, Chenildieu, and Cochepaille, look this way." All those who heard the voice felt chilled to the heart, for it was so lamentable and terrible. All eyes were turned in the direction whence it came: a man seated among the privileged audience behind the court had risen, pushed open the gate that separated the judges' bench from the public court, and stepped down. The President, the public prosecutor, M. Bamatabois, twenty persons, recognized him, and exclaimed simultaneously, "Monsieur Madeleine."

CHAPTER XI.

CHAMPMATHIEU IS ASTOUNDED.

It was he in truth; the clerk's lamp lit up his face; he held his hat in his hand, there was no disorder in his attire, and his coat was carefully buttoned. He was very pale and trembled slightly; and his hair, which had been gray when he arrived at Arras, was now perfectly white; it had turned so during the hour he had passed in the court. Every head was raised, the sensation was indescribable, and there was a momentary hesitation among the spectators. The voice had been so poignant, the man standing there seemed so calm, that at first they did not understand, and asked each other who it was that had spoken. They could not believe that this tranquil man could have uttered that terrific cry. This indecision lasted but a few moments. Before the President and the public prosecutor could say a word, before the gendarmes and ushers could make a move, the man, whom all still called at this moment M. Madeleine, had walked up to the witnesses, Brevet, Chenildieu, and Cochepaille.

"Do you not recognize me?" he asked them.

All three stood amazed, and gave a nod to show that they did not know him, and Cochepaille, who was intimidated, gave a military salute. M. Madeleine turned to the jury and the court, and said in a gentle voice,—

"Gentlemen of the jury, acquit the prisoner. Monsieur le President, have me arrested. The man you are seeking is not he, for—I am Jean Valjean."

Not a breath was drawn,—the first commotion of astonishment had been succeeded by a sepulchral silence; all felt that species of religious terror which seizes on a crowd when something grand is being accomplished. The President's face, however, displayed sympathy and sorrow; he exchanged a rapid look with the public prosecutor, and a few words in a low voice with the assistant judges. He then turned to the spectators, and asked with an accent which all understood,—

"Is there a medical man present?"

The public prosecutor then said,—

"Gentlemen of the jury, the strange and unexpected incident which has disturbed the trial inspires us, as it does yourselves, with a feeling which we need not express. You all know, at least by reputation, the worthy M. Madeleine, Mayor of M——.

If there be a medical man here, we join with the President in begging him to attend to M. Madeleine and remove him to his house."

M. Madeleine did not allow the public prosecutor to conclude, but interrupted him with an accent full of gentleness and authority. These are the words he spoke; we produce them literally as they were written down by one of the witnesses of this scene, and as they still live in the ears of those who heard them just forty years ago:—

"I thank you, sir, but I am not mad, as you will soon see. You were on the point of committing a great error; set that man at liberty: I am accomplishing a duty, for I am the hapless convict. I am the only man who sees clearly here, and I am telling you the truth. What I am doing at this moment God above is looking at, and that is sufficient for me. You can seize me, for here I am; and yet I did my best. I hid myself under a name, I became rich, I became Mayor, and I wished to get back among honest men, but it seems that this is impossible. There are many things I cannot tell you, as I am not going to describe my life to you, for one day it will be known. It is true that I robbed the Bishop; also true that I robbed Little Gervais, and they were right in telling you that Jean Valjean was a dangerous villain,—though, perhaps, all the fault did not lie with him. Listen, gentlemen of the court. A man so debased as myself cannot remonstrate with Providence, or give advice to society; but I will say that the infamy from which I sought to emerge is an injurious thing, and the galleys make the convict. Be good enough to bear that fact in mind. Before I went to Toulon I was a poor peasant with but little intelligence, a sort of idiot; the galleys changed me: I was stupid, and I became wicked; I was a log, and I became a brand. At a later date indulgence and goodness saved me, in the same way as severity had destroyed me. But, forgive me, you cannot understand what I am saying. At my house the two-franc piece I stole seven years ago from Little Gervais will be found among the ashes in the fire-place. I have nothing more to add. Apprehend me. My God! the public prosecutor shakes his head. You say M. Madeleine has gone mad, and do not believe me. This is afflicting; at least do not condemn this man. What! these three do not recognize me! Oh, I wish that Javert were here, for he would recognize me!"

No pen could render the benevolent and sombre melancholy of the accent which accompanied these words. He then turned to the three convicts,—

"Well, I recognize you. Brevet, do you not remember me?" He broke off, hesitated for a moment, and said,—

"Can you call to mind the checkered braces you used to wear at the galleys?"

Brevet gave a start of surprise and looked at him from head to foot in terror. He continued,—

"Chenildieu, who named yourself Je-nie-Dieu, you have a deep burn in your right shoulder, because you placed it one day in a pan of charcoal in order to efface the three letters, T. F. P., which, however, are still visible. Answer me—is it so?"

"It is true," said Chenildieu.

"Cochepaille, you have near the hollow of your left arm a date made in blue letters with burnt gun-powder; the date is that of the Emperor's landing at Cannes, March I, 1815. Turn up your sleeve."

Cochepaille did so, and every eye was turned to his bare arm; a gendarme brought up a lamp, and the date was there. The unhappy man turned to the audience and the judges, with a smile which to this day affects those who saw it. It was the smile of triumph, but it was also the smile of despair.

"You see plainly," he said, "that I am Jean Valjean."

In the hall there were now neither judges, accusers, nor gendarmes; there were only fixed eyes and heaving hearts. No one thought of the part he might be called on to perform,—the public prosecutor that he was there to prove a charge, the President to pass sentence, and the prisoner's counsel to defend. It was a striking thing that no question was asked, no authority interfered. It is the property of sublime spectacles to seize on all minds and make spectators of all the witnesses. No one perhaps accounted for his feelings, no one said to himself that he saw a great light shining, but all felt dazzled in their hearts. It was evident that they had Jean Valjean before them. The appearance, of this man had been sufficient to throw a bright light on an affair which was so obscure a moment previously: without needing any explanation, the entire crowd understood, as if through a sort of electric revelation, at once and at a glance the simple and magnificent story of a man who denounced himself in order that another man might not be condemned in his place. Details, hesitation, any possible resistance, were lost in this vast luminous fact. It was an impression which quickly passed away, but at the moment was irresistible.

"I will not occupy the time of the court longer," Jean Valjean continued; "I shall go away, as I am not arrested, for I have several things to do. The public prosecutor knows who I am, he knows where I am going, and he will order me to be arrested when he thinks proper."

He walked towards the door, and not a voice was raised, not an arm stretched forth to prevent him. All fell back, for there was something divine in this incident, which causes the multitude to recoil and make way for a single man. He slowly walked on; it was never known who opened the door, but it is certain that he found it opened when he reached it. When there, he turned and said,—

"I am at your orders, sir."

Then he addressed the audience.

"I presume that all of you consider me worthy of pity? Great God! when I think of what I was on the point of doing, I consider myself worthy of envy. Still, I should have preferred that all this had not taken place."

He went out, and the door was closed as it had been opened, for men who do certain superior deeds are always sure of being served by some one in the crowd. Less than an hour after, the verdict of the jury acquitted Champmathieu, and Champmathieu, who was at once set at liberty, went away in stupefaction, believing all the men mad, and not at all comprehending this vision.

BOOK VIII

THE COUNTERSTROKE.

CHAPTER I

M. MADELEINE LOOKS AT HIS HAIR.

Day was beginning to dawn. Fantine had passed a sleepless and feverish night, though full of bright visions, and towards morning fell asleep. Sister Simplice, who was watching, took advantage of this slumber to go and prepare a fresh dose of bark. The worthy sister had been for some time in the surgery, stooping over her drugs and bottles, and looking carefully at them on account of the mist which dawn spreads over objects. All at once she turned her head and gave a slight shriek. M. Madeleine had entered silently, and was standing before her.

"Is it you, sir?" she exclaimed.

He answered in a low voice,—

"How is the poor creature?"

"Not so bad just at present, but she has frightened us terribly."

She explained to him what had occurred, how Fantine had been very ill the previous day, but was now better, because she believed that he had gone to Montfermeil to fetch her child. The sister did not dare question him, but she could see from his looks that he had not been there.

"All that is well," he said. "You did right in not undeceiving her."

"Yes," the sister continued; "but now that she is going to see you, sir, and does not see her child, what are we to tell her?"

He remained thoughtful for a moment.

"God will inspire us," he said.

"Still, it is impossible to tell a falsehood," the sister murmured in a low voice.

It was now bright day in the room, and it lit up M. Madeleine's face. The sister raised her eyes by chance.

"Good gracious, sir!" she exclaimed; "what can have happened to you? Your hair is quite white."

"What!" he said.

Sister Simplice had no mirror, but she took from a drawer a small looking-glass which the infirmary doctor employed to make sure that a patient was dead. M. Madeleine took this glass, looked at his hair, and said, "So it is." He said it carelessly and as if thinking of something else, and the sister felt chilled by some unknown terror of which she caught a glimpse in all this. He asked,—

"Can I see her?"

"Will you not recover her child for her, sir?" the sister said, hardly daring to ask the question.

"Of course; but it will take at least two or three days."

"If she were not to see you till then, sir," the sister continued timidly, "she would not know that you had returned; it would be easy to keep her quiet, and when her child arrived, she would naturally think that you had returned with it. That would not be telling a falsehood."

M. Madeleine appeared to reflect for a few moments, and then said with his calm gravity,—

"No, sister, I must see her, for I am possibly pressed for time."

The nun did not seem to notice the word "possibly," which gave an obscure and singular meaning to the Mayor's remark. She answered in a low voice,—

"In that case you can go in, sir, though she is asleep."

He made a few remarks about a door that closed badly and whose creaking might awake the patient, then entered Fantine's room, went up to the bed, and opened the curtains. She was asleep; her breath issued from her chest with that tragic sound peculiar to these diseases, which crushes poor mothers, who sit up at nights by the side of their sleeping child for whom there is no hope. But this painful breathing scarce disturbed an ineffable serenity spread over her face, which transfigured her in her sleep. Her pallor had become whiteness; her cheeks were carnations. Her long, fair eyelashes, the sole beauty that remained of her virginity and youth, quivered, though remaining closed. Her whole person trembled as if she had wings which were on the point of expanding and bearing her away. To see her thus, no one could have believed that she was in an almost hopeless state, for she resembled rather a woman who is about to fly away than one who is going to die. The branch, when the hand approaches to pluck the flowers, quivers and seems at once to retire and advance. The human body undergoes something like this quiver when the moment arrives for the mysterious fingers of death to pluck the soul.

M. Madeleine stood for some time motionless near this bed, looking first at the patient and then at the crucifix, as he had done two months previously, on the day when he came for the first time to see her in this asylum. They were both in the same attitude,—she sleeping, he praying; but in those two months her hair had turned gray, and his white. The sister had not come in with him: he was standing by the bed-side, finger on lip, as if there were some one in the room whom he was bidding to be silent. She opened her eyes, saw him, and said calmly and with a smile,—

"And Cosette?"

CHAPTER II

FANTINE IS HAPPY.

She gave no start of surprise, no start of joy, for she was joy itself. The simple question—"And Cosette?" was asked in such profound faith, with so much certainty, with such an utter absence of anxiety and doubt, that he could not find a word to say. She continued,—

"I knew you were there, for though I was asleep, I saw. I have seen you for a long time, and have been following you with my eyes all night; you were in a glory, and had around you all sorts of heavenly faces."

She looked up to the crucifix.

"But," she continued, "tell me where Cosette is? Why was she not laid in my bed so that I could see her directly I woke?"

He answered something mechanically which he could never remember. Luckily the physician, who had been sent for, came to M. Madeleine's assistance.

"My dear girl," said the physician, "calm yourself; your child is here."

Fantine's eyes sparkled, and covered her whole face with brightness; she clasped her hands with an expression which contained all the violence and all the gentleness a prayer can have simultaneously.

"Oh," she exclaimed, "bring her to me!"

Touching maternal illusion! Cosette was still to her the little child who must be carried.

"Not yet," the physician continued,—"not at this moment; you have a little fever hanging about you; the sight of your own child would agitate you and do you harm. You must get well first."

She impetuously interrupted him,—

"But I am well! I tell you I am well! What a donkey this doctor is! I insist on seeing my child."

"There, you see," the physician said, "how violent you are! So long as you are like that, I will prevent your having your child. It is not enough to see her, but you must live for her. When you grow reasonable, I will bring her myself."

The poor mother hung her head.

"Doctor, I ask your pardon; I sincerely ask your pardon. In former times I should not have spoken as I did just now, but I have gone through so much unhappiness that I do not know at times what I am saying. I understand; you are afraid of the excitement; I will wait as long as you like, but I swear to you that it would not do me any harm to see my child. Is it not very natural that I should want to see my child, who has been fetched from Montfermeil expressly for me? I am not angry, for I know very well that I am going to be happy. The whole night I have seen white things and smiling faces. The doctor will bring me Cosette when he likes; I have no fever now, because I am cured; I feel that there is nothing the matter with me, but I will behave as if I were ill, and not stir, so as to please these ladies. When you see that I am quite calm, you will say, We must give her her child."

M. Madeleine had seated himself in a chair by the bed-side; she turned to him, visibly making an effort to appear calm and "very good," as she said in that weakness of illness which resembles childhood, in order that, on seeing her so peaceful, there might be no difficulty in bringing Cosette to her. Still, while checking herself, she could not refrain from asking M. Madeleine a thousand questions.

"Have you had a pleasant journey, sir? Oh, how kind it was of you to go and fetch her for me! Only tell me how she is. Did she stand the journey well? Alas! she will not recognize, she will have forgotten me in all this time, poor darling! Children have no memory. They are like the birds; to-day they see one thing and another to-morrow, and do not think about anything. Had she got clean underclothing? Did those Thénardiers keep her clean? What food did they give her? Oh, if you only knew how I suffered when I asked myself all these questions during the period of my wretchedness! But now it is all passed away and I am happy. Oh, how I should like to see her! Did you not find her very pretty, sir? You must have been very cold in the stage-coach? Can she not be brought here if only for a moment? She could be taken away again directly afterwards. You could do it if you liked, as you are the Mayor."

He took her hand and said: "Cosette is lovely, she is well, you will see her soon; but calm yourself. You speak too eagerly and put your arms out of bed, which will make you cough."

In fact, a fit of coughing interrupted Fantine at nearly every word. She did not object; she feared lest she had injured the confidence she had wished to inspire, by some too impassioned entreaties, and she began talking of indifferent matters.

"Montfermeil is a rather pretty place, is it not? In summer, pleasure parties go there. Have those Thénardiers a good trade? Not many people pass through the village, and theirs is a sort of pot-house."

M. Madeleine still held her hand, and was looking at her anxiously; it was evident that he had come to tell her something at which he now hesitated.

The physician had left, and Sister Simplice alone remained near them. "I can hear her, I can hear her!" She held out her arms to command silence, held her breath, and began listening with ravishment. A child was playing in the yard, and probably belonged to one of the workmen. It was one of those accidents which constantly occur, and seem to form part of the mysterious *mise-en-scène* of mournful events. The child, a little girl, was running about to warm herself, laughing and singing loudly. Alas! what is there in which children's games are not mingled?

"Oh," Fantine continued, "'t is my Cosette! I recognize her voice."

The child went away again. Her voice died away. Fantine listened for some time, and then her face was clouded, and M. Madeleine could hear her murmuring, "How unkind that doctor is not to let me see my child! That man has a bad face."

Still, her merry ideas returned to her, and she continued to talk to herself, with her head on the pillow. "How happy we are going to be! We will have a small garden, for M. Madeleine has promised me that. My child will play in the garden. She must know her alphabet by this time, and I will teach her to spell. She will chase butterflies, and I shall look at her. Then, she will take her first communion; let me see when that will be."

She began counting on her fingers,—

"One, two, three, four,—she is now seven years old; in five years, then, she will wear a white open-work veil, and look like a little lady. Oh, my good sister, you cannot think how foolish I am, for I am thinking of my daughter's first communion."

And she began laughing. He had let go Fantine's hand, and listened to these words, as one listens to the soughing breeze, with his eyes fixed on the ground, and his mind plunged into unfathomable reflections. All at once she ceased speaking, and this made him raise his head mechanically. Fantine had become frightful to look at. She no longer spoke, she no longer breathed; she was half sitting up, and her thin shoulder projected from her nightgown; her face, radiant a moment previously, was hard, and she seemed to be fixing her eyes, dilated by terror, upon something formidable that stood at the other end of the room.

"Great Heaven!" he exclaimed; "what is the matter with you, Fantine?"

She did not answer, she did not remove her eyes from the object, whatever it might be, which she fancied she saw; but she touched his arm with one hand, and with the other made him a sign to look behind him. He turned back and saw Javert.

CHAPTER III.

JAVERT IS SATISFIED.

This is what had occurred. Half-past twelve was striking when M. Madeleine left the assize court of Arras; and he returned to the hotel just in time to start by the mail-cart in which he had booked his place. A little before six A.M. he reached M——, and his first care was to post the letter for M. Lafitte, and then proceed to the infirmary and see Fantine. Still, he had scarce quitted the court ere the public prosecutor, recovering from his stupor, rose on his legs, deplored the act of mania on the part of the honorable Mayor of M——, declared that his convictions were in no way modified by this strange incident, which would be cleared up at a later date, and demanded, in the interim, the conviction of this Champmathieu, evidently the true Jean Valjean. The persistency of the public prosecutor was visibly in contradiction with the feelings of all,—the public, the court, and the jury. The counsel for the defence had little difficulty in refuting his arguments, and establishing that through the revelations of M. Madeleine, that is to say, the real Jean Valjean, circumstances were entirely altered, and the jury had an innocent man before them. The barrister deduced a few arguments, unfortunately rather stale, about judicial errors, etc., the President in his summing-up supported the defence, and the jury in a few moments acquitted Champmathieu. Still, the public prosecutor wanted a Jean Valjean; and, as he no longer had Champmathieu, he took Madeleine. Immediately after Champmathieu was acquitted, he had a conference with the President as to the necessity of seizing the person of the Mayor of M——, and after the first emotion had passed, the President raised but few objections. Justice must take its course; and then, to tell the whole truth, although the President was a kind and rather sensible man, he was at the same time a very ardent Royalist, and had been offended by the way in which the Mayor of M——, in alluding to the landing at Cannes, employed the words "the Emperor" and not "Buonaparte." The order of arrest was consequently made out, and the prosecutor at once sent it off by express to M ——, addressed to Inspector Javert, who, as we know, returned home immediately after he had given his evidence.

Javert was getting up at the moment when the messenger handed him the order of arrest and the warrant. This messenger was himself a very skilful policeman, who informed Javert in two words of what had occurred at Arras. The order of arrest, signed by the public prosecutor, was thus conceived: "Inspector Javert will apprehend Monsieur Madeleine, Mayor of M——, who in this day's session was recognized as the liberated convict, Jean Valjean." Any one who did not know Javert and had seen him at the moment when he entered the infirmary ante-room, could not have guessed what was taking place, but would have considered him to be as usual. He was cold, calm, serious, his gray hair was smoothed down on his temples, and he went up the stairs with his usual slowness. But any one who was well acquainted with him, and examined him closely, would have shuddered; the buckle of his leathern stock, instead of sitting in the nape of his neck, was under his left ear.

This revealed an extraordinary agitation. Javert was a complete character, without a crease in his duty or in his uniform: methodical with criminals, and rigid with his coat-buttons. For him to have his stock out of order, it was necessary for him to be suffering from one of those emotions which might be called internal earthquakes. He had merely fetched a corporal and four men from the guardhouse close by, left them in the yard, and had Fantine's room pointed out to him by the unsuspecting portress, who was accustomed to see policemen ask for the Mayor.

On reaching Fantine's door, Javert turned the key, pushed the door with the gentleness either of a sick-nurse or a spy, and entered. Correctly speaking, he did not enter: he stood in the half-opened door with his hat on his head, and his left hand thrust into the breast of his great-coat, which was buttoned to the chin. Under his elbow could be seen the leaden knob of his enormous cane, which was concealed behind his back. He remained thus for many a minute, no one perceiving his presence. All at once Fantine raised her eyes, saw him, and made M. Madeleine turn. At the moment when Madeleine's glance met Javert's, the latter, without stirring or drawing near, became fearful. No human feeling can succeed in being so horrible as joy. It was the face of a fiend who has just found a condemned soul again. The certainty of at length holding Jean Valjean caused all he had in his soul to appear on his countenance, and the stirred-up sediment rose to the surface. The humiliation of having lost the trail for a while and having been mistaken with regard to Champmathieu was effaced by his pride at having guessed so correctly at the beginning, and having a right instinct for such a length of time. Javert's satisfaction was displayed in his sovereign attitude, and the deformity of triumph was spread over his narrow forehead.

Javert at this moment was in heaven: without distinctly comprehending the fact, but still with a confused intuition of his necessity and his success, he, Javert, personified justice, light, and truth in their celestial function of crushing evil. He had behind him, around him, at an infinite depth, authority, reason, the legal conscience, the public vindication, all the stars: he protected order, he drew the lightning from the law, he avenged society, he rendered assistance to the absolute. There was in his victory a remnant of defiance and contest: upright, haughty, and dazzling, he displayed the superhuman bestiality of a ferocious archangel in the bright azure of heaven. The formidable shadow of the deed he was doing rendered visible to his clutching fist the flashing social sword. Happy and indignant, he held beneath his heel, crime, vice, perdition, rebellion, and hell: he was radiant, he exterminated, he smiled, and there was an incontestable grandeur in this monstrous St. Michael. Javert, though terrifying, was not ignoble. Probity, sincerity, candor, conviction, and the idea of duty, are things which, by deceiving themselves, may become hideous, but which, even if hideous, remain grand; their majesty, peculiar to the human conscience, persists in horror; they are virtues which have but one vice, error. The pitiless honest joy of a fanatic, in the midst of his atrocity, retains a mournfully venerable radiance. Without suspecting it, Javert, in his formidable happiness, was worthy of pity, like every ignorant man who triumphs; nothing could be so poignant and terrible as this face, in which was displayed all that may be called the wickedness of good.

CHAPTER IV

AUTHORITY RESUMES ITS RIGHTS.

Fantine had not seen Javert since the day when the Mayor tore her out of his clutches, and her sickly brain could form no other thought but that he had come to fetch her. She could not endure his frightful face: she felt herself dying. She buried her face in her hands, and cried with agony,—

"Monsieur Madeleine, save me!"

Jean Valjean—we will not call him otherwise in future—had risen, and said to Fantine in his gentlest, calmest voice,—

"Do not be alarmed: he has not come for you."

Then he turned to Javert and said,—

"I know what you want."

And Javert answered,—

"Come, make haste—"

There was something savage and frenzied in the accent that accompanied these words; no orthographer could write it down, for it was no longer human speech, but a roar. He did not behave as usual, he did not enter into the matter or display his warrant. To him Jean Valjean was a sort of mysterious combatant, a dark wrestler with whom he had been struggling for five years, and had been unable to throw. This arrest was not a beginning but an end, and he confined himself to saying, "Come, make haste." While speaking thus, he did not advance: he merely darted at Jean Valjean the look which he threw out as a grapple, and with which he violently drew wretches to him. It was this look which Fantine had felt pierce to her marrow two months before. On hearing Javert's roar, Fantine opened her eyes again; but the Mayor was present, so what had she to fear? Javert walked into the middle of the room and cried,—

"Well, are you coming?"

The unhappy girl looked around her. No one was present but the nun and the Mayor; to whom, then, could this humiliating remark be addressed? Only to herself. She shuddered. Then she saw an extraordinary thing,—so extraordinary that nothing like it had ever appeared in the darkest delirium of fever. She saw the policeman Javert seize the Mayor by the collar, and she saw the Mayor bow his head. It seemed to her as if the end of the world had arrived.

"Monsieur le Maire!" Fantine screamed.

Javert burst into a laugh,—that frightful laugh which showed all his teeth.

"There is no Monsieur le Maire here."

Jean Valjean did not attempt to remove the hand that grasped his collar; he said,—

"Javert—"

Javert interrupted him: "Call me Monsieur the Inspector."

"I should like to say a word to you in private, sir," Jean Valjean continued.

"Speak up," Javert answered; "people talk aloud to me."

Jean Valjean went on in a low voice,—

"It is a request I have to make of you."

"I tell you to speak up."

"But it must only be heard by yourself—"

"What do I care for that? I am not listening!"

Jean Valjean turned to him and said rapidly, and in a very low voice,—

"Grant me three days,—three days to go and fetch this unhappy woman's child! I will pay whatever you ask, and you can accompany me if you like."

"You must be joking," Javert cried. "Why, I did not think you such a fool! You ask three days of me that you may bolt! You say that it is to fetch this girl's brat! Ah, ah, that is rich, very rich!"

Fantine had a tremor.

"My child!" she exclaimed,—"to go and fetch my child? Then she is not here! Sister, answer me,—where is Cosette? I want my child! Monsieur Madeleine, M. le Maire!"

Javert stamped his foot.

"There's the other beginning now; will you be quiet, wench? A devil's own country, where galley-slaves are magistrates, and street-walkers are nursed like countesses. Well, well, it will be altered now, and it's time for it."

He looked fixedly at Fantine, and added, as he took a fresh hold of Jean Valjean's cravat, shirt, and coat-collar,—

"I tell you there is no M. Madeleine and no Monsieur le Maire; but there is a robber, a brigand, a convict of the name of Jean Valjean, and I've got him,— that's what there is!"

Fantine rose, supporting herself on her stiffened arms and hands; she looked at Jean Valjean; she looked at Javert; she looked at the nun; she opened her mouth as if to speak, but there was a rattle in her throat, her teeth chattered, she stretched out her arms, convulsively opening her hands, clutching like a drowning man, and then suddenly fell back on the pillow. Her head struck against the bed-head, and fell back on her breast with gaping mouth and open eyes. She was dead. Jean Valjean laid his hand on that one of Javert's which held him, opened it as if it had been a child's hand, and then said to Javert,—

"You have killed this woman."

"Enough of this!" Javert shouted furiously. "I am not here to listen to abuse, so you can save your breath. There is a guard down below, so come quickly, or I shall handcuff you."

There was in the corner of the room an old iron bedstead in a bad condition, which the sisters used as a sofa when they were sitting up at night. Jean Valjean went to this bed, tore off in a twinkling the head piece,—an easy thing for muscles like his,—seized the supporting bar, and looked at Javert. Javert recoiled to the door. Jean Valjean, with the iron bar in his hand, walked slowly up to Fantine's bed; when he reached it, he turned and said to Javert in a scarcely audible voice,—

"I would advise you not to disturb me just at present."

One thing is certain,—Javert trembled. He thought of going to fetch the guard, but Jean Valjean might take advantage of the moment to escape. He therefore remained, clutched his stick by the small end, and leaned against the door-post, without taking his eyes off Jean Valjean. The latter rested his elbow on the bedstead, and his forehead on his hand, and began contemplating Fantine, who lay motionless before him. He remained thus, absorbed and silent, and evidently not thinking of anything else in the world. On his face and in his attitude there was only an indescribable pity. After a few minutes passed in this reverie, he stooped over Fantine and spoke to her in a low voice. What did he say to her? What could this outcast man say to this dead woman? No one on earth heard the words, but did that dead woman hear them? There are touching illusions, which are perhaps sublime realities. One thing is indubitable, that Sister Simplice, the sole witness of what took place, has frequently declared that at the moment when Jean Valjean whispered in Fantine's ear, she distinctly saw an ineffable smile playing round her pale lips and in her vague eyeballs, which were full of the amazement of the tomb. Jean Valjean took Fantine's head in his hands, and laid it on the pillow, as a mother might have done to a child. Then he tied the strings of her nightgown, and thrust her hair under her cap. When this was done, he closed her eyes. Fantine's face at this moment seemed strangely illumined, for death is the entrance into brilliant light. Fantine's hand was hanging out of bed; Jean Valjean knelt down by this hand, gently raised and kissed it. Then he rose and turned to Javert,—

"Now I am at your service."

CHAPTER V.

A VERY PROPER TOMB.

Javert placed Jean Valjean in the town jail. The arrest of M. Madeleine produced an extraordinary commotion in M——, but it is sad to have to say that nearly everybody abandoned him on hearing that he was a galley-slave. In less than two hours all the good he had done was forgotten, and he was only a galley-slave. It is but fair to say, though, that they did not yet know the details of the affair at Arras. The whole day through, conversations like the following could be heard in all parts of the town:—

"Don't you know? he is a liberated convict.—Who is?—The Mayor.— Nonsense. M. Madeleine?—Yes.—Really?—His name is not Madeleine, but some hideous thing like Béjean, Bojean, Boujean.—Oh, my goodness—he has been arrested, and will remain in the town jail till he is removed.— Removed! where to?—He will be tried at the assizes for a highway robbery which he formerly committed.—Well, do you know, I always suspected that man, for he was too kind, too perfect, too devout. He refused the cross, and gave sous to all the little scamps he met. I always thought that there was some black story behind."

The "drawing-rooms" greatly improved the occasion. An old lady, who subscribed to the *Drapeau Blanc*, made this remark, whose depth it is almost impossible to fathom,—

"Well, I do not feel sorry at it, for it will be a lesson to the Buonapartists."

It is thus that the phantom which called itself M. Madeleine faded away at M ——; only three or four persons in the whole town remained faithful to his memory, and his old servant was one of them. On the evening of the same day this worthy old woman was sitting in her lodge, still greatly startled and indulging in sad thoughts. The factory had been closed all day, the gates were bolted, and the street was deserted. There was no one in the house but the two nuns, who were watching by Fantine's body. Toward the hour when M. Madeleine was wont to come in, the worthy portress rose mechanically, took the key of M. Madeleine's bed-room from a drawer, and the candlestick which he used at night to go up-stairs; then she hung the key on the nail from which he usually took it, and placed the candlestick by its side, as if she expected him. Then she sat down again and began thinking. The poor old woman had done all this unconsciously. She did not break off her reverie for two or three hours, and then exclaimed: "Only think of that! I have hung his key on the nail!"

At this moment the window of the lodge was opened, a hand was passed through the opening, which seized the key and lit the candle by hers. The portress raised her eyes, and stood with gaping mouth, but she repressed the cry which was in her throat; for she recognized this hand, this arm, this coat-sleeve, as belonging to M. Madeleine. It was some minutes ere she could speak, for she "was struck," as she said afterwards when describing the adventure.

"Good gracious, M. le Maire!" she at length exclaimed, "I fancied—"

She stopped, for the end of the sentence would have been disrespectful to the first part. Jean Valjean was still Monsieur le Maire with her. He completed her thought.

"That I was in prison?" he said. "I was so, but I pulled out a bar, leaped out, and here I am. I am going up to my room; go and fetch Sister Simplice, who doubtless is by the side of that poor woman."

The old servant hastened to obey; he said nothing further to her, for he was quite sure that she would guard him better than he could himself. It was never known how he managed to get into the yard without having the gate opened. He always carried about him a master-key, which opened a little side door, but he must have been searched and this key taken from him. This point was not cleared up. He went up the stairs that led to his room, and on reaching the landing, left the candle on the top stair, closed his window and shutters, and then entered the room with the candle. This precaution was useful, for it will be remembered that his window could be noticed from the street. He took a glance around him, at his table, his chair, his bed, which had not been slept in for three nights. No trace of that night's disorder remained, for the portress "had done his room;" but she had picked out of the ashes and laid neatly on the table the two iron ends of the stick and the forty-sous piece, which was blackened by the fire. He took a sheet of paper, on which he wrote, "This is the two-franc piece stolen from Little Gervais to which I alluded in court," and he laid the coin on the paper, so that it should be the first thing seen on entering the room. He took from a drawer an old shirt which he tore up, and wrapped the two candlesticks in the rags. Still, he displayed no haste or agitation, and while wrapping up the candlesticks he ate a piece of black bread,—probably the prison bread which he took with him on his escape. This fact was proved by the crumbs found on the boards when the authorities made an investigation at a later date. There were two gentle taps at the door. "Come in," he said.

It was Sister Simplice; she was pale, her eyes were red, and the candle she held shook in her hand. Violent events of destiny have this peculiarity, that however perfect or cold we may be, they draw human nature out of our entrails and compel it to reappear on the surface. In the emotions of this day the nun had become a woman again; she had wept and was trembling. Jean Valjean had just finished writing some lines on a piece of paper, which he handed to the sister, with the remark, "Sister, you will deliver this to the Curé?"

As the paper was open, she turned her eyes on it. "You may read it," he said.

She read, "I request the Curé to take charge of all that I leave here. He will be good enough to defray out of it the costs of my trial and the interment of the woman who died this morning. The rest will be for the poor."

The sister attempted to speak, but could only produce a few inarticulate sounds: at length she managed to say,—

"Do you not wish to see the poor unhappy girl for the last time, sir?"

"No," he said; "I am pursued, and if I were to be arrested in her room it would disturb her."

He had scarce said this, ere a great noise broke out on the staircase: they heard a tumult of ascending steps, and the old servant cry in her loudest and most piercing voice,—

"My good sir, I can take my oath that no one has come in here all day or all the evening, and I have not left my lodge once."

A man answered,—

"But there is a light in that room."

They recognized Javert's voice. The room was so built that the door, on being thrown open, concealed a nook in the right-hand wall: Jean Valjean blew out the light and crept into the nook. Sister Simplice fell on her knees by the table, as the door opened and Javert entered. The voices of several men and the protestations of the old portress could be heard. The nun did not raise her eyes: she was praying. Her candle was on the chimney and gave but little light, and on noticing the nun, Javert halted in great confusion. It will be remembered that the very basis of Javert, his element, the air he breathed, was reverence for all authority: he was all of one piece, and allowed no objection or limitation. With him, of course, ecclesiastical authority was the highest of all: he was religious, superficial, and correct on this point as on all. In his eyes, a priest was a spirit that does not deceive, a nun a creature who does not sin. Theirs were souls walled up against the world with only one door, which never opened except to let truth pass out. On noticing the sister, his first movement was to withdraw, but he had another duty too, which imperiously urged him in an opposite direction. His second impulse was to remain, and at least venture one question. Sister Simplice had never told a falsehood in her life: Javert was aware of this, and especially revered her for it.

"Sister," he asked, "are you alone in the room?"

There was a terrible moment, during which the old servant felt as if she were going to faint: the sister raised her eyes and said, "Yes."

"In that case," Javert continued, "I beg your pardon for pressing you, but it is my duty,—you have not seen this evening a person, a man who has escaped and we are seeking,—that fellow of the name of Jean Valjean. Have you seen him?"

The sister answered "No."

She had told two falsehoods, one upon the other, without hesitation, rapidly, as if devoting herself.

"I beg your pardon," said Javert; and he withdrew with a deep bow.

Oh, holy woman! it is many years since you were on this earth; you have rejoined in the light your sisters the virgins and your brothers the angels; may this falsehood be placed to your credit in Paradise!

The sister's assertion was so decisive for Javert that he did not notice the singular fact of the candle just blown out, and which was still smoking on the table. An hour later a man, making his way through the fog, was hurrying away from M—— in the direction of Paris. This man was Jean Valjean; and it was proved, by the testimony of two or three carriers who met him, that he was carrying a bundle and was dressed in a blouse. Where did he procure this blouse from? It was never known; but a few days before, an old workman had died in the infirmary of the sailors, leaving only a blouse. It might have been that one.

One last word about Fantine. We have all one mother, the earth, and Fantine was given back to that mother. The Curé thought he was doing his duty, and perhaps did it, in keeping as much money for the poor as he possibly could out of what Jean Valjean left him. After all, who were the people interested? A convict and a street-walker: hence he simplified Fantine's interment, and reduced it to what is called the "public grave." Fantine was therefore interred in the free corner of the cemetery, which belongs to everybody and to nobody, and where the poor are lost. Fortunately God knows where to look for a soul. Fantine was laid in the darkness among a pile of promiscuous bones in the public grave. Her tomb resembled her bed.

END OF PART FIRST.

9 783752 344417